MAPPA MUNDI

Also by Justina Robson

Silver Screen

MAPPA MUNDI

Justina Robson

an imprint of Prometheus Books
Amherst, NY

Published 2006 by Pyr®, an imprint of Prometheus Books

Inquiries should be addressed to
Pyr
59 John Glenn Drive
Amherst, New York 14228–2197
VOICE: 716–691–0133, ext. 207
FAX: 716–564–2711
WWW.PYRSF.COM

10 09 08 07 06   5 4 3 2 1

Library of Congress Cataloging-in-Publication Data

Robson, Justina.
Mappa mundi / Justina Robson.
p. cm.
Originally published: London : Macmillan, 2001.
ISBN-13: 978–1–59102–491–0 (pbk. : alk. paper)
ISBN-10: 1–59102–491–9 (pbk. : alk. paper)
1. Brainwashing—Fiction. 2. Genetic engineering—Fiction. I. Title.

PR6118.O28M37 2006
823'.92—dc22

2006016167

Printed in the United States on acid-free paper

Thanks

A lot of people helped me directly and indirectly in the making of this book.

On the science and culture side I was given information and help by Liane Gabora and Kerstin Dautenhahn, and by the books of Susan Blackmore, Steven Pinker, and Rita Carter. I have taken some liberties and made some imaginative leaps with the facts in order to make the scientific element of this story fit the drama. It's nowhere near as simple as I've painted it, and the actual chemistry and biology of detailed synaptic interaction is well beyond the kind of laissez-faire treatment my story depicts. Therefore all intentional and unintentional mistakes concerning the nature of memetics, cultural theory, and the physiology of the brain are my own. For a thorough and contemporary exploration of these subjects please refer to the original source authors.

I was also assisted by several kind members of the Cartographic Society on the Internet, most of which never made it to the final draft, but which was extensively useful in shaping the ideas underlying this story. I received valuable details from Nancy and Art Saltford about life in Washington, DC, and tips from the FBI Information Service on the Internet. Again, mistakes and fantasies concerning geography and the structure of the agencies concerned are all my own doing. John E. Koontz gave me advice about Native American names and language, as did Jordan S. Dill and the books of Serle Chapman; again, errors are down to me.

I'm grateful to Mary Corran for discussing the state of current mental healthcare and the experience of depression with me.

The usual suspects also appeared in advisory and supportive roles: Peter Lavery, Richard Fennell, Liz Fennell, Freda Warrington, Anne Gay, Eric Brown, Eileen Thomas, Piers Anthony, Peter F. Hamilton, John Parker, and Ruth Robson.

Thanks also to Colin Murray for editing the final version with a generous hand and to Nick Austin, without whom no sentence would be the same . . .

"Free will is an illusion caused by our inability to analyse our own motives."

Charles Darwin

Contents

Legends

Legend 1

Natalie Armstrong

Natalie was eight that summer. It was a dry season, a La Niña year. The Gulf Stream drove northwards, hauling hot Caribbean weather on its back, and brought day after day of hot sunshine and desiccating breezes. The breeze picked up the hay dust from the fields and blew it all the way to the edge of Nan's Wood, where Natalie breathed it in and sneezed and sneezed and sneezed.

"Tiggy one-two-three Nat-ta-lee!" shouted Karen, triumphant at the tigging tree fifteen yards away.

"It isn't fair!" Natalie came out of hiding and wiped her nose on the back of her hand, which she then scrubbed clean on her jeans. She was cross because Karen had won more times than she had. "You wouldn't have got me if I hadn't lost my patch."

Natalie was allergic to hay dust and grass pollen and wore a skin patch of drugs to prevent reactions but it had come off when they were playing spacewalking in the barn and now it was lost. Her eyes and nose were streaming.

"Yes, I would!" Karen said with contempt.

"Well, it's a boring game. I don't want to play it any more," Natalie said, swiping at her eyes with the tail of her shirt. "Let's go further into the woods where the air's cleaner."

"You're just saying that because you lost," Karen said, folding her arms and standing with her legs planted firmly. She was bigger and sturdier than Natalie, and Natalie hated it when Karen became stubborn, because she could stop and stand like a vast, angry piglet and Natalie could do nothing except wait or leave.

"No, I'm not. We can mushroom hunt and be the Spice Traders from the East," Natalie said quickly, naming a game that she knew Karen liked. "You can be Martinello, Prince of the Eternal Youth Mushrooms and I'll be Pongo."

Natalie didn't even like the sound of the name Pongo, who was Karen's creation, but Pongo was the Eternal Youth Truffle Hound and Martinello's companion, so it was the only part left. She hoped she'd got it right. Sometimes Karen preferred being evil for the afternoon and then Natalie would have to be Queen Primula Eustachio, Her Old Baggageness, because King Clive Eustachio the Ancient and Mighty had more evil powers in the story and that meant it had to be Karen.

Karen shrugged, "All right. But if we find any then you have to taste them first."

Natalie scowled and sniffed but she nodded. She hoped that they wouldn't find any so that she wouldn't have to start an argument with Karen. Pongo was only a truffle hound, not a truffle taster, and there was no way she was going to eat some nasty fungus while Karen gloated. And anyway, Karen only said that to pay her back for stopping Tiggy One Two Three.

They moved onto the small path that led from Karen's mother's farmhouse through the fields and the woods. Eventually it came out at Henhurst, but they weren't going that far. At the fork, they took a left down the hill into the deeper and thicker growth where fungi were more likely. Last year there had been large fairy rings, clusters of field mushrooms like white curds, dark magenta caps half eaten by slugs, and the rude, slimy revulsion of stinkhorns to discover and collect. This year there were only a few small *coprinus* on the grassy banks, their judge's wigs ragged and black with ink. Even they had dried out early.

Now the rustling, sighing wood showed nothing, for all their searching.

Natalie stopped kicking through the leaves beneath her favourite oak tree after only a few minutes. "There's nothing here."

"Keep digging, dog!" Karen insisted, doing nothing to help from her stance on the path where she was watching for enemy soldiers.

Natalie trudged through another small area, not really looking but watching Karen. She knew they wouldn't find anything here. The only place left where there might be a chance was down in the Bottoms where several streams ran close together and kept the flat ground moist long after everything else was browned. Karen did not like going into the Bottoms because of the treacherous climb out and the slippery log that crossed the beck. She didn't dare walk over it without using her hands. But Natalie was annoyed.

"I can't smell anything here. But," she sniffed dramatically, "I think there might be something in the Badlands."

"You're not looking," Karen said, her hands balled into fists, cheeks pink.

"There's nothing. The Empress must go without this year," Natalie intoned. "Unless we can brave the dark journey and bring back the mushrooms." She stared hard at Karen. She was bored of the game already but took some satisfaction from the easy way that a suggestion of cowardice could alter Karen's plans.

"But we must be quick," Karen said after a moment, "because the winter is closing in and soon the passes will be closed. Here, I'll ride," and she mounted the Prince's horse, the mighty stallion Arctica, and set off at a canter down the bank. Natalie followed her running. She didn't hold out much hope that there would be any mushrooms in the Bottoms either, but the running down the hill as fast as they could was fun, ending with a tumble down the last bits of grass at the end, rolling over and over as they were felled by the enemy's clever arrows.

Crawling along on three legs, bravely doing her best for the

Empress, Natalie soon lost track of time and her annoyance with Karen. She hunted through the black pits of Rasmora, dragging her injured leg, and scouted the wild garlic meadows of Ys in vain. They camped beneath the overhang of Cold Mountain and the season turned slowly to winter without the trace of a mushroom.

Pongo's leg got better, although he still had to walk with a limp, and the Prince's poisoned-arrow wounds slowly healed, although he was so weak he could only follow the dog around and stand in the safer spots, whilst the hound searched the banks of the River. Twice they were attacked by platoons of the foxhole diggers from Eustachia, who burrowed invisibly towards them through the soft earth and would spring from the shadows, armed with cutlasses. Twice the Prince fought them off with his bare hands. Twice Pongo tore them limb from limb with his teeth and they both feasted on the bodies of the slain to save themselves from starvation, although the black flesh was a taste they could hardly bear.

A cold snap of December turned into the gloomier, icier perils of January in Trogard. Vultures and crows ate the leftover foxholers until no trace remained. A princess appeared, but was forgotten. Poisoned winds roved, preventing their return to the castle, whilst the futile searches continued and the Prince spoke of an end to the kingdom as the queen grew old. And one day Pongo looked up and saw that a great darkness was coming out of the East.

"What time is it?"

"I don't know. My watch has stopped."

They stood and stared west, where the last of the sunset was fading. Although only a few minutes ago they had noticed nothing, now they both saw clearly that deep shadows were mustering between the trees. Where the bank had been green and gold, a soft powdery blueness was creeping uphill, blade by blade. The soft, fleecy warmth of the evening was gone suddenly, as if stolen. In its place cool air clasped them and made the dampness of their arms and faces feel icy. Natalie shivered and Karen abandoned her watchful post at the camp and came over to her, walking hurriedly, quietly, through the twilight.

They looked towards the path, where the bank's broad back was flat and dark against the glowing royal blue of the sky. From their original station it was only a half mile of track and field to the yellow lights of bedtime. Now, however, there was another half mile of sparse woods and the vile steepness of the bank itself between that safe place and the dank grasp of the Bottoms. As they looked they listened to the calls of the last birds to go home. They strained their ears for a human sound, but the tiny noises of grass and leaf and the chatter of a blackbird were all they could hear.

Karen was afraid of the dark, Natalie knew. She was afraid of it herself. Out here there were no lights of any kind, not even a glow from distant streets. If they waited any longer they might not be able to see the way home. And in the failing of the light, the stories of Trogard and its legions of enemy foxholers, its orcs and lizards and hungry vampires, took on a strange weight in her mind, so that although she knew they were only products of her imagination, it seemed as though the world in darkness would be soft and pliable, and would yield them up from the sticky mud beneath her feet. Robbed of light, all hard edges failed. Surfaces broke, insides slithered, anything unseen and untouched might turn to the substance of Trogard itself, pulpy and fungal, oozing into a shape worth being frightened of.

Karen clearly felt it, too, because she moved even closer to Natalie, until they could feel each other's warmth. Now that they had broken into silence, it was impossible to cause any untoward noise. The woods were listening, waiting.

Karen signalled, "Let's go home," with a wave of her hand, but she didn't move. Without wanting to they both kept listening, straining their ears against the slight rush of breeze in the leaves. Fortunately the engine of a tractor in the distance burred for a moment like the beat of bee-wings. Because it was mechanical it proved that the ordinary world still existed and released them for a few moments. Natalie began to hurry towards the bank, her shoes heavy with the sticky, almost cakelike mud of the stream's tiny delta.

She heard Karen panting behind her, breath light with terror, feet heavy as they blundered forwards. With the abandonment of their game the banks and bushes lost their glamour and returned to their true dark and gloating selves, slow as sloth and strong as stone, patient yet crafty. As soon as they turned their backs the awareness of the Bottoms' ancient hostility was as sharp as eyes upon them and every nerve between their shoulders was alive with prickling fear.

Before them the tussocks of the bank shifted like sea waves and vanished in sargassos of shadow. Natalie slipped in her haste and she and Karen cried out, their voices shrill and squeaking, as they both went sprawling with their hands on unfamiliar dirt and sticks. Their faces thrust into the chilly leaves so closely that they could taste them in the back of their throats; blue the smell of the night air sinking towards them.

"I'm scared!" Karen said, her voice breaking into a whine laced with real fear.

"It's all right." Natalie got up quickly, wiping her hands on her trousers, trying to talk lightly and not sniff although she wanted to listen, listen harder to hear what was coming.

Karen began to make snuffling, squeaking sounds that Natalie realized was weeping. She had to shut her up before they were heard. "It's all right," she said again, trying not to let her anger at Karen's weakness show. "There's still time. The twilight is safe. When the world goes blue there's nothing allowed to chase or hurt you. It's magic. As long as the blue lasts we'll be okay."

"How do you know?" Karen asked. She was still getting up clumsily, trying to get ahead of Natalie on the slope so that she wasn't the one closest to the Bottoms.

"It's old country magic," Natalie said, lying but convincing even herself as she said it. "Everyone in the country knows it really. Things can be there, but they're not allowed to come out until it's properly dark and you can't see a thing. Come on."

"Yes, as long as the blue lasts," Karen said in a stronger voice and she was off and running through the trees, Natalie at her side in the scramble for the top.

They made it to the path and the lane.

To either side the creatures gathered. They watched and listened for their chance, but with every step the girls got closer to home and still the blue light lasted in the west. Somewhere in the running and talking, where they reinforced the rules of the Blue World, Natalie almost forgot that she'd made it all up. Karen believed her so wholeheartedly that hearing her own lies repeated made them seem true. By the time they reached the yard and the house she was so immersed in the magical lore of the twilight that she could feel the force of it like an invisible barrier, heavy against her back with the pressure of everything it was holding at bay.

Later, much later, after they had gone to bed, Natalie stood at her window and looked out towards the wood. It was dark and she could see nothing at all beyond the yard, which was dimly lit by spilled light from the kitchen window. The whole wood might not exist, or it might have walked closer and be just out of the light pool, waiting for unbelievers to go to bed and dare to sleep. Anything might come in dreams. Anything might be true there.

With their deserted bodies lying open to harm there was nothing anyone could do to stop *it* coming in and running its fingers through their hair, whispering dreams in their ears, telling the truth about the Blue World and the places and things that lived and thrived in darkness, when nobody was there to banish them by being awake.

Natalie wondered if the wood was angry with her, for creating the story of the Blue World and so curbing its powers to terrorize and claim her. As if it wasn't bad enough that daylight and ordinary people could steal its soul away. Now she'd pushed it even farther away towards the place where nothing existed, where even the Bottoms had no power, no space, no life.

Natalie knew about that place. She could go there when she held her breath and shut her eyes and nobody knew where she was. She knew that was where the old powers went when nobody wanted them. By seeing things and putting your hands on them, by making trees into doors and cupboards, by chopping wood and cutting grass, that was how you kept your power to say what could be done. You banished old bad spirits by tidying them away from your mind with order.

But Natalie was too young to hold on to that notion all the time. She could play and pretend in the wood as long as she believed she could. But her belief was weak when she was alone, even in the daylight. Sometimes she couldn't believe strongly enough that the bushes were only plants with no feelings, or that the trees were recent additions, not an old forest with a mind of its own. Sometimes she felt the belief of the wood pressing in on her and its belief was stronger than hers. It wanted to exist, and she was in its way.

Then she'd have to wait for a sound, a call, her mother's angry voice looking for her to release the spell. And now she'd challenged the wood to save Karen, made up a lie that Karen could use against it, and it didn't even matter that it wasn't true. As soon as she'd said it she'd felt the fabric of reality shift to let it in. Now it was true whether it ought to be or not. She had used magic and the wood spirits would remember her strike against them.

Natalie twisted the net curtain in her hands. She saw the dog come out of its kennel and look up at the wall that protected it from the land beyond, listening, ears cocked. She heard the chink of its chain as it looked, longingly, at the house door, and then slunk back inside the dark hole of the little hut. Inside walls, in a space full of people who did not believe, that was the best protection there was. Even the dog knew it.

She briefly wished her dad were there (he was the ultimate non-believer) but he would have had no time for her either, so it was better he was not around. He was the kind of man who could sit by the bed-side, reading his paper, while his only daughter was eaten by ghosts he did not believe in.

Natalie moved backwards, into the room, and got into bed without taking her gaze off the window. Curled and chilly in the comforter she stared at the stars and listened hard to the sound of her and Karen's mothers talking in the kitchen below, the chink of ice in a glass, the drone of the television where Karen's dad was watching a police programme. Beyond it all she could hear the wood. A silent vastness, brimming full of ancient secrets and chaos, waiting, eating the lie of the Blue World, looking towards her with clever eyes that had already calculated the total of her crimes against it.

And she wondered, lying there and waiting for the defeat and terror of sleep, whether the wood could be kept at bay entirely by lies. If making up a thing and having it seem true was all there was to making things true. If the world, without a witness, was infinitely malleable.

That was why Karen was so desperate to talk the protection of the blue magic into being. That was why everyone constantly talked and shared and agreed on so many things that she, Natalie, didn't understand. Money, politics, current affairs, gardening, housework, laundry. Did their saying make it so? Had they created everything that way? They spoke with the conviction of knowledge.

But suppose that the fragility of it all was something they had forgotten with age? Then they would be safe, because their certainty in their own stories was absolute, and certainty was protection magic at its height.

Natalie was not certain. She longed to be, but how could she pretend she was when she knew the truth? That the safe world was a web of lies, beneath which the shunned reality waited, a master of infinite patience and terrible revelation.

Legend 2

Jude Westhorpe

It was the winter of Jude's senior year. He and George Kilgore and Ru Tanner were in the Maine woods a few miles beyond the boundary of the school grounds, out hunting. It was the first day of the Christmas holiday. They were together because Jude and Ru were friends, and George was loud and aggressive and had delayed departure especially for a chance to roam the forest with his firearms and prove to his father and himself that he wasn't a candy-ass liberal whose eventual Senatorial status would lead him by the snout and pecker into debauchery and casual morals. His was a complex ambition that Jude had no hope would be satisfied by this or many other similar outings. But, he told himself as they'd loaded up, it wasn't as though there was anything else to do but wait for his flight back West.

George had driven them out along the back roads and they had walked a mile or two farther through a new snowfall, as thick and deep as its descent had been soft and silent. Jude sank up to his knees before the powder compressed sufficiently to make a noise, juddering through his feet.

George had been lent three guns from Daddy's collection—a carbine and two rifles. Jude didn't much like George and was only along because he was Ru's friend. Ru was simple, for a straight-A's guy, and he'd never been on a hunt. Both he and George, from white families of long-line descent, imagined that bringing Jude along would be lucky, although they wouldn't say so in front of him. Nobody in their right mind would really believe that Native American blood would make anyone a better tracker or more attuned to the woods, but Jude was conscious of being watched for any signs of wolflike stealth, sixth sense, and all the rest of that shit. It made him clumsy. He stumbled in the lead, not knowing where he was going, confident of not getting lost only because they were creating such an obvious trail that it would be easy to follow it back to the truck.

Some hours passed and George decided they were nearly in the right spot.

"Okay, Tonto, halt-o," he said with the deliberate affability of someone delivering a true insult, and got out his binoculars to scan the landscape.

Jude ignored him and walked on, staying in the tree line beside an open meadow. He saw Ru hurry up to his side and glance at him with an apologetic look. Ru sure was in the shit. He wanted George to approve of him and he wanted Jude to stay friends with both of them. Jude nodded in resignation at Ru's stupidity, the rifle he was carrying so cold that it had numbed his hands through his Polartec gloves, its weight leaden and uncomfortable no matter which way he held it. After a moment or two, when George had noticed them carrying on, Jude heard him yomping quickly to catch them up. It was a sound of huffing and rasping, floundering, but with a weighted intent that made the hair on the back of Jude's neck rise.

"Holdja horses!" George grumbled and yanked on the hood of Jude's parka so that he could pass them both and get up front.

Ru said, "Hey, what was that?" and pointed away into the tall, skinny poles that led off to the right where nothing moved except a slither of ice crystals falling from a distant twig.

The wind curled an invisible finger around the lightest top layer of the powdery snow and flicked it into a swirl around their legs.

They slipped and stumbled into hidden potholes under the soft fall. They made enough noise to scare everything from here to next Tuesday, Jude reckoned, and he was glad. He hoped they didn't see a single animal. He would far rather shoot George, who kept talking about how he really wanted to go up into Canada and pot himself a Poley-Bear, a real be-Jeezus berserker.

George was from Boston, but he liked to feign a Kentucky accent for hunting. Jude watched Ru's eager leaping in George's wake with sad jealousy and foreboding as Ru giggled and hooted, finding the idea of George shooting a polar bear very funny. George was dead serious. He glared at Ru, "Get that fucking carbine out of the snow, willya? It's never gonna work if you get it covered in shit."

"Shh!" Ru said, lifting the gun up to his chest. He was going to study English Literature in Oxford, England, come fall. Jude thought Ru had some kind of fault in his head, maybe Asperger's, anyway, something that made him different and susceptible. He looked at Ru wiping off the short barrel and patting the stock of the gun, and wondered what would happen to him over there.

Around them the woods stretched silent as death. Overhead the sky had a greyish-white pallor that spanned the world, preparing to release another load of snow should the cold let up a little. The air had a frosty nip, and it felt like it cut Jude's cheeks every time he moved too quickly. He blinked, watching his breath plume and vanish, a few crystals dropping out of it towards the deep trough that George and Ru had made, like ploughs, in front of him. Trees stood or leaned in spindly profusion, crowding around them as they circled the meadow. They saw nothing.

The rest of the day blurred in Jude's mind when he recalled it; wading through the powder, sliding into a chest-deep trench and being hauled out by Ru and George; looking through the same trees and flat, empty white ground in all directions, not believing the compass when it told them they'd run in a circle until they found their own tracks; sitting under a rocky overhang with feet like ice blocks and gritted teeth, George not letting them eat the Hershey bars they'd brought in case a bear smelled the chocolate and woke up from hibernation right underneath them, ready to spring.

"You gotta see a bear to shoot it," Ru pointed out, handing round the half bottle of bourbon George had opened. Jude didn't drink any, he just pretended to. He was so cold all he could think about was going home.

"We ain't in a market for bears today, Ruby," George said. "Deer."

George had a big, foot-long hunting knife he'd spent two weeks sharpening and showing off. He'd talked in the dorm about using it to butcher an animal or "finish it off" with a big swipe across the jugular. He kept it underneath his mattress, next to a notebook like a girl's with a lock on it, and some survival magazines. Jude didn't doubt that with some more whiskey in him George would be the most dangerous thing in the whole forest. He wished something would happen so it would be done with and they could leave. It didn't occur to him that he didn't have to wait for George, that he could just go.

They saw the deer a moment later, walking cautiously along the edge of a clearing where dense overhead branches had caught some of the snowfall and left weak tufts of bleached grasses to show their heads. It was a doe, a big one, and she was alone. Her ears turned in their direction as she heard the chink of George's bottle when he put it down on the rock.

"Yassuh," George murmured and began to sight, sinking the gun butt into his shoulder. His grin was fixed. He looked like he was going to bite the wind.

At that moment Jude realized, with a shock of sudden revelation, that there was something deeply wrong with George. He wasn't just a jerk. He was broken, deep down, and even when he tried to, he couldn't work properly. This behaviour of his was a result of the fault in him, and he hadn't always been like that. Someone had done it to him, a long time ago. Someone had broken George and now George, instead of being poured from a whole jug, just seeped out of the cracks any which way he could. Jude had known him, at a distance, for five years and he'd never seen it until now.

Quickly Jude glanced at Ru, looking for a moment of old familiarity, but Ru was quivering with excitement, fumbling with the carbine, his arms shaking so much he couldn't have hit a barn door from the inside.

"God shit!" George hissed. His brand-new telescopic sight had misted with the warmth from his eye—he'd forgotten he should have kept it in his pocket to stop it getting so cold. He fumbled at it with a cloth as Jude watched him and saw the pouchy middle-aged destiny already beginning to unfurl in George's hopeless face. His rubbery lips were split with cold, but looked like they were deteriorating in a more permanent way; old seed cases whose time had come to open.

The deer stepped carefully to the edge of the grass and pawed away some snow. She put her head down to nibble.

George settled again. Ru squinted along the carbine's length, careless of gluing his skin to the metal with cold.

In a way, the wrong way, Ru and George were right about Jude—he did have more experience with guns than they did, although he'd never have told them that it was his fifteen-year-old sister who had taught him to shoot. Carefully, because he could hardly feel his hands, he slid the rifle bolt into place, listening to George start murmuring love to the deer, "C'mon, baby, turn for Daddy, one more step to the side . . . that's it."

Despite the insight and the pity that Jude had felt a moment before, he hated George in that moment for this whole production. Not for the simple fact of hunting, although Jude loathed the idea of killing as sport, but for George's idiotic machismo and his second-hand barroom talk learned from TV shows and T&A magazines.

Jude swung the barrel of his rifle well out to the side and, as the deer turned and George's finger tightened jerkily on the trigger, squeezed his own hand into a fist.

The deer crouched and leaped. Ru gasped and dropped his gun into the snow, a strip of skin peeling off his cheek with it. George's shot went off in the moment's dead air that followed Jude's.

"You fucking asshole, whaddya do that for?" George flung his rifle down as the deer vanished into the distance, her bounding wallow through the snowdrift silent and slow, like an art film of some moment of salvation.

"I liked it better alive." Jude met George's stare with a flat gaze that said if he wanted a fight he could have one.

Ru was looking at them both in a puzzled way, not sure what had gone on but using George's moment of distraction to pick up his borrowed gun and dust it off, humming with pain at the raw patch on his face as he did so.

Jude held out the dead weight of the rifle to George, "Here."

"What?" George batted at it, spitting as he spoke. "You brought it out here, you can take it back."

Jude dropped the gun in the snow and stood up, legs aching and weak from the long time they'd been crouched under the overhang. He looked at Ru, who was a mass of indecision, then back at George.

"*You* take it. It's yours."

"Jesus! What's the matter with you? Fucking everything up. Pick it up. There's still time to find another one."

"I changed my mind." Jude put his hands in the pockets of his coat and started to walk away.

"Jude?" Ru called after him. "Are you going?"

"Nah, he ain't going," George's voice said from close behind him.

Jude turned round just in time to receive George as he slammed into him in a headlong tackle. They fell down through the soft snow onto a shallow bank and rolled over and over, struggling to hang on and drive each other off at the same time.

Jude wound up on his back, George quickly getting astride his chest and digging his knees in on either side. Jude put his hands up, unable to see because of the white crystals sticking fast to his eyelashes, and got a punch in the mouth, a blow harder than he'd have believed George could deliver. It felt like he'd been struck with a rock. His head slammed against something hard under the snow.

Needles of pain radiated across his face and deep into his skull. He realized he had to do something, but when he opened his eyes he saw black flowers exploding in slo-mo in front of the runny, shaky vision of George reaching back to deal him another blow. This time Jude's lips and the left side of his face exploded in heat, like the sun had come out and was shining just for him.

He dashed a hand across his eyes and looked up into the empty white sky. Through the fierce glare he saw the silhouette of George's hand raised above him. He couldn't believe it was holding the hunting knife, but the fine length of steel blade reflected white snow and the yellow streak of Jude's scarf.

"George?" Ru said from somewhere above them both, hesitant, ready to laugh if it were a joke, hoping it was a joke, not knowing what he would do if it wasn't.

George grabbed Jude's hair and stretched his head back to expose his neck, grinning down at him. "You're gonna pick up that fucking gun and take it back to the truck, and then you're gonna walk back to school on your own." He was calm now, like he'd had it all planned out for some time. He brought the tip of the knife down to the base of Jude's neck and tapped at his collarbone with it where the anorak was pulled to the side.

Jude's bone told him that, regrettably, the knife was made of harder stuff than it was. At the same moment, in a combination of sensations so peculiar he thought he must be imagining them, because they couldn't be right, he felt George grinding his pelvis in a slow, suggestive way down onto his crotch.

"And I'm gonna tell everyone how you chickened out of shooting a pretty little Bambi in the woods, Mohawk boy." He balanced the knife on its point against Jude's collarbone.

"George," Ru said, pleading. "The deer are all getting away."

"No, they ain't."

Jude knew that George wasn't joking. It was one of the reasons Jude had had to foul up his shot, why he couldn't bring himself to let pity stand in the way of stopping whatever it was that George's cracked mind had decided it wanted to do. He didn't even think George was gay. If he were, he wouldn't have known that fact about himself. He had too much invested in being George Kilgore, American Man of Purpose, for that.

He made himself look straight into George's slate-coloured eyes but he didn't know how long he could keep it up: the returning stare was vivid with an energy that hadn't expected to find itself a way out like this so soon. It was building up behind the face, getting ready to take form.

"Let him go," Ru suggested, quietly. "Nobody needs to know anything. I'll take the gun back."

"No, you won't." Jude stared at George. "Get off me, you homo freak." He hoped that getting him angry would make George go off early, and save them something nastier. He was so angry himself that he didn't think to be afraid.

George looked down at Jude and poked his neck with the knife. His hands were numbed and his reactions slow. Jude felt it cut his skin quite deeply and the sudden new pain made him furious. Without thinking he brought up his heavily gloved right hand, grabbed the blade and twisted it round in George's grip. For a second they struggled with it. Then George heaved up and sat down with all his weight on Jude's chest and cracked one of his ribs.

With the sudden, terrifying weakness in his right side and the fear of what the dry, snapping sound might mean, Jude lost his hold on the knife. George brought it round in a wide swipe, cutting a gash behind Jude's left ear. Full of pain, Jude panicked, thinking he was going to die, hearing his own breath come in tiny gasps. He felt George getting ready for something else.

There was a cracking sound, like a branch breaking, and that was when George fell off him, stunned, a swelling the size of a baseball starting on the back of his head. Ru stood over them, shaking and green, with the carbine held like a bat in his hands, butt end out.

When George woke up they all carried the guns back to the truck, stopping often for George to rest and be sick and to adjust the blood-soaked scarf around Jude's neck.

Jude never saw George again after that day, and the last he heard of Ru he was teaching English in Newport Beach, married, his wife expecting a child. In his mind Jude returned many times to the white day, the silent winter, the dead land. In his memory there was a black and white bird sitting on a branch. It wasn't his gun going off but the bird saying *chakk-chakk-chakk* that scared the deer away. The branch stuck out of an old dead birch, like a hand-rolled cigarette from the mouth of a tall, lanky man.

In Jude's imagination his father grinned out from the birch trunk as the hunting blade flashed down. In this, the inwardly true version of what had happened in the woods, George's knife plunged into Jude's chest and cut his heart in two. It hurt. But not in the way Jude expected. It was like an icicle, cold and fierce, parting him in the middle. It made a division between two zones, each forbidden to the other. The knife stuck in his breastbone and the bone closed around and over it like a hand, holding it in. As George let go of the blade his face became boyish and lean again. He smiled at Jude with pure happiness, and the wind scattered him into a million crystals and bore him away.

This understanding, and not the facts of the actual incident, became the stronger part of Jude's recollection, although over time he thought of it less often.

In the last few years he hadn't recalled it at all, unless he'd touched the scar behind his ear, and then it was only a distant whisper of brilliant cold, a fragment of a broken and buried thing.

Legend 3

Mikhail Guskov

In a mind the past and the future, dreams and imagination, are seldom well regulated.

Mikhail Guskov, as he is now, was born fifty-five years ago, in November, in a small town outside Sarajevo. His mother was a Turkish Muslim and his father was a Christian Serb who returned from a holiday to Turkey with a wife whom nobody could understand and whom everyone suspected of being payment for some dark deed Mikhail's father had done for her family.

The wife, Ain, spoke none of their languages, although she soon learned, and along with the words came the nonverbal realization that her husband was a violent alcoholic, given to depression, insomnia, and bouts of deep self-pity rooted in a fierce patriotism for the old country, in which he still lived physically but was forever emotionally exiled from by its redefinition as communist Yugoslavia.

Ain's anxieties were complicated for her by her own devout religion, filial piety, and keen sense of personal preservation, which she extended to her baby son when he arrived nine months to the day after her wedding. She could see that she wouldn't be alive too much longer if she stayed and so she packed up Hilel, prising up a floorboard to take the secret stash of drinking money from its biscuit tin. On foot and by train she fled across

Bulgaria to settle at Igneada, on the Black Sea, a place she had been to as a girl and where she'd eaten the sweetest candy she'd ever tasted.

Hilel doesn't remember the story of how his mother and father met and married, so that section of history does not exist. There was something about a business deal, he thinks, some kind of bride-for-favours arrangement (the local beauty the only wealth the poverty-stricken grateful parents could bestow) and perhaps his father had killed a bad man. In his mind he imagines the little family of two leaving Sarajevo on a stony road, the city shot-blasted with despair, as it will be again in the 1990s thanks to the shells of the warring factions. Behind him his father, a colossus seated on top of their small white-painted house, polishes a gun, his movements betraying the covetous evil of a monster. His mother drags the little boy (him) along by his hand and he can't keep up with her and his arm is nearly pulled out of its socket. But that's not a real memory, that's only a dream.

Something he does recall is that his father had big red hands, and his mother bore their marks on her arms and shoulders and back. He did actually see that.

In later years he remembers Ain as a stern voice that is always angry, because she never manages to be angry at the right time with the right person. The only person she is not angry at is Allah, but this is the person whom Hilel comes to be angry with the most, because he is always on the receiving end of her rage, when really he thinks it should be Allah under that hand—who else has given her this unsatisfactory life? Her hands aren't red, though. They're tough with work, but they're kind in his memory. Even though they hit him many times. He was a naughty child.

Ain's family are reasonably well off, as it turns out. They send her enough money to start a modest business in carpets. For ten years nothing much happens, or, if it does, he doesn't recall it.

But then Ain leaves Igneada and returns to her family home in Istanbul, to begin a new marriage with an older man who owns a fleet of lorries. There's a lot of conflict there. Hilel's aunts have many older children who aren't pleased to see him and he's expected to pray and go to the mosque which, given his antipathy to Allah, is the proverbial last straw on the camel's back. Hilel runs away from home two years later. He was the top of his class at school, so it's a disgrace as well as a mystery. Ain never sees or hears from him again. When he looks back on this decision it's in the light of the knowledge that his act would lead directly to her death in the cab of a dark green delivery truck loaded with red capsicums. Poisoned by diesel fumes and carbon monoxide, Ain has at last agreed with him and discarded her faith, but at the time all he could think of was escape from the prison that is the world as it's created by the minds of her family.

He moves across the city and deals hash, heroin, and other types of opiates. He's a delivery boy at first, but quickly he learns to skim money—ignorant of his heritage he's nonetheless a born scammer, like his father. It's dangerous, but he's much smarter than his masters, which isn't saying an awful lot, so the gap between them is even wider than they grudgingly suspected. They would soon learn its real extent—to their cost.

By the time he's seventeen Hilel is called Mahmood. He owns the house and the street and the old man who gave him his first parcel to carry across town. Although he doesn't know it he also owns the truck in which his mother killed herself, and the delivery business as well. By now, though, he has more pressing matters. His life is in danger. Rival associations are closing in on him, and they have many more men and guns than he has, so again he takes all he can carry and leaves. He follows the Black Sea coast, heading into the Ukraine on a false passport.

This crossing entails the first of his true transformations in which he alters his appearance via the scalpel of cosmetic surgery and his ways by a lot of book-learning to become Pavlo Mykytiuk. It's his first moment of genius. He understands that he can lose more than his appearance. He can lose his entire history.

Pavlo is a hopeful young Communist. Mahmood had leanings that way, but he was never able to really break with his old Islamic background. Pavlo has no background, except in his own imagination, hence he's free to be an idealist. He joins a young people's commune in Volgograd and learns to speak Russian.

Of course, nobody there believes he's Ukrainian, but they don't care because they are young and all are glad that someone has come so far to join them for their beliefs. In this respect they're as blinded by fervour as the drug dealers of Istanbul. Also, although Pavlo has taken a lot of trouble with himself, old habits die harder than mere identities and before too long he has to leave again, a wake of accusations and bad blood behind him. He takes most of their money and feeble possessions with him. What was his was theirs, and what was theirs was certainly his.

When he remembers it in the far future this part of his journey is like a dark forest of festering emotions, mostly fear and loathing. He walks a gritty track. On all sides large houses shut him out. People won't speak to him. His lip-service communism only gets him so far, because already new values and different kinds of systems are sweeping through the country. He tries his luck closer to the centre, in Tula, but the times are so hard he falls foul of both the reigning criminals and the police and finds himself sent to jail pending trial, where the investigation into his alleged crimes uncovers his third false set of identity papers.

Finally he is entered into the Kodeks—the database of Soviet criminal records—as Alexei Kurchatov (naming himself after one of their most notable physicists from an article he's read in an old magazine) and is incarcerated for theft, drug dealing, running a prostitution racket, and a variety of other trumped-up charges that the KGB select from the approved list. The KGB have got in on the act because false ID constitutes an internal "crime against the state." He's lucky he isn't sent to a Gulag, but instead he's transported to Moscow for further investigation at the request of a judicious immigration officer. In

Moscow his papers are lost and he's left on the remand wing of some pit of a prison, trying not to catch TB as around him men drown in their own arterial blood.

Ironically, it's inside that Alexei meets the people who will succeed the Party to rule Russia in the 1990s—the Mafiocracy. As for the KGB, they soon lose interest because in October 1991 their organization is dissolved and they've got their own futures to worry about.

The key figure Alexei meets in prison is Jurgenev—a man with all the physical presence of a rat's shadow, who is both intelligent and corrupt to the marrow of his bones. Now Alexei, unlike Pavlo, is an old hand who has been down the route of youthful idealism and wisely spurned it in the name of self-interest and survival. By conceding to the only two moral imperatives of the Russia of that moment he has finally become the genuine article.

Alexei immediately understands that Jurgenev is a powerful player in the prison community—most of whom are seething with righteous anger at their scapegoatings: these are servants of the state who have been sacrificed to the public anxiety mill by their fellows. Some of them, including Jurgenev, used to hold key positions in the government and they are all determined to escape jail and exact some vengeance of their own. Alexei is lucky to share a cell with Jurgenev, because this association prevents him from becoming one of the slaves who provide sexual satisfactions, scrub toilets, slop out, and do all the other filthy and degrading jobs.

For his part Jurgenev can see that Alexei is a born criminal, with an unusually sharp mind. Perhaps with dreams of family and empire he organizes private tutors for Alexei from other areas of the prison. Then, as Jurgenev's personal assistant, Alexei is taught science, languages, mathematics, and how to rule from beneath the foot of the oppressor; what Jurgenev slyly names, in a voice that is proud and contemptuous in its clever understanding of the world, "the woman's gambit."

So, it's inside jail that Alexei ascends almost directly to the right hand of a small and ugly god, and for three years they organize and plot and bribe and threaten until at last they are freed and strut into Moscow at the head of a little army of ruthless men, as savage as street dogs, who begin to cut, shoot, and stab a path to wealth and power.

Jurgenev has an eye only for the cash: he's no philosopher. He's using Alexei's superior understanding of politics and humanity as his own, and will continue to do so as long as it suits him, or until he has no further use for it. Alexei sees that Jurgenev's power is growing so this day, in which the munificent father rat will turn on and cannibalize his son, looks likely to arrive. Alexei could dispatch the old bastard himself, but he's got no interest in being another Muscovite scum-sucker in Ferragamos and Dior. Kurchatov has served his purpose and may as well kill himself as try to escape Jurgenev's claw.

Alexei Kurchatov's body, face blown off, is discovered afloat in a Chechen ghetto storm drain after a gun deal goes awry. That very night, in another Moscow precinct, a new student applies to study at the University, his application and genuine examination certificates gratefully received along with a fistful of US dollars and a heavy crate of Russian cash in notes so used that the grease of many fingerprints has turned them almost completely grey.

So begins the career of Yuri Ivanov, well-heeled Muscovite scholar, with plenty of surprisingly helpful mafia connections and friends in positions that count. His only danger remains discovery—but Jurgenev, once his protector, has enough to occupy his mind with a sudden and depressing fresh interest in his activities due to the police's new crackdown measures on organized crime, so that's taken care of for the time being. Alexei has gone forever—his corruption and his despair with him, drowned in the filth of the sewers.

Yuri, on the other hand, is a sophisticate. He understands the mafia and deals with its business cordially, distantly, a good servant and a polite master. He would never soil his own hands with violence directly, not like Alexei, who has shot more men than he could name. His interest is science and the mind and he sets to studying it with the zeal of a true convert. The guns of ex-brothers hold no fear for him. Some of them even admire him from afar.

Yuri moves into psychology just as the boom begins and grants, prizes, and awards come his way from several areas, including the FSB itself, successor to the KGB, that is beginning to see a use for someone capable of great deceptions. They ask him to travel and study in Germany, to spy on the West and to continue his work.

It's in Germany that Ivanov meets the first of the people who will change his mind, instead of his changing it for himself. This person is a professor and future Nobel winner, Nikolai Kropotkin. It was the millennium year, and everything had a feeling of starting afresh. When they put their heads together they realized the direction that this newness was taking.

Ivanov understands that it's not, as he thought once, that God is the master; nor, as he thought once, that *he* will be master; nor, as he thought once, that ideology is the master; nor, as he thought once, that money is the master; nor guns nor knowledge nor power nor democracy nor any state. The master of mankind is so much larger than all of these very small, very ancient, very wrong-focused ideas.

All these ideas are what you get when you stare the wrong way down the telescope. The right ideas are the ones you get by seeing yourself not as a player in a game or a mote in the eye of god but as a world, an entire universe, within which all things are possible and all sources found.

Kropotkin and Ivanov altered the map of everything with their view. They posited that the driving forces that dominate individual lives originate deep in the structures of the brain and its layout, in our ancient heritage, whose shadows stream backwards from man to ape to older ages when we were as blunt and formless as jellyfish and aware of nothing more than the rhythmic swing of the tides.

But neither of them would have seen this if Ivanov had not once been Hilel and all those men after. Because that was the story that gave him his clue and conviction.

Kropotkin and Ivanov put together the physiology and the psychology and assembled them with memetic theory and they realized—although, like all revelations, it was only a hypothesis and not the whole truth—that the master of man is the idea of progress and improvement and betterment and ease, and that this whole memeplex, which is the fancy articulation of survival itself, has us all enslaved. To put it another way, the development of Mappa Mundi, as all such developments, was a necessary result of our own nature, as irresistible as evolution itself. What we can change, we shall change. What comes to hand, we shall use. What we see, we presume to understand. When the basic needs are satisfied, the restless mind turns itself towards improvements.

Yuri Ivanov saw the whole cultural flow of those days—the self-absorption, the self-examination, and the constant self-flagellation towards the perfection of our physical bodies and our "holistic" persons—as exactly the same impulse as the drive to religious exactitude and national fervour that had made Ain and his unremembered father so damned irritable and so impossible to reason with or placate.

If we are right, we shall be saved. If we are good, we shall be saved. If this, that, and the other, then we shall be saved. Perfection and purity, fame and the life everlasting. What was the difference?

And, as Ivanov only suspected then, there was nothing you could do that would save you. Death, like taxes, was certain. Nothing survived. It was the final, unbelievable insult.

Ivanov and Kropotkin knew there'd be no solving death in their lifetimes. So, they reckoned, they might as well forget about it. Meanwhile there might be something in trying to free human life from the slavery of survival.

Their work was not received gladly. Soon Kropotkin moved to

richer projects back in the motherland and the CIA approached Ivanov and suggested that a new country with greater wealth might suit him, if he would only assist them in a few military projects. But although he did go and became a US citizen, he maintained all his old contacts and told them it was merely a front, a double act, another face to add to his collection.

Because they knew some of his story, they believed him.

Legend 4
Mary Delaney

Mary was thirteen when she visited what had once been the old family home in Centralia, Pennsylvania. Her sister, Shelagh, was with her. They hadn't wanted to come, but the funeral arrangements for Gerry Delaney had specified a ceremony to take place on the old site of St. Ignatius's, beside the cemetery where his parents had been laid to rest.

The Trailways bus moved slowly, in an endless grumble, through places of passing familiarity to both girls—Washington, DC, Philadelphia—and then, much later, through towns Mary had never heard of, with names like Frackville and Shenandoah.

In between the towns, each smaller and more grindingly stricken by economic failure than the last, the road meandered along hills lined with the soft grey-brown of winter trees stitching a white sky to the ground. Mary tried to see through the masses of narrow trunks, but at that time of year the light was poor even under their leafless branches and within a few yards a greyness became blackness, became nothing at all, until the bus seemed to move on a narrow belt of solid ground between two gulfs of unknown space.

Gerry had been their uncle. He had died in Allentown, another name on a map that Mary had to fill in for herself, like a blank outline in a colouring book. She imagined small houses of gray clapboard outers and white window frames, streets traced with the black nets of electric lines and punctuated with tough, upright telegraph poles, occasional garish notices for McDonald's and the laundromat, but it was vague and flat in her head like a packed-up film set. The only 3-D image she had was that of Gerry himself, a heavyweight man who might have been a boxer in other lives, dying at the gas station where he worked, lying in a pool of unleaded as the tanker hose he'd failed to lock down bled copiously over him until the vapour-autoback system shut off the flow. The coronary had started as he'd bent to fix it in place.

"They were lucky there wasn't a spark," Mary's mother had said, her first words after some moments of reflection on the news. Mary'd looked at her in appalled silence. So they were, but was that the only thing to say?

Gerry was the hallmark of the Delaney clan. He'd served in the army, then got the GI Bill and studied to be a realtor, making the mistake of remaining in the old mining towns of his youth, where property and goodwill both came cheaper than usual. The business had fallen through because Gerry didn't have any skill as a negotiator. He was a nice guy. He'd then moved into insurance, but hadn't the heart to press his policies on people already stranded by life's high tide up in the hills. He ran a bar and diner for a while in Jim Thorpe, the Switzerland of America, but had to leave after a New York ski instructress accused him of sexual harassment. He ended up in Allentown, dispensing gas, working late nights, building up the gutful of fat and disappointments that had smothered him.

Well, that was how Mary imagined it from the news she heard at the dinner table. In fact, her mother insisted that Gerry *liked* it up there in the middle of nowhere, had friends, and didn't miss the money or the success that he'd once hoped for.

Driving up in the bus, however, Mary couldn't see it that way. Here it would be an event if a cat crossed the road, she thought, looking out the window at the remains of an old post office, the tatty flag outside swinging listlessly in a cold breeze, the columns of its once fancy wooden portico flaking green paint into the wind. A few yards further on, outside a bar called The Blue Moon, a yellowed sign advertised a Saturday clam bake to a broken-down old Chevy that had died next to it.

Clam bakes. For God's sake. Everything about these mountains was creepy. The places were choked with weeds and man-made remains: machinery rusted in stacks, tractors sank into the fields they'd once worked, farmhouses slumped into the earth, tiles, tires, old iron, gut lengths of electric cable, rubble, kids' toys, plastic containers, and household rubbish sat everywhere in hillocks, grave mounds for the spirit of the coal industry. She couldn't stand looking at it all. What a mess. What a God-awful, pitiful, shit heap. And in its midst, scratches of life—a hair salon, a car wash. A clam bake. Pennsylvania and Transylvania had more in common than a few syllables.

In the valley below the place with the post office, which once had been pretty, the scars of old rough-cut clearance were growing new coats of healthy trees. A little white church and a few headstones stood alone there, overlooking the wealth of empty silence in a long, narrow valley. Nobody was about. Mary hoped that Gerry would get to rest somewhere like that, decent and forgotten. She wanted to forget him and intended to, instantly, as soon as the return bus hit Pittsburgh.

She glanced at Shelagh, who was humming the aimless repeated phrase of a chart song, her dreamy gaze focused inwardly on Mack, no doubt; Mack of the surveyor's building downtown, who had to stay in the office over the weekend and was going to pay for their wedding on a loan he'd work off for the next three years. Mack and Shelagh were going to have children (raise a family, as Shelagh put it) and settle down to obscure deaths on carefully paid-up Medical Plans, which Mack would have already set in place at some pathetic weekly rate of pay under the names Mr. and Mrs. M. Smith. Shelagh had Gerry stamped in her soul.

Mary looked at her sister with suppressed anger and resentment, with a pity that robbed her of the power of speech. She felt the same when she looked at her mother, her father, their house and their neighbourhood with its credit-card debt and its small-time dreams and its grinding sense of dead ends, as though everyone who'd come to live there was the losing player in a game where they'd never figured out the rules. She wanted to forget them all.

The bus came to a halt at last with a toad's-death croak of brakes, and Mary and Shelagh stepped out for the first time onto the steaming hot asphalt of Centralia, Pennsylvania. The journey had taken almost a day and they were exhausted and aching, but they forgot that in the first moment that they set eyes on the place: Centralia had burned out, big-style and long ago, and it was still burning.

Aware of the danger it was in, the bus hastily turned around and left them on the town's edge, where a large yellow sign advised: Public Notice—Danger from Subsidence and Toxic Gases, State Liability Ends Past This Point. Two black cars were parked a little further along beside an empty space where the church of St. Ignatius had stood, before it was torn down for its own safety. Anxiously waiting were the rest of the family, who'd travelled up to stay for a few days, and the priest. Mary saw them jigging from foot to foot on the scalding earth, their figures mere shadows wreathed in flitting smoke as the listless breeze sent sulphur vapour and other poisons on a tour of the town.

There were no buildings at all. Mary looked across the cracked tarmac and then across a narrow slot of grass, pitted with holes where smoke and steam rose. The grass was nearly all dead. By the church's old site the blackened and bleached trunks of birches leaned sideways in all directions and Mary saw that the gravestones had nearly all fallen and been absorbed into the fire below.

She knew then that she could do whatever she wanted in her life and not have to feel guilty. The dues had already been paid in this wasteland through the immolated lives of the living dead.

Shelagh took a tentative step towards the others and Mary followed her into the stinking steam. She tucked her face behind her coat collar, pretending not to like the egg-reeking smell but really hiding the fact from the others that she was grinning fiercely from ear to ear.

After the very brief ceremony, and the subsequent undignified and hasty exit from hell, Mary found herself taking a liking to the area, although her plans to go skiing and whitewater rafting there would never come to anything. At the lawyer's offices in Mount Carmel she found to her surprise that Gerry had left her something personal, something of his own, besides the insurance and compensation payouts from the gas company that were going to send her to college. She received it by post a few days later on her return to Charlottesville—a small, lead-crystal replica of the space shuttle *Columbia*, the one and only remaining element of Gerry's once-powerful ambition.

She kept it close always.

Legend 5

Ian Detteridge

Ian was a casual believer leading a relatively unexamined life. He attended church three times, once when he was christened, once when he was married, and at his parents' funeral. His own small family of self, wife Dervla, and daughter Christine struggled most of the time against debts for the car and the house and a yearly holiday. But they didn't struggle too hard and by the time he was forty Ian had paid off most of his troubles except for a vague dissatisfaction with life that religion might palliate but wouldn't solve. He didn't want a sop for his soul. He wanted something more permanent and genuine. Sometimes he lay awake as Dervla snored quietly at his side, thinking, trying to figure out if there was more to life than market-town living somewhere out beyond the galactic rim of Halifax, Huddersfield, Batley, and Dewsbury where his building work took him on regular tours of lives like his own.

Ian drank a bit. He liked an occasion. He wanted to find something that he could only describe as "grand." "Grand" was a day out at the seaside of his boyhood, kite in hand on the beach, running in the thin surf and splashing his legs with icy salt water as the kite string tugged him on, up, towards the sky.

Dervla watched television. Soaps mostly. She had a life inside the box, Ian always said. He'd come in from work and find her glued to it, making tea or ironing, her movements dreamy, remote-controlled. He couldn't get into that stuff. It was simply more of the same that he'd already had. House and car, buy the shopping, out with the lads on Friday and Saturday, rugby on the Sunday, a fortnight in Lanzarote, watching his belly grow year after year, inch by inch, keeping the books and putting up and pulling down pieces of homes; he tried to understand what it meant, because it had to mean something.

Christine liked to read. When Dervla watched the screen Christine had her face stuck between the pages, pushing her glasses up her nose with regular, precise movements of her index finger every two or three minutes. She told him all about her books. Fairies and elves, pixies and witches, some boy who was a wizard and had adventures at school. Ian didn't understand her either, although he thought he understood that both of them, each in their own way, was trying to fill in that vague empty place inside, the one they'd brought with them from wherever they came from, the one that never had quite enough.

When he was a lad Ian had wanted to be an astronaut, or fly a hang-glider—something that took you out there where freedom was. One wet Wednesday night, when Dervla was at her sister's, he saw a documentary on climbing Everest without oxygen. A reporter asked the man, "Why did you go up there to die?"

Dervla would say that.

"I didn't, I went up there to live."

Ian wanted to be the person who would say *that.* As soon as he heard it said, he knew that the man on the mountain was filling up the dissatisfaction with real, solid stuff. Ian wanted to be a better, braver, more useful person. Someone who could say, "I have lived."

Meanwhile, outside in the rain, the gales were only warming up to their night's performance, lashing the windows and bending his cypresses into sickles of writhing green. Tonight a slate will break and slip.

Tomorrow Ian will get out the ladders and climb up to fix it. The rain will make the slates and their slimy load of lime-tree sap as slippery as an ice rink.

Ian's used to roofs. But tomorrow he'll be thinking about climbing Everest as he reaches the top of the ladder and tests the guttering's mettle before trusting his feet to the tiles. The first slip is the failure of a crampon in the ice. Has he the resolve to continue in such harsh conditions? The camera crew and narrator standing behind him relay their feeble doubts to the awestruck audiences in a million homes. Ian sticks to the task.

The audience gasp at his daring.

As Ian places the slate and reaches for a new pin to hold it down, he's really fixing a bucking tent to the sheer North Face in a howling gale. Mallory's ghost has risen from its rocky cairn to give Ian a thump on the back for his courage in the teeth of the storm.

As it happens, however, Ian will place a foot on a mossy chunk stuck between two slates, lean down, and then feel a huge crevasse open up beneath him.

As he falls he'll look up and think, "I wish I—"

Legend 6
Dan Connor

When he was five, his mother gave him a hat with a woolly tassel.

When his heart beat, the tassel moved.

In the corner of his eye he saw its shadow.

Wiggle. Wiggle.

In his ear, sheltered by the hat, he heard a sound very faint. Ba-dum. Ba-dum.

Ba-dum. Wiggle.

He laughed. He could see his heart beat.

All day, with the hat on, he kept this power.

At night the hat was put away in the closet in the hall.

At night he didn't see the tassel's shadow.

He didn't hear his heart.

He wondered if you were dead at night and alive in the day.

When he heard a story about vampires he saw they were the opposite.

They were Un-Dead. That made him the Dead.

The kitchen knife made a sound inside his skin like nails on a blackboard.

He didn't hear it with his ears, but with his mind.

The blood that came out made a sound, too, like the sea.

Deep inside it he could hear his heart. Ba-dum.

That was a huge relief.

They stitched him up into silence.

The quiet of enforced silence built like a distant wave.

Eventually he learned to silence himself, hiding in the closet like his hat.

Ha ha. That was a joke.

Funny Dan.

He looked for love.

He found it not.

He looked for love.

He found it not.

He looked . . .

Fuck this for a game of soldiers.

One day, a year later, Dan saw a vampire in the street.

He was old and hideous with age and neglect, beautiful as he glittered with his crisp shell of overnight frost. He had curled up beneath a bridge, after trying to cover himself in newspaper and boxes, like the mice at the pet shop. He had a hat on, quite a nice one, that some kind person had given him. It had five long tassels of gold, brassy and faintly ridiculous, like the Three Kings get to wear in a nativity play.

The tassels moved in the wind, across the man's crystalline, rat-coloured cheeks. Dan heard the vampire's Un-dead heart in the wind making a sound like cars whooshing past on a wet road. It sighed with the burden of things unsaid and undone, ashamed of itself.

He decided to do something to help. At the Careers Centre they offered courses to tempt the unwary into new lines of work. Dan chose psychiatric nurse. It had a long training time, and college meant he could leave home.

The Universe rewards a good deed. His mother told him so. His father, who spent his life building cars on a production line as an overseer of robots, died of a heart attack in the pub when he was fifty-two, taking part in a steak-eating competition where you could win a tray of uncooked meat, big as a butcher's window, to take home. His last words for posterity—"Another sausage!"

Dan, remembering a broken arm, the closet, and too many clouts to count, figured his mother was right.

Compass Rose

White Horse woke up in the middle of the night, choking on smoke. She opened her eyes and the hot, searing pain started tears running down her face. It was almost a relief. She'd been expecting something bad to come her way ever since she'd broken into that car in town. At last it had happened and she could deal with it.

She groped around in the ink-dark familiarity of her bedroom, and for the first time thought she was lucky to have had no electricity for a month—she knew her house and she could walk through it without sight. She found her bag first, just beneath her hand where she always left it. Inside it the machine she'd stolen from the car clunked heavily against her wallet and the snaplock holder with her Pad inside it. At the end of the bed she found her jeans, put them on, and slid her feet into her boots. Her jean-jacket was on the back of the hardwood chair. Coughing, she wriggled into it, on hands and knees, her face an inch from the floor as she crawled towards the door. She kept her face in the zone that was supposed to be less smoky and reached out for the handle but when her fingertips made contact with the thick wood panel the heat seared her skin. Now she could hear the fire, as well as smell it. From the narrow crack below the door a roaring, white-noise sound came, like the aftermath of an explosion, and as she hesitated there, she both heard and felt a part of the first floor crack and begin to give way.

Without warning she was sick, violently, and her next intake of breath was pure poison. She backed up as fast as she could and hauled herself over the bed to the window. The drop wouldn't be too bad, down into her yard grass, although the house was higher on this side where the land fell away into a dip.

Opening the window gave her a few moments to breathe. She couldn't stop coughing. It felt like the house had come loose from the ground and started to spin and buck, like a boat, but she was still moving. She got one leg over the frame, then the other. Her bag stuck, catching on the window lock. A gust of hot air and ash plumed up, from the outside this time, engulfing her in orange sparks. Sharp pain scored across her hands where it touched her and in surprise and fear she yanked the strap hard. It came loose, dislodging her, and she was only spared a head-first plunge to her death when the seat of her jeans snagged and ripped on the catch. She hung helpless for a second, thankful for the rivets and seams cutting into her flesh, and then began, very cautiously, to try and lever herself free.

As she wrestled with the tough material that was stopping her from falling free, she thought she heard someone outside shouting and crying, doing some kind of wild dance in her vegetable patch. Her head was spinning. The cloth gave suddenly and she slipped down, grating the front of her body against the sill, gasping with the unfair shock of this new pain in her breasts and ribs.

Deep within the house's old, dry innards, a fundamental element surrendered to the flames. She felt the wall and her window frame sway slowly inwards and heard the huge, crashing noise of the roof falling.

Gulping air, her hands shaking, White Horse tossed the bag out into the night. Her eyes streamed and seemed to bleed. She couldn't see anything properly. The air was thick as she pushed out with all her might, away from the house and into midair and the spiral of yellow and orange sparks.

She had her knees bent for the impact-and-roll but it was over before she expected. Her feet met the ground with the solid impact of two concrete blocks. Shooting pains darted into her knees and hips as she rolled, crying out, onto the cold earth. As she panted, trying to get her breath back to shout for help, she realized there was a strange smell all around her and that she was wet—soaking, in fact.

She tried to yell, but her voice was empty. Instead of her usual tough holler a tiny frog croak came out of her throat, dislodged a bubble of spit, and scraped her gullet so sharply it felt as though a cat was clawing it. But someone had heard her.

Another voice from somewhere in the swirling clouds of smoke said her name in familiar Cheyenne.

"Vohpe'hame'e! I see you. Little devil. Get your butt out here and burn!"

White Horse couldn't recognize the voice, but she understood what it meant by the wet grass that wasn't alight yet and the smell of gasoline all over her.

A fear so deep it made her bones hurt shot through her. Gasping and trying not to breathe, but coughing all the time, red coughs of agony, she searched desperately for her bag. She had to get it. The machine, her evidence, was inside it. She looked everywhere, holding her eyes open in the stinging wind, but all she could see was a tiny pinprick, like a dying star, that she knew was the powerful beam of Red Hat's garage light. She was nearly blind.

Footsteps, heavy and with a kind of drunken doggedness, came closer. She heard them. She felt the tremor in the ground, muffled by the dying spasms of the house.

"At last!" said the voice. It was turned in and gargling on itself so it was an inside-out thing. "There you are!"

White Horse looked up at the same moment her right hand found the bulky shape of her bag. A shambling figure, silhouetted against the glare of the fire, veiled in drifts of heavy, poisonous smoke, stood in bearlike calm over her, its arms half spread.

White Horse stood up. Ice-cold pain shot up the core of her right leg and through her lower back. She started running away from the house, coughing, gulping, throat on fire, and in three strides had lost all sense of direction. There would be the fence and then the road.

The fence hit her at an angle and sent her sprawling to the ground. She landed on the precious bag and something in it broke. The machine. The stench of the gas made her giddy and the voice was suddenly right behind her,

"Wait up, wait up!" It was laughing.

White Horse heard the sound of a cigarette lighter being flicked, flint on metal.

She screamed, and the little frog in her throat whispered, "Help me! Help me!"

The propane tank behind the house exploded with a gigantic bang and the singing scream of metal fragments spinning through the air. Its fireball gave off a hot burst of blue and orange light that reached through the smoke and showed White Horse the woman standing over her, staring at her lighter with an almost comic perplexity as it refused to catch. Her absorption with it was childishly complete.

White Horse pushed herself upright, so frightened she could hardly breathe. *Snick-snick-snick* went the lighter wheel under the woman's heavy thumb. Sparks darted eagerly across to them, as though wanting to help.

Then, in her only lucky break, White Horse felt the paling against her lower leg move easily and knew she was nowhere near the gate, but by the loose rail, away from the road and the light. She was in the hollow where even the neighbours wouldn't see her, in the dark where the pumpkins sat Halloween-fat in Fall.

The lighter was still flicking. *Snick-snick*. It was so familiar. In the part of her mind that wasn't panicking, she knew that sound.

"Martha?" she croaked out. She couldn't grasp that it was Martha, but as soon as she heard that *snick* she knew. It matched that silhouette, that voice, if you turned it right-side-out again. Martha Johnson, family friend, storekeeper. Martha Johnson was trying to burn her.

Instead of trying to get through the fence's easy gap beside her White Horse was paralysed by this realization. It didn't make sense. She'd been in Martha's store the day before yesterday, buying bread. It couldn't be the same woman. This wasn't real.

"Damn thing," the voice had changed now. Martha was peevish.

"Martha . . ."

"There we go!"

In a moment of unconscious and complete necessity White Horse let go of her bag and closed both hands around the end of the loose rail.

She heard rather than felt herself take light. It was a soft "whump" sound and then a rush of wild, hot wind against her skin. It showed her Martha Johnson's livid, gleeful face holding the lighter and grinning at her own cleverness.

White Horse swung the rail. All the nails that had failed to hold it into the post sank into the old woman's smile with a jarring crunch that smashed her grip loose.

Martha Johnson fell silently, without even putting out an arm to save herself.

White Horse screamed and the fire swooped eagerly into her mouth and down her throat to drown her. For the first time she felt herself starting to burn, and the pain was unbelievable, unbearable.

Something knocked her over, rolled her into the ground, and crushed her flat.

She woke up in hospital in Billings four hours later, but it was another two days before she could talk properly, and in that time she decided that she couldn't keep this to herself any more. She had the machine that was responsible for the deaths and the violence. She couldn't make it work, but she knew what it was, and she knew that the men who'd brought it were government because they'd talked in the diner about it when she was waiting tables.

White Horse was going to have to call her half brother. It was good that she had so long to think it through—she had time to think of all the ways she could start and throw them all away. No lousy Pad call was going to fix things between them.

A week later she discharged herself and took her leave of her friends. With the bag safely packed up inside a new rucksack and with credit-card clothing all over her and debts she was never going to pay, she left for Washington, DC. In the bag, the object that had cracked didn't look like it was broken enough to be useless. Whatever it was, Jude would know. He'd help. He had to.

In her hand mirror, as she travelled on the bus, White Horse looked at her reflection, its long hair all gone, replaced with a tight-braided pseudo-African look to hide the fact that most of the hair was fake. Funny, she thought, and giggled, hoarsely, to herself. Cheyenne hiding in African guise. Like her brother, she had two faces now.

Map

One

"Where the *fuck* have you been? I've been on this line ten minutes now and nobody has the good grace to even fucking speak to me and this is supposed to help? For all you know I could've topped myself and you wouldn't fucking care. Who do you think you are? You know what you are? A bunch of fucking prissy, pointy-headed little shits who think they're better than the rest of us telling us what to think and how to act and how much to drink and not to take any drugs and not to feel better—you don't control us! I know you think you do and that's what you'd like to think, you like thinking you're some kind of fucking elite class who can talk down to us from your fucking ivory towers, don't you? Well, I'll tell you what you know about life and reality outside your theories and your fancy talk. You know what you know? Nothing. *Fucking nothing . . .*"

A deep breath is a cleansing breath, Natalie thought, taking one and letting it go as the ranting continued, without pause or loss of volume, for another solid minute. She waited, drawing an angry face on the flatscreen of her Pad, giving it stabby, straight-up hair and sticking-out eyes, a big screaming mouth with a storm of angry bees coming out of it.

After the day she'd had a few hours on the Clinic helpline was all she needed, but she felt sympathetic. This man on the other end was hopping mad, and she'd been that way, too, all day, but unable to say anything like the stuff he was coming out with. Hearing it said with such sincere violence made her feel a little better. And he was justified, she thought. She was a psychiatric psychologist, with social-science and nanotechnological qualifications coming out her backside, but that didn't mean she knew anything about anything when you came down to it. Then again, maybe she was just brimming with self-pity because her father had told her point-blank that her research was nothing more than a load of superstitious, dangerous rubbish, based on unscientific, invalid data and pie-in-the-sky dreams.

When the caller paused for breath Natalie said, not meaning to speak aloud, "A-men!"

There was a moment of stunned silence.

"Sorry, sorry!" She quickly erased the strict vicar she'd sketched, his pulpit sprouting directly out of Angry Man's hair, which was doubling as hellfire. "I've had a bitch of a day. Now, you were saying?"

But after that Angry Man's abuse became a bit sheepish. At last he began talking about how much he missed his kids, who'd gone to Australia with his ex-wife, and how he drank too much and ate chocolate under the bedsheets at night, reading *Wonder Woman* by torchlight because that was the only way he could get to sleep. As he spoke his voice softened by stages until it had moved from the gruff regret of a stoical man to the disappointed helplessness of a small boy.

Natalie filled in her parts of the call-log on-screen when he'd gone and dried her face off on the same manky piece of paper towel she'd used earlier to wipe up a coffee spill. She blew her nose on the last dry bit and chucked the vile thing into the wastebin. There was a moment's blissful silence.

"Goodnight, Dr. Armstrong!" the last of the day nurses called as she passed the open door of the helpline office. Natalie answered, yawned, and thought she might go and try for another coffee—Rita would be in soon to pick up the shift and she could go home.

The line rang. She picked up the handset. It was a woman, and for five minutes, as the switchboard signalled urgently and Natalie felt the will to live draining out of her, the caller went on and on about how her son's tantrums—strictly humdrum, to Natalie's mind—were becoming unbearable and why wasn't there some prescription drug she could give him to make him calmer and more rational?

"If there was," Natalie imagined saying, "don't you think we'd all be taking it?"

She wrote the words in a speech bubble and gave them to a praying mantis to say.

Natalie said, "It can be very traumatic to experience this, I know, but if you put yourself in his position . . ."

As she talked her mind ran another track entirely. It said, "Have you ever had that experience where you're trying hard to make yourself understood to someone and they just don't get it? And you realize, in the middle of whatever the hell it is you were going on about, that they never will, and you get this sudden awful feeling of being completely and utterly alone? But it's *more* than alone. It's a kind of cosmic *Fuck you, there is no God, and even if there were he wouldn't notice you* kind of alone. You're talking to thin air. You're making noises that don't mean anything to any other living creature on Earth."

The caller said with reluctance, "Well, quite, that's exactly it. He will not listen to reason. But maybe he can't, like you say . . ."

Natalie continued in her mind, blanking out the mother's rationalization.

"And then, right on the heels of that, the last of the fucking rug gets ripped out from under you because you realize that now, even *you* don't know what the hell you were trying to say. And because this idiot's not fucking listening, you've lost it forever and it's like you don't exist. That's why two-year-olds throw fits of rage, because they don't get the last part yet, they still think that they're the focus of the universe. And that's why they get shy and twisted at three, 'cos they figure out that, actually, other people *can* make them not exist.

"That's what's happening to your son. That's all. So don't worry, he'll never get over it. He'll live a straight life, no rocking the boat, no confronting salesmen on the doorstep, no taking the first or the last biscuit in the tin. Just like the rest of us. He'll be normal. Which may be good or bad news, depending on the rest of your family."

Natalie drew a series of ever-decreasing sheep, until the last one was a dot, crushed under a ballooning fatness of a woman with posh hair and a complacent smile, light aircraft circling for a landing on her stomach.

Or had she actually said that?

Natalie sat up suddenly, realizing that there was silence on the other end of the line.

Had she actually said that stuff? Shit. She didn't want to believe it. Her heart was hammering. It would all be recorded. She could be given the sack . . . it might get in the papers. She was exhausted, but that was no excuse. Might she, in a moment of microsleep, have forgotten the training and said that?

"Well, if you think it's normal . . ." the woman's voice said, very hesitantly. "As you say." The call ended.

Natalie kept her hand pressing the handset down and banged her forehead on the tough surface of her desk, once, took a deep breath, thought—*a deep breath is a cleansing breath, stay awake, you silly mare*—and picked up the next caller from the queue, after which she definitely would have to get coffee, or possibly some form of surgery to stop her mouth running away with her. She smothered a yawn with the back of her hand.

"I'd like to speak to Doctor Natalie Armstrong," said a man with a bold American accent.

The voice was clear and strikingly calm, but hiding inside it were tension and anxiety; the stress of a mind wound so tight that Natalie thought she could hear the creaking of imminent implosion.

She felt her back prickling. The voice had spoken her name. The helpline was anonymous at both ends to preserve confidentiality and security. They gave only code names on the hotline in order to avoid the constant attentions of the area's chronic fixators. How had he known to ask for her? Maybe he was an ex-patient. Or maybe it was more than that.

She moved her hand nearer to the Flag Call button, which would ask the police to trace the location. As she hesitated over the button, she said, "Natalie isn't here today. Can I help you?"

"Oh."

Disappointment.

In the pause Natalie's mind veered off. She wondered whether her flatmate, Dan, would have already eaten the microwave pasta and spent the rent on taking one of his boyfriends out to the pub. Or perhaps the kitchen was gleaming like a new knife and he'd remembered not to switch on the shower because of what it did to the people downstairs. She could have a fantasy, just as well as the next nut.

"Who am I talking to, please?" Her American had gone cool and efficient on her.

"This is Jennifer," Natalie said, and waited.

The waiting was the worst. Not knowing if you would hear a sudden scream, a whimper, a tirade of abuse, explicit sexual lusts, or detailed stories of mutilation and eventual horrific death—yours, theirs, or someone else's. Or fear. Or, most commonly, despair.

The silence scared the shit out of her every time, in case whoever was on the other end of the connection was something beyond imagination, a thing that was so virulent and deadly it would travel down the digital band with the smooth effortlessness of a snake and kill her just with the potency of its thoughts and the soft, repetitive sound of its breath.

"Well, I need to speak to Dr. Armstrong on a professional matter of some urgency, and I'll only be in the UK a while. I'm sorry to call you on the toll-free and I won't take up any more of your time. If you could pass on my name and number I'd be grateful. My name is Jude Westhorpe and I'm a Special Sciences Agent with the FBI."

Of course you are, Natalie thought, comforted that he wasn't going to blow tonight. She picked up her pen and began adding to the doodles. He was just a fantasist. Sounded relatively harmless. Probably keen on police procedural, crop circles, and extraterrestrials. He might even be entertaining, although she should try to get rid of him in case the next one in line was seconds away from jumping off the top floor of a high-rise.

She began to draw a cowboy hat.

"Can you take this down or is it recorded?"

"Oh, it's recorded," she said in her most warm and comforting doctor-tone. "One week turnaround, then it's erased once it's been checked. But I'm ready to go here with the pen. Fire away."

"My personal number," he announced and a rapid series of tones dashed into her ear as his Pad transmitted.

She wrote the numbers down automatically by hand, as she'd been trained to do in her student-job days as a night-shift 999 operator. It was a hard habit to break and it made her spoil the fancy hatband and feather she'd been colouring in. She scowled but said "Mmn" with interested politeness.

"And I'm staying at the Hilton in town." He hesitated.

She thought that he was waiting to see if she could swallow that or was about to try and call his bluff. *Classy fantasy*, she thought. *Rather like the old guy who keeps calling me Miss Moneypenny. Which is an improvement after some of the names I've had today*.

Natalie decided to let him off. He wasn't hurting anyone as far as she could judge. Probably lived at home with his aging mother and never went out of the house except to sign on at the social and verify his continued existence to someone in authority. The cowboy received two dots and a flat, short line for eyes and mouth.

"When will you be able to pass this message on?"

"I'll do it right now," Natalie said, admiring his consistency. She slowly scrubbed out the numbers with the round end of her stylus, and replaced the hat with a black crow flying clumsily across the twirly landscape of scribble—Jude Westhorpe. What a name! Very old-rural. It spoke of incest and barn-burnings and the grinding love of toil.

"If I need to call again is there some other office number you can give me?"

Safe ground now, he was having trouble finding excuses to hang on.

"I'm sorry, we aren't allowed to—"

"Okay, okay. Just pass it on as quickly as you can, Jennifer. And thanks. You're doing a great job."

He hung up.

Natalie heard the click with a mild surprise. That was pretty concise, for a dreamer. He must really be tripping out on it. He'd got the accent—although he could be a real American, no reason they couldn't be as insane as the rest. Professional-sounding. Very polite. Only slightly controlling with that last compliment and the use of her name, and he'd even managed to say it like he could have meant it. No hints of masturbation in the background. Nice. She could even look forward to hearing from him again.

"I'm doing a grr-eat job here!" she told the desk and the walls, trying to mimic his accent. Where was it from? Not New York. Not Texas. No, she didn't know.

Natalie signed against the call details and glanced at the clock. It was ten to nine. She should have finished ten minutes ago but she couldn't go when it was like this—the switchboard lights flashing in that red, bloody-dot morse: SOS. She yawned, picked up her handset. *A deep breath is a cleansing breath.*

Natalie reached the flat at ten to midnight. She made her Keycard swipe with the clumsy stabbing action of a casual maniac. The light flashed green—here's your chance, lady!—and she shoved the door with her shoulder, but it was swollen with all the unseasonal June rain and all it did was judder against her with a shiver of repulsion and then jam tight on the hall tiles.

Natalie took a step back into the puddle that was the top step and heel-toed off her good shoes. Balancing on her left leg she karate-kicked the door on its fattest part, just by the handle. Her foot throbbed with protest, but the door swung back and slapped the wall with a noise like a gunshot that echoed in the hall and down the street. If she hadn't been doing it every day for two weeks it would have shocked the daylights out of her. It was easier to shut—she heaved against it with her bottom, her wet feet slipping on the cold floor. She leaned on the angry wood and rested. Only the stairs now—six flights, but carpeted.

Her fantasy of domestic bliss had not come true. She could tell that much just by standing in the tiny hall and looking through the various doorways.

There were odd sounds in the living room and a smog that told her Dan was in and not alone. The kitchen lights were on, showing that spag-bol had been enthusiastically cooked and then left to boil over.

She picked up her case and barged the living-room door open, making plenty of announcing-herself noise. The lights were out but as she passed the sofa reflected gleams of flame (from *her* fancy gothic candelabra and *her* candles) shone pale off three legs, an arm, and a tangle of throw-cloth on the sofa, items which her brain all-too-easily resolved into Dan and his guest *in flagrante*.

She lifted her case right up next to her face to block them from her sight as she stumbled through the piles of clothes on the floor.

"Didn't see anything, didn't see anything!" she repeated in a quick burst.

Dan mumbled from somewhere in the many-limbed hillock, "'S all right, we're just about done anyway."

From behind the thin panels of her own door she thought that the other voice sounded like it belonged to Slow Joe, the alleged deejay who was either always one night before or one night after a really good gig that somehow Natalie or Dan never managed to get to—"You work freakth are alwayth thtuck in the offith, like. No freethtyle happenin'!" The voice had an affected lisp on top of its affected accent that was supposed to make it sound artistic. Definitely the man himself.

Natalie put the radio on to a talk station so that Joe wouldn't find an excuse to come in and start moaning about music. She opened her case and prised out the box of fried rice she'd bought on the way home. No cutlery. Well, she wasn't going through Mata Hari's boudoir scene again.

She was eating, using two pencils for chopsticks, with her face halfway inside the carton when Dan put his head round the door. His shaggy-brown-dog hair and spaced-out expression were perpetual, as though he was living in his own portable Barbados. She envied it with all her heart.

"Hello, Smiler!" He beamed at her. "How's things at the mad factory?"

It always annoyed Natalie that he talked as though he didn't work there himself, as though he had nothing to do with the place and could just leave it without a second thought, which was true. He could. She, on the other hand, had responsibilities . . . but she'd had enough martyrdom for one night.

She scowled. "What's that stuff in the air?"

"Joe brought it. Cuban something. 'S useless, anyway. Bit late for you, though. Swinging from the rigging all over town, are they? Weather brings it out in people, I reckon. Rain all the time. What they need is some serious smoke." He seemed to notice that she wasn't joining in and gestured with his nose towards the papers and electronics scattered around her, "You never know when to quit the job, do you?"

"I'm fine." She scrubbed her feet against the carpet and nodded towards the door with a look that asked when Joe was leaving.

"Yeah, you look it. Left your shoes downstairs again? Joe's just going. I'll get 'em." He vanished, leaving a puff of incense and poppy ash in his wake that boiled up in the stale air of her room and then vanished.

"Your cheap conjuring does not impress me, Doctor Connor," she said, eyes narrowed, and then sighed and looked around her. Even pantomime villains did better than this.

Peeling wallpaper, still not fixed after two years. Dirty clothes on the floor right. Part-used on the floor middle. Washed and dried but not ironed, floor left. Washed and dried, no chance of ironing *ever*, hanging on each post of the bedhead like two dead angels moulting. The incense covered most of the faint smell of mildew coming from the sash windows and it made her sneeze.

She got up to see if Slow had gone yet, and got an eyeful of bare buttock trying to squeeze itself into tight trousers that were made of some material that glowed blue in the dark. He had a sixth sense for any kind of attention and turned on her with a sneer at her grey work suit.

"Fashion pathing you by again, ith it?" he said, the effect spoiled as he hopped to put his shoes on. He gave her a twirl when he was done, and had to thrust a hand out to the table to stop himself falling over. Cologne, alcohol, and fresh sweat wafted off him. A nervous giggle passed his lips and was stifled. He glanced to see if she'd noticed.

"It's pathed you on the way back again," she retorted, unable to prevent herself mimicking his lisp. "Where did you get that shirt? It looks like it's made of cheese."

"Pith off." He grabbed his coat from the darkness on the sofa and gave her the fingers.

She gave them back to him without any interest. "Got any gigs lined up?"

"Got any life lined up?" he shot back over his shoulder as he groped around in the half-light, picking things up and stuffing them in his pockets.

Natalie watched him, trying to see what items of debauchery he'd brought with him, or if he was stealing, but it was too difficult and besides, she didn't know what she or Dan owned that was worth the bother. She hadn't got enough energy left to make a witty response to his last dig. Instead, she chewed her rice at him vacantly, following his every move until he made for the door, his trousers giving him the revolving hip action of a carriage clock. It looked painful and she was glad. She thumbed the lights and the TV on and sat down, with only a trace of revulsion, in the warm crater that was the sofa.

It was good to be home.

She felt even better when Dan returned with her shoes, rescued from the puddle outside. He put them to dry under the radiator and sat down next to her. They both stared at the big-screen doings of some US police show involving a team of trained dogs. Dan liked the programme: it reminded him of *White Fang*, but less romantic.

"Some bloke called," he said after a minute.

Her heart sank; she knew no one. "Who?"

"I dunno. Some American."

"Shit. When?" An efficient stalker she could live without. "What did you say?" She put the rice down and searched around for the remote. Dan was sitting on it.

"Important is he?" Dan said, feigning lack of interest.

"Move your arse. I didn't say that."

Dan turned his head and looked down at her, "Got a fancy man, have we? All tucked away at the Hilton when she says she's going to do the volunteer hotline. And such a virtuous cover story, too."

"And if I did, why would he be calling here?" Natalie leaned over him to make a grab for the house controller but he picked it up first and held it out of her reach. "Dan!"

"If you tell me . . ." he began.

"He called the hotline!" she snapped. "Tonight. He called me there and he knew my name. I don't want some mad git knowing everything about me."

Dan's taunting grin softened. He let her have the remote.

Natalie cued the answer service. It was the same man. There was no image, only voice. It played over the silenced pictures of slo-mo malamutes on patrol.

"Doctor Armstrong? I've gotta see you straightaway. Please call. Here's the number, in case you didn't get the message at the Clinic. I'll be at the hotel."

"You think he's a nut?" Dan asked, using his toe to pick up a sock from the carpet. "He sounds normal. Could have got your number from the Clinic registry."

"Not the flat number," she said. "And they always start by sounding normal. Mostly. And here, what would you bet on it? He says he's an agent for the FBI, but he's in Britain. He says he has to see me, but not why. He doesn't give any proof of ID. His name, for Christ's sake, is *Jude Westhorpe*. Allegedly."

"Now you mention it, it does sound something of a long shot." Dan drew a thumb and forefinger around his nonexistent goatee and narrowed his eyes. His heavy fringe came down like the fire curtain at a theatre and made him look like an old sheepdog. "Ten quid he's real."

"Done." She finished her rice and threw the carton onto the table.

In the dark and the quiet the room smelled terrible; smoke and sweat, sex and old dust. The TV dogs bounded down an alley and leapt a six-foot chain link fence. Soft rock accompanied their flight as Dan cued the sound. Natalie stood up to open the window and let a blast of cold air in. She looked out at the night across the roofs of the terraces opposite and wondered where life was going. She'd done nothing important in six months. She had her interview with the Ministry to wait for. If that went bad then she didn't know what she'd do. She didn't like to think of leaving, not when Dan was here. Without her, what would he get up to?

Under her sore, door-karate foot she felt something unidentifiable, but moist and a little slimy. It was, curiously, the most sensual and attractive experience she could remember having in recent weeks.

"I'm off to bed."

Dan snorted, "What, and I threw Joe out for one mad bloke's phone call and two minutes of mind-numbing conversation? Jesus, it's more fun at work."

"Yeah," she said and was already more than half asleep before her head hit the pillow. As Natalie slid out of the waking world it occurred to her that half asleep was the state she lived in these days. Awake was something she wouldn't know if it bit her on the ankle. Awake people noticed that Dan needed her attention and she didn't do that. She tried to get up and apologize but it was too late for that. Her mind slipped from her and into the dark.

Jude Westhorpe stood on the long straight section of Haxby Road where the spiked iron railings that surrounded the York Clinic for Psychiatric and Psychological Research were overhung by mature lime trees offering a small measure of concealment. He idled for a minute or two to look, his jacket slung over his shoulder, expression vague, pretending to be a curious tourist. The trees formed a single row that bordered a wide swathe of grass, landscaped in curves and dips so that it held the old red-brick buildings as though in the palm of a protecting hand. He recognized the pattern as one that made fast running impossible and mowing a trial. On the far side of the compound the parking lot was a maze of thorny bushes, again giving no clear escape routes.

Jude began walking slowly along the lane. Closer to the gates he noticed that there was a uniformed security official/greeter at the door, who was connected by lapel mike to the ones manning the barriers at the fence. He made as though to tie his laces, reaching through the rails at the same time to recover the tiny surveillance unit he'd left the day before. He had a feeling his high-tech espionage was all in vain. From the aerials and dishes on the flat roof of the modern block to the suspiciously large number of people who moved around the doors, he didn't think there was going to be an easy way in, and this Armstrong woman wasn't going to call him, not with the approach tactics he'd used so far.

Once he was out of sight of the Clinic he paused to sit on a bench, wood grey with age and wear, on its back a bronze plaque that said "Mrs. Phillip Sillitoe, MP." He used his Pad to check Armstrong's picture again—by now it was almost etched on his brain. He looked for her everywhere he went: a small woman, early thirties, slim, with a red-purple crop cut and a face made elfin and bold at the same time by sharp cheekbones and a powerful, long mouth that she usually lipsticked in shocking colour. Her mouth fascinated him. It looked like it would open onto something more than just teeth and tongue. It looked as though something wicked and erotic, sharp and lethal lived inside it and could leap out.

The surveillance unit hadn't managed to get any sightings of her. Jude sighed with annoyance and made himself start walking towards the city centre. The hangers-on he'd seen must be Ministry agents or plainclothes police, and he had maybe two days left before someone noticed that he wasn't on vacation at his mother's house in Seattle. He had to do something more drastic.

Considering exactly what this could be lengthened his walk until he was almost through the centre of the impossibly tiny town, approaching one of the bridges that crossed the river. Unwilling to go further he took a turn down to the waterfront and bought a drink at the small pub there named the King's Arms, which seemed to be one of the attractions he ought to visit, judging by the number of students and pot-bellied men loafing around it.

The barman, a genial, overweight, utterly unremarkable man in some new, sleazy shirt whose material played video images across the pockets, served him a pint of Theakston's; a dark beer, it smelled faintly of vinegar and old, watery cellars. Jude watched the windows on the man's chest, sun setting behind the clouds, a flight of black-winged gulls. He wondered what the images were supposed to tell him and briefly wondered what he'd put on his own pockets if he had the bad taste to try it. Probably a picture of some fabric, the same as the rest of the shirt. Ironic, but not very original.

Jude sighed with annoyance at his own predictability, took the drink outside, and sat at a trestle table that was covered in old glasses and sandwich packets, drinking the beer very slowly. In obedience to his wishes and the alcohol in his otherwise empty stomach time stretched out and developed holes, beckoning him to fall into them.

He stared at the river. The water was high enough to be almost level with his feet. Brown and thick, it was full of unpredictable currents, slow on the surface, racing underneath. It looked almost like you could walk on it. Getting into the clinic would be like that, too—like walking on water.

In the pocket with the disk of stolen files he'd brought to give to Doctor Armstrong was the photograph from his sister's backpack. He took it out and looked it over yet again: his mandala. Funny how objects could freight meaning like cargo-craft, a scrap of paper as heavy as a safe full of lead. This one carried that kind of weight and served to remind him of all the great justifications he had for being here, lying to his partner, lying to his boss, getting his mother to cover, getting false papers and a bogus ID to use, just in case. In case Armstrong wasn't easy to get hold of. In case he was pushed to the point he was at now, pinned to it. And, God, he didn't want to do a cover number because that was an easy way to get caught out, but soon, in an hour or so, he was going to have to.

The photograph showed White Horse's wood-framed house, burned to the ground. He'd spent summers there, riding and hiking with her and her mother, while his own mother worked nine-to-five at a Seattle accountancy practice to keep him in school and his friends got sent to summer camps and private villas in Europe. Deer Ridge #32 was a second family home to him. He'd never realized how cheap and fragile it was until he'd seen this image.

Where the sitting room used to be a few brittle spars of black char reached up from the cinders; four fingers outstretched for help and no thumb. On the left side the washing machine was just recognizable, its door slimed with oily smoke, frame melted. Here and there were fragments of other things: the corner of the piano lid, the funny, homemade metal casket that had held the TV and radio unit, springs from the lousy guest bed that always made his back feel like he'd gone ten rounds in the ring still holding their shape like giant cartoon hair. Rills of grey smoke gathered in the shape of snakes where the table and chairs had been.

With the house out of the way and the branches of the Scots pine next door crisped up you could see a clear view of the mountains. The sky was brightly blue over their summits, a trail of cloud like a puff of cigarette smoke blurring from their tops, and the sunlight glinted in a tiny flash from the valley where the reservation wire-fence line ran alongside the narrow dirt road towards the highway.

That place was about six thousand miles away but Jude only had to touch the picture to smell the ash on the breeze and feel the tremor in his sister's hands where the camera shake had blurred the foreground into a mess of green and brown. Five years ago he'd never thought he'd see it again.

They'd had their last fight when he left the marines and joined the newly set-up Division of Special Sciences in the Federal Bureau of Investigation. There was no government agency more symbolic of all that White Horse hated about the state, and rightly so. Their father had died in one of the skirmishes during the occupation of Pine Ridge in the 1970s, and by a government bullet. Leonard Peltier eventually went down to Leavenworth for the two agents who were killed, because somebody had to go, and even though she was barely one at the time this miscarriage of justice was the primal force in shaping the political activist and passionate cultural advocate who grew up to be White Horse Jordan, Jude's half sister.

It was this part of her, and not the other parts that liked him better, that had barred him from entering that now burned-down place ever again. Many seasons ago, when it had still been standing, and about the time that Martha Johnson had opened her second store downtown, they'd exchanged their views.

"You've joined the fucking enemy!" White Horse screamed at him, her face dark with fury as she physically pushed him off the step and onto the path. "There's nothing between us any more! Nothing! Go back to your mom's rich white family and live a great life doing good for the state that loves you so much. You don't deserve Dad's name!"

Jude had been too angry to speak, but she could see what he wanted to say and cut it off with a slicing motion of her arm.

"You're betraying us. Everything. You spit on us and our history! All for your money and the power to shove little people around!"

"I'm not the one who said they were little, remember that."

"Fuck you! Traitor."

"And what are you? A cultural dinosaur! A fascist preservationist! Holding back everyone who follows you by forcing them to stay on bad land, in poor housing and with no prospects when they could be a part of the future and not the past. You're always whining on about history. Well, that shows there's no point in clinging sentimentally to old ways as if you were still living in the goddamn' stone age. Everything changes! Talk about spirit? You haven't got the monopoly on that end of the world. You don't own it because of the color of your skin like some fucking multiple-entry permit. Don't you think we have to change as well?"

For once he'd reduced her to jaw-breaking silence.

He didn't say the final thing in his heart, which was that he'd agreed to ditch the marines and sign on with Special Sciences because it seemed like a chance to set a thing straight that was broken; to work from the inside and force what he could of the FBI into a better, more just kind of shape. It was the sort of foolish ideal, like her own, that

White Horse would have instantly leaped on and shredded in contempt. Jude hadn't been sure that he'd have enough conviction left to carry it through. But when she got angry he pushed aside his concern that a single person made little difference inside the huge politics, especially a minor servant like him.

They had shared a final stare of mutual loathing with their chins stuck out at mirror-identical stubborn angles on that doorstep, and then, amid puzzled looks from the others standing on the lane—Jim Johnson and Marie from one lot over, Rising Wolf on the opposite side who waved and grinned because he hadn't heard what was going on—Jude had got in his car and driven out of there and never been back.

He wasn't even sure that this whole operation wasn't some big apology. But that would be like backing down, and he couldn't do that. So it wasn't. It really wasn't.

Jude put the photo back in his pocket and finished the beer. It was warm and it tasted homemade, like the stuff he and White Horse brewed one summer vacation when they thought it would be cool to copy Sam Adams. He liked it and got himself another. At the other tables tourists in flimsy pastels, dressed for a summer that never seemed to quite get started, shivered as a cloud crossed the sun. He put his jacket on and watched a few pretty girls and some curious-looking dogs pass by—slipping into the time hole with the ease of any river-bank animal.

"So, just remind me again what we're dealing with."

Ray Innis, ginger crew-cut shining glossy as a racehorse in the weak light of the King's Arms back bar, leaned over the table towards Dan. His leather jacket creaked over the bulky shape that didn't quite fit under his armpit.

Dan looked across the table at Ray with dislike, trying not to think about the gun. Ray's bland, dispassionate face hid a core of exploitative, insensitive self-interest that was certifiable and Dan knew better than to get on the bad side of it. He kept his voice as low as he could and separated the sides of a beer mat to make something to write on. In blotchy ballpoint he illustrated his explanation with a diagram.

"NervePath is like a computer. It's hardware. It goes inside the nervous system and the brain, right? This thing we're working on and testing is like the software; what makes the NervePath work. It's going to be called Mappaware."

"What for?"

"It's Latin." Dan thought he managed to say it without hinting that Ray was an ignorant, uneducated, barbarian bastard but it was hard to tell. Ray had a mind like a cheap personal organizer with low processing power; what it didn't deal with now it stored for later. Somewhere inside it was a ledger with all of Dan's credits and debits painstakingly printed and Dan had this feeling that he was in the red.

"And you think this stuff will start to take off when?" Ray pocketed the half-mat without looking at it, his pale blue eyes fixed on Dan the whole time.

"I don't know. Like I said. A while."

"And it has potential for a bit of creative marketing? You could write some of this yourself? Dreams, fantasies . . ."

"It's not porn, for fuck's sake!" Dan hissed at him, unable to prevent himself. He looked around them both quickly, but nobody seemed to notice them. They knew Ray and his dealings.

Ray's stare didn't waver.

Dan said, "It'd do something more like make you happy, if you were down, you know? Make you like your job. Make you better at, I don't know, typing or something." He wasn't prepared for what Ray did next. He was hoping that he'd be able to put off Ray's interest long enough for Dan himself to get out of what he owed him and out of the United Kingdom before Ray cottoned on to the full potentials of black-market mind control.

Ray took a brown envelope from his pocket and put it into Dan's pocket.

"What the—" Dan started to say. He didn't want favours from Ray.

"A retainer," Ray said, holding the envelope in its place and daring Dan to do anything about it. The cheap finish on his hair gleamed like new pennies. "Got to keep you on my side, haven't I? Got to keep things businesslike, old son. Here's a little bit of interest. More where that came from. All you do is keep me informed. I can't say fairer than that now, eh? And we'll say no more about what you owe me."

Ray wanted a lot more than that, Dan knew, or would do when the time came. He was thinking big, for a small-time dealer. Dan opened his mouth to object, but nothing came out.

"You know your trouble, Dan old son? You think too much." Ray eased out of his seat and let a fiver fall from his fingers to buy Dan another drink. It lay on the table like a dead leaf.

From his six foot six he looked down and Dan felt himself about five years old; that small, that naive, that weak. Ray didn't need to say anything else. Dan knew it all. But Ray was "feeling his verbals" today, as he would have said. He maintained eye contact with Dan for a few more seconds. He was smiling as he bent low to Dan's ear and whispered, his breath as sweet and pure as a baby's, "It's all porn, love. In the end."

Dan waited until he was sure Ray was long gone and stood up, feeling ill. He went into the men's room, locked himself in a stall, and looked in the envelope. Five thousand in used notes and a grand's worth of doctored heroin that gave all the high and none of the trouble after: pure gold.

Dan's guts tried to turn over. Ray really was thinking of becoming the next black-market baron. Dan was going to be his court fool. It all seemed so far from that time he'd been off his face and had mentioned the NervePath to Ray's associate, Ed. Why had he said anything? Maybe it had been to get some coke when he was on his bad ride, during finals. Maybe it had been then. Christ.

When he heard another man come into the room he got out of the stall and made to wash his hands. He washed his face with cold water too and looked at himself in the mirror: happy-go-lucky floppy-haired Dan, the lad with no harm in him. Reminding himself of this character made him feel better. He didn't mean any bad. He wasn't able to. Not him. Was that the beginning of lines around his mouth? He sneaked a tube of Estée Lauder Active Regenerator from his pocket and rubbed it in carefully. The first sharp start of the day's beard under his fingers made him wince.

Outside the pub on the riverwalk the crowds were already thickening as the sun came out, teasing the boat crews of the cruisers with hints that they might come back for the afternoon sailing. As he hesitated between going back for another drink or returning to work Dan saw an exceptionally handsome man on his own, sitting staring at the river. He wouldn't have paid attention—Dan knew when he had a hope and when he hadn't—except that he didn't look English, he looked American. There was something about the way he wore his dark, expensive clothes. No English person put a turtleneck and an open-collar jacket together that way. And he was kind of exotic, a half-and-half of some kind, and better-looking than anyone Dan had seen all year, even with that haircut that didn't know if it was long or short. In fact, he looked like Dan would have wanted to be—calm, professional, at ease, enjoying the afternoon without a care in the world. Dan watched for a full thirty seconds but he didn't get an eye contact. Straight, too. Bad luck.

Shrugging his own jacket closer around him, Dan set off for the bus stop. He wondered how he could tell Natalie about Ray. She might be able to help him out of this. But no. She was already in enough difficulties with the project itself and the keen interest of the Ministry—and her "stalker." It would have to wait. And there was the Ministry woman, too, always on his back about the Clinic and the staff. But she could wait and all. He didn't like so much being on his mind at once, he just wanted it all to go away and not matter. If only he could get enough money together he could cut and run and go somewhere where it wouldn't matter. At the travel agent's on Market Street they were offering flights to Australia for only a grand and a half. Really, thinking of it like that, he could go any time, if things turned that bad. If it weren't for Natalie he'd go today.

Dan got on the bus at Micklegate Bridge and watched the streets wind him around and around until he didn't know which direction he was facing.

Two

"I'm sorry," said the man from the Ministry, "but it's out of the question."

Natalie ground her teeth together and tried to appear normal as she did so but that, too, was getting beyond a joke. "I don't see how you make the distinction," she said finally. "It has no scientific basis."

"No, maybe not. But it has a priority basis. The Ministry doesn't view your research as immediately relevant. Selfware," and he paused, rolling the word around his mouth like a gobstopper that didn't taste good. "It's theoretical, even metaphysical. Its consequences may be profound for the individual, but they have no obvious immediate application outside some kind of self-perfecting or self-advancing endeavour, and that's not something our paymasters are interested in right now."

"It's no more theoretical than the Mappa Mundi project!" Natalie retorted. "It shares a lot of fundamental technology. It rests on exactly the same conjectures. My whole contribution to that arena—a highly successful project so far, I might add—has been in terms of the work I've done on Selfware. You must see that. My work is an extension to Mappa Mundi. It isn't different in any way."

"Yes. And excellent work it's been. Here," and he pointed at the paper files on the desk, "are many recommendations and notices from your bosses. I can see that where the two different areas overlap you've done pioneering and invaluable work." He smiled at her with genuine admiration and Natalie wondered, *Why? Why soft-soap me and talk when you won't give in? And it's all right for you, you've got your job saying no to people like me and there's nothing I can do.*

She tried her final, desperate card. "This clinic has to turn away patients my research would potentially help. Depression on its own robs the whole country of millions of man days a year, blights lives. That could change. Even in the army people must get depressed . . ." But it was a losing wicket and she gave it up, because the light in Glover's eyes hadn't changed a bit. He was unchallenging, calm, approving.

"No licence, then?" she said.

"I'm sorry." He gathered her papers together and laid them in his case, edges lined up under the Top Secret stamp that looked to Natalie like something you got in a kid's detective set. "Of course, you can still practise and assist in the work that your father will be supervising. The Mappa project as a whole continues. And the majority of your work, even in Selfware, is effectively being tested in our trials on that, isn't it?"

"When, then?"

He spread his fingers out on the closed lid of his briefcase and tried not to look at the wall clock. "I can't say. I'm sure that once Mappaware is fully licensed for commercial use, say in another five or six years, that it wouldn't be that long. Personally—" he relaxed, letting the stiff line of his shoulders drop forwards "—I found your reports fascinating. Expanded states of consciousness, hyperperception, evolution of the mind, testing the existence of the soul: real superman stuff. If it was up to me . . ."

"Yeah," Natalie said around the six- or seven-year-rock in her throat. "Thanks."

"Well, then."

And it was over for another year. The Ministry interview.

Natalie heard the door close behind her as she stood in the plush corridor of the offices wing and wondered how many more interviews it would take, and at what date and time the Chinese or the Americans or some backstreet genius would beat her to publication and patent. On top of that she also had her father to face again, and wouldn't *he* be full of consolation? Most likely he'd snort derisively and that would be the verdict on her entire career: wasted on a futile direction of enquiry more suited to vicars, gurus, and other snake-oil merchants. She set off back to her own section of the Clinic.

At the drinks machine in the Research Sciences Lounge she typed for a can of cola and got lemonade. Popping the seal and swigging the nasty, oversweetened fizz inside, she reflected that, of course, she shouldn't be in it for herself. What did it matter who helped who first as long as someone got saved? Her pager went off in her pocket, vibrating with the sudden urgency that always made her imagine a small animal wired to the eyeballs on caffeine. She glanced at the screen note it displayed, which was from Reception. It said, "Man here to upgrade Treatment Rooms. You to meet."

Natalie felt ready to throw in the towel. There was no way she had time to take anyone into BioSafetyLevel-$_4$ areas, with their showers and suits and all that palaver. Anyway, it was Dan's job and where was he? He should be here by now with the sandwiches—he'd been gone fifty minutes. It was almost half past two and she had meetings all afternoon.

She took another mouthful of her drink and then tossed the half-full can into the bin on her way to reception, trying to fight the desire to give whoever was there a mouthful about their timing. She'd heard nothing about any upgrades from the supplier although, given the week's record, that was nothing surprising. Once she reached the desk however, she changed her mind.

The NervePath systems engineer was gorgeous. Not just merely handsome or kind of attractive in an interesting way but pulse-jacking, heart-crushing, punch-in-the-gut primordial.

Natalie slowed right down on approach to let the blush fade and took her time watching him, wondering if maybe she could skip the catch-up parts of the meetings and only return for discussion, giving her an easy hour of clear time. She knew it wasn't possible with a project as complex as Mappa Mundi, but she wished it were.

The systems engineer was talking to Dan's friend, the senior nurse, Edie Charlton, who was so intent on him that she didn't register Natalie's arrival until she noticed him looking over her shoulder. Edie muttered a quick introduction, and Natalie saw his soft, interested gaze sharpen as he noted her name, although she was too busy noticing him to wonder why.

Until now she hadn't had a type or even looked for one. Men were an oblique concept, people with different outer casings whom she barely noticed in a sexual way. Natalie had work, like Slow Joe said, not a life. Maybe now that her chance for fully fledged independent research was gone again the neglected bits of her brain were waking up. Whatever it was, she felt suddenly self-conscious and despairingly hopeful, acutely aware of her sexless appearance in the lab whites and grey suit, the fact that she forgot her lipstick, the sweat trying to leap up all over her as she played it cool.

"I didn't realize an upgrade was due out yet," she said, thinking, *Yes, keep it businesslike, you've no chance anyway.*

"It's a bug fix," the engineer said easily. His accent was one of those transatlantic ones that drifted about between English and American. His name badge identified him to her pocketpad as Jason Hilbert, PathSystems Employee No. 14781, certified engineer rating 04, MoD-cleared.

"Not in the log," Nurse Charlton murmured, although she didn't seem very bothered about that minor security niggle either. She broke from smiling at him to share a glance with Natalie; the visual equivalent of a wolf whistle.

"I should check with your office, if you don't mind," Natalie said, face straight. "We don't have you on our file."

"Please." He nodded, his big, blue $BSL\text{-}_4$ oversuit rustling as he set his case down and smiled—a big, white-toothed smile that Natalie, just for a second or two, thought was nervous. When he smiled, though, he looked even better. He looked dangerous.

You are such an idiot, Natalie reminded herself. *Stop it.*

"New to the job?" she asked. There was something familiar about him. But she knew she'd remember if she'd seen him before. He was quite a lot taller than she was—wasn't everyone?—and athletic under the coveralls. It was the eyes that caught her, though. They had a sparkle she only associated with someone showing genuine interest, even though that might more usually be directed at the figure of Charlton than herself. It was confusing her.

"Three months in," he said. "Takes a long time to pass the exams."

The PathSystems office machine returned a verify code and Natalie had to be satisfied.

"Where's Dan? Have you paged him?" she asked Charlton.

"He's on his way back from town. Why don't you open up the systems and he can take over when he gets here? I wouldn't have asked you only," and she smiled wryly, "Mister Hilbert says you have a friend in common."

"Oh?" That seemed very unlikely.

"Charles Dyer, at Cambridge," Hilbert said quickly.

Natalie nodded, "Oh yeah." She gestured towards the walkway that led to the heart of the clinic and they began moving towards the doors into the Therapy Centre. He moved confidently at her side, carrying the weight of his case easily, although she could tell it was heavy. Charles Dyer had overseen her PhD work. It was possible Hilbert could have studied in the same department, but why would he choose to be an engineer when he'd been taking blue-sky courses at university?

"I know. I did MA work there after you'd gone," he added. "Professor Dyer helped me out a lot and you were mentioned. I used some of your past research papers."

"Really?" Natalie was suddenly feeling less confident than she had a moment ago. It wasn't because of Dyer, or what he was saying, just something about the voice. "Which ones?" She held open the doors and Hilbert and his case passed inside. She swiped the inner doors to the treatment areas with her security pass and showed him through into the airlock.

"'Memetic Mapping of Ground State Axioms' and 'Metaphoric Process Conversion Theory.'" He didn't slip in saying it. She listened to the lilt of the syllables.

As they were forced to pause for air filtration and test, Natalie put her security card in her pocket. *Fuck it*, she thought. *Perfect and bonkers.* She turned towards him and looked into his dark, honest eyes.

"You don't know Charles Dyer, do you?"

Natalie Armstrong was not as Jude had imagined her in the flesh. She resembled her pictures only in a strictly technical way. In fact, her whole face was split dramatically down the middle: animated on the left, deadpan on the right. Its large, tilted grey eyes were still and focused. They looked straight through into the core of him with unnerving calm. Under her spiky magenta hair the effect was startling and direct. What the photographs had failed to communicate, and what he hadn't been prepared for, was the fast-snapping intelligence that sat right behind those eyes and expressed itself so vividly left of centre. He didn't think she'd bought his story for more than half a second straight. He felt the beat of blood in his neck beneath the suit's tight collar.

"No," he admitted and put his cases down. "I went to MIT, did biology, went into the marines, and got poached into a special branch of—" He hesitated, seeing her face wrap itself around a sardonic look as she mouthed silently, ". . . the FBI."

The line of her extraordinary mouth encompassed humour, resignation, and disappointment all at once. He found himself staring at its muscular precision with unprofessional speculation.

"Yeah." It was a moment or so dawning but he realized that she must have been the one he spoke to that first night on the hotline. "Listen, I guess this isn't a very good start, but I tried a legitimate way and—"

"Okay." She held her hands up and already looked infinitely sick of pretending to believe him. "You've tried very hard to get hold of me. We're here for five minutes anyway because of the safety systems and the airlock prep-time for the BSL-$_4$ zone, so you've got that long. I have to be in a meeting and I don't have time for whatever spying, blackmail, or looney-tunes you've got. So make sure you fit it all in."

Jude rubbed his face with his hand. He suddenly wasn't sure he could persuade her, and he wasn't even sure that what he had was worth her contempt. The weariness of the last seventy-two hours crept through him, numbing his limbs, but he took out his Pad and showed her the screen. Shakily he cued a photograph and she, looking bored, gazed impassively at it.

He took a second to register his own irritation with her attitude and it gave him the energy to speak forcefully, "This is me and my sister, aged eighteen and seventeen."

"Mmn." Neutral. She glanced at his face, gaze flicking across it like she was examining a portrait for likenesses.

Jude pointed at the screen, "This is her house. That in the background is Deer Ridge. This line is where the reservation's boundary runs and this—" he changed views "—is the town of Deer Ridge itself. Bar, bingo, stores, gas station. Your average American backwater."

"Mmn hmm." Still listening, but watching his face more than the Pad. Maybe she thought he was crazy. He'd thought so before now.

"This is her house as it is now." He showed her the Polaroid from his pocket.

Armstrong took it and looked it over. Her left eyebrow dropped fractionally into a demi-frown and was corrected. "Nasty. She wasn't in it?"

"No. That is, not fatally." He changed the slide view on the Pad again, his fingers stumbling on the keyboard. His voice threatened to waver and he had to breathe hard, "And this is who burned it down."

They both looked at the picture of a mild-faced, middle-aged Native American woman in a colourful waistcoat and jeans, smiling at the camera, her hand holding the rope of a stout brown pony on which a child was riding backwards.

"Her name is Martha Johnson and she lives, lived, half on the res and half off, because she has two stores in the town and she did door-to-door deliveries for twenty-five years. Three weeks ago she had a visit from some government guys—claimed they were Feds, but no way—passing through, looking for some of the young troublemakers—you know there's some tension between the res kids and the others, the usual stuff but recently someone wrecked the stands after the high school ball game and they're both blaming each other. Anyway." He realized his time was getting short and Natalie Armstrong's expression was still only polite.

"After they've gone Martha starts getting aggravated. By the time they find her dead in one of the dry creek beds, shot with her own .22 pistol—not very effectively, it took her a few hours to die—she's stabbed three people and tried to burn down five properties, including my sister's house. She also shot nine domestic cats, two dogs, both survived, and her husband. Married twenty-one years. Had five kids. One in college, one in prison, three with good jobs—that's Georgie there in the picture on the horse, she's the one in prison. Six-hour operation but husband didn't survive."

He paused for breath and risked another look at her. His hand holding the Pad up was turning white and numb with tension.

Armstrong glanced up at him and Jude saw that fast mind turning what he'd said over and over, already trying to see what she might have to do with it and reaching for the vital clue. At least, he hoped she was.

He forced his bloodless hand to work and changed the views. He had a gallery of police mugshots, native, white and black, some of them dead ones, naming them as they passed. "These people all exhibited peculiar and undiagnosed mental illnesses in that same week. Their statements and circumstances were all catalogued in detail by officers at the local station, but then confiscated by another FBI unit sent in for investigations. No charges have been brought for eight murders, four attempted murders, one rape, three counts of burglary, twenty-one counts of assault, and at least fifteen other crimes including animal cruelty, vandalism, and incitement to riot. All the suspects here have been arrested and held without trial since two weeks ago Thursday, under the Mental Health Provision. Until the day of that visit though, all these people were absolutely okay. Since their arrests there's been no repeat of the violence and disorientation in any other people in that town. One affected person was a traveller from out of state. He was arrested last Tuesday in Wisconsin for trying to rob graves and was committed to state care indefinitely. No prior indication of any kind of mental or stress-related disorders."

Jude met Dr. Armstrong's gaze again, the grey-green stare focused on him with disquieting precision. "I've met him," he said, careful not to glance away. "In the hospital. He wasn't even able to give his own name. The doctors have no diagnosis. It doesn't fit anything they've ever seen before. I can give you the report. They said his mind was just—scrambled, like someone had stuck a spoon in his head and scooped it around."

He didn't think he'd ever met someone so compelling to look at, nor so difficult to read. Even now, when he had seconds left to make his case, he found himself wishing they could have met under other circumstances when he could get to know her.

"You mean altered at a physical level?" she asked. "Did they scan it?"

"It's in the report. Yes." He knew five minutes had to be up. "And there's one other thing, in case this doesn't interest you." He stumbled through putting the files from his pocket into the Pad and getting them loaded. He wanted her to tell him they were irrelevant. He wanted to see how her face changed when she looked at them, even though he'd have no idea what she was thinking.

"Here. My sister stole these from the arresting agents. I thought—that is, I was told by my colleague in Washington that you'd know what this is."

As the files came up Armstrong took the Pad out of his hands and stared at it. Both sides of her face set like stone. Only her eyes dashed back and forth as she read line after line of the code he hadn't even been able to identify.

After a second she said, "What colleague in Washington?" Her voice was cold and direct, like a general ordering an assault on a hard target.

The door locks beeped, to show that they were ready. She didn't move, but paged down the file in slow, regular sections.

"I can't say." Jude had thought this over a lot before he came here, knowing she would ask. He'd decided that, if the worst case was true and the files were bad, she couldn't betray what she didn't know.

"And what made you come here to find me, instead of going to a NervePath expert in America?" She was still reading as she spoke, multitasking, though he had no doubt she was listening to him very closely.

"I thought it may be a piece of government work. Everyone I could talk to there may be involved. They either wouldn't confirm what it was or they'd know someone had found it out. Usually we're not supposed to tread on the toes of National Security. But this—" He struggled to justify such a huge break with procedure, even to himself. "It's personal. I got your name on a Netsearch. My newspilot chose you as the most likely candidate to help me."

"I must have an interesting profile, then," she said and looked up at him, almost joking. The laughter drained from the right side of her face, lingered a little on the left. "This could have you arrested and indefinitely detained right now." She handed the Pad back. "Did you know that?"

"It was a chance."

She nodded. "And if I help you then you won't be the only one breaking the law. They still kill people for less."

There was nothing he could do but wait and watch her. Her gaze didn't break once from his, although her eyes narrowed as she strove to see into his soul. If she said no, then he was out of ideas and he'd have to go home and admit failure. He thought of his sister's face and the red, furious scars that splashed it.

"I'll need to read this in detail to know whether or not it's responsible for the activities you've mentioned," Armstrong said after another ten seconds had passed. She jammed her hands in the pockets of her white lab coat, shrugged as if to be rid of the weight of the decision, and keyed the airlock to open the outer door. "Before I do—what are your feelings on this kind of technology? If it were to turn out that your suspicions are right and your government is creating this for military or national use, then what? And what happens to me?"

It took a second or two for him to realize she had agreed.

"I was kind of hoping it wouldn't be that," Jude said slowly and saw her cynical nod at his silly idea. In his relief he was able to grin and say, "You know, you're a very difficult person to talk to when you're not being Jennifer on the emergency line."

"Not always," she said. "Only when I'm being asked to commit treason." She gave him an oblique glance, kind of shy, he thought, not understanding it.

"So." He felt a weight lift from his shoulders and sink right into the centre of his heart. "It's real." He thought he was going to have to sit down or fall but there were no chairs, only the tough floor.

"I think we'd better finish this conversation right here," she said. "Clever of you to pick an airlock. No mikes." And she inclined her head towards him, conceding the point.

Jude found he was still smiling at her.

Natalie looked at Jude carefully and saw someone who had just received a shock. She asked, "Jude's your real name?"

"Yeah."

She nodded slowly. He had started out by telling the truth and taking a risk. The lying had only been a necessity. On the other hand, there were so many unanswered questions that this raised she didn't feel like touching it. She'd surprised herself saying yes—probably because she wanted an excuse to see him again. She could feel the far-reaching consequences of this stupidity twist inside her, as if she was a puppet being tugged by strings from the future, as she said, "Okay. Leave this with me. But I want to know exactly how your sister got hold of it. What she told you it was, what it did, why she thinks so."

"You think she might be lying?" Now he was surprised.

"You don't?" Natalie shook her head in disbelief. "You think people carry this stuff around in the open? No way. Was it in this format when she got it?"

"What do you mean?"

"On a disk like this, or is this a copy?"

"I assumed . . . I downloaded it from a machine, some kind of remote control thing like a PocketPad but a bit bigger."

"Come with me," Natalie said. Her pager went off like an epileptic mouse, reminding her that she was supposed to be heading for the conference suite. She switched it off.

They marched quickly to her office where she took down a worn catalogue of glossy pages from a locked shelf unit. Opening it up to one of the early pages she pointed at a black object, halfway between a Pad and a gun in style, with a keypad and a single-line command screen. She lifted her eyebrows to ask the question. They weren't going to give away information, because aside from the airlocks and wash-down facilities in the BSL_4 section, the Clinic was monitored.

Trying not to notice the effect it had, she leaned close to him so they could whisper.

"Like that," he said, his breath touching her face with the scent of peppermints. "What is it?"

Natalie wasn't immediately able to reply, and not only because she was imagining the breath to be a kind of kiss. It was her turn to experience a shock. All she could see and hear for that second was the Ministry guy saying "out of the question" and she was thinking, *How can it be out of the question? If Mappaware's already out in uncontrolled trials somewhere. What the hell are you saying this to me for? How can you sit there and pretend when you're already using this crap, addled, defective version in the real world? Or don't you even know, you dickhead?*

She felt the soft exhalation of Jude's patience against her cheek. She put her lips next to the soft wing of hair over his ear and said, almost noiselessly, "It's a handheld version of the big stuff in our treatment centre. Definitely not for public use."

"Who makes it? Is that its serial number?" He asked these questions by pointing.

She replied by showing him the page in the catalogue and added, "I don't know about that number, I assumed it was the price."

"How many?" he asked, waving his fingers.

She held up five fingers and one thumb, then lifted another finger, not sure.

He indicated the machine in the picture and did an elaborate shrug—*What does it do?*

She looked at him and realized it didn't need a full-on explanation. With a half-smile kindled by self-consciousness and lust she took his head in her hands, fingertips to his temples and face in the old Vulcan mind-meld, hoped he knew the show, and rested her forehead against his. *It reads minds.*

The intimacy, no practical need for it beyond her own desire and his permission, had a delicate-as-eggshell quality, a high voltage that made the hair on her head stand up. They stared into one another's eyes. He blinked slowly and checked out her right side, her left side, looking to see which eye she was hiding behind. Natalie could feel his carefully controlled breathing. Another two inches and they would kiss.

She flinched back, remembering herself, but he'd understood her well enough.

His expression was growing more serious all the time. Lines had begun to appear on his forehead.

"And it writes to them," she added, drawing on his forehead with her finger.

She doubted he'd know what she wrote, so fast and so vaguely. *Kiss me.*

The one good thing about having been institutionalized-mad was that it was a great excuse to use for any moments of real slippage, when the meanings of fantasy began to emerge in the real world. Slippage hadn't happened to her for an eternity. The thrill of making it happen now was a charge so intense she had to turn away in case he saw that she was unable to contain it. She pretended to execute some commands on her desk station.

As Natalie got her wits back she considered that her information wasn't as impressive as it seemed. Mappaware could just about write *Kiss me* and anything that wasn't more taxing than the equivalent of Peter and Jane books. It wasn't like a command-code yet. But maybe, from what she'd just read in the airlock, her knowledge was sadly lacking in that department.

Jude stared at her and at the catalogue page for a second or two, his mouth ajar, and then it closed. He took out his Pad and wrote on the screen, showing the note to Natalie, his face full of concern, "My sister still has it in her bag." He paused and then quickly scribbled after it, "Do they come fitted with radio-locators?"

Her pager was hopping mad in her pocket. "I have to go." For an answer to his question she shrugged, but her expression wasn't very hopeful. He nodded and worry erased what was left as a result of their brief contact.

With more speed and quiet than she had imagined he'd be capable of he was halfway out the door before she ran up to him and jammed her hand in his overalls pocket, taking the Pad. She expelled the file disk with a flick of her thumb and put it in her lab coat, signing that she'd read it more carefully and call him. He looked at her with misgiving but then nodded.

On second thought, Natalie was almost sure that every piece of

PathSystems equipment came with GPS and could be lasered to a bubbly mess from orbit within a range of accuracy of less than a metre, but it didn't seem helpful to say so, and by the look of Jude he had already guessed as much. She followed him far enough to see that he was going okay and not being arrested by security, and then turned back. Behind her own closed door she waited and breathed for thirty seconds, even in and even out. *A deep breath is a . . .*

But at the end of it she didn't feel clean. She felt sick. There were so many unknowns and sudden, nasty traps: he's lying, he's a plant, he's a double agent, a foreign agent, a test from the MoD, or he's telling the truth. But which one? And the physical fact of him had confused her more than she'd liked. Well, that wasn't strictly true. She'd liked that by far the best, which was unprofessional, stupid, and had already got her in trouble.

Composing herself, Natalie sent a message to the conference room explaining that she would be late by another ten minutes because of a Pad failure. In that time she ought to be able to see what this file was exactly. Although she'd read it in the airlock she'd been so distracted by him she wasn't sure.

With shaking hands she loaded it into her own Pad and started reading in earnest.

Dan's second lunch meeting was outside the Clinic, but not far away. It took place over a secure Pad link, and the lack of glamour in its location—a park bench—was more than made up for by the pay. Not that Dan was short of money now, but he knew it was going to take more than a measly few hundred thousand to get rid of Ray's interest in him during the foreseeable future. This job had the added bonus of being legit.

Shelagh Carter worked for the Defense Directorate as a watchdog, a person who kept an eye on Ministry business from within, making sure there were no unfortunate leaks or sudden departures of key people. Her job title itself was hazy and Dan didn't remember it, but her credentials were impressive and the small good deeds that she asked him to do, keeping the country honest, made Dan feel better after his much less virtuous dealings with Ray Innis.

Carter opened the channel on the dot of two and issued her instructions. Dan's Pad accepted her files and transmitted his answers to the last set of enquiries she'd made: personnel movements, work hours logged, service records for the major equipment, dull admin stuff like that. She never asked him to do anything underhand, such as actual spying or recording of conversations, and he was grateful, because he probably would have done it and that would have crossed the line into Bad Dan mode again.

Her face, if it was hers, was calm. "Good work, Dan," she said. "I'll be in touch. Usual time and place."

No, it wasn't Shelagh Carter who had made him late, but the fact that he'd forgotten to get the sandwiches, and by the time he remembered the shop was all out and he had to walk another half a mile to find something. He ran back to the Clinic at full trot, head down, fringe hanging, out of breath and smacked full face into some engineer coming out of the revolving doors with a big metal flight case in his hands. The security guard had to get involved to pick up all the things that fell out of the case—and the egg and cress, which had to be scraped off the carpet and reinstalled between its slices of bread.

Another dilemma. Egg and cress was Natalie's sandwich. Dan's was cheese and pickle. Should he change them? Would she notice a few nylon fibres? No, she probably wouldn't. She had a stomach for two-day-old pizza and cold curry. Natalie could take it. She'd think the shop had done it.

When the sandwiches were all together again, like Humpty if he'd ever managed to get back on his wall, Dan met the bloke's eye and thought, *He looks familiar, wasn't he sitting outside the pub an hour ago?* But it couldn't have been. That guy was slick and this one was older, rougher, and tired. He gave Dan a weary look that wished him heartily under a bus. However, when Dan apologized he said, "Hey, no problem. Take it easy next time," and his voice was as darkly American and friendly as Dan had imagined.

He wondered if this were something to mention to Carter. Then he realized he was an hour behind schedule and started to run indoors again, the guard shouting at him to slow down. Well, what Shelagh didn't know wouldn't hurt her. He made a note to tell Natalie instead. In fact, if the guy was hanging around on business, Dan would be interested in meeting him again.

Natalie was in her office. She snatched the sandwich, unwrapped it and took a bite without taking her eyes from whatever she was working on. "La' fr'a mee'ing," she said around it and pointed at him with an index finger. "You are a bas'ard. Fu' off an' do some wor'."

"I'll see you at home time, then, sweetie," he said. "Enjoy!"

Natalie. She was a brilliant mate. Dan was smiling from ear to ear as he swung himself out and down to the staff lounge for a coffee.

Three

Jude dumped the engineering clothes, equipment, and ID immediately after he was sure he was clear of the Clinic and its crowd of security personnel. He checked out of the Hilton and moved to a guest house on Fulford Road. It was the kind of place where he felt like he was living in someone's home—small, fussy, and full of overdone feminine decoration—but it was very close to Wenlock Terrace, where he knew Natalie Armstrong lived with the same guy who'd run into him outside the Clinic. The risks of staying in town had increased enormously now that he was recorded by the Clinic AI security system, but he thought he should be okay for another twenty-four hours. His Pad, on the other hand, wasn't a good machine to use for calling White Horse; he knew it was tapped by at least one set of people back home. To call his half sister he had to find a public phone somewhere that wouldn't give anything away by filling the background with locational details.

He was thinking about this as he returned to York's minuscule downtown, trying to keep his mind from speculating on what Natalie had seen in the file. Instead, he thought about the way he'd got the message. Natalie Armstrong's hands on his head and that point-blank stare; the way they'd been able to communicate without speaking, the subaudible conversation their minds had been having across the black bandwidth of the iris . . . it made him walk faster, his heart accelerating. He'd never had anything like that happen before. He wanted to know what it meant (although some piece of him knew that he already knew and just didn't want to admit it because he wasn't comfortable about it). And he'd sooner dwell on the curiosity of that than on the last piece of information that Natalie had given him about the scanner itself—which meant that there was something else White Horse had lied to him about.

The city was busy despite a light rain that seeped from the sky in condensing droplets, as though just over the hill an ocean was slowly rising to the boil and the town was immersed in its steam. Chinese and European tourists fought for space on the slippery cobbled streets of the oldest sections along the Shambles and the bizarrely named Whipmawhopmagate, where the local storekeepers were dressed for the thirteenth century to give "color." Jude was caught on a dozen photographs and surveillance cameras before he reached the relatively unpopulated space of a modern building that supplied offices on short-term lets and tried the public phone there. He called his own apartment, willing his sister to be there, but all he got was the answering service. Her personal number zeroed him out with a Receiver Not Active signal that could mean anything from death to battery failure.

He had a feeling that she knew damn' well he was trying to call and didn't want to know. Now she'd got her investigation moving and her teeth well stuck into him she was only interested in seeing results, and even if he had gotten through she would have reamed him out over trying to question her methods. He slammed the handset back down in its cradle and cracked it. Even thinking about her pseudo-Marxist bullshit was enough. He didn't have to have the actual conversation because he knew how it would have gone:

HIM: You stole that thing. Where did you get it?

HER: I told you. I found it at Martha's store, in the back.

HIM: That's bullshit.

HER: What the hell does it matter anyway? You've got it and it has to be part of the trouble. Hard evidence. Just like you always sing on about. You can't get it for your stupid case against that Ivanov guy you've followed for five *years*, but I've got it and now all you can do is bitch your ass off.

HIM: Just tell me the truth for once in your life. Where did it come from?

HER: Do your job since you wanted it so much. When are you going to risk yourself for anything worthwhile? When are you going to take a chance? Scaredy cat. Do you think they're going to come and fall in your lap and confess?

HIM: You know I'll find out. Can't you make anything easy?

HER: Easy. Easy. Hah! Your whole life is too easy!

WHACK! Burrrrr . . . the handset cracks.

And in the heat of the arguing Jude wouldn't even have managed to tell her to get rid of the cursed thing any way she could before it saw her swallowed up into the prison system—or dead. She should know that it could. But he could see the stubborn look on her face, her contempt for danger and official ways and anything that said You Can't. He would bet she had it on her all the time, like the Polaroid of the burned house that he'd taken from the inside pocket of her jacket when she was in the shower—and that had told him she'd been lying, too, because there she was on his doorstep, hands still smutty with ash from thousands of miles away, hair five inches shorter and crispy at the ends, and she'd never mentioned that there was no house on the res any more. Not until he asked.

Jude turned around and looked through the plate-glass doors of the office block out towards the river, which had swollen even more in the last few hours. Its sludgy quality had thinned and he could just see the table on the bank where he'd sat before, its legs partly submerged and the pub doors sandbagged shut behind it. His mind returned slowly to the problem of Ivanov, his long-term investigation that had been running before this came up.

Yuri Ivanov was a man who moved like that river, in currents unseen, his curious touch reaching out much further than seemed possible from one minute to the next. Ivanov was only one of his forms, the first in which Jude had encountered him. He had many other shapes and names; how many only the man himself could know, and uncovering them didn't just mean following simple paperwork trails of birth certificates, passports, photographs, licences, and addresses. His chameleon-like changes of identity were comprehensive—at least one intensive course of plastic surgery had transformed his features from their previous state into Ivanov's present appearance: thick, Mongoloid features and straight black Chinese hair. On its own such a thing would be enough to interest Jude in a suspect, but when you added in Ivanov's vast swathe of qualifications—scientific, philosophical, criminal—the man became a living enigma that demanded someone solve his puzzle. He also happened to work in exactly those fields that Jude also picked and winnowed: breakthrough technology, social adaptation, Perfection.

A woman in a raincoat came hurrying in to make a call. Jude left and turned at random onto another street.

Perfection hadn't really got a toehold in England yet, he thought, watching a colourful pod of umbrellas chase each other along the bridge just ahead of him. And he was glad. He liked this place, with its quiet, kooky corners, its tiny, unbalanced buildings, its sense of deep age and permanence, however illusory that might be.

Thinking of Ivanov made him aware that it was time to check in with Mary and see how their case was going in his absence. His enthusiasm was as damp as the sidewalk underfoot. He wasted ten minutes with a coffee from a Burger King, thinking it would remind him of home, but it tasted nothing like American and made him long for Washington's humidity and stifling summer heat. This abiding damp and chill in summer couldn't be right. The coffee tasted of muddy river water. The piece of him that had talked silently to Natalie Armstrong took it as a sign that the mission was as good as dead.

If he had any brains he'd leave right now on the next taxi to the airport, no looking back. It was inconceivable that he was going to get away with it. He shrugged his collar higher as it began to rain in slow, small drops, but he was thinking of Natalie Armstrong again and he knew that it was too late to go home.

At a café outside the city walls on some suburban road lined with dripping sycamores and verges thick with grass he made a coded Pad call and reached Mary at last.

He sat with his back to the window and mapped out the York scene, replacing it with footage of Seattle's Capitol Hill so it would seem he was where he claimed. On the screen Mary was tired, her coppery mane of hair looking faded in the sunlight as she stood in some anonymous early morning corner of an Orlando mall parking lot and confirmed, to his disgust, that their genetic sequencing lab had gone AWOL on them.

"Everything ripped out. They're long gone. The paperwork still links them in with the baby-fixing people at Fort Lauderdale but there's no hard evidence of Perfecting crime taking place. Unless I can find where they went and someone to talk, I think it's over." She yawned and switched the Pad to her other hand.

"Can you ID them from a genetic forensics sweep?" Jude didn't hold out a lot of hope: the databases for national recognition were mostly put together from people already inside the penal system, not ordinary citizens like science majors, and the machines the information was held on were notoriously hackable. Ivanov could delete what he wanted, given time.

"We're trying it but the place was cleaned out." She shook her head and he imagined he could see the heat of the distant day bobbing in the coils of her hair. "No sign of him," she added, knowing that he was going to ask her about Ivanov before he had to say anything.

Jude cut the call short with a few niceties. The fact of his lying made him unable to talk with her in a normal way, because they were friends. He hated the situation and its cheap, greasy feeling and he didn't want her to see any signs of tension in him, so he constructed a little fable about sailing on the Sound and heading into the Olympics for a few days to get some walking done, asked her how she was, and said goodbye with a smile on his face, remembering to make his eyes do the smiling, too.

Outside the rain eased and the sun began to come out. He drank a cup of English tea and felt the headache effects of his lunchtime beer roll across his forehead. He wanted to do something so badly instead of sitting around that he walked to the guest house and changed to go out for a run to watch the river's slow rise towards a spell of casual destruction.

The action was good, it felt like progress and it eased the crushing anxiety of the long wait for Natalie to call. He ran a long way, right out of town and into the countryside where another shower soaked him to the skin. Later on, drying off from a real shower in his bedroom, he attempted to reread the huge data files on the Ivanov case and within two minutes fell asleep on the bed, the Pad in his hand, opened to the gene sequencing notes, the logs, the times, the sightings . . . all the inconclusive details that had to add up to something. But what? What? And if there was no evidence in Orlando, then where and who and how?

Mary Delaney snapped off the call to Jude with nervous irritation and walked the last few yards to her car. She took a deep inhalation of the air-conditioning when she turned on the engine and waited for the spec analysis of the call to come through from her Netwatcher. When it did she found herself chewing the ends of her hair in frustration. Not from Seattle at all, but the transmission had ended too soon to pin down. It was a fix, that background.

She stared out of the car window, thinking how generic everything looked these days and knew Jude had the smarts to do that for sure. But where was he? What was he doing?

She closed her eyes and prayed for one minute that it wasn't anything to do with Mappa Mundi. She prayed hard, with all her heart, but when she opened her eyes there was no relief, only the frontage of WalDrug and a kid eating a Popsicle, staring at the blacked-out windows of her Porsche in mesmerized delirium and staining its T-shirt with blue drips.

The icy air from the vents was starting to make her blouse feel like cold water on her skin. She turned the jet down and flicked over the Pad to send in her report to their boss in Washington—Conchita Perez, head of Special Sciences. Then she tapped in the code for Nothing to Report and sent it to her other boss, also in Washington, but in a very different environment.

It was a lie.

In fact, both messages were lies. The FBI report was nothing but what she had made up for Perez and Jude to read. It said that by the time she and her team had raided the lab in Orlando it had been cleaned out. There would be no more DNA resequencing to produce souped-up babies either with secondary sex characteristics straight out of Net porn or with brains tweaked for intelligence. The USA was back to production as usual, and all the chaos that Nature threw up, because that was better than planning ahead, and Perfection Law said so in spades. So Perez would be pleased at least with the lab's closure, even if Mary had failed to make an arrest. And her other boss, the secret one, back in the Pentagon, would give her a big, fat reward. All for lies.

Mary was used to lying and it had become merely tiresome to be inventive nowadays, instead of nerve-racking. Her hand on the big metal knob of the Porsche gearshift wasn't even breaking the mildest of sweats. She drove out of the lot and took the highway back in the direction she'd come, listening to the engine rev high and throaty, waking up the commuters.

The report contained elements of truth. The gene-sequence lab was cleaned out as well as she could manage, given the time, and now she had all the seized paperwork to go through and sift, making sure that any incriminating details never found their way into Jude's investigation. That was what made her foot start sinking to the floor. Lying to Jude.

The thing that made her want to scream was that in all the years they'd spent working so hard to pin Ivanov to the wall, Jude had never once realized that the core of his problems sat next to him, worked in the same office, smiled as she put down his coffee on the desk, kissed him goodnight on the cheek, hugged him after a crisis, drank beers with him on Fridays at Goodenough's bar, sat with him at baseball games and passed the popcorn. He was smart, but when he wasn't being so smart he was stupid. Stupid in the best way; blind when he'd given his loyalty. He'd never make time as a double agent like her. And she wondered what that was like.

She flew a light changing to red, got blipped automatically by the local traffic AI, flipped it her code, and watched its terse warning vanish from the Porsche's onboard system.

Jude was the nicest guy she knew. She liked him enormously. Sometimes she even thought she loved him, or could have if her life had allowed it, which was why he must never find out that the gene-sequencing lab Ivanov had been running wasn't only perfecting the DNA of privileged unborns all over the USA. It had a secondary purpose, far more ethically suspect, that it carried out in the name of national security. She was sworn to protect it but she wanted to protect Jude, so he would never know anything about Mappa Mundi. Ever. Not if she could stop it.

Her foot on the accelerator was pushing so hard, she had to draw it back consciously, stockings sliding in her shoe, heel digging the floor. The car slowed from eighty to fifty. The roaring in her ears subsided. With the loss of velocity Mary felt the first faltering of her confidence in her ability.

She knew it was too late. In her jacket she was aware of the weight of her gun, holstered neatly below her left arm.

She wondered if there was some other way out. Jude could be redirected. Or maybe this was supposed to happen, this discovery, part of a larger plan that small movers like Mary weren't clued up on. She knew that not everybody in the NSC had such rosy views of Mappa Mundi as her boss did. If they'd decided to take counteraction from the top then perhaps Jude finding out some silly clue was no accident. They'd leak something and then sit back smugly to watch her as she was forced to fry Jude for it. The key to the truth must lie in the way that he'd found out, if he was lying to cover for a trip to England and not something dumb like a dirty weekend in Rio.

The more she thought about this, the more likely it seemed, and she convinced herself it wasn't just ego. Research would tell, however. A little bit of research.

At the next lights Mary pulled a U-turn on red and headed back towards the airport amid a squeal of tires, an angry cloud of black exhaust smoke, and a parade-day applause of car horns. This time the traffic AI recognized and ignored her.

She flicked her Pad to hands-free mode to call in and check with her support services—yes, the calls and instructions to England had gone out OK and no replies about anything worth noting had arrived, she was told. Her mood lightened a little and she accelerated smoothly into the inside lane before dialling the number of a general, a personal friend at Fort Detrick, to whose offices she was put straight through.

"It's Mary Dee," she said.

"Well, Mary. What a nice surprise. Kinda thought I'd be hearing from you sooner though," said General Bragg, his voice gravelly and rounded, like a friendly grandpa's.

Mary wished she could see his face to clue into exactly what that meant. "Oh yeah?" She kept her grin on. "I've been busy on my cover. It's not all expense accounts and private planes on the federal side of the tracks, y'know."

"Oh, now, Mary, I can't believe you haven't got some fancy runaround all to yourself, a big girl like you." But he sensed she wasn't quite levelling with him among all the bantering and added, "So, what's rockin' your boat?"

"I'll tell you, Jim," she said, and this time she wasn't fooling. "I need to know how the test on CONTOUR went."

Once she'd told him the codeword for their business she heard him take an uneasy breath. "I thought this was no straight ace," he said.

Mary's chest felt like the steering wheel had hit it. She veered sharply and almost struck a slow-moving van on her outside. As far as she'd known until that moment, CONTOUR had never been tested—and it was supposed to remain untested until it had been stabilized. As she was correcting the car with a savage jerk of the steering wheel that almost sent her into the central reservation General Bragg said, "There was an authorized—authorized out of your bosses' offices, that is, NSC-approved—single, low-percentage prototype test using a simulation verified system."

"Where?" She knew there wasn't a site on Earth that was sanctioned for this and especially not inside the continental US. Some bastard was playing tricks right at the top.

"Zone Five. But this came from your—" General Bragg was beginning to be upset for her, and this she could do without.

"Verify that," she answered, smooth and confident, as though she'd only been checking a fact. "Get you later, Jim. I've got a plane to fly."

With her mouth clamped shut on the Happy Jockette routine and her foot making the car's engine scream, she left black marks on every turn between there and the terminal.

She'd clear things with Bragg later. All that mattered was that some bozo had moved to a live test of Mappaware. If she didn't know that meant her boss hadn't known either. She pulled off at the next service point and sent a message in before making arrangements to leave Orlando within the hour. She abandoned the Porsche to its fate in a short-stay parking lot, keys in the exhaust pipe and a pager message to the hire company. By late evening she was waiting in an outer office at the Pentagon, buttoning the sharp cut of her suit to its most uncompromising. She'd had a few hours to figure things through and she was well prepared by the time Rebecca Dix summoned her.

Rebecca had been called out of a presidential dinner and looked fit to spit bricks. Seated on the edge of her desk she nodded at Mary and gestured at the wall display where the CONTOUR message was displayed. "Your analysis, Agent Delaney?"

"General Bragg confirmed he received a notification of an authorized live test of CONTOUR on a small, isolated, and insignificant population within the bounds of the A12 Testing Agreements—"

"I can fucking read it myself," Rebecca said in a mild voice. "What I want to know is, what you think this is in aid of."

Mary met the severe dark stare of the First Adviser to the NSC with calm certainty.

"Bust the project open."

"Has anyone got hold of it yet?"

Mary saw Jude in her mind's eye. "No."

"If they do—" they both knew what Rebecca meant, because of the test site and Jude's connection "—you'll take care it goes no further."

"Ma'am."

"Mary?"

Mary looked at Dix's face, trying to show no feeling.

"Do you want me to replace you? Don't worry if you do. I can arrange that—"

"No, ma'am," Mary said firmly, looking straight ahead, at attention.

Dix nodded slowly. "When it gets too much, Mary, don't be afraid to ask for help."

"That's okay. Thank you, ma'am."

After she'd finished the sandwich, Natalie had about ten minutes to read the files, or less. She was familiar with the language they were written in—because she'd helped to create it—but what she saw wasn't easy to interpret for two reasons. First of all, it was badly written. Second, it did things the logic of which she didn't understand until she ran the program in her simulation suite and saw their effect blossom.

In her Patient, starting at a normal position, the emotional centres at first shut down to almost insensitive levels and frontal-lobe activity dropped off the scale. Then the program worked to link and stimulate all those things about a human being's makeup that act subtly to darken the heart. The result was something like paranoid schizophrenia. The program itself was a crude recipe for making someone mad, as sophisticated in comparison to Natalie's work as a skateboard was to a space shuttle. But she betted it worked, after a fashion, well enough that it would make anyone burn down a house or shoot themselves just to escape the sudden and incomprehensible spiral of misery and mania their lives must have become.

Natalie erased it from her machine. Why was it so simple to do the worst for people, when fixing exactly the same naturally occurring fault was so bloody hard? These fifty shitty lines: enough to screw up anyone they touched, and it would take years of work to scratch the surface of a solution. If she'd written this, how long could it have taken? A week? A month? But here it was, brute, short, sharp, and ugly as raw sin, sitting on top of her years of labour and those of all the others on the project; taking their technology's power, its potential for healing, its immense subtlety, and making a dumb gun to blow brains to hell.

Natalie removed the disk from her systems, taking it in thumb and forefinger, and dropped it in her pocket. Filth. She certainly would be seeing Jude again, no mistake about that. But for now he would have to sit and spin because she was about to lose the only job she'd got left.

Grabbing the notes and her Pad Natalie ran the three corridors from her office to the conference centre and took her place just as the satellite feed from the USA kicked in and their boss of bosses, Mikhail Guskov, came online to address them and give the state of play.

The meeting at the York Clinic was for the entire country, and not just for Natalie and her local crew. The centre was packed with over a hundred attendees and her lateness was only noticed by the auto-logger at the door who checked her credentials and gave her a tired kind of Ministry spiel about the sort of standards expected of premier contractors. She was deleting it when the address lit up the big screen of the auditorium and a hush fell.

Mikhail Guskov was in his fifties, but with the vigorous energy of a younger man, perhaps even of two or three younger men. His blue eyes glinted with it, and it quivered in the thick hair of his beard, his rough moustache, and the heavy and ill-cut nest that crowned his head in brown and grey. He reminded Natalie of an alpha wolf, and no doubt that was how he felt about himself, because his paternal pride was detectable even through miles of transmission. She didn't know where he was—none of them did—but for the duration of the link his presence was here and they, despite their own egos and achievements, waited on his every word.

"Dear Friends." He began, as he always began, in warmth and good humour. "A delight to see you all again and to have read your reports, every one of which, I am pleased to say, has edged us further towards our goal of mapping the human mind. In the last hour a simulation run has achieved a sixty-percent-accurate translation between the neural function and the synthesized theoretic model. Only you and I can know what that really means." He waited, not disappointed, as a flurry of whispering and excitement rushed around each room he spoke to; sites across the world were suddenly enlivened, with fresh enthusiasm on tired faces and quick movements from exhausted bodies.

Natalie watched the energy dynamic run and circle, flow like a tangible fluid. It brushed through her and she, too, was lifted, even though she was a watcher, not a participant. She calculated very quickly that Guskov's message meant that the time-crunch problem was no longer an issue. There had been a burning uncertainty about whether the real-time cross-mapping of mind and matter in an individual was a calculation that was NP-complete or not. NP-complete problems required more time than existed in the universe to solve. But their excitement was unbounded now that he revealed the sixty-percent correlation. Only forty left to go! Six years on from the inception of NervePath technology, and ten years on from the successful development of nanomedical gear, the biggest and most ambitious scientific endeavour to date was going to finish.

There would be a comprehensive science of the human mind, even, if they dared think further, of the very essence of every person alive. Natalie didn't believe in souls, but if she had she would have been afraid now, because even that final, sacred thing wasn't going to be outside her reach any more. It was measurable, definable, and mappable. Soon she would be able to point to it, or its absence, just as she could point to the image of a mind and say, "There, Mrs. Jones, that's why you're feeling so awful, the crossmatch between your worldview and experiences is failing right here. Don't worry, it's only a nervous breakdown and quite natural, you'll be fine as long as you can wait it out."

And if Mrs. Jones couldn't wait it out, then Natalie would be able to prescribe a therapy to hurry things along. But she knew as well as the man next to her that this leap forwards now brought them up against the hardest of problems—Mappa Mundi would enable them to alter people's minds. As she'd written on Jude's forehead, so she'd be able to rewrite neural paths in a process that amounted to the direct creation—and deletion—of people.

Natalie had been so sure, until now, that this was good. Despite the potential for harm, there were so many positive things it could be used for, to free individuals from biologically induced or incident-oriented mental torment. As a tool for self-understanding and development it would be invaluable. She believed in it absolutely. But in her pocket the disk sat, butchered, incompetent, a solid piece of ill-will. Its existence—certain from the start to come about because they were all only human—made her doubt their illusions of control. Mappa Mundi was protected by European and US governments, under the strictest security. But so what?

Natalie was hardly listening to Guskov, she was so immersed in the problem of what to do with her knowledge. Because maybe he already knew. Maybe there were wheels within wheels. It didn't take a psychiatrist to understand that people were creatures of many identities, many loyalties and weaknesses. Someone in this meeting was responsible for the abomination she had just read through, and showing her hand might be the least useful thing she could do.

A keen feeling of danger and anxiety almost made her want to run out of the room. She scanned faces, knowing nothing about what went on behind any of them, and found the plastic shape of the disk with her hand, holding it tightly: *you're going nowhere, son.*

Knowing their conclusions, Guskov was saying, "In a few short months everyone's view of the world is going to change. The last frontiers of our inner worlds are about to be laid bare, our truths—general and individual—will be plain for all to see, and our lies, our fables, our myths, and our fears. Do not doubt that this will not be greeted with joy in all quarters. When we know ourselves at last, the truth of certain faiths and beliefs will be undone and fallacies of all kinds will be brought to light, their perpetrators with them. We will have to face reality as it is, and not as we have believed it to be, or hoped it to be, or wanted it to be. Difficult times lie ahead. No doubt this work will attract its share of destroyers and naysayers and people who want to use it to repress and control others. When that time comes we must be ready." He paused and stared directly to camera.

Natalie thought he was slightly overstating the case. Mappa Mundi was hardly the end point of the venture, more like the beginning, but grand words got cranked out easily these days, especially when you had five-star generals and corporate project managers from pharmaceutical giants sitting on both sides of you, all of them wanting the good news about where their two hundred billion dollars had gone.

It was a winning speech—a kind of desperate speech, now Natalie thought about it: the sort of thing you said when you had to rally the troops for a final assault on a highly defended fortress and the odds were ten to one against coming out alive. She wondered what it was that prompted it now, when actually the news to report was so incredibly positive. Did nobody else think it peculiar? But around her faces were glued to the screen, suckers to the pitch, every one.

Guskov began speaking about the powerful synergy they had all participated in, the gestalt experience of working as a greater mind with a greater purpose, and Natalie started to worry.

Nobody he was talking to needed a hard sell. They'd all bought in a long time ago, despite their valid fears. So who was he talking to? To the generals and the people from Global NervePath Systems and the counteragents among them from envious foreign powers. He was saying everything and nothing. He was being uninformative to the point of boredom and they listened because nobody loves an adventure story like a hero-in-waiting, and that was what they all secretly wanted to be.

Meanwhile Jude's sister was getting burned alive in her own home.

Natalie got up in disgust, walked down the aisle stairs and out into the conference-area foyer. Maybe she was wrong. Maybe Guskov was chivvying them along into the last great effort. She just didn't understand what the rush was. Then again, she might be holding the reason for it in her hand.

Four

Jude woke very slowly from a sleep of exhaustion that seemed more like a blackout. Waves of unconsciousness beat him back from awareness of the room repeatedly, and the quiet sounds of traffic on the move were blurred by the window and net curtains into whispers just beyond his understanding. Alternating moments of near-waking made him think he could open his eyes and see the street light falling in a yellowed band across his feet, the gleam lighting the room in a dim bronze. He tried to get up, to move his hand, to roll over and he thought he had, even up to feeling the texture of the coverlet under him as his skin moved onto it, but a second later, a black second, he was as he had always been, a gold statue in a bronze frieze, his body as unresponsive as solid metal. Hours passed in the flickering of his mind. A thousand times he tried to wake up, to get up, to create a noise, to pinch himself, to be free, but a thousand and one times he blinked to see that all his victories were imaginary. He was that guy, what was that guy? That guy with the rock who got it to the top of the mountain and turned his back only for it to roll right back to the bottom.

He got up and dressed.

He got up and switched on the lights—they didn't work.

He got up and tried the TV. A horse race came on. The horses ran in slow motion in the dark with RayBan black lenses over their eyes. The commentary was lucid and clear, like a bell tone, but in no human language he knew. He thought that the commentators might be horses, too.

He got up and called his mother. "Hi, Jude! How's the investigation going, hon?"

"I'm not in Washington, Mom, you know that, I'm in . . . I'm in . . ."

He got up and dressed and started to go downstairs to find a restaurant.

He got up.

He got up.

But each time he woke he'd never gotten up. He saw his legs and feet next to each other, willed them to move, but they existed in another universe.

A sense of panic and breathlessness closed its grip slowly on his chest, increasing in intensity with each repeat: each repeat that he never quite remembered was doomed until the next blink, the next awakening into the same room and the same problem. He couldn't remember how to breathe. His body started to twitch with oxygen loss. His lungs were collapsing, there was a pain in his veins that was increasingly slowly but surely, their flimsy casings swelling like fat worms about to burst under their own greedy pressure.

He woke up and there was a hand on his shoulder. It was warm, but not familiar. It rested on his cold arm and it was weighty, like a real hand, and the fingers squeezed, and he felt his skin and muscles give in and sink down like obedient dogs waiting for the master's word. Jude was damn' grateful to that hand, because at last he was going to wake up for real and remember how to breathe.

There was the warmth of whoever's-it-was body behind him, too, and the drop of the mattress where their knees were digging his back and the stirring of the air from their moving and breathing. The sound of their breathing made him listen hard. It was like his, a slight panic in it, or maybe a sob, like it was forgetting, too, or like it was being smothered.

"Shit!" he thought. "That's it. The house is burning down and they're here to get me out. I gotta wake up right now. I have to get out of here!"

He smelled smoke; the acrid poison of burning paint and plastics, the boiling tar bite of furniture foam. He heard a splintery crashing of windows and TV screens and the roaring gasp of flames licking around his door. The fire came out of a gigantic mouth, open full as a June rose directly beneath the floor, tongues lashing, ready to swallow.

He was struggling with all of his nervous system at full scream in the effort, when to his horror a soft female voice said,

"I'm sorry. I'm so sorry . . ."

He felt a sensation on his cheek that was cool and hot; breath, lips—a kiss.

The floor under the bed collapsed. Jude's heart broke and he screamed in terror as he started to fall, the orange and red fire-mouth laughing him in, up to the billowing wet steam of its eyeballs.

He woke up.

Street light fell in a yellow band across his feet and lit the room in dim bronze, as still as though it had been cast for a hundred years. He tried to move his feet and they parted. He pushed back against the mattress and sat up. Although he could never have explained it, this time he knew it was for real. The other times had been so unlike reality that he couldn't imagine how he'd made the mistake of thinking they were true. This was a hundred times more detailed, more tactile, and the TV worked and it was showing the evening news and what was more he understood every word they were saying.

But he was breathing hard and he could swear that behind that last dream someone had really been there with him.

Jude touched his cheek, almost scared to, in the place where he had felt the kiss. Nothing. Not even a residual flutter in the nerves.

Then he became aware of how cold he was, nearly as cold as the dead. That woman, she had been kind of familiar, right . . . but he didn't know anyone like that. He didn't recognize her voice, even though she had spoken straight to him in a way that suggested they were—the first thought that came to mind was *lovers*. Was he dead and she alive? Could he have made her up or had she invaded his dream, like a psychic spy? His mind had a lot of tricks it could pull. He'd always told White Horse her "visions" were imaginary things but at this moment he wouldn't have said it with anything like the old certainty.

Jude rubbed his face in his hands and looked around, trying to get some bearing on the rest of the day that wasn't muddied with bizarre beliefs in nonexistent women. He was starting to feel better until he switched on the light next to the bed. With the judder of bad brakes his heart ground to a halt.

There was a paper file lying on the vile chintz counterpane, a manila folder of a shape that he recognized immediately as an American office standard.

The sight of it erased every other scrap of awareness he possessed. He stared at it and was too confused to be afraid. The TV changed its show. The room became blue, with soft lights playing across the bed like tree-shadows moving in moonlight. Jude steeled his nerves and reached out to pick up the folder. His grip wasn't too sure, though, and a slew of blue, pink, and white pages slithered out of its guts. He dropped the rest and put the main room lights on. His hands were shaking. The new brightness made him aware that he was naked. He scrabbled to put his clothes on and not take his eyes off the papers. There were photographs attached and he recognized them as personnel documents. He thought they looked like government issue.

His Pad rang with a six-note, the one he'd set for priority incoming. He picked it off the dressing table and looked at the ID. Natalie Armstrong.

On his knees in front of the bed, half dressed and stunned, he answered it straight away, running a hand through his hair and hoping he didn't look too bad, although he must have done.

Her face materialized on screen and, with the familiar ease of people who spent a lot of time talking over distance, she wasn't looking at him, but at something in her hand.

". . . Whatever this is and where you got it but it's something I want to know more about and I assume that there's no such thing as a secure line considering the situation, so . . . I'm sure you know where I live and I'll leave here in half an hour. If you catch up with me, we'll talk then." As she finished she glanced up at her own Pad camera with a quick practical nod, not attempting the false eye contact that would only have been polite, and then her hand came down and switched it off.

Jude had the impression of a messy, cluttered room around her, that she'd been reading something on a display screen, and that in the hard light of its rays her unique face looked sharp, other-worldly and dangerous. He broke from staring at the empty Pad screen a second later and looked up at the files.

His mind oscillated between Natalie, the file, his dream, and this awful, disgusting, chintz-covered room with its frills and furbelows, tassels and cushions and overblown flowers on every surface surging up at him like tangling thickets of genetically modified people-eating roses. He experienced a sense of disorientation so strong it was worse than zero g. He decided he couldn't stay there.

As fast as he could, Jude started gathering up the papers, stuffing them back in their folder. He put that and the Pad in his case and finished getting dressed in the darkest clothes he had. Natalie was right, he did know where she lived and he was going to get this whole business done and out of the way and go home tomorrow with an answer that would get White Horse off his back. Back to real life. Yes. Definitely.

Jude took the case with him when he left. As he jogged down the steps in his good shoes he thought that he never had to go back, and that made it possible to throw off the whole experience like an old skin left behind. On the damp street his step lightened as soon as he turned the corner.

Dan was glad that Natalie hadn't said anything about the sandwich and that she seemed to be alive as usual when she got home, shoes in hand, at seven-thirty. Therefore he was able to say, as innocently as possible, "That bloke who came for the upgrade thing that wasn't. That was him, wasn't it?"

Natalie stopped halfway across the living room and turned her head. "You'd know that if you'd not had two hours off for lunch, now wouldn't you?"

"Has he got the hots for you then, or what? Is he mad? Did you send the police after him? You know, I bumped into him as he was leaving, because you can't really miss a guy like that, can you now? And I saw him in town—" But he broke off there because to go on might entail mentioning Ray or coming up with some lie, and she was too good at picking the truth out of them. It was almost like a second-sight thing with her. Dan looked down and pretended to glance at the *Radio Times* that was upside down next to him.

"Where?" was all she said and he knew he'd blown it.

"Just in town. You know. Walking around. Probably sightseeing." He glanced up carefully and saw that she was losing interest, so it was safe to add, "But smart casual, not in the work suit, and, you know, I often wonder why it is," and he could lift his head now and grin, "that they issue such awful things as boiler suits for uniforms, I mean, they don't even—"

"It was a BSL-$_4$ suit, you moron." She started moving again, but at the doorway she hesitated and dropped her bags there. She fixed him with an uncomfortable glance and Dan knew he'd scored. "Did he recognize you? Did he say anything?"

"Yeah, he asked me to ask you if you'd go out with him."

Natalie nodded, face stony. "Piss off and die, Dan." She turned her back and disappeared into her room.

"You like him!" Dan singsonged. "Yes, you do! A-ha! At last, the ice queen genius of Yorkshire shows she isn't absolute zero."

Her head reappeared, "You went to see fucking Ray Innis, didn't you?"

He stopped singing.

"I knew it. You're such an idiot. You know that if you ever give him one sniff of anything to do with work you'll end up in jail for the rest of your life?"

Her voice was pleading despite the gunlike assault of its words. Dan knew he was an idiot, but it was only when she was like this that he ever actually felt afraid. His head seemed full of woolly clouds that needed a focus but weren't able to find it by themselves. Natalie never suffered that. It was pure light in her head, razor-bright. She couldn't understand it. He didn't understand it, he only knew that some stuff helped and other stuff made him forget that he was, despite his ability to do his job, fundamentally dumb in a very important way that meant he'd never make the grade.

"I didn't buy anything off him. I didn't give him anything." At least that was the truth. He could say it and look her in the face and not flinch or giggle, but he sounded like a child, even to his own ears. He smiled at her, winningly, "Want a beer?"

"I've got work to do," she said. "Maybe later."

"You're always working." Ah, this was better ground.

"I like it." And she'd let him off the hook, he could hear it.

"You need more play," he said, sliding down into a more comfortable slouch. "You need a night out with Mister Mad American, or whoever. Jude the Obscurity."

"You stick to those pills, son," she called in her Old West Doctor voice, and he heard her switching her machines on. "Let me do the prescriptions around here."

"Tea though?" Maiden Aunt.

"Aye, a'right." Northern Farmer.

Dan was happy as he got up. He knew that if the American had really been mad there was no way the conversation would have got that far. And did that mean he was some kind of agent? Maybe he should mention it to Shelagh Carter after all? But he thought, *Nah—if Natalie likes him, then he must be okay. She'd spot a phoney in a minute.* Which reminded him . . .

He took the tea through and set it on her wobbly old desk. "You know what? I saw Knitted Man do something weird today. Funny."

"Oh yeah?" She used her leg to steady the desk and started rummaging in one of her bags for something.

Knitted Man was Dan's name for Bill, one of the Clinic's chief programmers for the NervePath systems. Although he wasn't qualified in psychology, or any other mental science, his technical skill with the hardware and software was constantly called on as the doctors and researchers struggled to get their ideas down into practical code. He wore a tank-top sweater on many of the cooler days and it was this, combined with his pinkish indoor skin and round body that made Dan think of *The Clangers*; an old show about a race of knitted aliens who whistled. Bill also whistled when he thought he was alone and Dan had recordings of him taken with the office webcam that could guarantee a laugh with almost anyone else in the Clinic whenever things started to get a bit intense. When work was going well Bill whistled "La Marseillaise," when badly, snatches of opera, and when things were going *really* badly he made a kind of slowly repeated "piu" like a finch on the verge of dropping off the twig.

Dan watched Natalie produce a generic disk and jam it into the driver of her personal machine. She seemed not to like it, for some reason.

"Yeah. He left early, said something about going to get some money for his holiday, but walked out of the parking lot towards the Haxby Road end instead, whistling the whole time."

"I thought you said it was weird. That sounds about normal for our place." Natalie tapped at the grey keys of her 'board and flicked on the switches of her graphics processors. As they came up to speed she took a sip of her tea.

"D'you want to know the big news?" she said. "Stages One and Two have now been cross-mapped properly." She made a face at him that said Ta-DA! and waved her hands in the air.

Dan paused, forgetting the funny story about Bill and the security system, and looked at the gobbledegook that had suddenly cluttered the screen in the terse, efficient Courier font that meant he couldn't read anything properly without putting his lenses in. "Stages One and Two?" He wished he listened to more of what she said. It would make life so much simpler.

"Physical Event Map and Mental Event Map," Natalie grinned like a maniac and waited for him to get it. He waited. She said, "You know, it means that we've stuck together the real world of physical events like chemicals and electricity and the nonphysical world of mental life. It's the big kahuna. The foundation for a genuine working theory of consciousness. Dan, for fuck's sake! The Holy Grail, man!" Her voice had risen on the last phrases as he'd kept his face straight and now he could grin, too.

"Gotcha." He nodded wisely.

"Yeah!" She made a fist with her right hand and pumped the air. "That's what you call a goal. It's a game of two hemispheres. The lads is over the moon!"

"You said it was a grail. Now it's a goal." He gave her shoulders a quick rub as he slipped briefly into Jewish Mother mode. "Goal, grail, schmail. Ishmael! Fetch me a whale. Grail, and still she sits in her room at the little screen, popping her eyes out and not a husband in sight. Oy, why have you sent me such a daughter? The least she could do is put on a dress and try to act normal before her ovaries are withered down like raisins and her face would pass for a dog's bum!"

"Well." But Natalie was in a good mood. "It's not quite the Grail yet. More a sort of plinth thing that the grail will go on. But you get the idea." Her graphics cards had revved and produced a slow pair of pictures, side by side, on the screen. As the images built themselves in layers, forming a rough 3-D of two naked brains, she added, "That does sound weird for Bill. He must be feeling the pressure. A week in Malta will sort him out."

"Yeah maybe." Dan wasn't sure. But he'd mentioned it and his conscience was clear. "Anyway, you have to come out for at least a celebratory tipple, hon, or the whole thing isn't cricket. What're those?"

"The right one is a sample of Tony Clearwater, the schizophrenic with paranoia who was up the other day for part of the volunteer therapy programme in retracking that my dear old dad is involved in," she said. "Do you think it looks like this other one here? Just by zone colour?"

What they were seeing was a representation that used different colours for different levels of activity, roughly delineating the pattern of a few minutes' thought. Dan glanced back and forth and rested his chin on the top of her head. "Yeah. Pretty similar. Not over here . . . but mostly in the temporal lobes and this thingy here."

"Amygdala," she said, trying to shrug him off.

"Yeah. Close enough for government work. You should wash this you know," he plucked at her two-inch tufts. "Makes it an entirely different colour."

"Good," she murmured, not hearing him at all. "And not good."

"Come again?"

"I am going out after all," she said, spinning around in her chair so fast she almost knocked him over. He grappled with his tea and only burned his fingers slightly.

"Oh, great."

"Yeah. But on my own."

"Natalie!"

"I'll meet you. At nine. In . . . the Black Swan."

"Why? Where are you going?"

She stood up and started heaving him towards the door. "Go on now. I need time to change."

"Natalie, what's going on?!" But she wouldn't explain, only shoved him harder until he had to move or fall over. The door closed in his face.

"Nat-ta-lee!" he howled but she didn't respond. He paused. "Will we be eating out or shall I just chew on this six-month-old carrot from the last time anyone shopped?"

"We'll eat," she conceded. "But you can lick the stove clean as you're waiting."

He thought, listening carefully, that she was making a call to someone. With his ear pressed to the thin hardboard he could almost make out the tones.

"Dan, piss off!" she yelled. "I can see your shadow under the door."

Reluctantly he drifted to the sofa and put the TV on. He felt a bit flat and left out of things. Natalie couldn't have a secret life, it wasn't on. It was very unnecessary. *He* didn't have one. He told her everything. On the other hand, they were going out tonight, so there was that to look forward to. Only a couple of hours to kill. Still, curiosity was a new one and he was finding that it itched him something ridiculous. He could, of course, satisfy himself and follow her.

He could. He didn't have to.

Natalie found a dress too airy, a skirt too girly, and a blouse too much like a secretary's garb so she did a black-leather-trouser-and-shirt thing, stuck midheeled boots on her feet so that she could run if she had to, and found a decently cut jacket to sit on the top that was just about the same colour as her hair. The bootleg software disk went in her inside pocket, Pad on the outside. She checked her face in the mirror and re-lipsticked two shades darker. She only knew one make-up routine, but it seemed to have worked and made her look marginally less peculiar; like someone out of a French film rather than Catwoman's madder, more deformed sister.

With the basics taken care of, and five minutes to go before she'd said she'd leave, what she was doing started to look very dodgy indeed to her. As a precaution she logged a call with her personal datapilot service, Erewhon, leaving a closed message about her whereabouts in case of emergency. It was hard to get a secured line and she was late by the time she managed to scoot out past Dan, who was already into his bathroom routine. At least, as she tugged on the handle of the outside door to close it, there was no rain, only a heavy atmosphere of extreme dankness from the river and a mild scent of rotting greenery. She didn't want to go that way tonight, thought that more populated streets would be better, so she started towards the town end of the road and walked at a good pace. He'd better be on time, or he was going to miss entirely.

The trees overhanging Fulford Road dripped on her as she passed underneath and once her boot skidded on wet leaves, but she didn't slow down or alter course. Natalie strode past the first row of shops and then took a branch path towards Fishergate and the city beyond the walls.

Jude Westhorpe caught up with her as she walked in the darkest part of the way, alongside a church and its close-packed nest of gravestones where the vast shapes of old, nameless trees hung low over the pavements, screening out the street light and cocooning them both in shadows so dark that when Natalie looked back it was as if they had surged together to create his shape, as if he'd not followed her at all but been waiting here under the branches for her, immaterial until she'd come by. She couldn't help giving a shiver of fear and excitement.

Jude walked up to her and lifted a hand to her shoulder. To her astonishment he didn't speak but leaned down and kissed her shock-open, like a fish mouth.

"We're on a date, right?" he murmured in that husky American burr and she realized that it wasn't real, only their cover, for the sake of anyone who might see them there. Her unexpected emotions sank out of sight so fast she felt sick.

"Uh, yes, yes." She was shaking. She'd thought for a moment that he really was shadows made flesh. It had seemed magical, wonderful. As she faked a professional smile and tried to smother the giveaway emotion he might see in her eyes—*you fool, you pathetic shithead*, she snarled internally to herself—she couldn't help but feel the disappointment cut her to the heart.

There had been a time when she'd believed in such things, been a girl with a destiny, a special person, caught in the reality of her own imagination so strongly that it had turned her whole life towards the effort to discover the truth about the world of human meaning. Still, there was no reason not to take advantage. She wasn't so lacking in self-worth that she couldn't at least see how to have an interesting time, if not the one her imagination wanted.

Under the dark hands of the trees on Fishergate, Natalie put her hands on either side of Jude's face for the second time that day and kissed him, standing on tiptoe, as she'd wanted to the first time; kiss the darkness that hadn't come that long-ago day, welcome it like a long-lost friend, despite its promise.

Five

Fifty yards behind Natalie, dodging two kids on a bike—one on the seat with his hands in a genial strangulation grip on the front lad, who was pedalling so slowly that he was almost tipping it over—Dan couldn't see a bloody thing. She'd gone along the darkest bit of the road, like a nutter, asking for the local rapist to pounce, and that long-striding s.o.b. had gone in after her, accelerating to the kind of speed that Dan would have had to run to keep up with, and so far no one had come out the other end. Worse than that, it was starting to rain again.

He was going to give up and circle round the block to approach the other side of the church when he saw another man standing still on the corner, where the last house cast a long shadow. He, too, was looking fixedly at the trees and his figure had a heaviness and a still confidence that Dan didn't like the look of at all. The man wore a long, thick coat that was too hot for the weather and a wide-brimmed hat that cast the face in even deeper shadow. If he had noticed Dan he gave no outward sign of caring that he was there, nor did he waver when a clutch of students strode past within spitting distance, on their way into town.

It was a foolish thing to do but Dan couldn't stop himself. Shrugging into his jacket more deeply and shaking hair out of his eyes, he stepped off the pavement and grubbed around in his pocket, only then realizing he'd stopped smoking again three days ago. It was too late, though. The man had seen him coming and was starting to turn his shoulder, the hat brim angled to guard against any chance of eye contact. Dan pushed forwards faster, almost tripping over the curb. He caught his balance just in front of the figure and stood taller. He was tall, he could do that. He wished he hadn't, but his mouth was already continuing the pretence.

"Got a light?"

The man grunted in the negative and Dan saw a smooth-shaven jaw twitch side to side as he tried to see around and over Dan. Dan weaved an opposite pattern. The man stepped aside smartly and said, in a voice of rasping grit that hadn't a human feeling in it, "Sorry, mate. I don't smoke."

"Okay," Dan hesitated foolishly. He glanced at the man's face and felt sick. The flat stare was drinking him in just like Ray's did, only this one was even emptier, bigger, like a thousand Dans wouldn't be enough to fill it up. There was something weird about the eyes. They seemed focused and full of intent, but inanimate at the same time with a dullness that had scoured out their insides, numbed to pain or pleasure or anything Dan could imagine feeling. They made Dan's skin want to slide off his back and slink into the drain cover to escape.

The dead gaze flicked away, towards the trees.

Dan knew there was no way this person meant any good. He had to make sure that if he was watching Natalie or that American they'd get away. Would Natalie have had time to leave yet? Dan dodged around in front of the man, pretending doggy friendliness that hadn't noticed any hostility, blocking his view of the church.

The response was instant: two hands came out of the man's pockets. They lay on the front of Dan's shoulders with all the muscle tone of defrosted fish. The indifferent voice said, "Look, I don't know what your game is, mate, but I'm minding my own business and I'd like it if you got the fuck out of my face."

The hands shoved Dan backwards with a casual force that made his collarbones bend. He staggered back, doing a kind of quickstep, and hit his shoulder and head on the lamppost behind him. His shadow danced and its head lolled, rag doll–silly. It gave him the idea, not a brilliant one, of acting drunk—drunks might get smacked around but they didn't get blamed long-term, or remembered.

"Lend us a fiver?" he asked plaintively.

Shit. Shit! Why had he said that, why? Now he was being looked at with the beginnings of a genuine interest. With hardly any sign of movement the man's right fist darted out and punched Dan straight in the stomach. The man had a long reach and Dan was at the end of it, but it still landed like a horse-kick.

Dan doubled up, gasping, holding himself. He was convinced his solar plexus had ruptured or a broken rib had punctured a lung. At the same time he tried to look up in case there was more coming. Natalie had better have gone. He wasn't sticking around for any more, but his legs wouldn't take him away, even though he was trying for real now. He tasted his own stomach acid and saw a Kit-Kat wrapper floating in the gutter that made him try and smile—something ordinary in this horrible minute.

"Get lost before I lose my temper." Without another look at him, the man—all heavy overcoat, like it was just a bit of clothing over a couple of rigged dustbins, moving smoothly, oiled to silence—stepped out of the dark into the street light. He began walking towards the church at a fast march. Dan was powerless to stop him, but in an instant he heard the footsteps stop and the man swore under his breath; he had a cultured accent, the intonation of the kind of thug that is only produced by a good school, where a dirty word sounds out of place and never comes out right.

Huddled against the garden wall, looking back over his shoulder, Dan saw by the line of the shadows that nobody was standing under the trees. He cowered there, retching on nothing, gasping, until the crisp sound of the man's new shoes had faded out far away against the background of cars and voices.

Rain was falling harder now, bouncing and sparkling off the road. A group of girls on a night out passed him by in a perfumed clatter of high heels and one of them said, "Is that you, Dan Connor?"

He saw it was Edie Charlton and grinned, straightening up and trying not to let his face warp as a fierce stab of agony shot through his midriff.

"Hi. I was just, uh, checking the road signs here. Little hobby. This is still YO2, and nearly outside the walls, did you know that? Amazing. It's part of my extensive research into postal districts and the distribution of urban decay."

The nurses giggled, because they were from the Clinic and the District Mental Health Unit and all knew him well. Edie took hold of his arm. "We're for Lendal Cellars. Are you coming? Come on now, don't be shy. You'll find more nice lads down there than in this gutter."

"Aye, and don't be selling yourself round here, these bastards haven't got any money anyway!" cried another girl at the top of her voice. Amid a vague fog of Pernod and Obsession they piled up on both sides of him and, laughing all the time at his dizzy stupidity, they dragged him with them into town.

Dan looked in every opening and down every turning, but of the clean-shaven dustbin in the coat, of Natalie or that American, there was no trace.

On the other side of the low churchyard wall, in a bed of soaking weeds, with the American agent's body heavy on top of her and his hand loosely over her mouth, Natalie had to admit surprise. She waited a minute and then touched his palm with her tongue. He took his hand away.

"I have to say," she ventured in a whisper of conscious irony to the ear that was conveniently located next to her mouth, "this is faster than I usually go on a first date."

"There was a guy following me, or you, or both of us," he whispered back, "but something distracted him."

"Oh yeah. Of course." She ignored the feeling of water seeping slowly up around her back and neck and concentrated instead on the tough muscle sliding against her legs as he started to get up. It beat the sensation of whatever she'd encountered on the carpet the other day. "I'm sure he hasn't gone yet."

"Yeah, he has." He didn't notice what she'd meant.

Natalie thought crossly, *That could have been the best ten seconds of my life. And it's over already.* The part of her that wasn't a wise-ass felt faintly disgusted at the sentiment. Genuine emotion scared her.

They stood up in the almost complete darkness and brushed themselves off.

"I'm sorry," he said and sounded it. "That was kind of dumb. I'm so jumpy tonight. I don't know why. Probably he wasn't following. There's no one even there." He looked around quickly.

"No, don't apologize." She reached down and collected his case, which was sticking out of a clump of nettles. "Is this what you're looking for?" She thought he was smiling and then she heard him laughing very quietly. In a second she was laughing, too. She handed him the case. "I hear you Yanks use any excuse."

"Busted," he admitted. "But really. I think he was someone from your Clinic."

"Yeah, I'm sure you're right. After all, this is serious. National security. Top Secret." Saying it made her feel silly. She knew she had to take this much more seriously, but she couldn't.

"It is. It is." He was calming down now and so was she. Natalie took a few deep breaths, but not for any cleansing effect.

"Oh, your jacket," he began, making a half-hearted brushing motion that didn't connect.

"No, that's okay." She held up her hand. "It's not really all wool, it'll be great, just needs to dry." The trees were dripping more heavily now. They could hear rain pattering hard against the canopy, like being in a tent. "I think it's that way." She pointed at the flagstone path.

Jude waited for her to go first. He kidded himself it was because he wanted her to show the way, since she obviously would spend lots of time hanging out in the corners of local graveyards. He knew it was because she'd unaccountably kissed him like he was the last man on Earth and he was waiting for her to do it again. He felt as though the situation had made something slide out of position in his head.

"Okay." His heart was hammering. And that stunt with the wall—had it really been necessary? Of course it had. Lost the tail, hadn't he? Anyway. He had the case, although part of him would have liked to lose it then and there. He thought of the file and he knew where the slippage had started; in a world of such things, nothing could be real.

Water ran freely down Jude's face. They were standing in the stark black and white dapples of the church security light, near the gate. Everything in this goddamned country smelled of water and mud. He glanced at Natalie. She was looking at him patiently, face tilted up, doll-pale in the glare, two points of white shining right in the iris of her eyes as they closed down, centres blacker, zeroing in on him. The left side of her mouth was still smiling, the right was wry; she wanted to like him but she thought he was playing with her.

He said, "Anything ever happen to you that was really impossible?"

She pressed her lips together, evening out her lipstick to give herself time to think, and both sides of her face united in genuine interest.

"Like what? Meeting a spy and being thrown into a graveyard?" She coughed and laughed breathily at her own sarcasm.

Jude realized he must have really crushed her. He felt a fool. A real fool. He hoped he hadn't hurt her. He shook his head.

"Like . . ." But if you couldn't say a thing like that at a time like this to a psychiatrist, then when? "You had a dream, but part of it turned out true. I mean, like an object was in the dream and you never saw it before, but when you woke up it was still there."

Left eyebrow shot up in surprise, right edged down with mistrust and he had to smile.

"No. Not like that." She became self-conscious and flattened her expression in a practised way.

"But something? Or have you come across it, you know, in your research?" He didn't want to sound nuts or begging but he was both at the moment. The rain fell on his head. He felt water run down the back of his neck, making him shiver with its ghostly touch.

She thought hard. "No, nothing that you couldn't say wasn't just your imagination playing tricks on you. Nothing laboratory tested. But tell me more. I have a lot of material on this kind of paranormal event . . ."

Jude shook his head, scattering water. "This is going to sound too dumb to you. You're a scientist, much more advanced than I am. Paranormal. Christ. That's exactly what I *don't* want to know about. As if the rest of it wasn't bad enough."

"Not a believer?" She shrugged and ran her hands quickly through the short spikes of her hair. Her mascara had run in the damp and formed two dark half-circles just under her eyes, making her look vulnerable and vampish at the same time. "C'mon. I promise not to tell anyone, and it's the least you can do after what you've done to my jacket."

He grinned. "I guess so." It was strange, her taking it seriously like that, but he was relieved.

They began walking again, passing through the heavy, rotten arch of the lych-gate and into the street. A few yards later they emerged onto a broad, well-lit road full of people walking in both directions, umbrellas twinkling with droplets, raincoats rustling.

Jude started talking because it was easier now they were walking and he could avoid eye contact that might make him doubt his sanity.

"Okay. You're right. Just before I came out here I had this dream, I guess it was. Someone came and—" but he missed out the kiss part for some reason he didn't understand "—and when they were gone I woke up and there was a bunch of papers on the bed."

"Papers?" she glanced up at him eagerly. "Really? What did they say?"

"I don't know." It sounded so ridiculous.

"You're kidding. You didn't look?"

"I thought you were supposed to cynically give me an explanation of how material objects don't manifest out of thin air. To assure me that I was hallucinating."

"Hah!" She grinned. "I always try to do the unexpected. And you probably *were* hallucinating, unfortunately, although I've always hoped that one day I'd find a patient who wasn't, I mean, that it was real. Still got them?"

Jude stopped. They were on the edge of some main square, standing in the light from a travel agent's window advertising cut-price winter sun excursions to Florida. He held up the case. "D'you want to see?"

She looked deep into his eyes and then whirled around suddenly in a pirouette. "Shit, you're serious!" The fact seemed to delight her and he found himself smiling in a dumb way, starting that laugh again, because the whole world was nuts.

"Ah, you got me," he said, pretending it had been a joke, to see if she really did believe him or not.

People brushed past them on both sides and someone muttered not very quietly about idiots blocking the pavement. Jude let the case back down and started moving again. A few moments passed and he looked down at her.

She fixed him with a frank stare. "Speaking as a professional, you're an awful liar. And I'm friends with one of the best liars in the business, so I know the breed, and you, you couldn't lie your way into an under-twenty-ones night. So let's get something straight before we go on. You don't try to lie to me and I won't really lie to you. I believe you about the file. You'd better show it to me. But—" she pulled the wretched disk out of her inner pocket and flashed it in front of him "—this is bad news. I didn't believe you about it at first." She put it back carefully and steered them both down a smaller street where colourful lights were strung and restaurants alternated with small, exclusive boutiques displaying single shoes or fur coats to the drizzle.

They slowed down and Natalie took his arm. She spoke as quietly as she could and he listened hard for the verdict.

"Let's see now. Where to start. First of all, it's written in Mappacode, which is a specially derived language, requires a licence, and is only known by a very small number of programmers. But, of course, that doesn't mean someone couldn't have leaked it and hacked it—but then, they must have all the right compilers and those exist only on specific, nonlinked military machines, so if it *was* leaked it's taken a lot of trouble."

They turned a corner and had to skirt a small audience who'd gathered around a suitcase circus and were watching an old man juggle fire. Jude noticed it with another part of his brain. At any other time he'd have been delighted to find oddities like that but now it was only wallpaper.

"Second thing. It's not well done. Whoever wrote this isn't good at it. I'd guess that it's a botch—pieces of other programs copied and edited together. I'm sure of it."

"How come?"

"Because I've found sections of stuff I wrote inside it, that's why. You see, there are different areas of expertise. Some people work on the electrochemicals and the blood-chemistry side, some people on the nonphysical elements—nobody is an expert on everything. I write at the memetic level—the level of concepts. And at the patterning level . . ." She paused.

"The physical side of thoughts," Jude filled in. At least his memory was functioning clearly. He'd studied hard on the way over here and he was clear on the technicalities, if not on the fine detail of the subject. It was a gift he had pride in.

"Yes. That's my area. And some of my code is in this bastard thing. I even know the date I wrote it and where it lives inside the genuine article—it's an emotional patterner, a tool for studying and editing emotional responses to, and emotional causes of, specific memes; it tells me what the subject feels and what they're likely to do next as a result. Well, it would in theory. Anyway . . ."

"This is a patch-up?" He was adding in what she'd said carefully.

"It is. It's a patch-up that takes a normal person and makes them psychopathic. But it's brutal. It isn't the way this technology is supposed to work."

"Oh, like there's a good kind of psychopathic and a bad kind?" He wanted to laugh but he was thinking of White Horse and what she'd said about Martha Johnson and the laugh didn't get out of the starting stall.

They were passing some other kind of church. The first one was only small. This was huge, pale and ornate. Its stained-glass windows were lit up from the inside, but few people seemed to be about and the iron-studded doors were shut. A cathedral? Jude bent his head lower to hear Natalie as she whispered on, holding on to his arm.

"No. Not exactly. Like, there's a kind of psychopathic that retains personality and logical reason, people who stay coherent as characters, and there's—this. I don't even think it would have a natural analogue. I'm not even sure that you could really call whoever was targeted with this a human being in the end. It's . . ."

"Like stirring your brain with a spoon?"

"And leaving only the bad bits connected. The identity of the victim is going to be largely erased by this. It's moronic. As well as badly made. I think it was put together by copying pattern sets from someone very disturbed and then trying to duplicate them wholesale as activity lots in the receiver's head. As if this was just a photocopier for brains."

"It doesn't work like that?" He hadn't been sure about this point. The ideas and the experimental data on it had never looked like they matched up.

"No. It can't. Every brain develops individual patterns and connections from the moment the first cells start dividing. By the time we're adults, although we have a lot of commonality, we're all different. You might get the same outputs from two people when you ask them what a cat is, but how they think about the answer can be totally unique when you look at the patterning inside, the communication between the different parts of the brain. And even if we made everyone identical, with every moment that passes new and unique experiences are moulding new and unique structures, so they wouldn't stay the same. That's been the biggest problem we've dealt with. But now . . ." She stopped herself. "I can't tell you that."

"Now you've figured a way around that," he guessed, but didn't wait for an answer.

She smiled unhappily, turning her face away to look in the windows of a restaurant where normal people with ordinary problems were eating and drinking.

"And this is a piece of your project. A big military project. For mind control and identity control." He nodded. "I guess that beats my file story, although I didn't think anyone would top that."

"But this disk is not part of the project," she corrected him gently. "This is a . . . bootleg. This is trash. But someone in the project has done it. And if it's as you say, they've tested this. But whoever it was tested on must be primed with NervePath technology. It doesn't work on a cold brain. And NP is—"

"Controlled medical technology, illegal for use in the USA under the Perfection Bill."

"And in most countries across the world."

"You think GlobalPathSystems are in on it?"

"They're the ones who control the manufacture and release."

"But they're not controlled by the Pentagon."

"Maybe it's a commercial test?"

Jude stared at her. "There's a market for braindeath?"

She shrugged. "Or your people are testing this as a weapon, which looks a lot more likely. Despite, of course, all their signed pledges never to use it as such."

She didn't have to say any more. Jude thought it was pretty clear. It didn't even take the vision of White Horse in his mind, saying "We've had their pledges before," to make him place his bet on which supposition was going to turn out true. But now he and she had the same problem. They didn't know who else was in on it, and it was going to be very dangerous to find out.

They stopped, realizing that they had walked right out the other side of the town and were facing a major road. Above them was the heavy gateway of Micklegate Bar that had once been decorated with heads on sticks, heads cut off for less serious offences than they were discussing.

The rain had stopped and they were both damp. The rough stone of the arches dripped where it should have sheltered.

Jude realized that all White Horse's suspicions had turned out to be real. He'd come here to prove her wrong and now this God-awful rock had been turned over and he was going to have to do something about what was underneath it.

"I don't know about you, but I could do with a drink," Natalie said. She was shivering violently.

"Let's go." He tried to give her his coat but she was already jogging back the way they'd come, towards a lit doorway. He followed, the case heavy in his hand.

Mary Delaney stood in Rebecca Dix's outer office, listening through the open doorway as Dix and her secretary, Irina, had a standoff. Mary had requested a file and Irina hadn't produced it.

"What do you mean, it isn't there?"

"The Ivanov files are missing." Irina wasn't scared of Dix, and was equally as angry and puzzled as she was.

"It can't be missing. It's the only copy. Maybe Decker took it, d'you think? No, how could he have?"

"I had it only yesterday," Irina said, becoming calm first. Mary could imagine her attitude, hips jutting assertively, manicured hand to her face with four inch-long replicas of Earthrise from the moon perfectly painted on her nails. "I added the information from our agent in

Moscow and then I put it straight back. The locks have all functioned perfectly. Someone authorized has to have it." And for Irina that was it.

Dix put her head round the door and beckoned Mary in, allowing Irina to exit before she closed the door.

"I trust you heard all that? Good. Some bastard in the office must be doubling on us. Keep your ears sharp. We've got to get it back, fast. When we nail that Russian bastard to the wall we need to make sure nothing slips."

Mary knew that it was worse than that. Without the file there was little or no evidence that Ivanov was who they claimed he was. He could walk, easy, and take off with a stack of information in his head that had all been paid for from government funds. For security reasons no copies existed and the detail was all on paper. She had no idea where to start.

Dix looked at her with misgiving. "What made you request it now?"

"I wanted to add the Florida stuff."

Dix's stare became acute, lizardlike in its patience and depth. "Don't fuck with me over Jude Westhorpe, Agent Delaney."

Mary frowned. "I don't know where it is."

"As long as we're clear."

Of course Dix would have her followed from time to time. There was nothing that went unchecked. She must know they were close.

"One more thing goes wrong with this whole project and you're off the case."

"Yes, ma'am. If I might say something?" Mary didn't like asking permission to speak but Dix was ex-army and she liked things to run that way. "If you look for who authorized the CONTOUR release, you'll find who's causing the trouble on Mappa Mundi."

"Thanks, Einstein," Dix said, allowing a smile to soften her face. She waved at Mary to dismiss her, the worry of the theft submerging for a moment as she tried and failed to regret her stern attitude. "I'm on it."

Back in her day-guise at Special Sciences Mary picked up the heavy glass paperweight of the space shuttle *Columbia* and considered hurling it against the wall, but finally sat down to think instead, the comforting dense, smooth surfaces turning in her hands. Why do anything if nothing could be achieved by it? Throwing was her style, but she didn't need style right now. She needed to see the bigger picture that this sudden absence of the file and the live test of CONTOUR were both parts of.

She doubted that Guskov had had anything to do with the test. On the other hand . . . he'd screwed with the NSC before and won, and she would bet her last dime that there was even something in this latest genetics deal in Orlando that he was keeping to himself. When they interviewed she never got the final word in with him, nor did Dix, and now all the dirt they'd kept on him over all the years, tracing him back to his roots, finding every thug and pencil pusher he'd ever known—gone.

It was almost funny. She'd used Jude and his interest in this man to do her dirty work for her, snatching the meat from under his nose at the last second every time. And he was still faithful. And now she'd lost it, into thin air, and Jude with it for the time being. What was he up to? How would she divert him if the cursed thing had been placed in his hands?

She replaced the shuttle in pride of place and stared at it, willing it to vanish.

It was enough to make you start believing in the Philadelphia Project, it really was.

Columbia remained firmly material.

Mary began to hone the work on the details of Florida for the FBI, crafting something out of the almost-nothing she was allowed to use.

A message came through for her online from one of the British agents working for her. She read it several times before she realized the worst possibility had come true. Jude was confirmed sighted in England. They thought he'd made contact with one of the scientists involved in the project. He had to be investigating it.

In a single motion she swept up the glass shuttle and brought it down again with all her might on the desk. It broke into three pieces and a fine dusting of shards like powdered sugar. The nose section rolled away and fell onto the floor. The tail section had cut her hand.

Seeing it lie in pieces, when only a second ago it had been perfect, made her want to cry.

She didn't.

Six

Dan received the unexpected call from Shelagh Carter in the middle of his second pint. It wasn't a face-to-face, only a text note, so he didn't bother removing himself from the cramped end of the table where he and the nurses were wedged against the curving, low brickwork of the cellars. Music and lights provided a solid background of remorseless bright energy. This did nothing to stop Dan's heart from dropping into his shoes when he read the note's brief enquiry.

"Dan," it said in an innocuous, comic-style font. "Please register with the answering service if you have seen this man or know his whereabouts." An image was attached and Dan didn't need to blow it up to full-screen size to recognize it. Natalie's American. He flicked the message off and slid the Pad back into his pocket. The rest of his beer went down fast enough but it was another two minutes before he could squeeze his way to the bar and get some attention for another.

He was glad of the rapid drums and the general hilarity all around him as a hen night got under way. Paper streamers and pop glitter scattered all over him like fairy dust. Some female hand gave his bum an experimental squeeze and he almost spilled the beer as the barman handed it across the two heads in between him and the bar. Normally he'd have been in the thick of this sort of Grade A distraction, loving every second, but instead he made his way back to his seat and steadily poured the first of two extra lagers down his throat.

"What's matter wi' you?" Nurse Charlton elbowed him in the ribs after a minute or two. "You were all right a minute ago. Seen an old flame?"

Dan shook his head, actually unable to think of an answer for once, and grinned endearingly, which seemed to satisfy her for the time being. For some reason all the female nurses seemed to think his sex life was constantly evolving for their entertainment, envy, or discussion. It irritated him, although, he had to admit, most of the time he played the gay blade just as hard as he could. With his nose halfway down the glass and the drink beginning to take a bit more effect, he felt sick at himself. What was he doing here? And what time was it?

His Pad said half past eight. It would take ten minutes to walk to the Swan. Just time for another couple of drinks if he was quick. He flashed some credit across to Sister Johns, who was getting the next round in, along with a request for a lager and a Scotch.

Johns tilted her elegant brown face at him. "Are you sure? Night's still young."

He nodded vigorously and felt nauseous. He didn't want to have seen Carter's message. He didn't know what it meant, and if he drank a lot now he'd be able to forget it. It seemed to mean that Westhorpe was a kind of bad guy, but Natalie wouldn't have anything to do with one of those, so it couldn't be. Which meant that maybe Carter . . . but here his mind kept taking a U-turn all of its own accord. He tried to sort his thoughts out about the Ministry woman and it was like being magnetically repelled. He liked Shelagh Carter. Shelagh Carter was OK, a good guy, on the right side. He felt that very strongly.

But Natalie and the American . . . and there it was again. It was just like that sensation of levitation that he sometimes got when falling asleep. Floating just above the ground he'd be, and then, triggered by an image of a step off a cliff or a pavement, he'd plummet away into a terrifying fall and come to with a jolt. There was a fuzzy second of nothing. Then the only thing left in his gut and his mind was that Shelagh was right and he was wrong. He trusted her absolutely.

Except that he also trusted Natalie absolutely and the two would not, could not fit together any more. Dan thought of Natalie and knew she was smarter than he was. He could tell her about this—but no, a closed fist around his insides forbade him even to think it. He wasn't able to tell anyone about Shelagh. It was an Important Secret. Part of the government. It was vital not to tell.

In the back of his mind, in some unused pocket (and, he thought, there were plenty of those), Dan was dimly aware that he didn't usually think like this. He didn't normally have an impulse and then have another right on top of it that was contrary. He wasn't that quick or that complicated. Even Bad Dan only acted out one thing at a time.

Johns put his drinks down and he worked through both of them, even joining in the conversation until it was time to go. He said he had to meet Natalie and left, not remembering anything they'd just spoken about. As the cold air hit him he felt instantly that he was going to be very sick, but he didn't want to be because the alcohol was smoothing out the switchbacks that his head was trying to take. Through a haze of misery it was beginning to dawn on him that he knew what this was, he just didn't want to admit it as even possible. The symptoms, the reactions, the emotional jerking—they fitted the classic model. But he couldn't believe that it was true. This stuff wasn't in use yet. The project was hardly a third done. So it couldn't be that.

He had to get to Natalie and she would prove it wrong.

Dan was halfway to the Black Swan, managing to keep his stomach in order, insulated against the worst by his blood alcohol, when Natalie called him.

"Dan!" Her voice sounded agitated and it was sharp so that he couldn't protest. "I'm going to the old house instead tonight. I can't make it. I'll see you tomorrow."

Tomorrow was Saturday. Shelagh Carter would expect her call by then.

Dan vacillated, wandering in his patch of pavement as his focus left him.

"Dan, is everything all right? You look awful. Why don't you get a cab and come over, too?"

But his brain was slowly getting the hint. If she was going to the old house with whatsisname, then she probably had a plan that entailed being left well alone, especially by well-meaning meddlers like him. Natalie hadn't had a sniff of a date in eight months and he couldn't even remember the last time anyone had stayed over. His heart was full of pity for her, and a warm, affectionate feeling, even if the date did turn out to be an international spy or terrorist. Surely he must be a good one.

"No, no," Dan said, smiling and enunciating perfectly. "That's all right. I'm off home already. I'll see you tomorrow." Whatever was wrong with him could wait until she was back to help. He must have had it quite a while already, and he was still relatively okay.

With that decided he hung up and turned to his left where a raised flower bed had been conveniently positioned for inadequates to spew their guts into.

Mary Delaney played tennis on those Saturdays when she was in Washington, at the Lansdale Racquets and Clubs. It was an exclusive venue and membership was severely restricted. She felt proud to drive up through the gates and along the impressive gravel entryway, because in her childhood she'd played on courts more weed than clay, with balls that hardly bounced and no net except a washing line so narrow it was barely visible from either end of the playground.

Her morning fixture was regular, at ten, and always presaged some more businesslike meeting to be taken over lunch. There, amid the five-star dining rooms, or sequestered in a private suite lined with

English oak panelling, where floor-to-ceiling windows of bulletproof glass looked out over the vast greens of the eighteen-hole golf course, Mary felt most herself.

Out on court this morning she cracked the seal on an icy bottle of mineral water from the cooler and took a few sips as the condensation on its outside wetted her hand. She dried this on a towel and tested the grip on her racket as she waited for her opponent, Miles Roseck of the Montana Senatorial office, to double-tie his shoelaces.

He was a precise, intelligent guy who knew her in her role as a Special Sciences Agent, and he would be expecting her to discuss the state's reaction to the FBI investigation on Deer Ridge. She admired the strong curve of his quadriceps as he straightened; no doubt he planned a similar cross-examination for her. For now, however, it was enough to focus on the red clay, the feel of the ball, and getting out her aggression by hitting as hard as she could. That bastard who stole the file and Dix's subsequent pressure had done much for her energy levels.

They began the warm-up and she put together her game plan for the afternoon.

Mary had had to read the files on the Deer Ridge Accelerated Test (CONTOUR) twice before she realized that the entire situation surrounding Mappa Mundi had already moved into a new theatre of engagement.

This time it was not the Iraqi progress with NervePath, nor the Chinese successes with their animal-behaviour programmes (hamsters now served drinks in Beijing bars, balancing glasses on their backs, and in Guangzhou fish leaped straight from aquarium to frying pan through hoops of coloured flame), nor the steady leak-and-pilfer occurring within the community of larger military powers that had become such a commonplace that nobody bothered to conceal it.

The Deer Ridge Test was much more sinister than that. It was a strike aimed at bringing Mappa Mundi into the open and causing a scandal. It was set up for Jude to uncover and, in that crusading way he had, bring to the attention of the people. Then all hell would break loose.

Mary finished one of Miles's easy short balls with a punishing forehand that was pretty unsporting of her considering they were only making a rally. He got the kind of fixed grin on his face that indicated he figured she was already on a ball-breaking trip. She frowned and played some gentle, pathetic pops into his backhand. They came politely back, bouncing to her strings without her having to break a sweat. She missed the next one, clipping it into the net. Her mind would have to speed up if it wanted to think and play.

The current government could easily be toppled by the Republicans after that kind of revelation, dragging the military into the mud alongside it. The attempts at creating destabilizing political splits between pro- and anticorporate interest groups would be foiled and they would unite in outrage against Mappaware's potential for ending all that the Declaration of Independence stood for, particularly free will. The bubbling-under resentments of the computer-illiterate underclass would be stalled in their tracks and there would be an antitechnology backlash and a return to the "common values" of right-wing religious conservatism. A presidential impeachment would be forced.

It would also discredit the USA internationally. Despite the fact that everyone else was busy as bees on the same technology they would leap like sharks in a feeding frenzy to condemn the "inhumane control freakery" and "cultural colonization turning into invading ideology," thus diverting attention from their own identical efforts. It would provide impetus for a new wave of the powerfully effective reactionary factions to clog together under the banner of religion-fuelled anti-Perfectionism and demand a halt to all mindware research and biological innovations: exploiting the public horror over what had happened in Montana, they'd probably make the votes on that easily and pass a bill to outlaw it. If that happened, then the USA was finished in the race to get one step ahead with this stuff and there was a simple extrapolation Mary could use to predict where they would end up then: nowhere.

Furious development of those same technologies elsewhere would mean that they could not be first to market, and the first to market was sure to be the winner in this particular league. Such a consideration was, however, beyond the immediate comprehension of Mappaware's detractors. Few people in the world knew about the full potential of what they were creating, and Mary's bosses in the NSC wanted it to stay that way.

Miles came up to the net after they had rallied for a while, and Mary obliged him with a few easy balls to volley. They smacked down into the dirt on either side of her, not too ambitious and with only a little spin. Perhaps he would be holding back on things she didn't know about? Perhaps he was only pretending to play straight, but was really already involved with one of the factions opposed to military control of such projects, as an advocate?

She grinned at him and pocketed a couple of strays near her feet as their ballgirl ran to fetch the others. Miles wasn't even aware of such a split in the government as far as she knew. It was something like a secret society, and only those closest to the centre were in on the news. She couldn't ask him about that outright.

He moved back and she sailed a few high ones up for him to smash. The first one struck the edge of his racket and soared out of court. She saw him colour faintly pink and smiled inside, where it didn't show. The next four got killed with effective, careful blows.

She and Miles backed off towards the baseline to practise a few serves.

As she bounced her first ball Mary wondered how much power she really had. If she failed to control the situation then her expulsion from grace would be swift and fatal. She had enough authority via Dix's mandate to do a great deal, but coming down like a ton of bricks might not be the best way. She looked up, past a stray coil of hair, to Miles, who pummelled a straight shot down a few inches into the service box. The ball skipped on and made the netting rattle.

Mary threw hers high against the pure blue vault of the sky, her contacts altering immediately to protect her eyes from the hard sunlight, and sliced it hard. It swung violently out of court. Maybe this was going to be Miles's lucky day.

She watched him pin another one to the centre line and wondered if she should stand well back or try to catch it on the rise. She would stand forward, of course. It was the only way to go. Deer Ridge was a gateway straight into the Mappa project. She had to shut it.

They tossed a quarter and Mary won. She wanted to see if Miles would choke when he was put on the spot. She elected to receive, and the match began.

If she didn't close off access then the US couldn't win the race to be first to map the mind and discover how to control it. There was no way she could let that happen. Some other country calling the plays and the entire nation forgetful of two hundred and fifty years of history. She was hoping that she would be able to give Miles enough inside hints that he would help her calm down and discredit whoever tried to keep the story alive, particularly in the senator's ear. She could persuade him that the national interest lay her way, and leak only what she had to. But it was going to be tight.

Miles's first serve went wide and he spent some time bouncing the next, lining up his racket, balancing his feet. The second swung in towards her, but she was ready for it. Taking a neat step to the side Mary belted it with a backhand drive that topspun it over the net along the line, way out of his reach. Without meaning to, she felt herself grinning like a lunatic.

He could win it, as long as he didn't make her give it away, that was only polite. But before that happened, she was going to have some fun with him.

The house where Natalie and her father used to live was cold and unwelcoming. She was already regretting her decision to bring Jude there by the time the door was locked behind them. With her father gone to America these last seven months and nobody but the housekeeper to look after it the place had accumulated a smell of neglect that she associated immediately with the impersonal stench of the Mental Health ward. Both smells existed because of critical absence: one expressed the absolute lack of a physical presence, the other tried to disguise the physical traces of emptied-out minds, covering them up with chemical stinks of bleach and flowers as though smell alone could fool you into thinking they didn't exist.

In the house's deep silence Natalie thought she detected resentment, too. The place blamed her and Calum for the sorry state it was in, a shell without life. It missed Charlotte, her mother, after all these years. Bright and laughing, smelling of warm cookie dough and the faint fiery taint of the Aga's hot metal; long gone. The recollection made her falter but Jude didn't notice.

They sat by candlelight in the kitchen, once Jude had checked the place for bugging devices. He put the case on the table and she saw that he was shivering as he put his hands on the catches, their locks reading his fingerprints with soft licks of green light.

He glanced up at her, his face softer and younger-looking in the yellow glow as the candle flames ate the oxygen between them. If Natalie had had any doubt about his claims to authenticity she lost it then. She knew the look. It was the one she saw before a patient revealed something long hidden. Liars never did it right. They were always watching her too intently, caring too much. Jude was resigned to his own fear.

He looked down at his hands and opened the case, flinching as he saw inside it. He turned it towards her.

Natalie saw a brown manila folder, worn at the edges, sitting in the case like any commuter's package of homework. She wanted to laugh, because what had she expected? She heard him sigh as he thought the same thing.

"There could be a technology you don't know about," she began, doing her duty to explain away its perfectly ordinary appearance with speculation on the bizarre.

"Yeah," he said and let her know she needn't continue. "I heard about that." He grinned at her, doubtfully, and for a second she thought he was going to confess to faking it but instead he said, "I still don't know how to . . ." He looked down at the file and struggled for the right words. "This is *not* real."

He moved to touch it, but drew his hand back before he did.

"Let's open it." Natalie had the courage of beer inside her. She ignored the cold, penetrating damp of her clothes and spun the case to face herself. The folder was heavy. It took her both hands to get it out, but it felt ordinary; paper with smoothed patches from handling. Somebody had done a lot of work on it. She glanced at what else was in the case and saw some things she didn't recognize. Technology . . . but he quickly pulled it back and out of sight.

"You read it," Jude suggested. He watched her closely and she saw his nostrils flare with unconscious revulsion. Not at her, she felt—it looked much too unguarded for that.

With a firm hand Natalie flipped the cover open and saw inside it a stamp, similar to the one Glover had had on his files about her—Top Secret. *Welcome to espionage heaven. You have won the jackpot, crackpot.*

But her relief at finding evidence of a hoax was cut short as she saw the contents. The papers were official forms, with colour photographs lasered on, and fingerprints, too, lined up in neat rows of boxes. All carried holographic insignia of the Central Intelligence Agency, which made eagles dance above the page corners in the candlelight. The first one meant nothing to her. She read out the salient points, trying not to let her voice disintegrate into the penetrating cold of the kitchen.

"It's a boy. Turkish descent, but Yugoslavian. Hilel . . . I can't read the surname, maybe it's Muhammad. Islamic. Date of birth, nineteen fifty-five, Sarajevo. Left Yugoslavia in sixty-four. Mother took him back to Turkey, they settled with her family at Igneada on the Black Sea. Bright kid. Good exam results. One offence for drug possession, then—nothing. No records at all." Natalie looked at the headings. "It has the original police report attached, in Turkish, I think. What is this?"

Jude shook his head. He looked lost, bewildered. Natalie had to curb her natural irritation at his hesitating face and instead turned back to the files. She flicked through papers typewritten in Turkish, in Arabic, in something that looked Russian but wasn't. Then there was another picture, another front page tacked onto a wad of variegated papers.

"Pavlo Mykytiuk. Ukrainian. These ID papers of his are forgeries, apparently. He lived at Volgograd in the seventies, on a farming cooperative. Yeah, big guy. That diet of beets and vodka really makes them like bulls. What a neck!" She paused, looking at the photograph, and read on. "Looks like he wasn't popular there after a while. Stealing or something like that. He got blamed, anyway. Then he left and went to . . . Tula, where he was a railway engineer for a year. Member of the Communist Party . . ." Natalie looked up and joined Jude in staring at the photograph again.

Pavlo was young, pale, with idealism still strongly present in the set of his shoulders and chin, outthrust forcefully; he looked capable of taking care of himself, all right. He had stared into the police camera with complete contempt.

Jude's intensity in examining it almost made her eyes water in sympathy.

"Do you recognize him?" she asked.

"No," Jude said. He dared to reach across into the file's heart and lift half the stack away. An old, grubby card slid out and Natalie lifted it closer to a candle to read its faded handwriting.

"Russian, I can't read it," she growled, annoyed.

He took it gently out of her fingertips. "I can."

At last, Natalie thought, *the brain gets into gear*. She liked him again. She watched him read, the unconscious confidence of his ability. She wanted to touch him.

"This is a registration, an entry that's ready to be processed in the Kodeks," he said, wondering, turning the small, waxy thing over and over as he scanned both sides.

"Codex?" The word meant dusty documents and secret-society nonsense to her.

"A central database of criminal records kept by the Soviets, and then carried on by the Russians after the breakup of the Union. Alexei Kurchatov. Nineteen eighty-five. He must have gone down for years: theft, drug dealing, running a prostitution racket . . . the usual kinds of charges that the authorities used to throw at people they didn't like to get them off the streets," Jude turned the card over. "I wonder how they got this out of Moscow." Then he snorted with amusement. "I wonder whose this is, I guess I should say. Kurchatov. Like that's his real name."

"Why not?" Natalie asked.

"Kurchatov was a famous Russian scientist from the last century. I guess this guy could be another; there could be millions of Kurchatovs, but what do you think when it says here—no birth papers, no licence, no records of him at all . . . it's a fake." He leaned over the table and moved another wad aside, then suddenly grabbed one of the ID sheets as it fanned out from its friends, dragging it under his nose. "Shit!"

"Sorry?" Natalie leaned closer, trying to see.

"Yuri Ivanov," he said, in a tone of awe. "What's he doing in here?" Jude glanced up at her and shook his head. Inside his dark brown eyes she saw him at his most focused, his mind clear to her in that second, like an open book, like a child, but before she could see more he was back to his picture.

Natalie squinted at the photo. She saw a heavy, Mongol face, brow-shaded eyes glittering with ferocious energy. The man had a thick moustache and long, heavy hair of an intense blue-black. "Who is he?"

But Jude was searching through the other papers, finding a passport, identification papers from Germany, work permits, academic references. He seemed not to have heard her. Now his hands moving on the pages were still and precise and in the raw flame-light his face had become as serene as a church saint's. Natalie watched the blink of his long, dark lashes across his cheeks, the deep shadow his nose made, straight, clear; the precise outline of his handsome mouth part-opened over his white, straight American teeth.

"Ivanov is the one person I never managed to arrest," Jude said, suddenly glancing up at her, catching her at it, but not realizing he had, because his concentration was too intensely focused. "A bunch of circumstantial evidence and coincidence. He's an American academic: psychologist, biologist, polymath—a defector. Came over via Germany in the late eighties . . . complicated man. I met him once." But the memory must have been unpleasant because Jude made a face as though he'd tasted poison.

Again hesitancy and doubt did their unpicking of his confidence and he seemed to shrink in scale within himself. She knew that feeling and wondered what it was that he'd shared with his quarry—something significant.

Natalie looked down at the sliding heaps on the table. "But who's everyone else here?"

"I don't know," Jude snapped back and shook his head. He squinted at the sea of data.

"No coincidence now, though," she said and he looked up at her. "I mean, you getting this. It explains why, sort of. Here's a man you want. And here're some of his papers. Maybe this is what you needed all along to get some kind of conviction?"

"And God gave it to me?" he said sarcastically.

She shrugged and grinned. "Maybe."

Jude went back to sifting. Medical records. Immigration papers. Registration forms. Social Security. Natalie was glad this wasn't her job to sort out.

"Oh wait!" She flicked the papers her way round and almost spilled wax on them. Her whole body went cold.

Without a doubt, beneath the glowing eagle's wings it was a photograph of Mikhail Guskov.

"What?" Jude was staring at her now.

Natalie knew that this was something she shouldn't talk about, except now she was stuck with it and it was hardly as though the evening wasn't already a total violation of her signature on the Official Secrets Act. The Home Office were going to write her a permanent ticket to prison.

"This is Mikhail Guskov," she said. "He . . . works on the same project as I do. In America. Have you investigated him?"

"No," Jude kept on staring at her. "You know him? Well?"

"No," she said, getting her composure back with a bit of help from Jennifer the Hotline girl's diversion technique. "Not at all. Just his name and face. There aren't that many of us, really." Now the files disturbed her suddenly, and they hadn't before. She shoved the incriminating page aside—it was the last in the folder—and then as she glanced down it was as if her heart really did jump into her throat. Bawhamp. It stopped. Blood dropped into her feet. Her head swam.

It was there. After all these years. Right there in front of her. Bang. Just like that. Proof of the inexplicable.

"What?" Jude was demanding. "What? Dammit!"

Natalie couldn't believe it. She pointed at the folder's inner face and even Jennifer had no reaction to use as a cover.

"That," she whispered.

Jude read the scrawled words, crammed in between an elaborate drawing composed of pencil lines that circled and turned on each other, creating forms that seemed to try and leap off the page. "Due back: 15 June 2015." He shook his head. "That's today."

Dazed, a shock space inside of her bigger than the room she was standing in, Natalie traced the heavily scored lines of the doodle with her finger, her other hand holding onto her face, to check it was still there as much as to support it.

"You don't understand," she said. Her finger felt the gouges, followed as though it already knew the way and, after all, it did, because this was a picture of The Map.

"This is my handwriting."

Jude had, until that moment, not believed his own story about the file. It had become just that. A story. Even holding it and reading its extraordinary contents couldn't make him accept the way he'd come upon it. But Natalie's reaction changed him.

She began to shake—not the shiver he'd had, but convulsively, in whole-body jerks. Her grey-green eyes were glazed. Her mouth was open, her face expressionless, abandoned. It was as though she had left her body and was somewhere outside it, in recoil from the whole of the physical world. Only her finger remained under a conscious control in its sensory touching and retracing of the peculiar lines; a chant of form that was drawing her under its spell.

Looking at her awakened a primitive kind of fear, both for her and for him, because what was he going to do if she cracked up now?

Jude leaned across the table, knocking candles flying, and grabbed her upper arms in his hands with a grip as hard as he could manage. He tried to hold her still by force, shouted her name. "Don't go! Wake up! Natalie!"

Then, as fast as she'd gone, she was looking up at him again from the face that had been empty a second before. The right side of her mouth quivered in a shaky smile. "It's okay," she said quietly. "I'm sorry. It's fine."

"Fine." He shook his head. "No, that it ain't. So what is it? What was that?"

"I used to be mad," she said, offhand. She detached her arms from his grip with a brisk shrug, and stepped back. "Years ago. That drawing. It made me remember it. That's all. Don't worry. I'm fine." She moved towards the sink unit, drew up against it, and looked out of the window at the lights of the hotel beyond their garden wall, her back to him.

Jude sat down again and saw that wax had covered a lot of the Guskov picture. On the floor most of the other candles had gone out in thick pools that were slowly congealing. An edge of one page had taken light, but the paper was treated and it hadn't burned far. Three candles remained lit, their flames softly fluttering in the disturbed air, flooding the place with moving shadows.

He shivered and realized that he was cold because he was wet, as well as scared. This goddamned file. He wished he could burn it. He wondered if he should. The kitchen had an old-style, new-world fireplace that looked like it was sturdy. If he piled it all in there it would burn in minutes. He could bury the ash in the garden or whatever lay outside the dark windows and the surviving CIA decals could be sifted out and airmailed to some backwater country. If it had been his house he would have. He peered at the writing. Could she be lying? She had said she was mad.

He had just wasted his entire trip if she was.

He remembered her kissing him under the trees, her cool hands on his face, the fierce hunger she had that wasn't really for him, but for something much less ordinary.

It was all insane.

Natalie was opening cupboards. Jude watched her get out two shot glasses and a half-bottle of whiskey. She poured, clanking the neck of the bottle on the rims hard enough to break both, although neither gave.

"Want one?"

"Yeah." He crossed the room carefully, not stepping in the wax. He leaned against the units, alongside her, and they looked together at the pages littered in the pool of light.

Jude wondered how mad she meant, and how she could say it like that, like saying she'd once been a cheerleader, or a clerk. She thought he'd change his mind about her now. He didn't want to, but maybe he had. He took a drink and the sharp fire was a relief.

"It's late," she said. "You must be tired."

"I don't think I can sleep." He took another slug and held it in his mouth. The place was freezing and it was summer outside. He was tired. He was exhausted.

"My father never slept," Natalie said. "So he used to say. He'd go to the study and work. I think he did sleep, in breaks he wasn't aware of. His eyes would be open, but it was like nobody was in there. I used to wonder, where did he go? He was never happy when he came back, not after she died."

"She?"

"My mother. Charlotte. She was a travel journalist. Died in an air crash with the man she was having an affair with. Somewhere near Cape Town. It was in all the papers."

"I'm sorry." Jude didn't know what to make of this revelation, whether it was connected with the writing on the folder or not. Could that be the reason for her madness? It didn't on its own seem like enough. He took another drink and for a moment in his mind he saw a tall man, a lanky man, a cigarette in his mouth like a twig on the trunk of an old pine tree.

"That's okay," Natalie said, matter-of-fact. He saw her from the corner of his eye knocking back the whole contents of her glass. "I didn't mean that we should sleep." She glanced up and grinned; a wild, feral kind of expression that was a challenge directly at him. "I've got something to show you."

She was scary. He had to admit it.

The house had a wide staircase that led up two storeys and they negotiated it by the banister, carefully, his footsteps following in hers, thinking how glad he was that any city house these days was never really dark. On the top floor he made out three rooms. Natalie opened the one on the right and Jude saw nothing, as though she'd opened a door on night itself.

"Blackout blinds," she explained. "Step in and I'll switch on the light."

It was harder to do than he thought. His feet tested the carpet gingerly and he felt himself shiver as she closed the door behind them with a dead, muffled sound. He could have been anywhere in the world, with no idea where. His mind skittered with thoughts of serial murders, obsessional photography, collections of body parts, dead animals, or worse. His skin stood up in goose-flesh, not just from the chill of his drying clothes.

The lights were bright, but not blinding. He stared at the room. It was empty, but the walls—white underneath—were entirely covered in tiny, intricate networks of lines like those on the folder and equally tiny, precise writing.

"Welcome to my nightmare?" he hazarded, trying to keep it light.

"No, no," Natalie said, full of good humour now, apparently at his unease. "Welcome to Natalie Armstrong."

He stared around him. On the nearest piece of wall he took a closer look. None of the lines crossed. They were marked with numbers, reminding him of something. "This is a weather map?"

"In a way." She was smiling now and he wished she'd get on with it and let him in on the joke.

"These are isobars," she said. "Low-pressure and high-pressure areas, warm fronts, occluded fronts, storm systems—psychological ones. Sadness is a low. Love is a high. Other emotions are more complex figures. The writing and the names were representations, then, of everything that I knew."

"Then?" Jude moved closer and inspected a patch. He could see why the lights had to be so bright and even, otherwise he couldn't have read anything at all. The writing was minuscule.

"When I was seventeen. I'd just come off the ward. This was part of my cure, I guess you could say."

Jude was reading. His tiny entry, sited in the midst of an anticyclone, said, "Prakrti: reality of energy manifested as matter, a pocket of local fugue inside the Dance of Shiva." He had a vague idea that it was something to do with Hinduism.

"Why's this in such a state?" He pointed at its location. She didn't even need to look at it.

"I'm afraid the whole of me was in that state, really. Mum's death threw me a bit overboard on the mystic, though. That part of the wall is all about my feelings and theories on the nature of physical reality and death. Teenager stuff." She was grinning again, but this time she wasn't so sure of herself. He got the impression there was much more she would have liked to say but that she didn't think he'd want to hear it.

"But reading my ideas isn't why you're here," she added. "Well, it is. But not because I need an audience. Going back to your stolen program . . ." She activated a switch, using her Pad, and a section of the ceiling slid back to allow a large projection screen to unroll itself right down to the floor. Another panel in the ceiling silently passed to one side and a three-lensed projector moved into position. The lights dimmed and they moved together automatically, so that they could see the images better.

Natalie cued an image that Jude recognized easily—a coloured image of two brains, animated to show intricate patterns of activity.

"The one on the right is a volunteer, someone picked at random. The one on the left is a Zen Buddhist in deep meditation."

"Why?"

"Because they have a belief that underneath the shell of your self, all your defining moments, there is another entity that isn't bound by your human lifetime, it's an eternal, immortal thing, and they maintain that by bringing the mind to stillness, while conscious, you can make contact with it." She stepped up to the screen and plunged her hand deep into the Buddhist's synapses. "You can see the differences, but the key feature isn't just the pattern, it's the resonance. That's the blue in this picture."

"So what, though? Brainwave variations don't make a soul. Do they?" He glanced at her, striped with colour, and she nodded.

"No, of course not. But here the theta patterns are very pronounced, yet you can also see that this person is awake. And here." She indicated where and told him about areas where perception took place, processing the raw data of the senses into meaning. "Here, these areas are all in much stronger communication than in this test subject on the right."

He looked expectantly at her for the explanation and she punched up a film. "This is my subject, the Buddhist," she said and Jude saw a laboratory room, bare except for the old man on his sitting mat and another person behind him. They both held scimitars. In the corner of the recording the time slowly flipped along. They stood and sat, poised, motionless.

Jude could hear the faint white hiss of the soundtrack, thought he could just make out one of them breathing. Without a noise the man behind began to raise his sword.

"He's a Kendo master," Natalie said.

The master brought his weapon up for a short blow that would inevitably split the Buddhist's head. The Buddhist did not move. He seemed asleep. Not even a finger twitched where his hand rested open against the handle and the blade of his sword.

"Are those—real?" Jude said.

"I missed off the bit where they chop melons and stuff," Natalie said, so he wasn't sure if she was joking. "This is the interesting part."

"And these are test conditions?" He was so glad it wasn't dead bodies in refrigerators in here that he was actually getting interested.

"Oh yeah."

For an eternity the blade hung. At almost two minutes, with no visible changes taking place, Jude drew a breath to ask her what was going on and the two blades were suddenly together, half an inch from the bald man's head. The clash of metal rang clean and loud and Jude jumped off the floor.

"You've got to be kidding me," he said, his heart hammering.

Natalie pressed rewind, slowed it down, and played it again, "This from the man with Spontaneous Files," she murmured. But he was too startled to smile.

This time Jude saw the seconds passing more slowly. He saw, frame by frame on the third and fourth replay, that just before the blade above began to descend the Buddhist's hand took hold of his sword. With preternatural speed and no wavering, it put the metal between his head and the descending weapon, arriving precisely in position and remaining there as it took the shock, only dipping low enough to brush the skin over the man's skull with its blunt back.

"That's like—just a movie thing," Jude said, shaking his head.

"Yeah," Natalie agreed, and put the two brain pictures back on. "You see this flash on the left one, there? That's when his arm moved. The response starts simultaneously with the initiation of the movement in the man behind. There's no way any sensory information could have travelled from one to the other."

"So, this is like what?" He didn't know what to think now. He couldn't believe what he'd seen, but then, that was a common thing lately. He only felt slightly seasick.

"This is part of my project into human consciousness," Natalie said. "It relates to your programme because I've been developing a theory and a system—a programme of my own—that could, maybe, initialize this kind of deep perception in an ordinary subject at will. Part of that programme, a very little part, was in your file."

"What part?"

"The part that cross-links specific sensory processing areas. I'm guessing that the effect would be a bit like taking a shitload of acid or something like that. You'd get synaesthesia, but maybe worse; I don't really know, to be honest. My project requires precision. And it's never been tested. Other parts of it . . . are of interest at the moment, to your government."

"I'm not surprised," he snorted. "Can you show me what the whole thing can do?"

"Maybe." She switched off the projector and had it put itself away.

"Ah, maybe." He folded his arms. "Name the price then."

"The price is—" she paused, placing her Pad back on standby, "—that you don't mention me or anything I've told you to anybody else. I'm not an idiot. Someone's bound to know we've talked by now and they'll guess the rest soon enough. God," she sighed and shook her head. "I always thought the project would produce its share of shit, but it just goes to show what a fool you can be when you want to fool yourself. I didn't think of this and here it is. I don't know what the program is supposed to prove, and I don't know why they zapped people around your sister but it looks like less than chance odds to me, and I'm real good at statistics."

He wondered how he could ever have thought her crazy. Her fiery intelligence was right back, burning its way out of her face towards him, even making his freezing body feel warm.

"Something's gone wrong somewhere," she said and jammed her hands in her jacket pockets. He assumed she was referring to the file and its appearance, her writing; there was a mistake in the Universe. The harsh white glare of the room made her seem very small, very sharply coloured. "Although, given the odds against it, who could be surprised?" She grinned at his lack of comprehension. "I mean, looking at the project in the context of the world as we know it, of course something's gone wrong. Mathematically you could have computed the likely moment if you'd had the right data. Human behaviour is capable of being modelled very accurately, especially when it's large populations we're talking about, and not individuals."

"This is another part of your work?"

"No, just Sod's Law." She turned and looked at the room. "The past and the future exist only in our minds. That's part of my work now. The past and the imagination and the future, fusing identity out of experience and fantasy. Every one of us a unique product, constantly evolving along a narrative storyline that chooses us, as we once chose it, without knowing."

"I'm sorry?"

Natalie turned. Her smile flickered, feral one moment, self-mocking the next. It was mesmerizing. Her eyes were huge and intent. He stood still as she walked up to him, took her hands out of her pockets and put them gently on either side of his face. Her fingertips were icy. The third finger of her right hand touched the scar behind his ear.

"This gesture," she said, "is already part of my story and yours, you and me, it is one thing that we share. Third time today." She moved closer until he could feel the heat of her body. He was fixated, staring into her grey eyes, not knowing if they were more blue or more green, unable to find a name for the colour.

"But whatever it means to you," she said, long mouth wrapping the words before it sent them out, packaged like presents, into his consciousness, "I bet it doesn't mean the same to me. In reality, it's one thing. But we see it quite differently."

Jude smiled slowly. "Try me."

She stood on her toes and moved closer, until their faces were only inches apart. He felt her lean against him, her pelvis coming into firm contact with his. Her gaze never faltered and from inside its clear depths she watched for any sign of a change in him, a backslide, which he knew wasn't coming, then or ever. There was a peculiar sensation in the centre of his sternum, like something long and sharp was stuck there, vibrating.

"I'd have to tell you everything to find that out," she said, her expression now purely one of predatory instinct. He tasted the whiskey on her breath as she teased him. "You'd have to be me, and I'd have to be you."

"I've got a better idea," he said, every nerve ending in his face alert to the closeness of her. He put his hands inside her damp jacket, against the sticky fabric of her shirt. Underneath it her body was hot.

"Oh?"

He leaned back with his shoulder for the light switch. Pitch darkness enveloped them suddenly. "Want me to draw you a map?"

She felt along the scar just as she'd traced the lines on the file, careful, curious.

"Where's this?"

"Where we are," he said.

She laughed and then the cool vice around his head tightened. She kissed him and a shock ran through to the back of his skull, like the reverse of a blow from the butt of a carbine.

Seven

White Horse opened the venetian blinds with her fingers and peered down into the street, watching the traffic prowl by in restless fits and starts: one speed, then faster, then stopping again. It reminded her of a video she'd seen once in Medical 1 at college, of red blood cells moving along in a vein, but there was no life in the road or the city that she could see or feel to match this analogy. *If it has a heart*, White Horse thought, *then where is it beating?*

It disturbed her. She knew, she felt, that life's patterns moved together, the life of each individual only a part of life as a whole, but this surge and trickle wasn't the pulse of that kind of feeling. Something much more restless and unhappy impelled that endless energy that went nowhere. This was why she hated the city. It was the embodiment of the pointlessness of eternal activity, motion without purpose, purpose without feeling, feeling without a clear thought behind it, only the impenetrable leviathan of the Capitol, dead from the dollar-gland on down.

Washington, DC, she hated in particular. It seemed to ferment every corruption she could think of, like she imagined ancient Rome had done, crushing out the virtues of the people under the weight of its press, feeding the juice in as a wine to be drunk again—spirit death by distillation. She knew alcohol. On the res too many of her friends thought that they'd escape through the bottom of a bottle. Washington was the production centre of their despair as she saw it.

White Horse let the slats snap closed and paced the length of the long, pale cream room once more, her bare feet never getting used to how far they sank into its luxury carpet, nor to how easily it sprang back up after she had passed. She hadn't known carpets like this existed, and it was even stranger to find one in her brother's house, one of only a thousand gadgets, trinkets, and comforts she'd never imagined before.

At first they'd delighted her, but now she loathed them all. The apartment was a show home, an empty place. The gadgets existed to make life easy, but they required a duty of service, a payment of money, they came with obligations each one, from the mixer to the shower-pump system with its twenty-setting massage unit. Their existence made her soul itch.

Jude—she found it hard to think of him under the name Mo'e'ha, Magpie, anymore, since he'd left her that time they'd argued—had only been gone a couple of days. She'd only been here one more than that. But already she could feel the FBI catching up, following her easily from Deer Ridge to this apartment where soon they'd show up in force and drag her away. She knew them and their method. They were so close she could almost smell them. But she had to wait. It was unbearable.

On the smooth glass of the coffee table the neat, hand-size panel of the house's answering system was alive with messages. White Horse dared not use it and would not answer any calls. She didn't watch the TV and she didn't play music or games or use anything of the place, except the bathroom and the kitchen. Her own PocketPad was switched into collection mode only, to allow it to log calls but do no more. Last night she'd gone out shopping, come back, cooked. Now the rooms smelled more of chilli than polish, but it was all the impression she wanted to make. Her bag was ready, her boots by the door, always.

But how long should she wait? Jude had called her once, left a Pad message, no voice and no vid option. He hadn't wanted to talk to her and she, for once, didn't blame him. He had written, *Looks like you were right. Get rid of it.*

That had arrived four hours ago. White Horse had read it many times, even though once was enough to understand it entirely. She had not got rid of the ugly black machine, however. It was her only evidence now the program was in Jude's hands and there was no way she'd give it up. She wasn't even sure she trusted him a hundred percent not to turn his coat and hand it over himself. But she thought that the shortness and the routing of his note via ordinary domestic lines contained some element of wisdom. She should hide it. For the last four hours, she had thought of where she could go undetected, where it might be safe. Nowhere sprang to mind.

Scratching at the itch of her healing burns before she remembered not to, White Horse winced and cursed as the pain roared to life on her hands and arms. She went to the kitchen and took a pill for it, rubbed cream onto the skin carefully, and then she knew that there wasn't anywhere on Earth to go. The apartment was only safe as long as nobody knew she was there and that couldn't last. The doors would be watched, the AI systems governing the building's public areas alerted to look for anything odd. They were capable of sending her picture, files, and information direct to the nearest patrol car.

Then again, the FBI or whoever else was involved might find out Jude wasn't in Seattle at any time. The device itself must be fitted with some kind of tracking unit, she supposed, although if so it wasn't working. Maybe she'd broken that part of it when she fell on it back at the house. But she couldn't leave with it in case they located and destroyed it. Therefore, it must stay and she would go, to lead them away from it as fast as she could.

One thing she and Jude had in common was tidiness. It took her only a few moments of exploring to locate his tool kit in the cupboard with the cleaning equipment. Even the corners of that space were dust-free and everything he owned set in its place, as though it was never used. She felt sorry for him, alienated even by his own house. She felt that she had been instrumental in causing him to turn so far away from his right nature. This vacant space was his payback for turning. It was a punishment too much. She didn't understand why he couldn't feel this—or if he did, why he stayed. Was he so stubborn that he couldn't put down his pride and come home? She missed him. She'd always missed him, especially during those long summers when he was away at his expensive school and with his mother. They shouldn't have parted like that. She and he were one blood. His *wasichu* half couldn't be the core of the person she knew. It couldn't win.

White Horse opened the toolbox and lifted out its trays. She took the relevant ones with her and spread them out on the smooth, heavy-snow carpet that showed no trace of time. Then she went to her bag and extracted the machine.

Beneath the modern abstract oils of his pictures, and the display of old bone jewellery that was part Navajo, part Apache, part Cherokee, part Cheyenne—silenced to a whisper against the icy background of the walls—White Horse brushed her long, synthetic dreadlocks to one side and began to pick it to pieces.

She was glad to see that the dull black casing was not a manufactured type. It had been specially made. That meant it was more difficult to open without damaging, but it would also be easier to put together again afterwards. The thing had been intended to be serviced or upgraded, and she got it open after a few deft twists of the delicate screwdrivers, without even scratching its surface.

Inside she recognized some elements that were common to most electronic devices. Taking it to bits might render the thing useless if she ever got it to trial; they could say she'd manufactured it. But that made life easier, in fact.

She undid the mounts and removed the whole lot as a piece and then went to weigh it in the kitchen. She packed the casing with an equal weight of cardboard, cut out of a box of Cheerios, and a Pad battery. Then she replaced the switch systems and LED indicator, linking them together with the tiny battery from her own watch. When she was done the machine looked as it always had; press the switch and the light comes on . . . nothing happens, but then, it never did, as far as she was able to tell. It must be broken.

The machine's case went back into her bag. The contents lay on the carpet. White Horse looked around, guessing at wall cavities, false ceiling heights, the interior structure of the furniture, the likely gap size beneath the floor. Where should the device's innards go? Where could she hide them until they were needed? She moved silently through the airy rooms, touching walls, doors, cupboards, feeling the floors with the bare soles of her feet, open to guidance, waiting for a change in her feeling that would tell her she'd found it.

Mary Delaney had an audience with Guskov scheduled for three that afternoon. Dix never dealt direct with contractors. Instead, she had a team of negotiators that she shared with the Defense Directorate. Mary didn't come into that category, but after her job inside the FBI was over and Mappa Mundi was in the bag she hoped for advancement into their ranks. Hence she'd persuaded Dix to let her act more closely on the project this time, to keep an eye on it from both ends. As a reward or a punishment, Dix had decided to test her and give her the chance to act on her behalf. The authority was something Mary wasn't about to waste.

She pulled the appointment forwards half an hour, just to see what he'd do. They'd already met many times, and although she'd once or twice left feeling that she'd scored there wasn't any doubt in her mind that Guskov was always going to take the Grand Slam unless she was better than her best.

With winning in mind there was nothing left to chance. Mary wore her finest suit, had her hair, nails, feet, legs, and face seen to by a flotilla of experts, shod herself in perfect antique Blahniks, and when she checked herself in the office's private ready-room even she had to admit that it was unlikely the Russian was going to beat her at Best in Show. Brains, on the other hand . . . exact amounts of guarana, vitamins, and ginkgo were the maximum she was prepared to use in training. She slugged back her personalized mixture of three drops in a half-glass of water and checked again in the Ladies' Room mirror for traces of visible panty line. Beneath the silk lingerie she could feel her body trying to sweat, but under the control of the response inhibitor that functioned for her instead of an ordinary antiperspirant it wasn't making it. She grinned into the mirror. Time to go.

At exactly two-thirty Mikhail Guskov was shown in and they shook hands and made eye contact with matched firmness and determination, each registering the other's approval and engagement in the tussle with perfect understanding and the most subtle of shifts around the eyes. Mary loved meetings with Mikhail. They tested her to the limit.

"I'm sure that your contacts have already told you why this meeting has been called," she said, once greetings were over. They sat together in high-backed leather comfort chairs; hers with firmer cushions, but despite that he was as tall, as imposing, at ease. If he noticed the difference he affected not to. His blue eyes were amused and guarded, indicating readiness to fight, in that look that was more charged than any glance of sexual lust could ever be. Mary had long preferred it.

He gave a slight nod in concession to her guess. They both knew the contacts she meant; men and women working in the Russian mafia's network who owed him loyalty for old debts.

"I was shocked to discover that a decision had been taken here that would allow such a test to take place," he said, his American English almost perfect except for a haunting trace of Russian taints here and there; a style Mary was sure was deliberate. It made her think of wild Siberian winters, fur collars, log fires, and stone-built dachas deep in the forest. Nothing about him was not chosen. He was self-made in every detail. As she had, he had learned to abandon anything of himself that did not serve his purpose. But she checked herself in case he saw this admiration leaking out of her.

"It was a political ploy," Mary replied calmly. "A lever to test the mettle of the government. We should be grateful they chose CONTOUR. Less destructive than some other projects that are under way. Its effects are contained."

"Yes." Guskov let his head rest on the chair's support, easing his shoulders with a slow, sensuous motion. "And it served to prove that Mappaware is still far too unstable for any kind of real-world use." His face split slowly with a knowing grin at her, a sustained eye contact that he dared her to break in denial.

She realized that he knew about the Pentagon and CIA use of basic NervePath technology in the field. That was a surprise, and no doubt he'd seen the involuntary iris response to it as he looked into her eyes so keenly.

"The latest refinements on very limited and basic applications of Mappaware have worked much better than the test on Deer Ridge would suggest," she said. "Whoever constructed the programs used in CONTOUR . . ."

"*Kozyol*!" Guskov snorted, giving his opinion on that excuse for a person. "Yes, an idiot of the highest calibre. It astonishes me how so many of them appear to be employed in your most sensitive posts." His blue gaze suddenly became commanding and cold although his voice didn't change. "You must find them."

"We will." She opened the palm of her hand where it rested on the chair's arm, smoothing off a patch of imaginary dust, wiping them off the face of the Earth. His interruption had given her a mild case of annoyance, but she let it sink down again. He seemed to notice nonetheless.

"But this is not your worry," he prompted her. "So, the information leakage is as bad as I predicted it would be. But we haven't yet reached Stage Three. One or two more tiny slips will be all it takes for all our efforts to be wasted, given away to the world market. I thought you people claimed you had control." He was no longer amused. "This is no way to run a business, Ms. Delaney."

"My thoughts exactly." Mary smiled at him, using all the force of her wit to try and elicit a friendly response, not giving in when she didn't get one. "That's why we want to move to Isolation now."

As she had anticipated, he was not surprised by her challenge. He moved suddenly, lunging forward, resting his elbows on his knees as he considered her proposal. Finally he said, "The site is prepared?" He glanced up at her through his heavy, overgrown hair, cheeks and jaw very heavy at that angle, like a boxer's face that had taken her best punch and could take a lot more.

"Yes." Which was not strictly true, but she knew Dix could make it happen, because she had to.

He nodded. "And if we do this now, we will have to take in with us the extra personnel. It's outside the plans we drew up. These people will have to be imported, spirited in from all over the world. Can you do that?"

"How many?" Dix had warned her about this, and she dreaded the question. In order to go into Isolation the whole team working on Mappa Mundi would have to enter a closed environment, cut off from the outside world. The NSC had prepared for this eventuality a year ago, when the first stage of Mappa Mundi had been completed and it was already clear that the price of information was good enough to soften the resolve of more than a few. The site was limited, however. It didn't have the equipment or the space to allow significant alteration in a short time. Even getting it ready within a few weeks was going to drag out their resources to the limit.

Guskov didn't need to consult his notes. "Twenty-five."

Which was ten more than she'd bargained on. She laughed. "Twenty," and that was too many.

He shook his head, "Not at this level. There's too much to be done."

"Twenty," she said, wishing that she'd picked a lower figure.

His nostrils flared in contempt. "Not possible."

"Twenty. Five more would tip the entire system into a potential disaster. The site can't support that many. It's twenty."

And here she had him because the government called this one, whether he liked it or not, and he knew it.

"Choose who you like," Mary added, generously indicating the entire world with a half-shrug, "but by tomorrow I want a list of twenty names and not one more."

Guskov hesitated and then sat back, regarding her with a fatherly tolerance.

"Do you know that among my scientists many are deeply uncomfortable with the obvious implications of this project? It offends their moral sensibilities. They see immediately that for all your sweet words it is a perfect tool for repression. Of that twenty, at least half, or more of them, may quickly be pushed across the line where they refuse their labour and, once they are sealed in, then who will I use as they join the strike? Who will police them, so that they do not sabotage the work in a moment of misguided, heroic idealism?" He leaned his head on one side and looked at her through steepled fingers.

"I wouldn't dare to suggest anything to an expert in coercion," she said easily. "You can answer that better than I could." And now wasn't she on the back foot? She had to grit her teeth behind her cool façade.

"So," he mused, "you would take their families hostage, you would impound their assets. You, the American government, would use basic emotional router programmes and your inept, undereducated NervePath programmers to resculpt their personalities? All these tactics your culture stands against, first and foremost among all nations, and you will not hesitate? There is nothing so low that you will not stoop to it, to crush freedom's life out, without mercy?"

Mary felt her own smile go bitter cold now. "You can rely on that." As she said it and his smile intensified into one of warmth she knew that this one wasn't a bluff. She would. She could. The knowledge was a triumph and a disappointment, the two emotions so intimately entwined that she couldn't separate them.

"Then I will give you my list," he said. "Ten names. As we agreed."

She frowned questioningly at him.

Guskov smiled and disentangled his hands, spreading them out in the air. "There are some people," and his look made her aware that he suspected she knew who they were, "that even I would not trust, Ms. Delaney."

Part of her longed to ask if he would have included her on that list or not, but she'd already given enough points away on the day. She offered him a drink and they toasted their agreement with vodka.

When he'd gone and she had to send her news to Rebecca Dix, Mary paused with her hand on the Pad control. She had the sensation that she'd missed something, and then realized it was only the glass shuttle that had gone from its place. She shook her head to clear it of the feeling, and started calling.

Natalie stared at the ceiling of the guest room as dawn was breaking. Its faint, grey light came through the uncurtained window like the breath of an old animal out in the cold, weak and unwilling. From the street she heard the milk cart come whirring quietly, bottles chinking for houses other than hers.

She couldn't believe herself. What a moron. What an idiot. Talking like that and then . . . she cringed inwardly at the memory of her wanton behaviour. Oh my God. He'd think she was a Total. And then she thought of the file and today's experiment at the Clinic, which she'd conveniently forgotten about last night, and it was too much. She wanted to be safely away in her old life where nothing happened.

Beside her Jude rolled onto his back and reached over to touch her shoulder.

"Awake?"

"Oh yeah," she said. She turned her head on the pillow and looked at his face.

To her relief, he smiled and tucked both hands under his head. "I guess I look as bad as you feel?"

"Much worse." She was touched, surprised, glad when he pulled one hand out again and brushed the tip of her nose with one finger in a tender caress.

"Your science has done something to my head," he said wryly, but she didn't know this time what was meant. She wanted to think he was referring to a feeling he had for her that was more than friendly, something, not a headache or the problems of Selfware or gratitude for the project she'd told him about. But the smarter, self-preserving element of her wasn't awake yet. She said, "Do you always sleep with your informants?" and instantly regretted it.

He smoothed a piece of her hair down against the side of her head. "Actually, since my last girlfriend upped and left me for a baseball player with two houses in Europe and his own yacht, I've been working, and most of my informants ask for money or police protection instead."

"Silly me," she said, wishing there was a way to apologize. She should be thanking him.

"I'll leave you ten bucks when I go, if it'll make you feel better."

"When's your plane?"

"Nine."

"Then we should get going."

"Wait a minute." He drew his hand back. "What's the matter?"

"It's not you," she hated herself. "I'm just not used to—this." She pulled the covers up to her chin. "I don't do this. I . . ."

"Yeah, I know. You're mad." Jude rubbed his own face and sighed. "You told me. So, when will I see you again?"

"Don't joke," she said, trying not to be both pleased and hurt. She wanted any feeling that wasn't accompanied by its opposite.

"I'm not."

"You're playing a game with me." Why did she say this? Only actresses said lines like that. What did it mean?

"And what're you doing with me if I am?"

Natalie stared up into his dark eyes. They were night. And here was the blue of morning. She pushed the worthless parts of herself aside and decided on honesty instead.

"Well, how stupid would it be to say I've fallen in love with you at first sight, given that you're a hotshot FBI agent and I'm a bonkers woman in a lab coat whose most exciting regular experience is sticking electric shocks up other people's temporal lobes and watching them dance the cancan? That would have been attractive. Oh, and I could have told you about my lonely single woman's life, living with her closest friend, a gay man, in a flat-share that closely resembles the cliché of the age—the only thing missing is the cat and that's because ours ran away. I can see instantly that a man like you would go for that. Like a shot. Pow. Result."

"You talk too much," he said and kissed her.

"Stop it." Natalie loved the kiss but turned her head away. She wanted to believe him but there was herself in the way; the information didn't compute with what herself said could be true.

"What? Changed your mind? Okay, okay." He lay down again and sighed. "Get lost, Jude." He rolled over and sat up at the edge of the bed.

Natalie felt sick. She watched him get up, testing his clothes where they hung on the chair to see if they'd dried out, putting his fabulous body away and out of her reach forever. Worse than that, going away forever. They'd liked each other enough. She'd thought she could tell him about her life and she had. He wasn't making fun. What was she doing? This was pathetic.

"I didn't mean it. I'm acting like a fool." Natalie flung the covers back despite the fact that the house was cold and she was naked. "Stop. I mean. Come back. If you're not joking. The situation. I didn't think you could really like me."

He turned around, shirt half on, "I know. I listened to you, remember? I saw your Map. I heard your rat's-ass-crazy plan to enlighten everyone in the world by reconfiguring their brains *and* your weird conviction that given enough of a chance everyone on the planet will become a good person when they understand the Way. I know about the difference between a spiritual experience and physical reality and the validity of both of them, I've seen it on your machine. I've heard it all. I assume you haven't infected me with some software that turns me into your love puppet, so, now, can you see where I have it tattooed that I do everything you say?" He held his arms out to either side and gave her a questing look.

Natalie stared at him, her lower jaw loose.

Jude grinned and pointed at her with both hands in gun position, "Now you know what it's like to be on the other end of that. Do I do a good Doctor Armstrong?"

She nodded, drily. "Your pants are inside out."

He looked down at his naked body and she laughed.

They were dressed by five-thirty. In the kitchen Natalie felt her delight sink down as she saw the file papers. She helped Jude pick them up and put them all back and made a half-hearted attempt to scrape the spilled wax off the tiled floor. As the catches on his flight case snapped closed she stood up and put the knife she'd been using into the sink. It made a dull, bored sound that died quickly. She had heard it a million times, the peculiar tone of metal on metal in that place. The whole of the last twenty-four hours seemed utterly unreal. Being in that house, cluttered with memories, was only the icing on the experience. She looked at Jude and her heart almost stopped. He and she—but he was going. Perhaps that was what had made it so easy after all.

"Ready?"

"No," he said and walked out, sombre, his head bowed.

She followed him and they went out through the back door and along the side of the house where a small pedestrian gate let them out onto the road. They turned towards the road out of town and walked in the fresh morning light to the hotel at the corner, where Jude got a taxi to the airport.

As he watched the car pull up he turned to her. "I'll be in touch," he said.

"Yeah." She nodded.

He was still looking at her, his stare intense. "Take it easy."

"You, too." She closed the car door for him and then knocked on the window. It opened for her automatically, the taxi's engine rising to a waiting hum. "Hey," she said, "I'm glad you exist."

His face broke into a grin. "Ditto," he said.

She tapped the window and it closed again, sealing him in.

Natalie watched his car drive away out of sight. She listened—for shots, for a bomb, for anything. The morning was calm. Her face felt raw in the cool air, where his unshaven face had rubbed it. Her whole body felt raw. She shivered in delight and set off to walk home across the city.

If this was the way the real world got you to pay, it was worth it.

Dan woke up to a hammering on his bedroom door.

"Dan, you idiot. It's seven thirty! Get up!"

He recognized Natalie's voice and a glut of relief swept over him, almost dislodging the ferocious hangover for a second. Then he remembered why it was important to get to work early—today they were doing the Bobby X experiment.

The door opened and Natalie came in, holding out a mug of black coffee and a couple of white tablets. "Come on!"

"Thanks. What're these?"

"Just take them. I bought breakfast. Eggs, everything. It's in the kitchen."

The thought made him queasy. But he took the tablets and washed them down with scalding mouthfuls of the tarlike stuff in the mug. After only a few moments he started to feel better.

"What's in them?" he muttered as he dragged himself out of bed and into a dressing gown. Natalie shouted back something about a prescription but he wasn't quite tuned in yet. There was something last night that he'd been desperate to talk to her about. Now, what was it?

He sat down on the kitchen's only stool and watched her open a pack of bacon, lay the slices on the grill. When she turned around he noticed her face.

"Shit, Natalie! You got him!"

"Sound any more surprised and you can wear this spatula." She brandished it in his face and splattered a few drops of hot fat on his dressing gown, but she was full of an energy that Dan recognized easily and he wasn't impressed.

"I bet he was good. Was he? I saw you at the . . . I mean, I missed you at the pub. So, tell me." The little white tablets were good, he felt almost human.

She turned to him, "Saw us where? Oh Dan, you weren't . . . ?"

"Some bloke was following you, or him." At the memory of it he touched his ribs and felt instant pain. "I got rid of him," he said proudly.

Natalie was staring at him with concern now, which he liked a lot less than her anger. "Dan?"

"He hit me and I felled him with a knockout blow to the jaw. Iron Dan," he said, hoping she wouldn't push it.

"Are you all right?"

"I'm fine. Never better. Smashing pills, they are. Where'd you get them from? You could make a fortune."

"I stole them from work," she said. "Where do you think? And don't change the subject. Who was following? Why were you—no, forget that, I can imagine the answer. Just tell me."

Dan finished his coffee and looked into the mug, which didn't tell him anything. "I don't know who he was. A big bloke in a big coat with a big hat on. I asked him for a light, he punched me in the gut. That's it. Why? Is he really an FBI agent?"

"I think so." She turned around and checked the eggs absently. When she turned back she was frowning.

"Don't scowl. You looked happy before," Dan suggested. "And you haven't told me what happened. In fact, maybe that could wait." He'd suddenly remembered what it was he wanted to ask her. But that could wait, too, until they were at work and she had less mental energy to spare on grilling him about anything that might reveal the situation with Shelagh or Ray. She really would go mental if she knew the drugs had gone beyond a bit of weed and that the debts had changed the intensity of their grip on him.

"What?" She buttered some toast and handed it to him. "You're making less sense with every minute. I need you on top form today. No mistakes."

"I think he was probably from the Home Office or something like that," Dan said quickly. "Probably just wanting to make sure the star researchers aren't going to be compromised in the tabloids. So, how does he go, this guy?"

Natalie's face altered subtly. He saw its glow.

"Like a train," she said sweetly and trod on his foot, smiling as she ground her heel onto his toes.

"Your bacon's burning."

"Shit!" She got the grill tray out, using their one inadequate tea towel, and stood for a second, hopping as she licked her fingers and blew on them. Then she stood on his foot again as he giggled.

Dan wondered if his suspicions about himself and the man on the corner were true. It made it difficult to keep up the lighter side. It made him wonder if that one-way ticket wasn't a better plan than anything here, but then he looked at Natalie and knew that he couldn't go.

"Has he gone back?"

"Who?"

"Who d'you think? The Last of the Mohicans. Has he gone back to the loony bin?"

"Flew this morning. Two rashers?"

"Three, please. Never mind, darling."

"I don't mind."

"Ah yeah." He sliced into a tomato and watched her industriously cutting up her own food, focused right in on it, pretending she was all together and cool. "That's what we all say."

Mikhail Guskov placed his call to arrive in the United Kingdom at seven forty-five. He looked into the screen of his second, personal Pad as his contact there answered. Neither of them needed to confirm anything about the day's test or their plans. All that was required was Guskov's authority to proceed.

He'd given it a lot of thought since that meeting with Delaney. She liked to fool herself that she had that bunch of players at the Pentagon all in hand, but let her. He admired her balls for having the audacity to try it. But the sudden acceleration that this test had precipitated meant he had harder tasks than keeping her off his back. He had to find out if the Armstrong girl's test project was what he thought it could be. Despite his discreet backing of her, the Ministry there had still denied her a licence—not entirely surprising, given their already heavy involvement in Mappa Mundi and the fact that her work appeared to them to be no more than blue-skying: research that would, at best, produce marginal products and small revenues in the future.

But Guskov wasn't so sure. He had an idea that she might be on to the most radical and far-reaching science of her time, and before he could list his final team he wanted to know if she was going to be in on it. If she was, then maybe, just maybe, he could still stay one jump ahead.

He looked into the face of his contact and said simply, "Today."

His datapilot reported the line clean and the link was cut.

Calum Armstrong would understand later, even if he wasn't prepared for his experiment to fail so dramatically. Mikhail would talk him round. If he didn't—well, it would be difficult to lose a friend and colleague, but that would be his test.

Eight

When Jude had gone through passport control he called White Horse. There was no answer. He wondered if she'd received his earlier note. He left her another. The same.

On the flight back he had forty minutes to think about what had happened in England. He had his information, and didn't he wish he hadn't got it, because now his world didn't make sense. White Horse had said once—insisted—"You can't be two things. You can only be one. Live one way, in one world. You're part white, part Cheyenne. You can't live both. You have to choose."

Well, he'd been first one and then the other, and now the world of reason that he'd thought was good enough to see him through anything wasn't working.

It was not possible that he had the Ivanov file, although have it he did. But then, if Natalie hadn't told him about NervePath, Mappaware, and that it was possible to watch the flow of a physical action and know its meaning as a thought then that would have seemed equally as impossible a few days ago. But her other theories—that the self and free will were both illusory quantities, the results of imperfect understanding of the function of the brain and mind . . . he wasn't sure he could go the extra mile on those.

He looked across the clouds and thought of Natalie. She was singular. He liked her. She was interesting. If she was crazy, he liked that, too. "I'm glad you exist." He didn't think he'd had a compliment like that before.

"Champagne, sir?" the attendant asked.

"No, thanks." He didn't want to drink. He had to get—and keep—a clear head for Washington.

But as he tried to turn his mind onto the notes he was making he found himself thinking about Natalie's lopsided smile and what she'd said about Selfware, the system built to detect ESP, to facilitate intelligent understanding, to expand the mind's potentials to an unknown maximum limit.

To his reasoning self that, too, sounded crazy, like automated insight, like manufacturing spirit or personality. Could that be a good thing? Wasn't it another way for someone else to control you, or for you to do things to yourself that weren't wise at times when your fears got too much and the nights too long?

He knew that the technology could work, because of Deer Ridge. He just couldn't imagine what that would be like. Natalie's own connection to the problem was so personal, he even had sympathy for her father's views that she was too involved, making theories of her own psychoses. But she was only a part of the whole.

Deer Ridge was an early version of something his government had. Would that be good?

He'd like to think that. But deep in his heart he felt an older mistrust.

Even now the old treaties drawn up with his father's People had never been honoured, recompense never paid, admissions of bad judgement never made, and genocidal intent never acknowledged. Against his Cheyenne half the government had no record of good behaviour, just the reverse. If they'd had Mappaware back then there would be no Nation now.

Even if the technology had a good side, he didn't believe that was the only use it would see in the hands of the USA. Maybe Natalie's technology was a way to end all dissent—we will all be God-fearing, Bible-reading, materialist self-deluders. Everyone could buy in happily and be glad. If they were really happy, would it matter what they were? Wouldn't it be better than the present sorry state of Deer Ridge, with its eighty percent unemployment and a plenary judicial system that got government out of every promised benefit, with one weasel word after another, "respect for ancient ways" being foremost.

And there he was, Jude, channelling White Horse and not believing in the supernatural. He grinned and shook his head. One thing or another? He thought he'd rather have a lot of undecided things, and none of them quite right, than only two choices.

He sent a message to Mary, letting her know that he was coming back in a few hours' time. It was going to be difficult, finding out more without telling her, until he was sure that they needed to make an issue out of whatever it was that was really going on. One thing he had learned since joining the agency was to look before he leaped and he had to get Mary on side before he'd have a chance.

White Horse had no idea she was being followed. That was, she expected it, looked for it without trying to appear antsy, but recognized nothing—not that she knew what she should be seeing either, and that all added up to no idea in her view. Because she'd come that way and knew the roads, she headed back towards the railway station, tagging along behind two Ethiopian schoolkids with identical bright pink lunchboxes sporting the latest cartoon hero from TV, each one talking to its owner in perky tones of enthusiasm and in words she didn't understand.

She walked fast, businesslike, along the Mall, past the Museum area to the long strip where there'd be plenty of people moving and open ground. She liked land where you could see further than to the next block. She wanted to feel she could run.

Because there were six of them, linked by earpiece, expertly shifting roles around her in the morning pedestrian traffic, because they knew how to hunt in these conditions, she missed them all. But one of her senses, working overtime, prompted her to turn in and get a ticket to the Air and Space. Not that she had any love of aeroplanes, and the space programme was dead on its knees, more like a historical quirk than a living science . . . but she stepped inside and moved quickly towards a packed elevator. Her instincts made her examine the face of everyone coming through the doors towards her. One of them.

The doors closed and she felt the heaviness as she was lifted. Tiny box. She got out at the first opportunity and found herself face to face with a portion of *Enola Gay*. Photographs and montages of screaming, dying people walled her in on every side. She could touch the metal of the thing that had dropped the Hiroshima bomb. She did touch it. It was warm from so many hands, as calmly inert as the machine banging against her side.

Getting past the school tours was hard. She shoved more than once, got cursed, found a stairwell and ran down it, looking for an exit. One floor above her she heard the door open. One floor below her another door closed. She leaned over the rail but they were hugging the wall. The well of the stairs disappeared into darkness.

Behind her a woman came into view. She was tall and tough-looking.

"Here she is," the woman said and stopped, looking flat at White Horse. The woman's stance showed she was poised to leap down the flight and tackle her to the ground.

White Horse spun around and saw a man running up from below, the identical imperative to stop her in his eyes. She grabbed the handrail and kicked out at him as soon as he got within range, a mad gesture that packed more intent than power, but she was panicked now and ran straight into his destabilized body, knocking him aside as she threw herself down and down again.

She was starting to feel the first surge of relief as she stepped out into the museum foyer again. Then a hand took her arm from the side.

"No!" White Horse pulled away. She opened her mouth, ready to scream the place down if it would get her enough attention, but only the shocked face of an old man looked up at her. He backed away from her and she wanted to apologize but instead she walked quickly across and joined a group of people just being ushered into a space-simulation ride. Her ticket was good for that. She pushed her way to the end of the seated row as they sat down and heard herself cursed blue by Kentucky accents from one side of the auditorium to the other.

As the doors were about to be closed she stood up and brushed past the security guard through the exits. She was on a dark ramp, leading her back up to ground level. Hesitantly she walked up and tried to appear confident as she moved towards the doors. Could she have lost them?

They closed on her as she reached the street, a human knot who hemmed her in on all sides in a practised dance that looked like an ordinary jumble of different people whose paths have just crossed for a moment and in that moment a cold stab pierced the arm of her jacket.

They were so close that she didn't fall as the drug took hold. The last impression she had was of them sitting her in the seat of a large car, fastening her seat belt judiciously, undoing her treacherous hands from their grip on the bag and lifting it gently away.

Bobby X was not the real name of Ian John Detteridge but it was his name now. They called him that at the hospital and he answered to it—but he didn't answer them. He answered their voices, which came at him from the shifting, coloured holes in the world.

At first, when he'd woken out of the anaesthetic and the accident, he thought he'd lost part of his sight. He could make out the shapes of his bed and the equipment hanging around him in swathes of spaghetti tubing. He could see the curtain and the window and the walls of his room and its flickering, badly fitted light on the left. Clear as daylight they were. But then he'd noticed a patch that didn't seem right.

It was a mass of shifting tones and planes. He thought—a coat . . . no, a . . . —but here his thoughts ran out.

"Mr. Detteridge?" said a voice from behind the blur.

He tried to see around it, blinked, jogged his eyes about. (That hurt.)

Something touched his arm and that was part of the shapeless thing, too. It even had a strange colour to it, greyish, like rat fur, like dust. He cringed, "Nurse!" he called hoarsely.

"Mr. Detteridge?"

He realized the voice was coming from the grey, alien thing that he couldn't see.

He screamed.

It had taken some time to diagnose the problem and, even when they had, he didn't understand it. They said he'd lost the ability to recognize living things. And that grey, mouldy brown aura, that shapeless, undefinable, shifting mass that was a nothing—that was how he saw a living thing now. Didn't seem right that a brain could be mixed up that way just from a bang on the head, but so they said, and because he wanted it to be true Ian agreed with them and went along with it.

Bobby X was the name he got from going into special therapy. They said they'd fix him now and at last the day had come. They didn't use his real name because he was a kind of volunteer and the therapy was still a secret, just being tested, and he was going to test it for them and be a pioneer, would he like that?

He wanted things to be normal. Of course he'd said yes. What was the other option? Try to go home to your wife and children who now scared the living daylights out of you and looked—"abominable" was the only word to describe that mixture of revulsion and wrongness.

But now the time had come he was scared to his bones. He didn't want to do it. What if they only made everything into that rat-coloured nothingness? What if he didn't make it? Then he might be stuck in a mental home forever, living like this, a moron, an embarrassment. They might forget him and he'd die there, mouldering away to rat dust.

He listened to the TV to keep himself alert. Couldn't watch it, only listen. He turned his head away as the nurse brought in a drink and some toast. He knew it was her, but he couldn't bear to look. It was like knowing wasn't enough any more. He could "know" as hard as he liked, but when they came at him he saw—indescribable things. They said the ratty colour was his own repulsion, an illusion. But he didn't feel that was true. In their odd movements, their incomprehensible lack of sense to him, it was part of them, as real as their loathsome, sudden touch.

There would be no need for sedation. They'd filled his head with the tiny things that would do the fixing and it wouldn't hurt at all.

He wasn't sure. He just wasn't sure.

Bobby X. He'd heard it said so often it was more his name than the real one. Or if he stayed this way, it would be his name forever. Man of mystery, like a revolutionary. He liked the sound of it, but not the reality. If he was going to stay like this—he'd rather die than be alone with these things around him, talking as if they knew him, as if he knew them. If it didn't work, he'd find his way. Save some pills or something. He'd get out.

The semblance of a plan made him feel better.

He sipped his tea.

Natalie watched Bobby from the doorway and took her readings with the handscanner from behind his back. It had a reasonable range and she didn't want to upset him any more than he already was. If it were future days she could probably have pursued the entire treatment without him being any the wiser, but as things were Bobby X was a test animal and he was going to have to jump through the hoops for as long as it took to recalibrate the new tissues of his brain.

Seeing her father wasn't something Natalie was looking forward to, but she didn't delay it. She fortified herself with memories of the night before and took the results straight to the Therapy Suite where he was already deep in discussions over the last-minute details with Knitted Man, Bill, the systems supervisor. His satellite image was large as life on-screen from his labs in America. Either he or Bill could easily have read her data already from the network, but protocol demanded she announce it herself.

"The last NP check is ninety-four percent saturation. Ready to go," she said, breaking in when they reached a pause.

Her father nodded after a microdelay. "Thanks." He added, as an afterthought, "Your last paper in *Neurotechnology Journal* was better than before. But I think you should have given more graphics for the online version. An illustration in real time would have made your argument more conclusive."

Natalie raised an eyebrow. High praise indeed, and, as Calum sat down and began fussing self-consciously with already completed routines on the program, she thought she detected a smidgeon of guilt at his neglect of her over the months—no calls, no letters, and the excuse, as always, "a secret project demands absolute security."

Bill gave her the double banana of both eyebrows in quick succession and she smiled vaguely at him. He looked undeniably cheerful, instead of stressing out. His confidence was a credit, considering the numbers of Ministry roving about the place. Every corner she'd turned today had seen clutches of grey-suited officials milling in the lanes, loitering, and muttering into the microphones of their cuffs and lapels; glassy-eyed, they watched her pass, listening in to the neat earpieces that trailed a single wire into the trim lines of their collars. Outside they turned into black-uniformed police and some kind of soldier she didn't know the name of that carried small but effective-looking guns. The cordon was tight. She could almost feel it around her neck.

"I'll check the room prep," she said, although neither of them were paying her any attention now. It was the next task that had chimed up on her Pad. Her father looked up at her as she passed the camera.

"Mrs. Reed says somebody's made a mess of the kitchen up at the house. I take it that was you?"

God, that woman worked fast, Natalie thought, not too fondly. "It was hardly a mess. I knocked a candle over. I didn't have time to fix it this morning."

Fortunately he didn't have the imagination to wonder why she'd used candles instead of the lights. He grunted, "Okay. Now, let's get the patient cued up. It's nearly five to eleven."

Natalie wasn't required for this duty. She took the time to go to the staffroom and get a drink. She was thinking over Calum's unusually positive response to her work, wondering what it meant, or whether it was a soft-soap for a later attack, when her sleeve was tugged violently. She realized Dan was at her shoulder,

"Nat!" he whispered. "Where's the scanner thing?"

"It's in the Therapy Room, where do you think?"

"Can you get it back?"

"Why?" She scowled at him, hesitating with her hand on the door. What lunacy was he thinking of now?

"I want to borrow it."

"What?" Her scowl became a glare. "Don't be silly. Not now. Anyway, what for?"

"Nothing." He shifted from foot to foot. "Never mind. Coffee?"

"Dan!" She grabbed his arm and stopped him as he was halfway into the room. "What's going on?"

"It's okay. Nothing. I wanted to . . . look, you're right. Not now, eh?" He pulled away from her with expert grace and made a beeline for the drinks machine.

She stared after him, stupefied, and then shook her head. Whatever it was he was bothered about it would have to wait until this was over. She hoped it wasn't something to do with that dodgy mate of his, Ray. And speaking of Ray—she stepped up quickly to Dan's side.

"You haven't got anything in your locker, have you?"

"Espresso, hon?" He handed her a cup and met her gaze with a firm "no" glare. "I certainly won't have. Are they doing a search?"

"Oh, Dan, for Christ's sake!" Natalie kept her voice to a whisper, smiling over his shoulder at Charlton, who was giving her a grin. "You said you'd given it up. You can't use at work. We had a deal. Now go get rid of it before some officious prat from London sniffs it out and we all get dragged over the coals. It's my bloody job as well as yours!"

"Hold that." He gave her his cup and marched out at a fast clip. She could tell from the way he didn't meet her eyes that he was feeling guilty. Well, he could bloody feel guilty, he *should* feel it.

The mug started burning her fingers. She put it down and was immediately cornered by the nervous aftercare technician who wanted to know what they were going to talk to Bobby's family about on the viewing deck, once the show was in progress. Natalie kept looking to the door for when Dan would get back, wanting to follow him and make sure he wasn't caught. But there was to be no escape and he didn't return for what seemed a very long time.

Dan took a nonchalant stroll down to the cloakrooms and went in, glancing at his watch. He checked the locker area thoroughly—nobody about. Inside his locker he did have an old ounce of the good stuff tucked away, for moments when fortification was required. He hadn't used it for at least . . . well, at least a week. The practice of fishing it out and slipping it into his pocket, using a half-pack of biscuits as a cover was well worn in. He managed it without a hitch, locked up again, and made for the exit. His Pad rang when he was halfway there.

He answered it before thinking to check the line and with a sickening jolt saw Shelagh Carter's face looking out at him from the screen. "Er, hi," he muttered. "I'm at work just now, I can't—"

"That's fine, Dan," she interrupted firmly. "This will only take a moment. I understand that you're a good friend of Doctor Natalie Armstrong."

Dan's mouth, already a bit blanched from a morning of severe dehydration, went desert dry. He worked his throat for a useless second and croaked, "Well, yes, I suppose so."

"Not to worry." Shelagh smiled obligingly. "But we've had a report that somebody might have tried to latch onto her in the last week or so. An expert enemy agent, snooping for information on the work at the Clinic, particularly today's experiment. I thought you'd be the person to ask. I wouldn't usually, because it's hard to discuss a friend, I know, but it's for her own benefit. She's one of our best. We don't want anything to cause her trouble, or danger."

"No, no, quite," Dan mumbled, trying to think much faster than his mouth was moving. Maybe he should have told Shelagh earlier about the American. Was he American? What had Natalie told him? There was no way of knowing.

"Are you sure?" God, that was so weak. She'd know he was stalling.

"We're ninety percent sure. As you can imagine, the subject, the experiment, the whole field is red-hot at the moment. Anything unusual, Dan. Anybody. You don't have to name names if you don't know them, just any clue."

Dan dithered. Suddenly he wasn't sure about Jude. Natalie was sharp, but even she could be taken in by the right face, the right line. He knew *he* could be. What if it was as Shelagh said and maybe Natalie was in danger? But then, he had a reason not to entirely believe everything Shelagh said, either . . . He wanted to run back to the lounge and discuss it all, but Shelagh was looking at him from the screen and he dare not for fear she'd interpret any delay as tacit guilt.

"There *was* someone," he began. Then he quickly hedged it around with, "But maybe he was genuine. I mean, I don't know, do I?"

Shelagh nodded.

Dan decided not to tell the truth. "He was this Asian guy. An engineer from one of the big companies that make our computer system. I think they had dinner. Nothing else."

"Are you sure?" She fiddled with the controls on her Pad, momentarily blotting herself from view with her fingertips.

A heavy wave of blankness swept Dan's mind. It was like a pressure, it flattened his intentions down. He should tell her the truth. It was safer. It was better. He'd feel good again, if only he did.

"Maybe he was American," Dan said without any conscious desire to say it. It was as though the words had taken on lives of their own and were tripping off his tongue, pixielike, whether he willed them to or not. "Yes, he was. His name . . ." Dan fought back, trying to think of something inappropriate—think of any vegetable except a carrot! "J—" . . . any name, then, Jasper, John, Julius, Justin, Jack, Jonathan, Jason . . . "J-u—d-e." It was drawn out of him, as though she had caught the hook of the J and wound it up around her finger. "Westhorpe" followed easily, a second later. His head was fishy, swimmy. He might be sick again.

"Good work, Dan," Shelagh said cheerfully and he thought for a disoriented second that she was a sturdy WAAF girl in a wartime film, chivvying the boys along when the formation had finally landed, Jerry bombed to bits and only one man missing. It was the voice that was brisk, starchy, English to the core . . . except . . . except . . .

She must have cut the call from her end. He found himself sitting on the tile floor, the biscuits crushed under his hand. When he tried to remember what had just happened, it drifted out of his reach effortlessly and away into never. He had a vague feeling that he had done something very, very bad.

The ounce, that was it. He had come to get rid of the ounce.

With only a small amount of subterfuge he managed to sneak his way into the incinerator room where specialist medical waste, not allowed to leave site, was destroyed and popped the offending packet in. A few thousand degrees wouldn't leave enough residue for Scotland Yard to trace.

As an afterthought he put the biscuits in, too. They'd been open for months.

Back at the coffee lounge he pushed past one of the junior technicians and gave Natalie the wink. "Done it."

She stared at him, "What's the matter with you? You look awful. And what did you want that scanner for?"

"Scanner?" He didn't remember. "I don't know. I'm sure it'll come back to me if it's important."

She shook her head, "Get it together, will you? Honestly. Today of all days."

Jude got home and opened the door, immediately looking for his sister.

"Vohpe'hame'h," he called out, using her Cheyenne name instead of the English version, thinking it might please her better.

There was no reply. Her bag was gone, he realized, as he checked all the rooms, in fact, there was no trace of her at all.

No, that wasn't quite right, she'd left some hairs behind—short, broken-off ones—in the bathroom and on the pillows of her bed, but that didn't tell him for how long she'd been here after he'd left. He'd been away two days, three nights.

"Shit," he said softly into the mushy quiet that the triple-glazed windows offered. For a second he was at a loss. He turned around, looked through to the kitchen table or the pinboard for a note, but there was nothing.

He checked the message backlog:

"Hi, Jude, this is Mary . . ."

"Mr. Westhorpe, this is MasterCredit Customer Accounts calling. We'd like to . . ."

"Jude, Steve. Yannick's dropped out of the squash league and I was wondering . . ."

"Jude, Perez here. Check in when you get back from Seattle. I want to see you and Mary about the Florida case . . ."

"Would you like to know how to make a million . . ."

"Jude, this is Mom here. I know you're supposed to be here but your boss keeps calling the house for you and I'm not answering or returning her calls. You know, I think she's pretty uptight about whatever it is and although I know you're doing something . . ."

He listened to all thirty-eight of them, one at a time. There was no message from White Horse.

Jude got himself a glass of water and sat down at the table in the kitchen for a moment with his head between his knees, thinking.

Where the hell would she go? Was it to lose the machine, or did she have it with her, desperate to keep it because she believed he was going to betray her to the other side? With the house at Deer Ridge gone there were any number of friends all over the country she could choose to visit, most of them members of the American Indian Movement. Too obvious. If she was smart, she wouldn't take trouble there. Then where?

Just on the off chance he called her personal Pad number again.

A woman answered it, but it wasn't White Horse, he saw that in an instant, and he'd keyed the call off before he'd even registered the fact. Shock coursed through him like a strong shot of whiskey, numbing his feet and hands.

With clumsy fingers he recalled the image to the screen again and stared at it, searching for any telling detail. He asked his Fed Datapilot service to trace the location, if they could, but he didn't hold out much hope. White Horse's Pad was two years old and he doubted it transmitted so much information.

He didn't know the other person. She seemed to be in a vehicle. Maybe the Pad was stolen . . . but his guts didn't think so. He took a drink of the cold water and then sank even further into the conviction that White Horse was in trouble and had moved quickly out of his reach. Only the fact that his apartment seemed untouched made him think she'd at least walked out of it of her own free will.

He set his personal Datapilot, *Nostromo*, to analyse the screenshot of the face and to try to fix the location by zooming in on the scraps of detail that he might miss. As he waited for a response he called Mary.

"Hey there!" she sang out as she answered. "How was the Bay? Not enough sun for you? Or was the wind not catching the sails? You're back soon."

"Hey," he said, trying to make it sound double as peppy as he felt. "You know me. Can't stay out of a case for long. After you called I thought I should get back as soon as I could."

"I'm afraid it doesn't look like we were able to pin down anyone. They cleaned up too well. But there might be another piece to the puzzle coming in next week. We've been invited up to Utah to assess a new biodefense initiative. Sound familiar?"

To Jude's mind at that second, it didn't. "Okay," he said. "Listen, I'll see you tomorrow back in the office."

"Sure."

He hung up and sat in the silence that followed, trying to pin together a new defence initiative with Ivanov's baby-fixing business and not succeeding. At the moment, however, the pursuit of Ivanov from government-funded hidey-hole to black-market racket couldn't capture his interest. He had, in the file, Ivanov linked with Guskov and Guskov was linked with White Horse's black machine, with Natalie's programming, with so many things he couldn't make them form a picture at all.

Nostromo returned then with the requested information about the Pad and its place on Earth. Jude took the address and looked at it with despair and exhaustion.

Fort Detrick, Maryland.

A military base? He thought he was going out of his mind. She would never have gone there herself. She must be a prisoner. But the army? Who? Why? Why not a military prison? Hell, why not simple police custody? He'd thought the thing was a federal matter.

He groaned and put his head in his hands. This was so much bigger and uglier than he could have dreamed.

Nine

Natalie reviewed Bobby X's case for the last time as she drank her coffee. Bobby was a forty-eight-year-old builder who had fallen off a three-storey roof whilst trying to fix some tiles up there after one very bad January gale. Once the swelling of his brain had abated the problem he'd been left with was readily definable.

She watched one of his examinations on her Pad screen as he struggled with explanations. They showed him simple pictures on a video.

A chair was a chair but a dog . . .

"It's a brown, moving thing, textured, like a carpet? It makes noises—" Bobby paused, mouth working, plaintively, as he fought for a likely explanation "—from its motor."

A cooked carrot on a dinner plate was okay for eating, but a raw one . . .

"Is it, um . . . it's a spike, with feathers at one end. I . . . are they a rudder? No, a wing? You know, like for a propeller?"

They faced him, just once, with a mirror. Looking at himself Bobby cried out with terror at the moving waxy forms so horribly arranged there. Natalie wasn't sure that some part of him didn't recognize himself—in fact, she thought that this was what made that experience so particularly revolting. Whatever he felt about his meaning-gap in relation to other things it must have been ten times worse to realize that he was falling through the cracks in his understanding of himself.

Her readings, taken this morning, showed that his regrown neurons were fully functional. Restoring Bobby's old meanings to him was the second stage of development. It would demand, and prove, that their theories about the ability of the software to adapt to an individual mind were correct. Her work with Selfware had made this possible, and she was looking forward to giving Glover at the Ministry a tart letter when it proved to be the linchpin of their success.

Following on from Guskov's acclamation of the valid cross-referencing between the physical action and a mental event, this experiment would pave the way for the production of many other programs that would tailor themselves to fit the brains and minds in question. It required constant feedback analysis, which had so far tied it to lab experimentation only—where they were able to use the processing power of the basic expert-systems machines. If it worked in Bobby's case, with the feedback loops tracked and passed by the internal NervePath on its own, that meant it would only be a matter of time before the whole technology was fully miniaturized and mobile. Considering what she'd read on Jude's disk, however, they might be a bit late on the mobile . . . she shook her head.

Her Pad sent her a reminder that she was due to collect Bobby and take him through now. She left her half-finished drink and nudged Dan, who was engrossed in an upside-down copy of *Chat* magazine.

"Come on, you."

As they reached the door she added, "What's up with you, anyway?"

"I've got a headache," he mumbled. "I'm going to get something from the dispensary."

"Is that all?"

"What d'you mean?" But he couldn't meet her gaze. He let his fringe hide his eyes.

"Later," she assured him, pointing her finger at his chest and prodding. "I mean it."

Dan sloped off and Natalie had to take the other direction. She wondered if he'd disposed of the remains of his stash by eating it. It wouldn't be the first time he ended up in casualty. He was getting to be a real liability, and because she'd been so lax with him until now it was likely that she was going to have to pay when he finally made a costly mistake. *Just don't let it be today.*

She opened the door to Bobby's room.

"Hello, it's Natalie."

Bobby had his feet up on a heated rest. He put the magazine he was holding down and left his hand on it as he put it aside, taking comfort from it as he turned to focus carefully on the Pad she held in front of her. Natalie felt cruel, forcing him to confront what was difficult for him, but he had the long-term patient's air of resignation and patience by now—he expected no more.

"Hello." He was polite. The nurses had combed his hair and put him into a neat outfit of trousers and shirt. His face showed uneven shaving where they had hastily gone through the motions.

"I've come to take you through," she said, maintaining a bright and positive tone. "Ready?"

"All right, doctor." He smiled at the Pad, she wasn't sure why. It seemed that although he couldn't recognize her he was aware of her nervousness and was trying, even from his terrible position, to put her at ease.

As they arrived in the Therapy Suite the screens in the control room lit up with a living map of Bobby's mind. Natalie saw them display the damaged area as a silent, white zone. On the edges of its borders neurons fired, trying to break the barrier of silence, but the NervePath that saturated his synapses held fast to the new cells, and allowed no signals to pass.

She knew from experience in working with patients who had

received regeneration treatment that the fresh tissues could have found new routes that worked, or created substitutes by themselves, but that was an uncertain, lengthy business. This way, it was hoped, recovery to a near-original state could be achieved. She set the chair in position and put its brake on.

Bobby grinned. "I've been wondering what the hell you guys all look like after all this time."

"Well, don't hold your breath," she said, patting his shoulder. "Some of us are no oil paintings. I'll see you later, okay? Nurse Charlton is here to fit your VR sets. Remember the drill?"

"Yes. 'Bye." He was smiling in anticipation as she left.

Natalie put on a show face for the cameras and went into the Control Room. Dan arrived and glanced over nervously at Bill. She tried to get his attention but he seemed to be avoiding her. He busied himself with the test runs on her father's station.

Glancing up to the observation gallery she saw the Ministry's cameramen take up positions. Inside the Therapy Suite all was quiet, except for the faint tweets of Bill whistling. Natalie was watching Dan's tight shoulders flex with discomfort as he unplugged and reconnected the last wires, working under her father's directions coming through his earpiece from the USA, when she realized Bill's ditty was the "Marseillaise." *Bit premature*, she thought, turning back to her own part of the task.

She wondered, as she assessed the initial readings of the external equipment synchronizing with Bobby's NervePath, if Jude was in a good mood. He'd be nearly home by now. What would he do with the file and the program information? The only good thing about being locked in the Clinic was that until this was done she wouldn't be arrested or taken for a long walk off a short pier.

Bill's whistling cut short—the treatment had begun.

Natalie watched the readouts, spelling out the progression, the changes. The white zone sparkled with life, like fireflies winking at her as neurons signalled furiously, trying to forge a path through virgin territory.

Ten minutes passed. To Natalie it seemed much more like ten hours; the central heating's relentless eighteen degrees coupled with her anxiety made her feel breathless as she listened to Bobby's blithe confidence in his answers to the test questions. The Map of his working thoughts flickered and shaded itself in a kaleidoscope of hues. With her practised eye she watched him fighting with his own fear, his worry that it wasn't working, and the strange and unprompted effects that the activity in his new area was creating. She was glad she didn't have to live through it.

On the opposite wall the pictures that Bobby was seeing were displayed. It was a safari expedition, culled from a popular documentary on world wildlife.

"No," Bobby was saying. "It's a kind of a mottled tube with a thinner sausage at the end. A fishing float? No, a draught excluder."

The leopard in the VR simulation hauled itself up a tree and vanished among the leaves.

"Shit," she heard Dan mutter. He was stiffly rebuked by Calum barking, over the intercom, "Time out. Let's review for a moment!"

They pored over the instruments and the settings for the strength of the connection charges. Differences in Bobby's reactions should have been more immediate than this, and they all knew it. For the watching Ministry officials Natalie gave an impromptu explanation. "This is a recognized stage in the testing. We're pausing to assess and recalibrate the strength of the neuron boosters in the NervePath. It will only take a moment or two." Well, it was nearly true.

She inserted a time stamp in the therapy log and watched Bill make minute, fussy adjustments on his console. On screen in front of her an idle shuffling took place in Bobby's language comprehension centres. Dan had just caught her eye, and was trying to say something, when a sharp cry of fear shot through the connecting door.

It was accompanied by a sudden pink blurt on Natalie's monitor, like a small shell exploding.

As they all watched, paralysed with shock, Bobby spasmed, kicked over his wheelchair, and crashed heavily onto the floor, groping around him blindly. He was trying to get up and wrestle with the VR hood at the same time; Nurse Charlton was attempting to hold him still, pinning his arms to his sides to prevent him hurting himself or ruining the equipment.

"Quickly! I can't hold him!" she shouted.

Natalie dashed around the clumsy block of her station, guts turning to lead inside her, and was in time to see Bobby's face as he tugged off the thick head-cover. He was white and startled, sweating profusely, and red where the tapes had waxed his hairs off, yet smiling, teeth bared with a kind of hysterical glee.

"Doctors, I presume?" he said in a weak voice, trying to maintain his glib humour through the shock. He gave up and sank back down to the carpet, shaking. "Shit!"

"Are you all right?" Dan was plaster white.

He and Bill staggered together as they helped Bobby back into the seat, right way up. Through the video link her father was simply staring at Bobby with astonishment and the beginnings of a frown. The Ministry cameramen leaned closer, trying to catch it all on their headcams.

"There was a lion. A great bloody big bastard," Bobby explained, panting weakly. "Teeth and . . . big eyes. Claws like, like knives. I thought he was going to spring at me."

"Maybe filling the programme with predators wasn't such a great idea," Natalie said, not for the first time.

Her father's smug response was expected.

"We thought they'd be sharper triggers to the system." But his long, muttered, and redundant justification was cut off by Bobby peering excitedly around him and into their faces.

"Which is which?" he asked. "I must thank you. It's marvellous. Marvellous what you've done." Then he caught sight of her. "Doctor Natalie!" he cried. "There you are. There you are at last!" His eyes were filling with tears as he looked at her. "No oil painting!"

"Thanks." She patted his arm, unable to stop herself grinning like a fool. "Remind me not to call you for an opinion next time."

"Bill!" Calum grunted from the intercom as they collected themselves. "Let's go for a test on the effectiveness of the purge."

Bill twitched in annoyance, but did as he was told. Natalie watched him go, wondering at his sudden change of demeanour. But then she caught Dan grinning at her and such was the euphoria she grinned back, his sins forgiven. By the time they had completed their tearful recovery of Bobby and sent him to his room the tension that had been so oppressive had turned around completely. Dan was whistling the "Marseillaise" himself as he switched down the gear and back in the offices her father was laughing as he went over the details with Glover and his other observers via the livelink.

"Yes. As agreed," Bill was saying. "When the restorations are complete to ninety percent effectiveness, the system is closed down. NervePath deactivates at specific, preset values."

Glover walked across to her and offered his hand, "Congratulations, Doctor. A triumph. You must be delighted."

Natalie knew he wasn't only talking about the experiment here, but her code that had contributed to it. "I think it's a perfect start," she said, but her hand pumped his with the enthusiasm she hadn't let show in her voice. "I hope it's just the beginning of a whole new series of treatments for damaged or disrupted cases."

"And possibly, in time, it may have applications for ordinary people," he said.

"Or the military," she said and promptly cursed herself. "For treating trauma in the field," she added hastily.

"Yes." He smiled and looked genuinely pleased.

She couldn't keep up her iron facework much longer, but she didn't have to.

Her Pad signalled incoming mail. Excusing herself, she moved to the window and leaned against the radiator there to check it.

It was from Jude.

She's gone, it read. *Will be in touch. L. J.*

L?

Natalie glanced up to see if anyone had noticed her face redden or her sudden change of mood but they were all still involved in mutual back-patting. She looked down. Gone?

She felt the need to tell someone else what she knew but looking around the room she couldn't settle on any of them. Even her father—he worked with Guskov and Guskov was in that file.

At least the experiment had gone off well.

Natalie engaged for a few more minutes in the congratulations and then went to her own rooms to study the results in more detail. In the corridor she saw Bill shouldering his way out of the computer room doors. She readied herself to stop and say "well done," slowing to meet him and holding up her hand, thinking to give him a good-buddy punch on the shoulder. But he hurried past her, head down, not even noticing who she was.

"Hey!" she said, but not very loudly, sure he wasn't going to react.

Puzzled, she watched him reach the doors to reception and stride through them. She glanced at her watch. Five. Maybe he had an appointment somewhere. He often went suddenly introvert. Perhaps the pressure of the exposure to so many strange faces and inspectors had got to him. It had got to her. She wanted nothing more than a few minutes alone and some space in which to think about the file, about the disk, about Jude, and about what she was going to do with Dan.

White Horse woke up slowly and kept her eyes shut and her breathing light. She could feel that she was lying on some kind of thin mattress and there was no movement. The light coming through her eyelids was dim. Her burns had returned to itching and hurting. She needed the drugs in her bag, but she had no sense of that being close to her. She listened hard as her head cleared, but heard only herself as she breathed and the minute movements of the stuffing in the mattress.

For perhaps an hour she lay there, feeling stiff, needing to pee. No clues came her way until she heard a door open close by. Then a man's voice, brisk with authority and in no doubt she was awake, said, "Time to get up. We've got a few questions we'd like to ask."

She stalled another second but there was no point pretending. She figured she must be in police custody or something like that. Fooling around with them in the past, in younger days, had only got her a black eye and two broken ribs.

She moved slowly to a sitting position and looked around.

It was a cell, as she'd thought. The tanned white man in front of her was no police officer, however. He was dressed in khakis and built like Magpie had once been when he was a marine, before going Fed and losing muscle. In fact, he was bigger than that. But his face didn't hold the bland callousness she associated with authority. It was looking at her shrewdly, watching her every move.

The shift of shirt cloth on her arms made the burns flare wildly.

"Can I have some water? And my pills?" she asked, not really holding out any hope.

"They're in the interview room," her jailer said. "All you have to do is walk through there."

White Horse got up, easing her stiff knee that hadn't been right since she jumped out her window, and shuffled out in the direction he indicated. A short corridor of brown walls led to another room with chairs, a table, and several other men she'd never seen before. Two of them wore army uniform. Another was in plain clothes. On the table the contents of her bag and the bag itself were laid out.

They gave her the water and allowed her to swallow a dose they counted out from her tablets. Then they asked her to sit down. They didn't say who they were and she didn't expect them to. They asked her who she was and she told them the truth because no doubt they already knew it.

"White Horse Jordan. Deer Ridge. Montana."

The plainclothes man sat down opposite her whilst the others stood back. His grey suit made her think of robots and civil servants. His voice was amiable.

"Where did you obtain this device?" He indicated the black casing.

She wondered if she had any rights that were worth asking for. There wasn't even a recorder going. She didn't try it.

"I took it from an unlocked car, a Chrysler, in Deer Ridge."

"You stole it?"

She gave her interrogator a flat gaze, carefully neutral, and said nothing. What did he think?

He was writing with a stylus on some very new and fancy-looking kind of Pad.

"Why did you take it?"

"It was evidence," she said. "I needed it to press charges. I couldn't have waited for the cops to come."

She sensed the attention of the three uniforms sharpen. The questioner noted her answers with no visible reaction.

"What charges and against whom?"

"Assault with a deadly weapon, against the federal government."

Now his mouth did flicker in a kind of smile at her naivety. Anger made her stomach growl suddenly and its unhappy sound filled the silence. She took another drink of the water. Only now did she wonder if there might be more in it than water. Too late, though.

"So, this was the deadly weapon?" He indicated the machine with his stylus, not touching it. "And where were you going to file? Did you have a legal representative working with you?"

"No. Nobody. I didn't trust anyone close to home. They're all in the back pocket of the state police. I wanted to come to Washington."

"But you didn't find a lawyer there." It was a statement. They all looked at her.

There? So she wasn't in DC any more. It was a kind of knowledge, but so weak it didn't make her feel better. "Not yet."

"What were you waiting for?"

"I wanted to be sure that I had enough evidence."

"You went to your half brother's apartment. What is his job?"

"He's a Fed."

"Mmn. But not any Fed."

She was going to have to say it. There was no way out she could think of. She wondered who they were. If this were official surely there would be more stuff about legal protection—theirs not hers.

"He's SS. Perfection Technology Investigator. I thought he could tell me if I had a case."

"That seems reasonable."

She looked properly at the man's face opposite for the first time. He was about forty, only a little lined, white with perhaps a flash of Hispanic. His five o'clock shadow was light. She didn't trust him.

"Where were you going this afternoon?"

"Away from you," she said and reflected his own stare back at him.

The others behind her laughed and she heard them moving about.

"Do you know who we are?"

She shrugged. "How should I know? You might be the same people who did Martha Johnson. You might be against them."

"We are against them," the questioner said calmly. "Does that surprise you?"

"Doesn't mean you're with me, does it?" She finished the water. The pills were just starting to take the edge off her pain. She tried to sit very still so nothing made it worse.

"Not necessarily," he admitted. His face became sympathetic. "We need more of a case, as you put it, than we have so far. I believe that it's in your interests, and ours, that we pursue the same lines of investigation. That way, there's more chance of success."

White Horse reached out to take hold of the black machine and all three of the uniforms leaped forward to stop her. She pulled back her hand and smiled at them as they withdrew, stalking back a few paces,

"I see. Well, we've done treaties with your type before."

"Miz Jordan, this is not that kind of deal."

His focus on her was acute and its pressure forced her to pay attention in return, against her will. She knew there was no point in attempting to cross him. Whoever he was, he gave the impression that he had power. Far more than she did. He put his Pad aside, "I will tell you the terms. We will release you, together with this—scanner—to continue making enquiries as you were doing. We will see where the feathers start rattling and falling. In return, when we complete our own investigations, your work will be included as part of a much larger general prosecution against the present government." He paused to see if she was going to protest. When she waited he said the bit she was really listening for.

"If you betray us, or fail to cooperate in any way, then both you and your brother will be eliminated from the enquiry. The Deer Ridge reservation will also lose its current courtroom fight against the state, and the land will be turned over to the government for mineral and oil exploitation."

White Horse was cold. Before this, she'd thought they were some small group. If they could influence the court, they were much bigger. And still she didn't know if they were lying. It could all be an elaborate plot. But if so or if not—what could she do?

She nodded. "And if you—we—win?"

"Then you needn't worry about your land rights. Here." He pushed his Pad over and she read something about a granting in perpetuity; blah, blah, it meant nothing.

"You might not keep your word," she said.

"That's true." He drew back his Pad and switched it off. "But then, I'm afraid that's the way it is. What do you say?"

She swallowed, carefully clearing her throat. She wanted to spit in his face. "I guess that saying no leads to a much shorter ending to our conversation?"

"That's a possibility. You would remain here, in custody, indefinitely." He grinned. "Did you think we would kill you now? But then, maybe later you could change your mind. Then we would have wasted a good opportunity. Perhaps we could ask your brother to persuade you, when he comes knocking to find out where you are? Miz Jordan, I assure you this effort of ours is in everyone's best interests. Even the lore and language of your People would endorse it, were I able to explain it to you in full. Alas, I cannot."

"Enough talking, Abe," the big man with the keys said then. "Our window is getting short."

"Miz Jordan?"

She looked around at their faces, trying desperately to judge from what she saw, to see some good intents, some competence, something that could persuade her she had a chance. She saw only faces, men with worries, men who were already outside their own law.

"Okay," she said.

They put her things back together, gave her another shot, placed a dark bag over her head and carried her away. Throughout it all she didn't resist, not a single muscle fibre moved. She saved her strength and prayed, until darkness took her, for cunning.

Dan knew that he'd forgotten something important. He vaguely remembered a call about Natalie, from Shelagh Carter. At least all that was out of his hands now. The Ministry and their twerpy security guys, macho and strutting, were actually better at looking after Nat than he was. But he didn't feel exactly good as he sat at home. He felt as though he'd been very Bad Dan indeed.

To get over it he fixed himself a big gin and tonic. A big gin, rather. The tonic was just speculative.

At least the day had gone well. Bobby was staying overnight and would be released tomorrow, and for a while there would be fuss, but then Clinic life would subside to its usual starchy ebb and he would have some time to get himself together.

He called the local Chinese for a delivery and flicked through the *Radio Times*. Natalie had already been home and gone back again, leaving him strict instructions to stop fucking around and do something useful. She hadn't even been baitable about the American guy, and Dan's cautious and sensitive attempt to suggest he might not be whiter than white had gone down like a bucket of cold sick. Maybe she shouldn't have slept with him. After all, if he meant a lot to her, now it was only going to be worse. You definitely shouldn't do that with people you cared about. Far too complicated.

He shook his head wisely and prepared to spend the evening doing a very safe, very certain, nothing at all.

It was about two in the morning when the shrill of a repeating alarm stripped him of sleep. He woke, shuddering with horror, barely realizing what it meant. It wasn't smoke. It wasn't the house. What was it?

Dan floundered up off the sofa and hit his head on the corner of the table. The pain momentarily made him intelligent enough to slap the house controller and get the noise to stop. On the TV screen there was a message:

"Emergency Staff Call. Dan Connor. This is a Grade Five Emergency. Respond by return call to confirm your attendance before you leave home."

He went through the motions in a blur of confusion. Grade Five; that was an accident, a breakout, a contamination alert or something like that. No, not quite like that or they wouldn't be calling him in, would they?

Since he hadn't got undressed he didn't need to do much before he was ready. Bleary-eyed and half sick, with chow mein trying to regurgitate every minute or so, he stumbled down the stairs, wrestled with the door, got it to shut, and fell into the taxi that was already waiting for him at the curbside. He hoped nobody was going to breathalyse him when he got there.

Natalie was in her office, poring sleepily over the results on her own code at about one fifteen in the morning, having been unable to sleep for thinking about Jude and Mikhail Guskov, when one of the night-shift nurses burst in, out of breath.

"You've gotta come!" she said between gasps. "He's saying something!"

Since there was only one important patient on the wards it wasn't hard to guess who she meant, but Natalie was still figuring out why his saying something was so desperate by the time she reached his room.

Bobby was sitting, talking.

". . . Because the spaces and the forms are part of one thing. Like a jigsaw. There is no division between space and form, the void and the illusion of dense matter. Matter itself is an energy vibration. Resonance derives shape, property, and gravity. Matter is information.

"As the shadow is seen in the light so the emptiness of energy alone is animated by information, and all life is a supercollation of informative points, a brilliant invasion on the empty world; its voice and song . . ."

Natalie stood similarly dumbfounded as this spiel rolled out in a light, airy tone that was both animated and curiously monotonous, as though Bobby were the mouthpiece of a machine, or speaking in tongues.

But it was what he was saying that rooted Natalie to the spot. Despite many recent distractions her head was still full of the minute workings of Selfware, and her own hopes of it, and in hearing Bobby's voice she was slowly becoming sure that this was its doing.

A chill crept over her from the bones outward as she listened to the bizarre litany. Selfware was not supposed to be active in him. Hell, it wasn't even complete in the system they'd used on Bobby. He'd never been exposed to the full program. Besides which, Bobby had been normal when they had purged all systems in his head more than six hours ago. Everything had shut off.

It didn't sound like him, except for his local accent. They weren't words he would have chosen or things she would have thought him capable of talking about. This was no sweet-talk from the influence of a drug, or even from an overflow of neurotransmitters triggered by the activity of the NervePath.

Was she responsible for this?

"What do you think it is?" she heard the nurse behind her murmur uneasily over Bobby's continuing paean to life, space, and time.

Natalie didn't answer. She studied Bobby minutely.

He was sitting up, his legs crossed under the sheet and his arms raised, like a swami at prayer. His face was radiant with the joy of his beatific insights and his gaze was dreamy and distant, looking far from the little room, its mundane beige decor and stupefied, equally mundane staff. "Marvellous," his word for what they had done to him, echoed through Natalie's mind, because that was what he was seeing now, whatever it was.

"Let's get him sedated for the time being. Bring the portable scan unit in here."

She had to buy herself some time to figure out what was going on. She would have to call her father.

". . . the sign and the symbol are more than the signified," Bobby was now relaying.

"Through symbolization a single meaning becomes hyperplastic within the mind. The limits of comprehension are broken. The reality they strive to reveal, concealed within the illusion of words, is set loose."

Natalie took a sedative shot from the nurse and administered it herself, slowly, because she wanted to hear what he was saying. It sounded horribly like the kind of things she'd heard from speculating physicists and language theorists. It was the kind of thing she would have half-expected to hear from a person who was capable of witnessing and understanding the world beyond their five senses. Or, of course, some peacenik student out of their head on pot.

"The mind flows in constant dialectic between the inner universe of the single self and the outer, material universe, in twin streams of pure information, each shaping the other to greater specificity. And the hidden dimension of gravity and the dimension of spatial expansion and collapse that is Time . . ."

Bobby's lips stopped moving and his muscles relaxed. Natalie caught him as he fell back to his pillows and straightened his legs out for him, smoothing his blankets, tucking him in.

Serene, he slept. Natalie wondered if maybe he'd had a secret hobby—quantum mechanics and consciousness theory, perhaps. No reason he couldn't. For all they knew this might have been a dream state and he was babbling something he'd read in a magazine.

Contrary to what her father thought she believed, Natalie did not have faith in any theory of quantum consciousness, where all minds were united as one in a unified field that interacted weakly with the physical world. Some people even thought that consciousness itself had determined the entire feature set of the physical world. She thought that was too quirky, too coincidental, and altogether such an ill-thought-out wish-fulfilment version of the quantum world that she wouldn't have touched it with a ten-foot pole. Such ideas oozed a tacky mental ichor that contaminated everything it touched with a blight of dreamy false premises. On the other hand, if someone maintained that a person's awareness of the world defined the way in which they understood it and themselves, she was all for that.

All the same, Natalie hadn't entirely given up on quantum theory and a possible link with consciousness, despite the fact that a brain was too warm a place to allow the kinds of changes that such things demanded. It was possible that there was a quantum element that was crucial to conscious states, aside from the very obvious observation that since *everything* was made up of quanta then of course there would be quanta involved in consciousness. At any university there were hordes of philosophers prepared to argue the toss—if consciousness is not physical the metaphysical leaps gladly in—but Natalie wasn't sold on beliefs about insubstantial and nonphysical souls, minds, or spirits of any kind. She considered herself a scientist and she couldn't go that far. But sometimes she would have liked to. In the case of Jude's file, for instance, it was a tempting idea and so far her only one.

She left Bobby content in his bed and went to make contact with her father. His pet Ministry official, McAlister, a man of political ambition, had already been alerted and was waiting for her. As she arrived he was sitting in her father's seat, studying the large-screen wall monitor, where pictures of exactly what was going on in Bobby's head were displayed. He looked faintly amused and bemused, like a two-year-old watching television.

The sight made her stop in midstride.

Bobby X's brain was ablaze, and not with ordinary shifts of activity. It looked more like the Christmas, Eid and Diwali illuminations than a real-time scan of a mind at work. Surges raced from frontal lobes and around the dopamine pathways, drove through the hippocampus like juggernauts, sparkled in the language centres, flickered like fireflies inside the blindsight area, and shone with the force of minor novae in the key zones that gave Bobby his sense of self, his awareness of his own body, his sense of joy, and, last but not least, his awareness of living things.

Natalie didn't understand what any of that would mean. There was no precedent.

She also saw a classic spike-and-slow-wave fugue moving through his temporal lobes. It was the clear indicator of a person undergoing a profoundly spiritual and religious experience. The only area functioning at a recognizably ordinary level was his visual cortex and that, although his eyes were closed, was working steadily, manufacturing the visions of his dreams.

From what she saw she wasn't sure that Bobby could have been conscious; not in the way she and the others were at this moment.

"What *is* that?" McAlister asked mildly, frowning in piqued curiosity as she sent the messages to her father, quickly adding a screamer notice to get his immediate attention.

"I'm not sure," she said, feeling inadequate. "I can't tell if this is him on his own or the NervePath." She carried on, talking to herself, trying to think. "This couldn't be a hypothalamic overreaction. It's far too big. Maybe it's in the programming. I'm downloading from the NP now to see if it's really purged. Damn it. We were moving so fast because of this fuckwit Ministry pressure." She cast a look of loathing in McAlister's direction.

"If they *are* working then I think we'll have to go for some kind of reset and shut them down completely, destroy them, rather than risk any worsening," she added.

Her father came online with a chime of bells, and his image appeared alongside Bobby's fairground lights. His pale eyes were sharp and accusatory as his office camera obediently panned around to include her in its shot. "Did you look at the program? Have you checked it?"

Natalie was angered by his suppositions. She glanced up from the desk where she was watching the download and said shortly, "That's Bill's job, not mine." She turned to McAlister, watching him cock his head to listen to the earpiece that connected him to the wider awareness of the MoD. "Where is Bill?"

"No shutdown," McAlister said at the same time to her father, as though she weren't there. "If you do that we'll never be able to find out what's happened in there."

"Yes, James." Her father switched his interrogation from Natalie to McAlister in one quick move. "Where *is* Bill? I've been calling him for an hour. No answer."

Natalie saw her father glance at her and realized that he was more afraid than angry. She was so startled she barely registered that he was trying to signal to her, something about McAlister.

There was a second of silence in which McAlister's face reddened. "How would I know? We're searching for him all over the city."

"What?" Natalie glared at him, stopped in full flow, her fingers suspended over the inverted desk controls. "Since when?"

"He hasn't been seen since the experiment finished," her father said.

McAlister sat up and straightened his tie nervously.

Natalie stared at him, uncomprehending. "You didn't tell me!" She looked up at the screen and saw her father acknowledge his mistake with a sneer. "Jesus shit!" She circled the desk, shoved McAlister out of the way, and started summoning the code that had downloaded from the NP in Bobby's head.

As it streamed up onto the secondary monitor she sat back in the chair, which felt like it had just dropped down an elevator shaft and was still going strong.

"Well?" McAlister asked, unable to help himself. He was twitchy with eagerness or terror, she didn't know which.

Natalie shook her head helplessly, seeing Calum's rage about to incandesce as he also read the results from his Pad, "I didn't do this."

"I'm not saying you did." He kept himself under control, she didn't know how.

"What is it?" McAlister again.

Natalie resisted an urge to pick up the chair and break it over his head. She held up her finger, giving him no answer, and ran a quick diagnostic to find the fault. It took less than a second. No effort had been made to conceal it. It was a single, tiny change in the end-point section.

She put it on the large screen. "This is at the end of our legitimate program," she said. The purge command, which she had written herself and checked that afternoon, had been added to. The last line now read:

```
if (currentPoint.checkstate( )==END) {
    SelfWare.Init(INFINITY);

}
```

Her father's florid face went white.

"What does that mean?" McAlister bleated, insistent. He looked like he was ready to jump on the desk and start throttling her.

Natalie said, "Some bastard has taken my Selfware program and loaded it alongside the therapy session. When the purge was run it automatically started the secondary system. But that's not all."

Natalie used the laser pointer and highlighted the last word. "This parameter. It should be a small number. A finite series . . ." She trailed off as her mind struggled to understand what such an alteration could do. "I don't even know what that means, running it with no upper limit. I guess it just . . . carries right on forever. But the theory says it shouldn't be able to . . . there's a very large noise problem with higher numbers of iterations . . ." She spun in her seat and rounded on McAlister, her anger brightening. "It doesn't take a degree to spot who's done this, now, does it? And you've lost him!"

"Never mind that," her father growled. He turned to McAlister as she started accessing the scanner systems, "There's your proof of what's going on. I told you before. Now, let's get on with the shutdown before anything worse happens with that bloody voodoo software." He shot a baleful look of reproach at Natalie and then reached forward to break the link.

"No," McAlister said quietly from his position, half hunched against the desk as if he expected physical violence. "No shutdown."

Natalie froze in midtyping. There was a second of absolute silence. In it McAlister stood up and straightened his tie. She saw that he knew all about Bill somehow. It was in the way he tried to form a sickly kind of confidence and take command.

Her father sat back slowly, eyes narrowed, mouth a thin, lipless gash, "Bobby is my patient." His voice was calm, "And I will decide what is best for him now. We are going to shut down. Natalie?"

"The scan-and-transmit system is ready. I'll just take a handset to his room and get it done," she said, pushing back from the desk.

"No," McAlister said again, this time with more authority.

She pushed past him and he plucked weakly at her.

"It's Mikhail Guskov's orders!" McAlister bleated as they were about to leave him.

Natalie half turned, her hand on the door jamb.

"We keep it running. It's important. For the project. Mappa Mundi."

To her astonishment she saw that McAlister was holding a gun on her.

"I'm sorry," he said, glancing at the screen and then back at her. "You have to listen." He waved the gun a little bit and with difficulty put the safety off.

Natalie thought he was more likely to shoot her because of incompetence rather than through intent. She snorted and asked, "Since when do you work for him?" Although there were strong links between Guskov and the Ministry she doubted they'd jump to his tune.

"Please, maintain the experiment," he said. "A little longer."

She glanced at Calum and saw him calculating, listening.

"If you try to stop it in any way," McAlister continued. "I will have to prevent you."

"Do the Ministry know?" her father asked.

"Not yet," McAlister conceded with a significant nod that Natalie assumed meant he was in Guskov's pay before he was in the Ministry's.

He waved the gun between her and the door. "We will go to the patient's observation area and monitor from there. I'm sure the MoD monitors on this conversation will update those who need to know."

"Put that toy away," Natalie snapped at him. "You look ridiculous."

McAlister did so, sheepishly, she thought. *Now what?* she wondered. *Will we shut it off or what? We can't leave Bobby like that.*

But they did.

In the observation area she and McAlister sat at the nurses' station. Natalie watched McAlister watching her, trying to ingratiate himself again with a little smile or some insider comment about this being the real cutting edge.

Natalie didn't understand her father going along with something as brutally unethical. Could he be agreeing just because doing the right thing meant being expelled from Mikhail Guskov's inner circle? He'd never shown signs of that shallowness before. Was there more to it?

She racked her brain to remember anything from the files that Jude had shown her that might explain things, but nothing did. Meanwhile Bobby slept and they sat, and time passed and Natalie's whole being demanded she do something; stand up, dare McAlister to shoot her, grab the scanner now sitting so damn' close on the station top, and save Bobby from whatever her wretched system was doing to him.

Outside there were other agents from the Ministry, armed ones. If she tried it, would they be quick enough to come to her aid? If they did, who would they shoot first?

The clock ticked the world around to two-oh-five and she remained frozen with worry and indecision.

A minute or so later, still trying to work up the courage to dare McAlister's gun, Natalie found herself thinking, *Gosh, that's bright in there, who turned the lights up?*

"I'm going to switch the lights down . . ." she said, moving towards the control. But before she could she heard McAlister whisper, "Jesus wept! Are the cameras on?"

She glanced back over her shoulder at the same moment her fingers located the lights command and found them already switched into twilight mode. McAlister had leaped forward and now hesitated, his fingertips just touching the glass wall of Bobby's room, his mouth hanging half open.

Bathing his sweaty face in a pale lustre, the sheets around Bobby were glowing as though lit from within or as if they'd been passed under a violet light in a nightclub. Their super-whiteness stood out vividly, suffusing the room and giving McAlister a yellowish shadow that stretched up and over the control panel.

Natalie didn't understand what she was seeing. Turning around, she scrubbed at her sore, tired eyes with her hand, but when she looked up the brightness remained, slowly, steadily intensifying. She moved to the window, pressing her face to the safety glass, and saw the head, face, and shoulders of Bobby X shining like a low-budget movie special effect showing the waking of a saint or a demon.

The emergency alarm went off at the same moment, maybe triggered by her father's conscience or the sensitive nanodetectors in the room, Natalie didn't know. McAlister jumped at the shrill sound and started mouthing off some protest, dabbing at the sweat rolling off his forehead. In contrast Natalie felt cold as ice. In that instant her courage finally took form. She reached behind her for the scanner and shouldered through the doors.

As she fumbled with the control settings she saw the light on her hands and lab coat. Its quality began to change from the stark white of the shining, making her waste precious seconds looking up at the bed where she saw Bobby's whole figure begin to emit a violet gleam. She felt heat brush her hands and face and her eyes watered and hurt. She loaded the shutdown commands and tightened her finger on the trigger but the scanner kept returning a "Failed Send" message. Frantically she checked power and systems—they were all OK.

The heat became stronger and she had to step back, almost

blinded. She kept on trying with the machine, but it occurred to her then that whatever was coming off Bobby was probably distorting the scanner's signal and she might as well have been trying to make contact using a tin can and a piece of string. It was only then that she realized she was afraid.

She looked up and narrowed her eyelids to tiny slits as she backed off and saw Bobby's face on the pillow, his smile deepening as the glow increased. He looked deliriously happy.

Natalie felt sick. She had no idea what to do. In the distance she could hear McAlister making calls, urging her to come out, to get away, his voice as high and hysterical as a child's. She began to turn away, shielding her exposed skin from the glare. She heard the alarm change its note to the tones for a contamination alert. There was a soft pop and the light dimmed back to its twilight night-state, gleaming red in the alarm's added suffusion.

Natalie's eyes struggled to adjust, watering profusely. She turned back, thinking Bobby must be burned or dead, and saw the sheet on his bed drift lightly downwards. It settled into a series of fold mountains and valleys. It lay on the surface of the dimpled foam mattress that rose out of its human-made hollows to meet it. Bobby was nowhere to be seen.

A few uneven, racking breaths came to her aid and she let go of the scanner, hearing it clatter down onto the tiled floor although that didn't matter now. She stared at the bed and her mouth worked silently around some meaningless syllables of disbelief. She wanted to laugh, reminded instantly of Jude's file and the manner of its appearance; things seemed to be popping in and out of reality, like there was nothing to it, like it was easy, obvious. The gut-trembling that she'd never felt on seeing the papers and memos appeared now, weakening her knees. She groped around for something to hold on to. The bed was the nearest thing and the relief as her hand felt its solid presence was indescribable.

From the door she heard McAlister squeak, "Where the hell did he go?"

Someone called her name from far away. It was almost inaudible.

Natalie leaned on the bed, feeling its heat and the smell of Bobby's sweat seeping up around her. Of their own accord her hands spread out, confirming that he was gone. Now she did laugh, a kind of coughing gasp that wasn't a sign of amusement. It must be a prank—but nobody involved in this had enough sense of humour to pull a practical joke.

"Natalie? Doctor Armstrong?" The voice from far away zoomed in as it spoke, hesitant and frightened.

Baffled, she looked under the bed, and found what she expected: nothing.

She spun around, thinking how ridiculous this was, and halted dead in her tracks.

Bobby X was standing right in front of her.

"Doctor?" he whispered. He held out his hand towards her shakily, peering.

"Bo—" she began, relieved, hand on her heart, ready to say what a scare he'd just given her, when he faded.

It was like watching a ghost. Suddenly she could see the open door through him and McAlister's dumb, stupid shape standing there like a stuck pig, mouth catching flies.

"Natalie?!" Bobby's tremulous voice was fading, too. It sounded like a badly tuned radio station. He pawed at something in front of him as if he was being attacked, blinking and squinting.

She realized that he couldn't see her any more.

"It's all right, I'm here Bobby." Natalie reached towards him quickly, moving to grab his hands. Her fingers passed through his and closed on nothing.

"Natalie!" he cried. His beatific happiness of a moment before was gone. The shadows of his face were racked with terror, their uneven flicker making him look as though he was winking.

She snatched over and over again at where she could still see traces of his outline. Her fingers slapped into her palms, her fists clenching emptily right inside his arms. She could feel nothing but a faint tingling like pins and needles where they closed on a void.

In fear and despair Bobby threw himself at her, trying to catch hold, but just as her hands had, his hands swiped right through her. In that instant her whole body was engulfed with prickling tremors and, as sure as she was of her own name, Natalie knew that she and Bobby were crossing over.

Then he was gone.

In his place came a numb blackness. Natalie fell into it as though into a vast, open mouth. With her last moment of awareness she felt its hungry breath engulf her.

On the surface of another world McAlister was calling, "Help! Help!"

Ten

Jude met Mary at Goodenough's bar and restaurant, a place close to his home where they occasionally went for a quiet conversation out of work hours. He took care to arrive before her, walking in out of the stale afternoon and hoping that the smell of fried onions and a mesquite grill would be enough to put him in a better frame of mind. Closer to and the bar's scent of spilt beer and margarita mix sent an acid line up his nose.

Neither odour hit the spot and he didn't stop as Cole, the barman, gave him the nod and said quietly, "Hey, Jude," front runner in the longest, oldest running-quip contest. Cole's grin was soft with self-mockery as he vigorously polished a glass pitcher with his white cloth. His rheumy, lugubrious eyes, specially modelled, Jude thought, on bloodhounds, tracked Jude's movements to the end of the bar. Cole waited until Jude sat down and then flicked a thick finger towards the Red Hook pump, questioning.

Jude nodded. The music was softer at this end where one of the speakers was broken. It sounded furry. Cole put the beer glass down on a mat, noted Jude's expression and ambled off again to unpack a few more pitchers from the washer. Jude looked along the ranks of cold beers, bottled fruit drinks, spirits above them in line upon line of bottles of endlessly different shapes, sizes, colours, and promises. It looked like treasure. From far behind him he heard the click of pool balls and the thump of a cue landing on its butt on the floor. The men playing spoke in soft voices he couldn't hear.

He checked what his datapilot had to offer on Fort Detrick. He'd not got far when Mary swept up.

"Hey, Cole!" she called.

"Mary, Mary," Cole said, "how's that garden going?"

Jude stood and gave her a hug of greeting. They kissed each other on the cheek and she settled down, cool and graceful, her blue eyes sparkling with the promise of complicity he'd been counting on to lift his spirits.

"I'm sorry about Florida," was the first thing she said. "I guess I screwed it up some without you. It happened so quick in the end. I wasn't expecting them to bail on us that fast. They must have had insider knowledge."

"Yeah." He nodded. "Apology accepted. I read your account. Tough break."

"Lost your man again," she said, carefully checking him for reaction.

Cole took her order with another hand-signal. They both watched him pour and shake the cocktail.

"Seems like fate," Jude said. "I think we're not meant to get him. My guess is that the government find him too useful. Someone watches over him. I'm going to ask Perez for some casework that doesn't involve his areas next. Something simpler, like fraud."

"How about voluntary body-chemistry control?"

"That's a science already?"

Mary flashed her whitened teeth and laughed. "It will be now that they've finished perfecting NervePath systems. Glandular balancing using Micromedica for common disorders will lead to doping yourself with your own hormones in the time it takes to say Olympics, don'tcha think?"

"Puts self-help in a whole new light."

"And the drugs empires will have to pack up and get with the pace." She took a sip of her martini as soon as it arrived and fished out the olive to eat it. "So what do you think of this invitation to Utah?"

Jude hadn't given it any thought since she'd mentioned it. Fort Detrick, not Dugway, was on his mind. "Another army technoporn show," he said. "Probably something to do with the biothreat." They'd been invited to views before, where a new advance in defense or offense was wheeled out for inspection. They were allowed in because their work was supposed to uncover similar systems being produced on the black market. Jude had never seen any of the biogear outside a $BSL\text{-}_4$ zone so far, and he never wanted to. "When is it?"

"In a few days. Perez is going to send you the details." Mary shook her hair back behind her shoulders. "Anyway, enough about all that. Did you hear about this rumor of experiments at Deer Ridge? I thought you said you had family there?"

Jude was startled, but he knew not to show it. He'd seen a few reports on the smaller or more outrageous newsnets and it was in one of their itemized postings from their own FBI datapilots. "Yeah. My sister. Half sister. She didn't know anything."

Mary looked disappointed. "I was hoping maybe there'd be a lead there, into something."

"If there is," he said, "it's going to be some kind of government thing. Just like these Ivanov cases. We've never successfully prosecuted any other agency for use or development. They always pull that national security number." He reached over to her hand where it rested on the edge of the table and squeezed it briefly to console her.

"Sorry. I'm being a horse's ass, I know."

"Maybe, like you say, it's got nothing to it." She shrugged.

He watched her closely as they took a drink each. She didn't seem concerned. He wished that he could stop being so picky-paranoid. He needed help badly and she was cool in a crisis. He trusted her. So why couldn't he talk?

"She's gone AWOL somewhere, though," he said, trying out the idea.

"She? You mean your sister?"

"Yeah. I let her have the apartment while I was away, and when I got back, *nada*. Not even a note. But she's always been pretty flighty. Could have just gone off and planned to come back in a few days. She often does that."

"You don't sound convinced," Mary finished her martini and wiped her fingers on the napkin carefully, taking a moment over each one.

"Yeah, I'm not entirely. This business could get the media real edgy. I know she'd like to use it any way she can to push AIM forward. I'm worried she might go and get a few of the active ones and stage some kind of protest about it." And if that didn't sound like lying lame shit he didn't know what did.

Mary nodded. "She never had to stay on the Reservation, though, did she? I heard you say often you'd send her money and she'd send it back."

"Uncle Sam's filthy dollar," Jude agreed, snorting at the memories of White Horse's terse notes. "Thinks it comes with a debt attached."

"Who's the parent in common?"

"Father. Magpie Jordan. Used to be called Joe sometimes but he never liked Christianized names."

"You've got it as your second name."

"Yeah. But I don't use it. Not unless White Horse is around. She doesn't like my English name much. Mom chose that, and she hasn't got a lot of time for her either."

"Does it mean anything? You never told me."

Jude grinned at her, "Magpie's a name for someone who likes to tell tales and lies. Dad was good at all that. Very funny. My mom thought he should have written it down but he never did."

"Sorry." Mary put her hand on his shoulder for a moment.

"That's okay. Long time ago. Another drink?"

"Why not? You get them." She got up to go to the powder room.

While she was away Jude thought he probably would tell her. The weight of not doing so was almost painful and he felt deeply tired. He worried that White Horse was in so much trouble he couldn't even touch it. He didn't know what he could do to help her.

He ordered the drinks and was waiting, looking at the high screen where that day's baseball highlights were being cycled, when his Pad bleeped a triple tone.

He flicked it on to read the incoming information—a coded line, a private word.

It was from a contact of his at the Centers for Disease Control labs in Atlanta. A guy who'd helped him out a time or two before.

New Russian connection. Meet me.

It was flagged urgent and included the times of flights and a series of instructions.

Jude put it back in his jacket as Mary returned.

"New mail. Anyone I should know about?" she asked lightly, winking.

For a second something about the wink bothered him. It was like a flirt, but Mary didn't do that routinely. It was like a signal, but he didn't know what it meant. The news from Atlanta was still sinking in. He shrugged it off.

"Nobody nice," he said and picked up the menu, almost as an afterthought, so he didn't have to meet her eyes and get the third degree. He paused. "How high up are our investigations supposed to go?"

She sat back in mock surprise at the question. "How high? As high as it takes. We're here to enforce the law for everyone."

"Right." He flipped the menu. "Want to eat here?"

"No," she said. "Not yet. Jude, come on. What's bothering you?"

He stared at the list. "I think I got into something up to my neck and I can't get out," he said finally.

She nodded. "Go on."

"I don't know if I should." He stuffed the menu back into its holder and flicked it away from him across the bar before turning back to her. "We've been friends a long time and it's probably better you don't know."

"Jude, for Chrissake." She smiled and nudged his shin with the toe of her soft shoe. "Let me help. Is it to do with White Horse?"

"Not entirely." He linked his fingers together and turned his hands inside out, stretching, listening to his two loose knuckles crack. He felt he was at a critical point, an intersection in events, where his next move, one way or another, would precipitate an instant and inevitable plunge into the future, from which there would be no means of escape. He sighed, breathless at this insight, helpless before it. Like a person listening to an old recording of themselves they've forgotten ever making he heard himself speak.

"I need a couple of days to think about it, okay? I'm going to stay away from work and just try to get it done on my own, yeah?"

"But then, if it isn't done, you'll let me help you?" She sat forward and stared intently into his face. "If it's dangerous . . ."

"I don't know," he said. "I'll tell you later."

During the next hour, they drank three more rounds, talked about nothing in particular, caught up on some more details of her Florida experience. None of this could drag his mind from the file contents and Natalie Armstrong. He was barely able to keep up his end of the conversation. When she was leaving Mary said, "If you want to talk . . ."

"Sure. Thanks." Jude watched her go. He realized he liked Natalie because she was sparky, like Mary. He asked himself, as he worked his way through a fourth beer, why he'd never gone to bed with Mary. He wondered, feeling suddenly lonely, if she'd like to and why he was thinking about this now when he'd never thought about it much before, whether it was his fear trying to grab on to something—anything—like a drowning man reaching for a shadow in the waves that might be either driftwood or emptiness. And then he thought about Fort Detrick and his mind went blank.

By eleven that night he still hadn't come up with a plan that wasn't a hundred percent impossible to carry out, and none of the guys he'd once known in the army had had any clue what he was talking about when he'd called to poke around. So, for want of any other action, he booked his flight to Atlanta.

Jude was entering the details into his diary when a curious possibility about the files back at his apartment occurred to him. It was so obvious that he wondered why he hadn't thought of it before. Suppose that those papers were all in one file because they all related to one man? The combination of the idea and the drink made him dizzy.

He paid Cole and left, hurrying home with his head down against a light rain that had just started to fall.

Dan got to the Clinic and found chaos. Police and military vehicles clogged the gateway like a log jam in a sluice. When he was allowed in he found the corridors were full of people who were all but running, weaving around each other in both directions, talking to microphones and one another in blurts of request and instruction that bounced off the walls and roof to mingle into a senseless din. The alarms were switched off, but the resulting background of silence was more disorientating than their normal screaming. The lack of motivating noise was unsettling. He gathered from fragments he overheard that there'd been some kind of Micromedica breakout—a contamination—and that something had gone bad with Bobby X.

Dan's first thought was to find Natalie. But when he asked where she was the security officer scanning his Clinic card gave him a flat glance. "Report to your station. Someone there will inform you of your duties."

Dan had to bite his lip to prevent himself from saying "Fuck you" right into the little shit's face. Two minutes in charge and it was *Zeig Heil* all the way. He took his card and brushed through the knot of people at the doors to the Therapy wing, treading on more than one foot.

A temporary hub had been set up in the waiting area. He saw

familiar faces there. They all looked pale and strained. Nobody smiled. Standing among them were two officers in biosuits with air-groomers in their hands. Their headgear was hanging off and trailing down their backs, so obviously if there had been any danger of live NervePath in the air it was gone now.

He caught hold of one of the other technicians he knew as the man passed him—a guy from NervePath Neurosurgery. "What's going on?"

Roscoe's face was alert with a kind of excitement that didn't know if it was going to get itself smacked down but wasn't able to stop anyway.

"Bobby's gone, man. Clean off the face of the earth. He was being treated by Doctor Armstrong. Something happened to her, too."

"What?" Dan tightened his grip even though Roscoe was tugging against it, clearly keen to go somewhere else. They had never had much time for each other. "Where is she?"

"Q-1." Roscoe twisted himself free and shook off Dan's touch. He gave him the once-over and curled his lip. "You should sort yourself out sometime, Connor. You're gonna give the place a bad name. She's been far too good to you."

Dan gulped air, not at the insult, which was beneath him, but at the information. He was still in his overcoat and he had the feeling that he was wearing odd shoes, but he didn't bother to check. It turned out that Roscoe was right. In the observation gallery of Quarantine-1 Dan found Charlton standing on her own, looking into the room beyond with a faraway expression on her face. Her arms were folded tight around each other as though they were burrowing away from the light.

Dan stepped up beside her and breathed his gin-breath slightly to one side. "What's up?"

"Oh, there you are!" She half smiled and they both looked through together. "She's asleep. Well, maybe more like a coma."

Dan looked at the small body in the bed and he wouldn't have believed it was Natalie, except he could see the short spiky red hair standing out stark against the white pillow.

"Why?" was all he could say. He found his hands on the window frame, pawing at its solidity.

"Don't know," Charlton said softly. "Something about getting cross-infected." She glanced nervously across at him. "Doesn't make sense, though, does it? I mean, she already had NP saturation, from doing her own work. So even if there was a spill, it wouldn't make any difference to her, would it?"

Dan was looking down at the monitor readings. He wished now that he'd studied harder when he had the chance. Natalie looked healthy enough; her heart was good, her blood pressure only a touch high. "Is there a readout on those things?"

"Not allowed to have it on," Charlton said. "But if you've got an access code higher than me you might get it. They're working up in the main processing suite, finding out what happened. You should probably be there."

"Probably." Dan fiddled with his Pad, logging into the Clinic system, verifying his Emergency Code, the passwords to the scanners . . . it seemed to take a lifetime. As he waited someone checked with Charlton over the intercom.

"No," she said to them. "No changes."

"How long?" he asked, making a mistake with his clumsy fingers and having to punch in the word again.

"Just half an hour," she said. "Seems like a lot of fuss to me. They say she fainted. She was exhausted. You saw her tonight. Maybe she needs to sleep it off."

Dan finally got the response he was looking for. As he focused his aching eyes on it he had to watch for a good few seconds before he could understand what he was seeing.

"Fucking Ada," he whispered. Charlton's question followed him as he raced through the door and headed for the central suite. There was no way that could be right.

He got a much colder reception from McAlister and Calum Armstrong. Then he felt every molecule a dirty, unshaven, disreputable loser as they filled him in, their cold, clipped tones like those of robots.

". . . Sabotaged the experiment causing an overrun of an unplanned system."

"Some kind of transitory crossover occurred, causing the program to jump host systems—upgrade Natalie's own inert NP structures . . ."

". . . Don't fully understand the physical processes . . ."

Dan realized, after he'd heard them rabbit for a couple of minutes, that it all added up to one thing. Natalie was infected with a live Selfware system—that stuff she'd written that he thought was a recipe for making yourself more intelligent and had tried to persuade her to sell on the Internet—and it was still running and they were doing nothing to stop it.

". . . Searching for the primary candidate . . ."

"Just shut up!" Dan yelled over the top of their jabber. "Shut up a minute. Why haven't you shut it off?" He turned to McAlister, the only human physically present, and cast a look over Armstrong Senior and some other man he'd never seen before on the live-link.

"It's password-protected," McAlister informed him. He looked smug about it.

"And you can't hack it in ten seconds?" Dan was incredulous. He found he was striding up to McAlister, taking his jacket in handfuls and lifting the weasel off the ground and it felt good. "Shut it off!" He glared over McAlister's shoulder at Armstrong, "She's your daughter, for God's sake!"

Armstrong looked sick. Dan had never seen him so disturbed. He almost looked like he was going to lose consciousness.

The other man, a heavily bearded guy, spoke for him, "We're working on it." He had a strong accent. Dan didn't know what it was.

"Let me go!"

He ignored McAlister's kicking and instead shoved him up against the wall, bashing his head against the corner of one of Armstrong's many degrees and valedictory certificates. "You're saying you have your sneaky fingers up everyone's ass here and you don't know the passwords?"

"It's her private—"

"Well, Knitted Guy must have had them, right? Or how could he get access to it? Think of that? Jesus, I bet I even know what they are . . ."

"If you do, then use them!" Calum barked and Dan saw that he meant it, every word.

"It would be a total breach of securit—" McAlister began as he found his toes on the ground again.

Dan swung him around and, with a shove, laid him flat out across the desk, arms and legs spread, so that he went sliding across it like a starfish, knocking the stylus holder flying. Dan was already working on his Pad, trying to find the route in.

The Defence chaps weren't all evil. He was given a helping hand by the "expert" working in Bill's place who took him into the right areas and got him to the Initialize Edit screens in quick time. There was silence in the room as Dan sat and thought, wondering if his bet was going to be as good as it had seemed two minutes ago or if he was going to crash and burn out big time, taking Natalie's chances with him. His hands shook.

But Dan did know the passwords because she only had three different ones and used all of them to try and stop him playing games on her machines at home when she was out. If she'd used another one . . . but he didn't want to think about that.

The second try worked. It let them into the edit protocol and Dan watched as the engineer rapidly located the INFINITY parameter and reset it to INTEGER:1.

"If I set it to zero after it's already been active it may do something unforeseen. Can't tell without looking at its databasing." This was explained with a shrug that said the engineer wasn't sure there was a lot of hope with the figure 1 either.

But Dan didn't care. One change was better than a billion changes.

He was ahead of McAlister all the way down the corridor and into Q-1. The scanner system transmitted the new instructions and Natalie's multicolour flare reports died back to something like normal.

"I want all the Security systems reset immediately," McAlister was saying into his lapel phone as Dan turned from the readouts. "Yes. Every single one. Erase them all from the system and conduct full interviews with all staff before restoration of any privileges."

Gently moving Charlton to one side Dan took a swing and punched McAlister in the jaw. His hand exploded in pain but McAlister went down and stayed down, his tinny earpiece just audible as it fell out of place and flopped wormlike onto his collar.

"McAlister! Are you all right?"

Kneeling, Dan leaned down to the lapel and said, "Mr. McAlister is taking a short break. He'll be with you just as soon as he can."

Charlton nudged him with her foot. "Thanks," she mouthed and patted Dan's shaggy head.

"Woof woof," he said and looked at his bloodied hand. "This Lassie thing is much tougher than I thought. Shit on a stick, I think I need the vet."

"Come on," she helped him up. "Let's get it sorted out."

"I'll take that, if you don't mind." A large military policeman roughly the size and heft of a tank was in the doorway, hands on his hips. He glanced down at McAlister and then stepped over him and clapped a pair of handcuffs over Dan's wrists.

"Mr. Connor, this way please."

Ian Detteridge stood in the hallway of his own home and watched his wife backing away from him, her hands over her mouth. She had them clamped there quite tightly, but they didn't block the whimpering sounds.

He looked down at himself and saw a faint shimmer of light where his legs should be.

Something wasn't right. He didn't understand it. His mind was like the wind. It came and went in fits and starts. His body had become so pale and flimsy that light and air passed through it freely. All he could cling to was the firm sense of who he was, not what, but even that was shaky now, because he could see so much more than before and what he saw was changing him.

"Dervla," he said, making an effort to be still. "It's okay. It's only me."

He smiled and held out his arms. He longed for her to hold him and tell him it was okay. He was sure it wasn't. The feeling wouldn't go away and he was afraid. He couldn't remember how he'd got home. The will to be there and being there were the same thing. They'd occupied the same instant.

"No," she whispered, cowering against the wall. "Oh, Mary Mother of God. Get away. Please. Go away."

Her terror made him want to scream.

"Mummy?" Christine appeared in her bedroom doorway. "What's the matter?" She sounded very scared. She looked down the corridor at him. "It's Daddy," she said joyfully. But then her face crumpled up at the edges into the same awful uncertainty that Ian felt. "Why isn't he real?"

"I'm right here, darling," he whispered, crouching down, trying to put on his happiest face. "As real as can be."

In that single moment he saw the woman she would become, tougher and more intelligent than him or his wife, resourceful, but forever low on self-esteem so that she hesitated over opportunities and lived a life that was long, yet barren, haunted by hopes and fears that kept her permanently in a state of hiding from the world. The sudden cruelty of the vision made him feel sick with pity, for himself, for her, for the whole world of people who couldn't see what he saw: the heart of nothing from which everything poured out, instant upon instant rising and vanishing as space opened before and closed after, leaving them forever stranded on the knife-edge of the present. He longed to tell her that she needn't worry about not being good enough. Anything was more than good enough, for him or the Universe.

But Christine looked at her mother, shaking and unable to talk, and wouldn't come. She said, barely audible, holding her teddy bear closely in front of her in the clutch of soft arms he'd never feel again, "Are you dead now, Daddy?"

And Ian knew that in any way that mattered, he was.

White Horse reached Jude's apartment in the evening and looked around for him. He had been back. His bags were there. But he was gone.

She cursed in every language she knew, walked straight to the kitchen, and opened the freezer, taking out the bottle of Stolichnaya that was its only inhabitant. Pouring herself a shot she drank it in one go and bit down on the cold burn with bared teeth as she poured another. She'd heard some things in the car on the way back from wherever. She wished she hadn't. They made being alone now so very hard. They made waiting for Jude a torture. Her nerves felt like each one of them was pierced and hanging on its own fish-hook, soul stretched out to dry, thinner than tissue paper.

She took the second shot in two gulps and then took the third into her brother's tight-assed white sitting room, to the sofa that enveloped her like a snowdrift, and flashed on the news channels. Her burns were about due for another pill but they didn't go well with drink and she needed that more than she needed to escape the physical pain. Despite the knockout drug that was wearing off she felt high as a kite. *Got to get down. Got to spread this around so it doesn't burn a hole right through my head.*

And stay sober enough to talk sense when Magpie did show up. She picked up a deck of cards that were in the magazine rack and started shuffling. She'd play patience. She'd play it real hard. She was dealing her second game when the house system went off with one of the billion stupid signals for incoming calls. The notes of Beethoven's Fifth, rendered in flat chimes that were as witless as the original was thrilling, circled her and then faded into their announcement of bad news. Wherever Jude had gone to he must have switched his Pad off and it was rerouting here.

She listened as the answering service took a message,

"Um . . . Jude, old chap. Dan Connor here. Well, you probably don't remember me. That is, I live with Natalie. Armstrong. There's been a bit of a do. Ah . . . the thing is, there was this woman from, well, it doesn't really matter, from some agency or other and she was asking about Natalie and I . . . I might have told her, that is, I might just have mentioned your name once. I'm not really sure. But you should know that you might get a few questions about it and, er— she's going to be fine, just fine. Going home to, you know, and staying with her father a few days and, yeah. It'll be great. Fine. I thought you should know. You know. Okay. Oh, got your number off the autologger at the hotline, but I'm erasing it now. Okay. Bye, then."

White Horse looked down at the face of the Queen of Spades she'd just turned up. She wondered who Natalie Armstrong was and what she had to do with it. And what hotline? She dealt three more cards and took off the Ace of Diamonds. She kept on playing, watching the deal, lining up the suits.

Calum Armstrong was on a flight back to England already. He drank black coffees and listened to the engine sound change and the vibration echo in his body as they reached sufficient altitude to go supersonic. The tremor in his hands wouldn't die down. He kept thinking of Charlotte, his wife. She'd be cursing him now from her grave, for allowing Natalie to become fouled in this mire, letting Guskov take control of the situation with his persuasiveness. He didn't even recall now what had made the arguments seem so powerful.

He rubbed his shoulders against the seat where his back rested against it, as if he was trying to scour them. But nothing relieved the sensation that he was coated in filth. Of course it wouldn't, and wasn't that so interesting, knowing so much about psychology but still being its plaything?

He took two aspirin. They didn't touch his headache. He knew they wouldn't. He knew so goddamned much, but he wasn't the one to save her. That sly, fop-haired fool had done it. Dan, whom Natalie liked so much and kept in employment when no other lab on Earth would have him. It set him to thinking that maybe her judgement wasn't so bad after all and he smiled with unstoppable pride.

My girl.

What have I done?

But the accident was totally unforeseeable, that was true. As to its cause and the results of the Selfware run on Bobby X—he didn't believe the reports. They didn't add up to anything except hysteria and the accounts of eyewitnesses too confused to make sense. Human beings did not vanish into thin air. Any explanation claiming such a thing was pure wish fulfilment.

Calum ground his coffee cup down on its saucer and gripped the handrests beside his seat until he could feel the struts beneath the soft padding.

They didn't. It was a fact.

She wouldn't.

Would she?

Eleven

Jude walked home the nine blocks from the bar, trying not to breathe too deeply of the city's late-night humid air. Kitchens vented odours of Thai, Mexican, Indian, and Chinese cooking, one after the other. The popular Arabic coffee houses strung veils of smoke around his face on the next street. From windows above the scentsations of the evening's mellow legal highs drooped to road level in soft, invisible blooms. At times like this he remembered the high, clean air of Montana with the wind from the north, sweeping off Canada and its uninhabited vastnesses. The sophistication and choice of the city paled by comparison with that prairie air, even if the Arctic blasts did enjoy tearing warmth out of his skin and coating his hair with fine sheens of ice so that he could hear the strands chiming faintly against each other.

He was looking at his feet, not stepping on a crack, thinking about Fort Detrick and his suspicion that every face in the stolen file had at some time belonged to the same man. From his left pocket the ten dollars he'd put aside in change for the panhandlers went without his seeing a single one of their faces as they oiled up from the shadows, murmuring. Perhaps they were the same person, too, doubling back on the easy marks and relying on their desire not to look too closely to get away with it. He wouldn't have been surprised. There was nowhere like a city for learning how to see properly; what you had to notice and what you shouldn't, under any circumstances, allow to exist. It was an ability of the middle class that was ripe for exploitation.

Was it possible that Yuri Ivanov, Mikhail Guskov, and the list of other identities belonged to one man? What did that mean? Why had it happened? If they were, physically, the same person who had been cosmetically or otherwise altered that was one thing. But he'd read the entries more closely since the first night and there were far bigger differences involved than that. Nationality, mother tongue, qualifications, skills, and psychological profiles: all of these were unique. It was not as though switching them was as easy as changing clothes. Anyone could change a name or a passport or a face. But could anyone be so versatile that they were capable of moving from one life to the next in such a complete way—new job, new associates, new everything?

Jude was wondering what it added up to, and again why and, horribly, *how* he had obtained the information, when he was startled by the apartment messaging his Pad to tell him that White Horse had returned.

He ran up the steps two at a time and burst through the half-open door. He could hear music and there she was, sitting on the floor, playing cards and looking up at him as though she'd never left. He got down on his knees to hug her.

"Where the hell have you been?"

For the first time in an age she didn't immediately wriggle away and cool-stare him. He could feel a lot of tension in her that wouldn't yield, either. When he drew back and sat by her she shrugged.

"I got your message about the machine. I went to get rid of it."

"And and and? C'mon, that isn't it. You didn't go to Fort Detrick on your own." He sat back on his heels and scrutinized her face. As with many of the People hers was no easy giveaway of her feelings. But she was pale, there were dark circles under her eyes, and he could see her struggling to hold in what was on her mind.

"Is that it?" She nodded slowly and turned up another three cards, looking down at her Patience game. "I wondered where it was."

"Who was it?" Jude tried to look her over unobtrusively. She didn't seem hurt—no more than she had been when she left, anyway. Her rat's-tail dreadlocks were tied back with a bandanna and the burns on her jawline and neck shone hot pink and oily with medication.

White Horse thought a while and turned over more cards.

"If they told you not to tell me . . ."

"No," she said, interrupting him. She put up a Jack and two tens. "They want me to tell you to keep on investigating. They said if I didn't that we would lose Deer Ridge to the mineral development proposal." She'd got her cool back now. She finished her dealing and tidied the deck in her hands. "Can they do that?"

Jude's mind reeled. He didn't understand the connection at all, "You mean, can they influence the judge's decision?"

White Horse nodded and began another round. She waited for his answer, the cards moving with metronomic accuracy in her hands.

"I guess that goes a way to telling me who they are if they can. Why say it if they can't? Did you believe them?"

She nodded without looking up.

"Fuck." He ran his hands through his hair. "Are you okay?"

"Mmn hmmn." She took out a nine and another Jack. "They want me to get a case together like I planned. Find a big-time lawyer. Go to court. Stage demonstrations. Get AIM on the case."

Jude's mind felt like it had been blown out. He couldn't think. He'd already had enough to drink but he wanted another one. Instead of going to get it he leaned against the sofa and closed his eyes tight, listening to the insistent drum White Horse had chosen to listen to and the snap, snap of the cards as she dealt.

Deer Ridge. The oil exploration. The mindware test. The threat of eviction from the reservation. White Horse's abduction to Fort Detrick. How did they all add up together?

The coal and oil thing had been going on for over two years now. As domestic reserves had started to dwindle, following the boom development of India and the African Allegiance nations who had imported so much at such vast expense to fuel their industries and their motors, the search for new supplies had become more urgent. Having exhausted all its own land the government had begun to legislate so that search and development was permitted on private land.

Any contractor could go to the county courthouse, apply for a search permit in a limited area, and begin tests. People whose properties were affected had to be compensated and, if the search was successful, their cooperation with any subsequent extraction was rewarded with large cash handouts and substantial share options in their own "microcompany" that would be a subsidiary of the contractor's. Most people were glad to become overnight millionaires. Those who objected were allowed an appeal. If they were turned down they were evicted and compensated at the market rate for their land and homes.

Deer Ridge had fought and sabotaged its way through site testing by Thomson Cushener, a large consortium that had located some small oil and mineral deposits on the reservation. They were now at the appeal stage. Thanks to White Horse's vigorous lobbying, nobody on the land wanted to move out of their home, no matter how attractive the price. They knew that if they did then their land would become part of the USA in perpetuity—and that they would not tolerate.

Deer Ridge's appeal proceedings were in adjournment at the moment, pending further investigations on the "findings" of Thomson Cushener, but they were due to be heard in another couple of months. Oil prices from the Arabic suppliers weren't too bad right now, so it hadn't seemed like they would lose; other places had a lot more to offer. Jude had considered it a safe bet that the appeal court would find for the People. Considering the political blowback of not doing so when the Native American issue was a sympathetic cause for a wide range of voters, he didn't see it happening. He had certainly never connected it with this bizarre "test" of a corrupt medical system. Could they be linked? The oil wealth involved didn't seem nearly high enough. It couldn't be the money side. It just couldn't.

"I don't get it," he said finally and opened his eyes. White Horse's game was nearly completed.

"It isn't the oil," she said, looking down at the last five cards. "It's because of the FBI test. And it isn't just the Feds. The army, too." She turned her head and looked him in the eye. "I heard them say they had support everywhere. People who are against Micromedica being used as a Perfection tool. They want to stop the work. They made Deer Ridge happen so that you and I would start to ask questions about the government's research plans. They thought you would be high up and safe enough to cause trouble before the others found you. They want it in the media. A trial on TV and the newsnets. They want the Democrats out, too." She made a hand waggle that showed that last part was chickenfeed by comparison.

"They?" Jude wondered aloud.

"Christian Right. Conservatives on both sides. Worried minorities. Moral majority. Lots of people are afraid of Micromedica," White Horse said. "Like gene therapy. They don't want anyone to have it, unless they can control it."

Jude wasn't sure he agreed with her but he said nothing. It was true that people feared Micromedica as one of the "supertechnologies" that seemed to promise humanity, a godlike power over natural events, but most people were as yet unaware that there was an application for the mind as well as the body—NervePath. But he didn't think that a scare story about that would be enough to cause a public outcry—too technical and remote from ordinary affairs—although all those who'd complained for years about government mind control would have a field day. First he'd need proof of misuse and the willingness of the authorities to use it without individual permission.

"Will you?" she asked.

"Will I what?"

"Investigate."

And save Deer Ridge, he finished in his own mind. *And probably save you and me. I'd be surprised if that wasn't part of the deal, too. And save the free world.*

Jude felt once again the sensation of branching paths and set destinies as he looked into his sister's face; sensed that he was walking into something there was only one way out of. One way or another it would be a nightmare. A mess. It would chew him up and spit him out and he might never get anywhere with it at all. She would see it as him paying his dues to their roots and all the time he would be doing it because he would anyway. For no reason except that it was the Thing That Jude Does. What did it matter how you reasoned about your reasons? You were a list of habits recycling themselves or you were on a great quest in your own head. Who the hell knew the difference?

He was so glad she was okay.

"With forces like that ranged against us," he said, "how can we fail?"

White Horse nodded. A small, sweet smile flitted across her face and she turned the five cards face down on the floor so that she could clasp his hand in both of hers. "The People will help you."

"The People had better keep their asses out of this one and look for a new home," Jude said, suddenly exhausted by the day. "I don't think it has a lot of mileage in it." He wanted to go home even as he was already in it. Everything he'd said and done in the last forty-eight hours made no sense to him at all. It was purely reflexive. Never mind Ivanov, he didn't think he could have passed an identity test himself at that moment, not even the one that checks for a basic coherent personality.

"Is there any vodka left?" he asked.

"I'll get it." White Horse let go of his hand. But he was asleep before she got back.

Mikhail Guskov read the reports and accompanying files on the Selfware test and put them aside. It was the early hours and he preferred to do his thinking in total darkness to keep his sleep disturbance to the barest minimum. Sleep was precious and slow to come, as though his mind had accumulated inertia along with its knowledge and braking its momentum was a longer and tougher job than it used to be. Some kinds of knowledge had much more weight than others.

The footage of the incidents was possibly doctored, he had to admit that. But there was no motivation for anyone to do so, unless someone involved was trying to play a joke. The suppressed hysteria in the accompanying text suggested that they weren't, unless it was Bill doing the writing, but Guskov had no illusions about Bill's sense of humour. The man had settled to do the job for a mere two million and a glorious *dacha*, a change of identity and a supply of young women from any dubious source that his old colleagues in Russia could provide. It was the kind of price that expressed only the extreme mediocrity of the ideals of such a human being as would accept it. Whereas, if this were a hoax, it was delightful.

Guskov had played and replayed the recordings to see the mystery patient, X, appear to disappear. He'd seen something like a half-tone version of X's body tear through the same space as Doctor Armstrong's fully fleshed one. But it was possible to see all kinds of unreal things on film, or in life: the brain was a marvellous interpreter, and he had long since learned not to trust it. But in this case the convincing factor came from the output data of the NervePath scanner; first where it had read Patient X, and later when it had taken information from Dr. Armstrong herself.

Guskov understood that they had shut down the system infecting her and he was glad, and more than ready to cause trouble for the Europeans if they attempted to interfere with his instructions again. It was one thing to run on with Patient X as the subject—admittedly a loss to his family but hardly to humankind as a whole—but quite another to allow a talent like Dr. Armstrong's to be thrown away for the sake of data. If this was as it seemed, then there was nobody more potentially useful on Earth than Natalie Armstrong. He had already added her name to his list and posted it on to Delaney. He wanted to be sure Dr. Armstrong arrived as a participant, and not as a subject. To that end Calum Armstrong had been an invaluable partner, convincing the Ministry authorities to release her into his care instead of holding her prisoner.

Tomorrow Guskov would look more closely at the Patient X data. It appeared to show that the Selfware system's ability to reroute all meaningful information paths to maximum efficiency had taken the INFINITY command to heart. Like all mindware, Selfware relied for its information on NervePath's inbuilt monitoring capacity, taking its data from the output signals that detailed the electrochemical status of the environment surrounding individual NP machines and also from the NP Cluster Wizards that sat "offline" inside gaps between the neural cells, preprocessing information from small, localized areas for transmission outside the host.

The key difference in Selfware, from what he could see, was in the way it communicated with the NP programming, asking for specific tests between local and distant connections and then authorizing operations on pathways and patterns. Because it occasionally required the NP to undergo individual nanyte replication, as the system first had when it entered the host and saturated the nervous system, it was capable of dictating the relatively minor definitional change that allowed the NP to reengineer its own sensitivity to other cells in the body, making their communications capacity something that Selfware could use. Thus Guskov believed that Selfware had co-opted not only the Central Nervous System, but every cell of the body, transforming them into neural components by spreading the NervePath technology into the wider somatic ecology.

Guskov guessed that it was a definitional vagueness of what constituted "neural communications," sitting somewhere in the NP programs, that had precipitated the event, allowing it to range far wider than Armstrong had perhaps intended. He wasn't sure about her intentions, now he'd read her files from the mental health institute where she'd spent two years, nor after Calum's own testimony about her view of reality.

Whatever her intention, by the time of the critical incident Patient X's whole physical being was both a functioning animal and a holographic, fractal processing machine with a fixed goal, donated by Selfware's own embedded design, of coming to an accurate and comprehensive perception of the physical world. Armstrong had wanted, Guskov thought, to find out if there was more to life than physics, chemistry, and biology. Maybe she had wanted to find God, or his absence. Guskov would be interested to know the answer, not only because of its interest as a question but for personal reasons. If it hadn't been for God and his works, Mikhail knew he would not be here right now, lying and thinking, unwilling for dreams to come. He turned away easily from such thoughts.

How you got something like Selfware into a strip of coding no more than a quarter-second in transmission and that seemed actually to work without fouling itself up in recursive problems was a feat that he would have loved to be able to perform. Either Armstrong hadn't fully understood what she was doing or she was a genius. It didn't matter to Guskov, he would have her on his side, and now, before the Ministry or someone like Mary Delaney got to her and filled her head with the crude, repressive ideas (culled from the same stock as certain views of God himself) that he had worked all his life to erase.

Guskov was sure, if Natalie Armstrong could be brought in safely, without any further dramas or accidents, that she would fully understand the scale and importance of his project, perhaps better than anybody else could. She might even be able to help him succeed, and that was a dark task now that they had been pushed into the closed environment for the final stages. Too hard, he'd thought often. The trap was closing too tightly. From such a place how would he manage to whisk Mappa Mundi out of the Pentagon's grasp? Would he have to resort to the use of partial systems as they had, to ensure its success?

His Pad timer beeped to remind him to stop.

He composed his body in a comfortable position and cleared his mind. Muscles relaxed and thoughts softened, flowering out of him. Empty, inactive, he invited sleep to begin. Like death, it would come in the instant when awareness ceased to exist. Every night he watched for it and effortlessly it slipped past.

Would Patient X still sleep, or had he passed beyond this world?

He let the idea drift away into stillness. Silence. Darkness.

Natalie returned to a blazing light, finding her body in the middle of automatically turning away from its glare. She was in a room with a high window, long and narrow like a slit in a castle turret, and the sun shone through it onto the bed where she lay under a sheet and a blanket. The industrial toughness of the sheets under her fingertips smelled of overheated linen. Her own smell was rank and animal and she was damp with the remains of a heavy night sweat. Across her back the tags of regulation pyjamas tugged erratically.

For an instant she had no recollection of the last fifteen years.

She was fourteen again, on the mental ward at McKillick, waking to another day of grey hell. In response she pushed her face into the pillow to get away from the light's contrary insistence that the world was a bright and wonderful place. The sheets, their smell, their feel, the smothering depth of the pillow's impersonal softness; this was safety in its purest form and she would stay there until Nurse Williams physically dragged her out into the hostile emptiness of the room. It was one of the rituals of every long and miserable day.

McKillick was a mixed ward, locked to the outside, but well-funded—which meant a high level of staffing, daily visits from doctors, and a reasonable standard of hygiene in the toilets and bathrooms. Natalie had never given them much thought before, but now, with a sharp reminder that seemed old somehow, like a distant view, she suddenly remembered what ward life was like, what she had to face.

Right from the first day she'd learned what madness cost, when nature forced her to trail into a cubicle, only to find a foot-long turd sitting on the seat waiting for her, clumps of soiled paper scattered over the wetted floor and stuck to the wall. Brown fingerprints pattered all over the tissue box and continued on some of the sink surfaces. Natalie had backed out rapidly, baffled, expecting to turn around and find herself in some train-station waiting room, its benches providing roofs for sleeping tramps. She went to the desk to complain and a nurse found her another toilet, with only a few scattered drops around the seat, which she wiped off with tissue and water. "I'll get it done," she'd promised, and left Natalie sitting there, the door unlocked, having to hold it shut against intruders by stretching out her foot and pressing hard with the inadequate tips of her toes.

Self-pity and disgust welled up in Natalie until she thought she was going to be sick. How could she be left like this—sat on the bog in front of total strangers, letting them lock and unlock her in places? She knew she should be doing things for herself, that it wasn't normal to be like this, but the will to muster *normal* was absent . . . even before the thoughts had finished her anger subsided into the squashy, grey void inside. Her foot fell to the tiles. Numbness filled her.

She was pulling her knickers up when a man opened the door and stood staring at her. He didn't seem aggressive, only irritated. His face made it plain he was waiting for her to get out so he could go. As she fumbled with her clothing and moved towards the sink he shuffled past her, unzipping his trousers to let go with a stream of pee that splashed up everywhere from the slippery surface of the plastic seat, spattering her dull grey skirt. She looked at it and realized she had no idea where the skirt had come from, either. She ran to her room, changed the skirt for a pair of tracksuit trousers, and put it in the laundry hamper. But she was new to the routine and hadn't put it in her name-tag bag, so whether it was hers or not that was the last time she saw it.

Without the need for concentration that such expeditions demanded the quietness of her single room quickly brought back catatonia. At least, so it must have appeared. Physically she lay on the bed, stared at the ceiling, breathed. But inside her head her mind was rushing, racing at a speed she couldn't name. In fact, there seemed to be no distinction between her and the speed: it was the only sensation she had, strong and powerful as a river, unstoppable as a damburst, as though something had broken deep inside her and the outside world, all of it, was rushing in, the difference in levels between them so great that the flood might never abate.

There was no room for an identity in the deluge. No single fact, memory, or image rose from the flow unless she were made to sharpen her attention. Then the force receded to the back brain, letting her drift for a time like a stick on the surface of a stream, talking to her therapist, eating her meals, going to the toilets with new vigilance. But she knew that while she did ordinary things, all the time she spent on them was time in which the dam was refilling to the brim and that soon she must surrender to the rush or it would simply take her when it was overdue.

Natalie was genuinely surprised when ten minutes seemed to pass and no one had come. She rotated carefully again, seeing herself as a sickly turkey on a spit of disappointment, and then recalled with a curious black humour that she was almost thirty. Drugs, cognitive therapy, and flat afternoons of the TV tuned to uplifting and educational materials specially designed to engage those of short attention span were years in the past. In a flash, the events of the last hours came back to her and she opened her eyes, laughing softly with relief and despair at the same time.

It wasn't possible. Like Jude's file with her handwriting on it. Bobby X couldn't have walked right through her.

That was her first thought. The second was that they would now certainly section her again and send her straight back to McKillick. She stopped laughing and pulled the sheet up to her neck. Perhaps it had been a dream? Maybe, the dark voice of her mind said, she was still in McKillick and had been all the time.

"Natalie, I mean, Dr. Armstrong!" Charlton said, hurrying over. "You're awake!"

"Yes." Natalie's mouth seemed very furred and thick, as though it didn't want to work.

"Can I have some water? What time is it?" And then, to check the truth of her suspicion, "Bobby! Where is he? What happened?"

"It's nearly six," Charlton said, pouring a cup of water from the decanter in the bedside cooler. Natalie saw Charlton was wearing a quarantine suit instead of her usual nursing uniform. Her voice was muffled by a mask.

Charlton handed the water over and didn't speak until Natalie had taken a sip. "Nobody knows where Bobby is. Don't worry about that now. I must call your father and tell him you're awake."

Natalie started looking around for her clothes. She was pushing herself upright, groaning when she suddenly looked back at the light. Six o'clock? She caught at Charlton's arm and snagged a handful of loose suiting with an almost fatal lunge off the bed.

"What time did you say?"

"Six o'clock. In the evening." Charlton suddenly seemed to feel that the pretence of normality was out of order. Her stiffly held posture slumped. "You've slept fourteen hours."

"Wait a minute." Natalie, her mind feeling clearer with every second, took another look around and then peered back at Charlton. "What room is this?" It was an unnecessary question, but she asked it to put the doubt in her to its final rest.

"Q-1," Charlton replied uneasily. "They put you in here after you didn't wake up. Dr. Armstrong—your dad—thinks that something in Bobby's experiment might have affected you." She glanced sideways, leftward, down, searching for a convenient lie. "There's been a lot of . . . well, he can tell you."

Natalie made herself sit on the edge of the tall bed frame and set her feet on the floor. "What's been going on? How can Bobby still be missing?"

"It's all right," Charlton said, without conviction. She moved out of Natalie's reach. "I'll fetch him." She slipped through the door quickly and it closed with a hiss of air from the lock system. There was no internal handle on the quarantine rooms. From the far corner the tiny lens of a camera watched Natalie get up and search in vain for anything else to wear.

There was suddenly a very strange sensation in Natalie's mind, as if thoughts were gathering like bees, a heavy swarm soaked in sweet and sticky autumn sunlight. She opened her mouth to speak to whoever was watching, but the buzz and pressure took all the words right out of her mouth, out of her thoughts.

Shit, she thought. *Here we go again. And I thought this was all behind me.*

Natalie felt herself changing, being changed. She was herself. She was not as she had been, not even a second before. A word stood out in her mind, like all surprises in the world rolled into one, a big candy-cone, roller-coaster, nuclear-detonation word: Selfware.

She looked at the camera's sad eye, saw the lens oscillate and shimmer as though it was falling through water, and then there was only whiteness: a pure arctic blindness that swept in from all sides quickly followed by silence, pressure, dark.

Apparently she woke on the instant, back in the bed in Q-1 with the sheet tucked over her. This time she decided to take the hint for what it was worth and use the time to figure out exactly what was going on outside this damned room.

Natalie was looking at a scan of her own brain on her Pad a half hour later when Dan came in and gingerly sat on the bedside, rustling in his overalls. It was seven and the Clinic's offering of dinner had gone cold on her table. She glanced up at him and grinned. "Heard you stopped it. My hero." She looked at the scan in its still form as she put it aside. It was not like her old mind at all. She wasn't sure what it was like.

"But the little bastards are still in there and functional," Dan said in a kind of a question, nodding at the scan image. "They still changed from the old MapScan system you had into NervePath." He made a few big gestures that Natalie understood to indicate a magician pulling a rabbit out of a hat, and he shrugged, asking her how such a thing could be.

She shook her head to show him she was no wiser. "I guess Bobby infected me. But they're there. And capable," she said and pushed the scanner away to reveal some printouts. She twitched the paper forward for him to see. "Here, look at these. They're my art therapy."

Dan flicked through the multicoloured images of Natalie's brain, some rendered with 3-D graphics. "Scans of your own head." He hesitated, awkward and uncertain with his knowledge and the situation. She could tell that he felt like a stranger to her.

He said, "That's a lot of activity and the scattering is—"

Natalie interrupted him with a wave of her hand, as though nothing was of less concern, hoping to put him at his ease. "Yes. This one I particularly like." She held out one in lurid green and red. "I name them after what I was concentrating on when I took the image. They're *estoire* art. Named after medieval maps. Stories of what I was thinking. Maps of my lovely inner life."

"What is it, then?"

"That one's called *Fuck Off!* And this one is Open the Bloody Door, You Bastards. And this one is *I'll Get You All, See If I Don't.*"

"I don't suppose you've got one called *FU Dan, You Drugged-up Sod, You're Fired.*"

"Well, I have, but I'm not telling you which one it is."

She put the pages down and watched him closely. No, Dan wasn't involved in deliberate subterfuge outside, but he had become a pawn in another game. It was clear. How it was clear she couldn't have said in so many words. Since waking the second time she seemed to have new senses without physical analogues. She knew, and that was all. Of course, she might be wrong, or dreaming, or psychotic. Time would tell. She wished they could both go home and get drunk.

Dan's normally cheerful face fell and he slouched, pushing the pictures to one side. "I'm sorry, Nat."

"Yeah, I know." She patted his hand and they looked away awkwardly from one another for a moment. "Anyway, the tests they're doing at eight should be final. I hope you've cleaned the flat."

"Like a new pin." He gave her an attempt at a cheeky grin and then stood up. He looked tired and his eyes were circled with grey. She knew that he was kidding her. There was no way the Ministry would ever let her back to the flat.

"You on the soft stuff again?" she asked, looking at the breakdown patterns in his blood. Shot sclera. Puffy face. Dehydration. He was fried. She wished he'd eat a decent meal and get some rest.

"Not so bad." He shrugged and broke away from her gaze.

"What's the Ministry doing?"

"They've been breeding," Dan said, moving to scratch his head with difficulty through the suit's tough fabric. "In fact, I don't think there's anyone left here who isn't an agent for someone or other, including the other patients. And the police have all mutated into Special Branch or big green army soldiers with guns. They arrested me, you know, for punching McAlister. Well worth it." He managed a real quirk of the eyebrows, "The MP was very butch and he wanted my number. I think he might be interested."

"You get all the luck." She smiled, although it cost her something because there was no life in his eyes.

"Natalie, I . . ." he began, suddenly serious, staring down at the thick coverings over his shoes.

She waited but he shook his head, unable to say what was on his mind. As he looked up at her and she gave him a no-problems grin she was suddenly chilled by the kind of gaze he gave her. His fringe didn't hide it.

Dan had sold her out. She knew it.

She tried to speak but she couldn't. It hurt, worse than a stab to the chest.

"Sorry," he said, and stepped through the door into the airlock without looking back.

"No, wait!" she cried and got up to jump after him. But she was too late. The door shut in her face and no amount of hammering and kicking it made any difference.

Shattered, she paced the room, trying to go back to that moment of revelation and pick it apart, to see if there was more, but there wasn't. He'd done a bad thing, something to do with her. Maybe he hadn't wanted to, but he was weak and he'd done it. He hated himself.

Done what?

Natalie knew she had to get out of here. She'd go and make him tell her. Was he in worse trouble than she imagined? Could it be something to do with that tosspot excuse for a human being, Ray Innis? But now her head was hurting. It was so bad that she had to go and lie down. If she hadn't been sure there were no sensory nerves in the brain she would have thought she was feeling the NervePath mites kicking up a feeble resistance against their premature silencing. They wanted to stretch out further and see what was to be seen.

As she agonized about Dan, part of the anguish was for herself. She had just become the world's most important guinea pig. It was a situation that wasn't without its danger. All it would take was one person with a working program and a scanner and she was easy meat for any amount of tests and experiments. The only way out was to physically destroy the NervePath technology *in situ* and she had no idea how to do it without killing herself. She knew that the only option she had was to play it safe with the Ministry until a chance came up and then to leave and run. And even that was a fairly hopeless-looking scenario.

For herself Natalie had a theory about what had happened in those seconds in which poor Bobby had become a transubstantiate. She'd been saving it up for when her father got around to visiting. The daughter in her who remembered him signing her off into McKillick wanted to see if it would make his head explode. To her surprise, however, when the time came they didn't talk of it.

"Dad, where's Bobby?"

"I have no idea," he said and told her of the call from Bobby's wife he had received, in which she was talking about seeing Bobby round the house, of being haunted, of demanding that it stop. "And you?" He was stern as always, stiff as a post, not rushing in to throw his arms around her or anything wantonly affectionate like that.

Natalie nodded, matching him calm for calm as payment in kind. "I calculate that I am approximately only forty-eight minutes behind him in terms of the Selfware run. So, if you were to reactivate it, I think I might expect the same to happen to me. I assume that McAlister has already mooted this in some meeting or other?"

"Cynical of you." But he nodded slowly. "Of course, I wouldn't sign for it."

She waited for him to say something about how it was that Dan had stopped the system, and not him or McAlister. But he avoided her gaze and glanced around the room instead, inspecting it for correctness.

"So, you're in charge of me now? I'm no longer legally sane, is that it?" But she knew the answer. It was much easier to get everything moving without consulting her about what happened. It wasn't that they were suddenly back to the bad old days. *More's the pity*, she thought, *because then I'd really let rip at you, you old sod.* Instead, she said, "But I don't suppose your disagreement will stop them for long. How interesting that the very stuff I thought would once make people that much more themselves has now magically removed my status of personhood in one easy move."

Calum looked distracted, and not by her attempts at irony. He turned, glanced at the camera, and then looked back at her and spat an emphatic whisper. "If there was a way out of this, do you think I wouldn't have tried it?"

"You," Natalie said slowly, enjoying her moment, which had been many years in the making, "have done many things in the past to change me. There was a time when I would have thought this would be your golden chance to fix me up once and for all: no depression, no mania, no crazy ideas. NervePath would be your toolkit and you'd be some kind of puppet master, chiselling me a new, scientific head." She paused. His face was grim and he was obviously angry at being spoken to like that. His lip twitched but he didn't speak.

"But I see I was wrong," she said and reached out to hold his hand, which he gave her with a glance at it as though it was rebelling against him. "I know there's no way out of this. And it's my own doing. Selfware."

"It's not your doing. This is Bill's work," her father said with a degree of hatred she hadn't realized he was capable of. His fingers clenched on hers to the point of pain. "Guskov."

Natalie freed her hand and activated her Pad. "I got a letter from him this morning inviting me to join you all in your American hide-away." She showed him and he glanced at it. "A closed environment? Times are desperate for the project."

Calum glanced down in a blink of confirmation and held his eyes closed a long time, holding her hand. Part of his complicit silence was shame at her condition, because in the past he had wished her different than she had been, and his wish had been granted. He laid his head down on her blanketed knees and sighed.

"Charlotte," he said, an appeal to another time.

Natalie squeezed his fingers. "It's all right, Dad. I understand."

"Do you?"

She didn't know. She didn't understand his kind of silent love, the sort that could watch what it loved grow distant and do nothing to stop it, waiting for it to return as though it were a kind of homing pigeon that instinct would bring back to the loft if only there were time enough. And when Charlotte flew the coop he'd kept the gate closed on Natalie in a perfect reverse of the same mistake. But her love wasn't like that. Charlotte. Dan. Jude. It didn't let things die forgotten. And therein was its weakness. It didn't let things go at all. So as he was here with her, but lost in the past, she brought the past with her into the present, a frozen dream, disconnected from the reality where it wanted to exist.

Natalie could see the truth of that. Everyone is a web of dreams. What we call reality is the master web. But beneath the fragile ropes that connect us, beneath that—her father was an old man, tired and beginning to feel that those things that had seemed important once were perhaps nothing but shadows on his mind. Charlotte left because she couldn't be herself with him. She would never have come back. He'd used his determination to face the hardest truth with logical calm as a shield to insulate himself from what he feared. But the hardest truth wasn't out there in the physical. It existed in the realm of communal fantasy, the world he'd pretended not to enter.

Natalie thought about Jude. Had she been part of a fable for him? Was he nothing more than a romantic illusion for her? What did these questions even mean, when the person who asked was the context of the question itself?

Outside the high window the lozenge of visible sky was blue, darkening to twilight. Natalie watched it shift through the range of indigo colours and then become black. She placed her hand on her father's head and listened to his quiet, difficult breathing.

Twelve

Mary read the reports on the British NervePath experiments and received Guskov's list from Dix's office while she was at the gym at six o'clock the next morning. The thing that stood out from her Pad's audio summary of them both was the name "Natalie Armstrong." Its unhappy appearance was so surprising, yet not surprising, as it filtered through her earpiece in the Pad's pleasantly chatty style that Mary almost quit cycling halfway up her Appalachian mountain trail. Only a jolt of willpower flipped her concentration back to the moment so that she drove hard with her feet and saved herself from a major bail-out, the back wheel spinning and slipping as the Velotheatre simulated a loss of traction on loose dirt.

She used the bike's controls to switch the pleasant views and motivating scenes of snowy peaks ahead to some long, flat highway instead and then keyed up the reports on the screens in front of her. The words superimposed themselves on the landscape in brilliant colours, highlighted red for links to other information, blue for news that had been culled from secure sources, green for everything else. Dix's squad of investigative writers were lavish with their energies, she thought, remembering her own time of service in those offices, conducting arrays of pilots across the networks, reading up on everything from starfish to pharmaceuticals in a day's work. The FBI stint had been a significant promotion. Even now the flush of pride at being singled out for fast tracking up the power ladder gave her an internal hit of energy strong enough to up her r.p.m. over the ninety.

She skimmed over the details of Armstrong's daily life she already knew and thumbed the text down onto the guesswork about the Patient X situation, grimacing at the dated stuff her ex-colleagues saw fit to include.

"Theories of quantum consciousness suggest it is a possibility that . . ."

They did nothing of the sort and they'd been discredited years ago as deep improbabilities, Mary knew. The old squad could learn something from the Feds' Special Sciences unit when it came to doing hard homework. Most likely they were including everything they could think of to cover their butts, a not-unintelligent motive in the Defense Department.

"The tape may be a hoax . . . created by a foreign agency who have captured Patient X and are using him to conduct their own tests . . ."

Now that looked a lot more likely than the guy vanishing into thin air. But there remained the odd coincidence of Natalie Armstrong's condition:

"Doctor Natalie Armstrong (attending physician) was attempting to sedate Patient X when the incident occurred. As a consequence immediately pursuant—"

Pursuant? But yes: Shalonda Neuberg, whose icon headed this section, was an ex-legal. Dix was always writing terse little notes to her about writing in plainer American . . .

". . . Immediately pursuant upon this Dr. Armstrong lost consciousness. Examination using MicroScan revealed that her Grade 2.1 NervePath semi-prototype nanyte structures (installed four years previously under MoD sublicensee program for theoretical researchers) had, at some time since her last examination, been switched for Grade 7.8 NervePath Electrochemical Relayers. This incumbent NP structure was identically programmed to that of Patient X prior to his disappearance, and the system was active. Dr. Armstrong's system was deactivated forty-one minutes after inception, under the authority of Mikhail Guskov, acting through his proxy, Doctor Calum Armstrong . . . Natalie Armstrong remains in a Q-1 containment . . . may be our only surviving test subject of an advanced and exhaustive NervePath process . . ."

Mary didn't know when she'd stopped pedalling but she found herself stationary, staring at the big screen and wondering if Guskov knew more about this than she'd first thought. It was exactly the kind of idea that made her skin prickle with foreboding. If she screwed up on protecting Mappa Mundi this late in the day, by underestimating him, she was finished.

The saboteur at the Clinic had never been apprehended. His handiwork was more than a touch suspicious—implementing an untested and idiosyncratic mindware system that Mary'd never heard of until the day before. A system written by Natalie Armstrong, who was now infected with it. Some odd kind of theory about consciousness that Mary didn't understand lay behind it. She only knew that the Brits had consistently turned it down for development. But by all accounts that woman would be a prime candidate for trying it on herself anyway if only she'd had access to the right level of NervePath, which allegedly she hadn't. But there in cold letters a foot high—Grade 7.8, the latest and best, unlicensed for use outside Defense Department jurisdiction. No way she could have got her hands on it.

Which made it look as though the whole thing wasn't a hoax, but that somehow Natalie Armstrong had experienced cross-contamination. Could Armstrong have engineered the whole thing? That, too, was possible.

Mary hated this mass of uncertainty. She got off the bike and towelled herself down, switching the displays back to the alps so that her coach wouldn't realize she'd been working on the job. She took a long drink from her water bottle. A spare drip ran down her chin and tapped, icy, on her chest. Really, she hadn't much doubt that Guskov was involved in this setup. Using him for so many projects and for so long was a big risk that Dix had taken. Until now he'd never put a foot wrong, and that was maybe reason enough to suspect that he was hiding a big private agenda. She'd read the file before it went missing. She knew he was capable of outplaying maybe everyone else in the league—but he wasn't going to outplay her.

No way was Natalie Armstrong going to join his Mappa Mundi elite team. Not as anything more than a test subject of minor interest. And in the meantime Mary was going to find Patient X and screw the lid down on Guskov so hard he wouldn't be able to breathe without her knowing it.

With her new information dealt with she was forced to return to thinking about the reason she'd come for the mind-clearing properties of a tough physical workout in the first place. Jude had been to see Armstrong as well.

Mary knew that from her culpable little mole, Dan Connor, who was the easiest make in the world. With so many natural ways to shape him the NervePath and Contour-ing seemed cruelly excessive. He'd sung for free about Jude's visit when she'd pressed him, and now she was even aware—and, she hated to admit it, bone-crushingly jealous—that Jude had been off sleeping with the Armstrong woman.

To her certain knowledge he'd been a strict loner since the last girlfriend took flight for fields more lucrative and glamorous: California bodywork, butt-length blonde hair, burning ambition and all—her lazy mind had never suited him, although he hadn't noticed it until she'd played the You Don't Pay Me Enough Attention card and had him sent off the pitch. Jude was a focused man, obsessed with work, kind and thoughtful, but no girly girl would ever find him productive in the end. Mary'd thought of seducing him many times, keenly aware every time she saw him of what a crush she'd had on him the first six months on the FBI assignment, but she'd always held back from it. You never knew when that kind of dynamite could blow up in your face, and she'd needed to be sure of him. His going out with Lucinda had been irksome, but understandable—Lucinda was comfortably generic and no threat to Mary in any sphere she cared about. But the idea of him with another woman, especially a smart one who was as theatrically far-out-looking as Armstrong . . . Mary ground her teeth and poured the rest of the bottle of water down the back of her neck.

The most aggravating thing was that he'd almost told her everything last night, but he'd clammed up at the last moment and she hadn't dared push him in case he got suspicious. She could try again today, however. He'd looked strung-out to her. He'd have to tell someone soon. She was going to be there when he did, and then she might even find it in herself to feel gracious about him and Armstrong, sympathetic, a pal who could share the locker-room intimacy. She could pull that off—but it would have to be quick, because she'd decided now that the only way to exert sufficient control on this whole situation was to shut down the British end of operations herself. Meanwhile she'd distract Jude with the biological defense viewing, a handy and legitimate venture. She might even strike lucky and Perez herself would find them a new case to look at that took his attention right away from anything that touched on Mappa Mundi.

Mary opened the door of the Velotheatre and tossed her bottle and towel into the hamper outside. Her coach came rushing up to check times and fat readings but it was all academic to her. She let him earn his money and then left for massage and a full wax with the one therapist who could be relied on not to try and make small talk. Waxing was agony. It was the perfect preparation for a day of sharp action.

Natalie slammed the wall with the flat of her hand and turned to face her father. They were standing in the kitchen and it was the fifth time in ten minutes that she'd tried to call Dan.

"They're stuffing up the phones," she spat, meaning the Ministry, who had the house under close scrutiny, no doubt. Even closer than when she'd been here with Jude. Thinking of that odd, enchanting evening made her all the more furious because she was here again so soon after. But the event was over and gone, and instead of Jude there was her father, standing there morosely, hardly listening to her and wishing he was back in his bolt-hole at the US laboratory where everybody was in awe of and obeyed him.

Whatever Selfware had done for Natalie, and she knew it was a great deal, it hadn't improved her exasperation threshold.

Her father looked up from the tea he was making—very slowly, precisely, pedantically, it drove her crazy—and nodded. "You should feel lucky to be here. I had to pull in every favour I was owed to have you released. And tomorrow we're leaving. You should sort yourself out."

Natalie picked at a join in the wallpaper as she leaned against the Aga and tried to stop herself, but the fascination of the paper's resistance and texture was too intense. "You haven't even asked me if I want to go. The letter says it's a choice, not a summons." She was aware of sounding like a spoilt brat. Under the ministrations of her fingernail the old paper finally tore. She stuffed her hands in the pockets of her jeans and snarled silently at Calum's broad back.

"Will you go?" He turned and put the teapot and cups on the table.

Natalie didn't want tea. She didn't know what she wanted, but it definitely included getting out of this house and going and doing something very drastic and final and preferably quite violent. She sat down and the thwarted desire stretched out into her feet and began to tap and drum them against the floor. One foot played four-four time, the other five-eight.

"Oh, stop it!" he said.

She pressed her toes into the stone flags and held onto the table with her fingers.

"Seeing as going is about my only chance to have any say in what happens to me, then yes. What choice was it? But I can't leave Dan like this, without saying anything. I have to see him. You know they're going to fire him when they find out he was using at work."

"And quite right, too."

"Mmn." She knew that was true, but Dan hadn't had anything to do with the sabotage and she was worried that they were going to pin it on him. He was the most convenient scapegoat.

"What do the readings say this morning?"

Natalie snapped back to the present and looked at her father. Consulting the scanner readouts had become like consulting the bones or the cards and it was only the second day.

"Hidden Dragon," she said and poured her tea out first, letting him wait for the really strong stuff. "Do not act."

He glared at her.

"Well, they may as well be I Ching readings for all it tells us. It might say that. It's what I think, and isn't that a good enough readout for you?"

Calum looked like he was ready to walk out, but he made himself sit and pour his own drink and listen to her. She could see him having to force himself into it, just like she was, this civilized veneer.

"I have to get out of here," she said and took a sip. "I can't stand this. I hate it."

"Work will take you out of it," he suggested and she saw that he really meant it, because that was why he worked all the time.

"Yeah," she said, not sure, and got up, taking her cup with her. "Well, I'll try that."

She heard him sigh behind her but as she reached her blackout room on the top floor she heard his own study door shut firmly, the echo rising up at her back.

Hidden Dragon. That was exactly it.

She brought down her screen and called up her own data readouts and their accompanying maps and graphics, surrounded by the black and white isobars of her earliest attempt. She'd got her wish, made it at last, she thought, as she stared at the vastness of information hidden in its forest of lines, waiting to be understood.

The post-Selfware reading said many things about her that never used to be true. It showed her responses were faster, her hemispheres precise in their balance and switching of dominance, her memories more acute. She was now able to recognize more delicate degrees of change and process them. Her sensory processing was as refined as that of the most sensitive humans ever recorded.

Her mind didn't seem different to her. Perhaps a little more colourful. But then, all her memories came through this new lens of the altered Selfplex. How would she know if she'd changed? Between being a child and herself now she'd changed, but it was only the difference itself that made it noticeable. The degree. Minds only remembered and noticed significant alterations—everything not in that category caused them to create the illusion that the world was mostly stable. The illusions were the direct result of who dreamed them. As she had changed, they had changed and taken her memory with them.

A faint draught of air stirred against her neck. She felt it signalling to her skin with the exact shape of what had displaced it. Somebody else had entered the room.

"It's worse than you think," said a voice behind her, quiet and withdrawn, flutelike with an inhuman shallowness of tonal variation. "Or it gets worse."

"Bobby!" She spun her chair around, caught in a mix of fright and delight.

He was standing there, not in the clinic regulation clothes but in his own T-shirt and jeans, work boots on his feet. He slouched, half corporeal and half a blurred mass of flat colour that shifted idly; a sketch in progress. He gave a limp shrug, to apologize for his sudden appearance. Natalie could see it was a huge effort to sustain even this level of definition. With a pull she could feel in her own bones, the exultant dance of the atoms was trying to drag him into its chaotic glare. The lure of it made him dazed.

"I was right about the information and energy," he said morosely, thumbs hooked in his waistband, his head bowed. "The problem is the switching. Take off the information, it's hard to put it back. Too much and—" He paused and looked up at her. "Time's the trouble. You forget."

The fact that he had materialized wasn't lost on her. But because it was definitely him and because Natalie could understand what had happened to him she wasn't afraid; she marvelled at this even as she had to push it aside to get on with what had to be done.

"What's going on?" she asked, getting up and stepping towards him uncertainly.

Bobby circled and kept his distance, moving as cautiously as a cat trying to stalk, uneasy with his new perceptions.

"Matter," he said and looked through the window with evident curiosity, as if there was a tank of exotic animals behind it, "is energy plus information. You and I, our bodies are matter. Our minds depend on that. There is no part of mind that is not the flux of information and energy at the classical level. At the classical level matter of certain density may not share space with other matter. You and I cannot cross over. But at the quantum level, all things may pass through each other. But passing through causes a change in states, a change of information. Every change brings loss, creates anomalies. Losses pile up. Anomalies grow. Forgetting occurs. Without the information being isolated from the process, how can what was be made to the same pattern? It is similar, but it is not the same. New organization is possible, but old patterns are gone forever." He turned back and straightened himself. "The longer you stay at a quantum level, interacting with lower levels of organization, the more you lose. Perhaps it's better."

He looked around the room, reading it, looked at her, reading her. His face was tired and sad. If there was a person less enamoured of his own vision of reality, she'd yet to see it—and she'd seen many.

"Where do you go—what do you mean? How can you exist at a quantum level?" Natalie asked.

"You can walk through that door," he said. "I can walk through things that are solid to you. There's a lot of space, once you understand. At that level, there's all the space in the world." He grinned in a watered-down way. "The words don't say it right any more. They weren't designed for this." His gaze said that there was no way he could explain it to her. She wasn't built to understand.

Natalie didn't know what to say. Tragedy seemed to have distilled in him. Something had happened that was more than the actions of Selfware, she knew it. "You went home," she remembered that much.

He nodded. "Never again."

"They didn't see you?"

"They did," he said and shrugged again. "Maybe I am dead. I will be. What's it matter?" He gathered himself with a shake. "But I came to say sorry for causing it to come on you. That was my fault. I didn't know. But it was. I see you've not come as far. That's good. You don't know too much. You don't see it all like I do." He nodded at her and the trace of a smile ran across his face. "Good."

Natalie wanted to ask him a million questions. She had no doubt he could have answered everything she'd ever wanted to know about the world and human understanding. As he stood there, however, he swayed a little bit, not only back and forth on his feet, but more profoundly, all his tissues vibrating slowly in the motion of unseen tides. His eyes, meeting her regard, looked on another place at the same time, a place that he created and was destroyed by with every instant that passed: mountain becoming sand.

"What will you do now?" Natalie asked, feeling cold. She crossed her arms, but it was no better. She would have reached out to comfort him but he didn't want it, couldn't have stood it, the whole of his skin said so. Unknown people had stolen his life and, she realized, were on the verge of stealing hers. His answer, all too human, confirmed her perception.

"Make them pay. Be sure they don't have it all their own way. Will you?"

Natalie felt that she didn't know anywhere near enough to make a decision. But, at the same time, when did anyone know enough to be sure? She thought she had an idea about why Selfware had been run.

Bobby said, "It's a test. To see if it would work on anyone. Your system has the ability to match any mindware system to the brain it finds itself in. They'll use that, because at the moment their work can't fit itself to the subject. It's all but useless except as a rewriting tool that can fit one mind into the same shape as another. That's what they did me for."

Natalie agreed. He'd just spoken her suspicion aloud. She said, "Not far left to go, then, until Mappa Mundi is completed." She glanced around and then back at his despondent figure. "Did you read my mind just then?"

"Not really," he said. "There's a point where the scale of what you notice changes and then it's easy to see." His bravado of a moment ago seemed to be a futile gesture, she thought, a fist shaken at the back of a victorious enemy, and he agreed.

"I can't think of anything else to do, y'know," he said, hands outstretched. "Here I am, still alive, in my way. No family. No ties." He laughed in a hollow, breathy way, experiencing the irony. "I see—but underneath it all, the one that sees is still me. Ian. John. Detteridge. But what does that mean? Nothing, really. He was an idea in my mind. He's dead now, but he can't have been me, because here I am."

He turned fully to the window and looked out hungrily at the greying sky and the street. "I need something. I want to live." He grasped the window frame and she saw his skin whiten where it pressed against the painted wood. His breath came faster now and his shoulders trembled, his voice deepening with passion.

"And I want that to mean *something*. I know I could do a decent thing now, given the chance. I would. If I knew what it was. If it'd do some bugger a bit of good. But if that fails then, well, I'll do the next best and give the bastards a seeing-to they won't live to regret. I'll have had a reason. I'll make it make sense. It has to. You know why?"

He turned back, head low as if he was drunk and unable to lift it.

Natalie shook her own head.

"Because the truth is that we're the only fucking things that mean anything. The rest is a dance on nothing and when it's over it won't any of it have mattered a damn."

He grinned with half his mouth. "That's your answer, isn't it? Right there. Why you made it. You wanted to see if anything existed apart from you. You wanted to know if it was waiting to get you. It ain't, but it'll get you in the end anyway. Ah, fuck it." He wrenched himself around. "I wasn't going to tell you that. Why did I? You wanted me to. I owe you now."

"You don't owe me anything, in fact, it's the other—"

"No," he said. "No. I know what I've done. I'm the end of your dream. That's a kind of killing. Now I owe you and I like that idea. You can tell me what this thing is I'll do that can help. When the time comes."

Natalie didn't know what he was talking about but his eyes were vacant and his body was slowly losing its shape. She felt as though she'd been punched and hit, such was the shock of what he'd said. She felt sorry for him.

He faded and vanished right before her eyes, shaking his head at her.

Don't pity me, pity you, she heard him say, the faintest whisper. *You've a way to go yet.*

Jude's morning in the office was anything but easy. Perez kept him chewing over the Florida case when he should have been out investigating leads from Mary's still-untouched boxes of paperwork. Then Mary herself arrived, late and crabby from the beauty salon, looking like she'd spent a million dollars to transform her natural prettiness into a take on Mount Rushmore: stony and middle-aged. She wanted to keep the damn' papers to herself for some reason he didn't figure out, and then, when he told her of his potential new lead in Atlanta, she went ballistic about how much time he was spending loafing around on fieldwork and how much admin he'd dumped on her desk and how she was always having to explain to Perez exactly what they were spending their budget on so fast. And it went on like that for what felt like hours.

Then Perez took a fresh interest, hearing about the Atlanta tip-off by earwigging around their door, and agreed with him that he *should* go and check it, because after all they'd spent on the case it was only fair to try and salvage something out of it instead of looking like a bunch of losers who couldn't detect their own asses with both hands. Mary took umbrage, thinking this was a criticism of her casework on the laboratory seizure where she hadn't made any arrests, and then they all started arguing about the significance or pointlessness of trying to get hard evidence against the Russian.

Finally Perez shouted over the top of them, "Just cut the crap! Delaney, get your reports done and on my desk. I want all that paperwork screened to the last dot. Westhorpe, get your butt on that Atlanta flight and don't be there one second longer than you have to. I'm sick to death of hearing that goddamn' Ivanov name. I want him in court or out of my life—forever!"

Meanwhile, in the pauses, Jude was trying to contact a lawyer for White Horse.

By the time he did leave for the airport he was wishing he'd not bothered going in at all. The lawyers' office had taken a message. They would call White Horse to discuss the options, although they were prissy about it, because he wasn't able to tell them anything and they thought he was wasting their time. He thought they'd wipe him from their minds as soon as the link dropped. His sister was at his apartment, with orders to go nowhere and do nothing until he got back, but he didn't think she'd obey. Why break the habit of a lifetime?

And then he got the chance to try and decode what it was that Dan was trying to say about Natalie; what was the guy on? Jude couldn't try and contact her directly, he knew that. Instead he'd sent his best datapilot, Nostromo, on a search, using all of his security clearances, to try and gather information. It came back every half hour, turning up a blank every time.

The flight was mercifully short and uneventful. He reached the meeting point, at Café Primo on Peachtree, ahead of time and waited, tolerating the wet heat with grim patience and frappuccino, but as the minutes ground past and his man didn't show Jude began to sweat. He left it ten minutes and that was enough of feeling conspicuous among the hardened mall shoppers and the table of smartgang girls in the corner, where his suit made him look like an out-of-work actor. Call it spy paranoia, but he'd had enough.

He stepped into the mall itself, into the shelter of a secluded seating area marked off by potted sago palms, and called the number. No reply except his answering service.

At the CDC office line they said Tetsuo had gone out for lunch early but wasn't back yet. Maybe he'd stopped off at the pet store. He had a fussy kind of cat that needed lots of coat products and he was always buying it things. They weren't too bothered, because the lab was running a long-scale test and there was, in any case, nothing for him to be doing right this minute.

Feeling increasing foreboding Jude checked back with Nostromo's secure server where he kept sensitive data on informants and went to the listed address, getting the cab to drop him two blocks south of the building. He didn't expect Tetsuo to be in. He didn't expect to find anything. Wrong on both counts.

Tetsuo's walk-up was open. Not obviously, but Jude saw the slight shuffle of the shadow between door and frame as he got to the top of the step and waited after ringing the bell. A hot breeze, sluggish with exhaust fumes and the smell of rotting fruit, moved past him and into the shadows of the entryway as the door swung inward easily at his touch. The soft burr of the air-conditioners dulled the noises from the street. Jude's nostrils flared as he stood on the threshold, trying to detect anything.

"Tetsuo?"

The door opened onto a long corridor with a room at the end and doors leading off it all along its length. The end room was the kitchen, identifiable by the cupboards on the wall which he could just make out. At the sound of his voice a long-haired, giant-sized, and obviously gene-tickled blue-point padded into view on the threshold. It watched him unblinkingly with golden eyes the size of golf balls in its handsome, black-whiskered face. Jude had never seen such an enormous cat. It was the size of a human child. Its long tail, plumed with glorious silvery and lavender fur, hung low, tip twitching in sudden snaps of annoyance.

"Hey kitty," he said, hoping it wasn't aggressive. He crouched down and rubbed his fingers together in its direction.

It made an unhappy, basso "mmrow," and turned away in digust, dissolving into the lilac shadows.

Jude stood up and drew out his gun, sliding the safety off. He could smell fish and something else he didn't like. He began to try rooms, searching them one by one. The first was the man's bedroom, tidy, his desk covered in papers and diskettes in stacks. The second was the bathroom. The third was the living room and it was dominated by audio equipment and a vast climbing gym. Silvery fur coated the sofa and the gym surfaces like spider silk.

The kitchen was last. Knowing the cat was already there and not nervous he assumed no other strangers were in there either. A draught blew the front door shut and he jumped, fresh sweat springing onto his skin. He put the light on.

The cat was crouched by Tetsuo's head where he lay, spread-eagled and cock-eyed, between the units and the cooker. It was licking and grooming one of its owner's eyebrows with long, white teeth, half-heartedly nipping the skin. Jude scowled in revulsion. The back of the guy's head had been blown off and it looked like the cat had been making free with the bits.

Jude waited a few seconds for his gorge to settle down, then drew out a pair of vinyl gloves from his jacket and went to check if the body was still warm. It was cool on the surface, so he must have come straight home and been killed immediately. Blood and matter coated the doors behind him and had spread on the floor in a spray. The smallest spatters there that the cat hadn't bothered to clean up had dried in the arid air pumping from the con unit.

He searched Tetsuo's pockets quickly, found his Pad and a toy mouse with an elastic tail, nothing else. Had he come back here to get whatever it was he'd promised Jude?

Looking at the cat was making him feel sick. Jude moved to get its scruff but the cat sidled away from him with a sly look and padded across the body quickly, like a big fat lady trying to dash across the street in high-heeled shoes. It preceded him, looking back as he shooed it out of the room, but as he searched the cupboards and drawers he caught sight of it often, standing just near him, looking up with dilated pupils, calculating.

He found the cat chow and put a dish of it in the hall. The cat ignored it and continued to follow him from room to room, never closer than leg-length away, never further. Occasionally it made a disapproving sound and once he heard its claws ripping at the ropes on its playposts behind him as he moved through the living room. As he glanced at the gym the cat sprang with surprising lightness to a shelf at Jude's waist height. It rubbed its cheek against a wooden column and followed his gaze as he looked up to the higher surfaces. They were all clean.

Jude gathered by the lack of fur that the cat hadn't been up to the top in some time. He was admiring Tetsuo's dedication and invention in making the construction when he saw a toy, fur matted, lying on its side on the highest section where a long tube ran up to a small platform covered with plush carpet. He reached up and brought down a fat teddy bear with both eyes missing and most of its seams ripped out. Kapok stuffing hung in clumps here and there. At the sight of it the cat half-heartedly pawed at Jude's suit leg, its claws snagging the cloth. He swore, pushed it aside, and stuck his finger into Teddy's chest. There was something in there.

It was a small cardboard carton, labelled with CDC marks that had been hastily scrubbed out with a marker pen.

The cat made an ominous, caterwaul-type revving sound in its throat and he tossed Teddy at its head, "You can shut up, owner-eater."

Inside the box was a fine-foam container, about an inch thick. Inside that was a vial of smart-lead-lined safety glass of the type used to transport Micromedica products, sealed. Jude put the empty box back on the gym's high board and placed the foam container in his inside pocket. He called the police, anonymously, as he left, locking the kitchen so the cat couldn't go back in. It followed him to the door and stood staring after him.

Whoever had killed Tetsuo might not be far away. They couldn't have looked for anything, or Jude wouldn't have found it. They could even have planted it there. He didn't know. It didn't matter. He had to get back and test what he'd got. There was no help for poor Tetsuo now, especially since the cat had probably eaten most of the ballistics evidence. He shuddered at the memory of it sitting there, vacantly licking the man's face.

Outside, the sweltering sun had begun to go down. The air felt like a warm tongue, lying against Jude's exposed skin. He called a cab and got the hell out.

Nostromo still had no answers for him about Natalie or Dan. He called home. White Horse recognized his personal number.

"Everything's fine," she said. "Mary was here to see you. She's going on some trip and wanted to let you know. I told her she could stay, and she did a while, but then she had to go. She said she'd see you day after tomorrow. She's going to stay home and do the paperwork."

At least something was going right.

Late that night, just before they closed, he delivered the vial to one of the lab specialists at his offices who could deal with BSL-$_4$ and other organisms.

"You don't have any idea what it is?" Nell Rush looked down at the innocuous vial with deep suspicion.

"I think it came out of the CDC."

"Unauthorized?" she seemed unwilling to touch the foam packing with more than the lightest support necessary. "This looks like nano to me. Microware. Maybe not. He worked where, this informant?"

"Antiterrorist."

"Shit," she said and closed up the packing over it. "Okay."

"Nell." He caught her sleeve.

"I know, I know. Don't discuss until I've seen you. Give me tonight and tomorrow. I'll try and check it by then, but I have a ton of other work on from Meyer and his partner. Ghetto eugenics."

"Thanks."

"Don't mention it. Just keep sending the cheques."

Jude stood in the Washington night outside the building and looked at the sky. No stars were visible, only a wash of light pollution reflecting from the clouds. Out there somewhere a lot of things were happening, and he was glad right now that he didn't know any more about them. But as he turned his eyes towards the road and started walking to the Metro he couldn't shake the memory of the vacant stare of that big, fat cat.

Thirteen

White Horse knew of Mary, although they'd never met. Mary seemed pleased to see her, and annoyed when she heard that Jude wouldn't be back until later that evening. White Horse invited her to wait, thinking he wouldn't be long—he'd said by seven. They sat down together in the white room and let the TV play quietly in the background. White Horse drank coffee. Mary had tea, which White Horse couldn't find, but Mary knew the kitchen better and located it first look.

"Huh," she said, looking at the box. "Run out again. He never remembers to get it at the store." She was going to leave the empty pack out, but on second thought picked it up and put it back in the cupboard, manicured hands adjusting its position perfectly. White Horse glanced at her own hands, burnt and callused, but she made no effort to hide them. Mary could think what she liked.

At first the conversation was tough going but, White Horse realized, once they'd got onto the only subject they had in common—Jude—it was clear that Mary was closer to him than she was. She tried not to notice the possessive jealousy that grew on her as they spoke; it was her fault the years had gone by in silence. At least this terrible set of circumstances would give her a chance to fix that now.

Mary, relaxing in the couch, began to tell her about their long-term pursuit of this one guy, omitting details she said she couldn't mention because of their secrecy. White Horse could see how much the flippancy of her telling revealed the kick she got out of having access to power and inside information.

"We first came across him when we were trying to convict these Russian mafia thugs for running steroid simulants into their pet basketball players in the Leagues—you know they're big on sports here. These drugs, they'd been altered in some real clever way to fool the body into thinking it needed to produce more of particular chemicals itself. Then, after, there was another set they used to filter them out of the bloodstream, so that whenever testing was carried out there wasn't much chance of them getting caught. You know, after all that nandrolone hoo-ha was finally sorted out the legal ranges for a lot of "natural" chemicals had to be recalculated and they played on that . . . so, there they were, trading players and making money and Jude and I finally catch up with them in Detroit where they've got a warehouse full of this stuff and a laboratory set up in one corner churning it out . . . but the guy who orchestrated it all, Ivanov, is already long gone on to something else."

She paused and finished her tea and White Horse waited for more. She thought Mary'd assumed she wouldn't understand some of it and was deliberately dumbing it down but she didn't say anything. She wanted to know about Jude.

"No way to get a conviction on him, as none of them would talk and there was no documentation. So, a few months later we're looking into some suspected small-time anthrax brewing, down in 'Bama where they still think that either they can use it to finish the government or, when the time comes, donate it to the national defence effort if the A-rabs decide it's time we were napalmed for blasphemy or whatever." She shook her head of bright, copper curls and snorted a laugh, in the way White Horse associated with white politicians ready to make a condemning statement against some person they'd got it in for.

White Horse smiled and nodded, to show she agreed how stupid they were.

"So, we'd got these four real home boys down at the police station and one of them decides he's gonna be a patriot. No way is he gonna take the rap and not drag down the foreign guys who've set them up, over the Internet, with the necessary know-how. He starts talking about this group we recognize as mafia names, traders in all sorts of survivalist shit they bring over from Eastern Europe, you know, knives, ex-military guns, and those tool things and all that *Living in the Woods* baloney . . ."

White Horse nodded. She knew it very well. Mary meant International Publications, and she had some of their books. It wasn't the best woodcraft or country living as White Horse would have understood it, but it would have worked. They also had regular magazine issues on violent revolution and other activist, anarchist stuff. The way Mary talked she didn't think much of it.

". . . And we trace them through the Net to the places they're getting the original seed kits from and who is it but Ivanov's mob, another branch, ferrying chemicals and biological agents out of old Soviet installations and with old Soviet scientists working for them back in the homeland. A real industry of old weaponry and old ideology!" She grinned. "They were our biggest bust—we worked them through the mill together with the ATF and Customs. Jude did the best on that. He was the one who went undercover and got to know them so we could make some easy setups. His Russian is native speaker. Does he talk Cheyenne?"

White Horse was disarmed by the question. "He can," she said, truthfully. Then she added, "But he doesn't."

"I hear you had a falling-out a way back," Mary said, eyebrows raised in curiosity. "But it's something he doesn't like to talk about. Are you getting it together at last?"

Her interest seemed too blunt to White Horse but she made herself answer. "We're talking."

"Good," Mary crossed her long legs and twitched her top toe playfully. "To be honest, Jude takes work much too seriously. When he took off to his mom's . . . which parent is it you share?"

"Father," White Horse said, thinking *She must know that already, or has he said so little about me? Us?* Even though her image of Jude had been one of a white boy who'd sold her out, an image she knew was melodramatic and fundamentally untrue, she was disappointed by this. Had he been able to pretend she didn't exist?

Mary was blithe, "Yes, when he took off to Seattle I was glad, really, he had to chill out; even though it meant I was left on my own with the latest Russian thing—baby-doctoring, would you believe? The man has his fingers in everything."

"So why haven't you arrested him yet?" White Horse asked.

"He has government protection." Mary pulled a face to indicate that she thought that was too bad. "He must have. Every time we try to pin him down the evidence vanishes, the people shut up or die or . . ." She waved her hands around. "Hell, anything to make sure he escapes. Had plastic surgery, too, in his time—changed passports, houses, cars, everything."

"Why?"

"I wish I knew. It's a bitch." Mary rolled her eyes. "I think he must be bringing in expertise that the government likes to use, pulling strings they can't officially touch—there's more than one of that type of guy out there. They're allowed free rein as long as they occasionally drag in something that the DoD wants or needs. And if our investigation touches on those things, then they keep us out."

White Horse smiled in agreement: she knew about that. But she was curious; the machine and her house were on her mind. And her likelihood of survival. She rubbed carefully at a burn and tried not to appear very interested. She wasn't sure if Mary had followed this line for a reason, if Jude had told her everything.

"If you tried to pursue it, what would happen?"

Mary smiled, "I don't know exactly. Probably end up in an accident or get pulled in and fired . . . blown so low that nobody'll believe a word you say about anything. End up in 'Bama trying to make bombs to stick in the president's car and writing articles for the *National Enquirer*." She looked at her watch, "If he doesn't get here soon I'm gonna go. I have a stack of work waiting at home."

"More tea?"

"Just a glass of water."

As White Horse picked the mugs up Mary said, "Forgive me for asking, but, what happened to your . . ." and she indicated with her finger an area around her own neck, ears, and hands.

"There was a fire at my house," White Horse said. "Electrical. I got out okay. It's not serious."

"Looks bad."

"I have pills."

"Staying over while your place is fixed up?"

"Yeah."

Mary followed her to the kitchen and leaned on the breakfast bar, watching White Horse pour herself another cup of coffee. "Hey," she said, "you know, I'm not being a hundred percent with you. Jude told me, you know."

White Horse glanced at her and saw her making a goofy kind of face to cover her embarrassment. Under her pale skin a pink blush rose and fell briefly. She gave White Horse a sympathetic look and took the offered glass from her. "It's difficult for him, you know, to offer his help investigating like that. His job is on the line. Maybe his life, if it's as bad as you think." Her blue eyes were deadly serious and tiny lines around her coral mouth dug deeper.

White Horse felt guilty. "If we don't do something then the People will lose the land," she said finally.

Mary sighed. "Yeah. I understand. My parents got kicked out of their old home when the place was redeveloped for a much better paying market. They didn't understand that the lease meant they didn't have to leave. They thought a few hundred bucks was a good deal for a bunch of ex-coal pickers." She shook her head and her gaze was distant, misty. When she glanced back she smiled and gave a firm nod. "Luck o' the Irish, huh? You've got to try and hang on." She drank the water and handed the glass back. "Thanks. You know, if I can help you at all . . . you're going to need more than a shit-hot legal, someone who's not afraid of the worst that the government will throw. Someone who can pay for protection. You need a journalist. I can make a few calls, let you know."

"Thanks." White Horse showed her out, feeling that Jude must have done something right out here. "I'll tell him you were here."

"Tell him he'd better call me or there's trouble!" Mary waved from the hall.

She had a nice smile, White Horse thought.

Dan scrubbed the kitchen floor on his hands and knees. The soapy water was as hot as he could make it. His hands were sore. He felt a bit of an idiot, like some Catholic going through the motions in the stupid hope that it was going to make a sod of difference to what he was, had done, would be.

It was the last thing in the flat to clean. Everything else was polished, waxed, scrubbed, washed, beaten, aired, laundered, ironed, sent to the dry cleaner, or thrown out. He was exhausted. The clock on the wall that had ticked away every hour he'd lived there with Natalie said it was an impossible four in the morning. He was exhausted, but he wanted to carry on. He did the last four inches again. He didn't know what he'd do when he got to the last foot or so. Wait for dawn, the time to die.

Natalie would never come back. Dan sat on his heels and wiped his forehead with the back of his hand, feeling its spongy heat with both satisfaction and despair. The Ministry had sent her off with her father and he'd heard, from the rumour mill that was the staff lounge, that she'd agreed to go to America, on some faster, more perfect version of the big project. She hadn't called him and he hadn't been able to get through to her number or the house on the Mount which, until that man came, she'd avoided like the plague.

The way she'd looked at him in Q-1, though. She had been changed. She'd just *known*. He was a bastard. He'd told on her to that Shelagh and he couldn't tell her about it, but he hadn't had to. That system really had made her more intelligent or something. When she'd looked into his face—he shuddered and bent down to the floor, rubbing as hard as he could at a tiny yellow mark on the flooring.

"Out, damned spot," he said to himself. "Out, out, out," and laughed, because he was a fool and fools had to say this dumb thing and make that fatal mistake and then laugh about it. But Lady Macbeth had been an ambitious bitch, and that hadn't been his problem at all. Lack of ambition, really. A fatal kind of happiness in his mediocre lot.

Where was Natalie? He had to explain it to her. He had to tell her about it and fight whatever the fucking Shelagh-witch had put in his head. Yes, he knew it was NervePath all right. Didn't need a scanner now, did he? Obvious. A series of blocks in place much stronger than his own willpower would ever have been able to generate. He was well fucked, and only Natalie could help him. And he had to apologize. That first. She had to forgive him. He didn't like to think about it if she didn't. Joe and the others had called, but they were no good. Friends were what counted and he knew he only really had one.

Ray Innis had left him some messages about a meeting.

Dan hadn't gone. Now he had to watch the street. Screen calls. Wonder where it was safe to walk. Standing Ray up was a very uncool idea. At least the undercover men outside and loitering had kept him away from the flat so far. Dan was being closely watched. They were toying with the idea of arresting him formally. He knew that. It was only a matter of time before they got enough evidence together, and then he'd get no chance to see Natalie.

He paused and tried the numbers again. Engaged signals.

"Shit!" He threw his Pad into the hot-water bucket and it vanished beneath the bubbles.

Grumbling about the pain in his knees, he got to his feet and wiped his hands on his trousers. Before he had time to think it over he was getting into his coat, putting on his boots, and then going back to fish the Pad out and put it in his pocket. He went into Natalie's bedroom, opened the window, and climbed out down the fire escape into the back yard, which let out onto a narrow cobblestone alley between one row of houses and the next.

No doubt he'd been spotted but he didn't pause to find out. Walking as quickly as he could he headed down to the riverside and then along the dark banks of St. George's Field at the water's edge, where the path ran to the bridge. Above him wind moved restlessly in the horse chestnut trees and to his left the river's high waterline flickered in hungry, fast-moving ripples. He saw a couple of cars on the roads ahead, street lights casting their glow down on empty pavements. It was only a mile or so.

Ahead of him Skeldergate bridge reared its smooth arch and cast black shadows. A movement made him hesitate, but he thought it was only the reflection of the street light on the water reflecting upwards to dance on the brickwork. In any case, it was time to cross the river. He ran out onto the deserted parking lots that covered the land between him and the path to the bridge. A camera, mounted high on a metal post, tracked him silently and he felt safer, though what difference some video of his murder would make he didn't know.

He was sweating hard by the time he made it to the road, and the coat was unbearably hot, but he felt he needed its weight and protection. Midges scattered in his face as he ducked under the branches of a sycamore. He brushed them away, hands still stinking of soap, and then saw a figure moving towards him from the other side.

It was coming at a fast walk: a man, in dark clothes, face turned to the footpath, hands in pockets. Dan thought it was the same man who'd waited on the street corner for Natalie, watching her at the church. Different clothes but that bullish, squared look, the mechanical movements . . . he glanced behind him and two more people were on the pavement, a couple, walking together briskly, holding hands. They were about fifty yards back. No cars came. It was quiet. He could hear their steps. He didn't stop, but his heart began to hurt with anxiety.

He met the lone man first. He looked up, and it was the same man and he recognized Dan in the same moment that Dan recognized him, the gap between them closing to less than ten feet. Dan sprang into the road with a sideways jump that tore something small in his knee but he kept running for the opposite path. Behind him he heard the man swear and grunt into faster action. But then a woman's voice cried, "Hold it, you there!"

There were sounds of running now but a hand descended on his collar, heavy as a lead ingot. Dan twisted around, ducking. His coat came off and he squirmed out of the reach of the other huge hand that came for him and found himself up against the railings, looking into the ugly, determined face of the unknown agent. But at the same moment the two behind caught up with them.

"Who the hell are you?" the woman demanded, flashing some kind of Ministry ID in the weak light.

The man holding Dan's coat backed off a step and threw it on the ground. His eyes darted back and forth, looking for a way out, but the younger man was holding a gun and so he cautiously raised his hands instead of trying anything and gave them all a cold, searching look.

"Mr. Connor, where are you going?" the woman asked in a tired voice.

"It's a free country," he said weakly.

"But you are not a free man," she informed him. "You may not contact Dr. Armstrong. That *is* where you were going?"

Dan felt himself redden, "It's very important that I—"

"Go home, Mr. Connor," the man said. "Agent Day will call you a cab."

The woman began doing something on her Pad as the man started barking fresh questions at Dan's assailant.

Dan looked around at the quiet, predawn city. He felt only despair at the idea of going back to the flat and its last untouched square foot. Work and blankness loomed ahead, days and nights of being watched like a dog, tethered, and then caught. Maybe prison. Natalie was going soon.

While they were all involved with each other he saw his chance. Turning as fast as he could, feeling a sharp, shooting pain in his knee, he took hold of the ironwork balustrade, threw up one leg, pulled the other through, and was suddenly plummeting down.

Before he knew it he was in the water. It was far colder and more gritty than he'd expected. He thrashed wildly and broke the surface, finding himself close to the far bank. He tried to swim towards it, but his boots were terribly heavy and his knee sent stabs of fire so acute they made tears come to his eyes. Slowly, inexorably, he watched the bridge pass over him. He kept reaching for the bank, but his legs were caught in a faster, deeper current and they spun him around, drawing him further out. Soft, tangling things tugged lazily at his feet.

Dimly, as he fought to keep his head above water, he thought he heard a shot and some shouting. Then there was another splash.

It was irrelevant—he had to keep trying for the bank. And he did, all the way past the cycle path and the warehouses until he was parallel with the path's turn to Bishopthorpe. There he managed to catch hold of some reedy things growing in the slow edge of the outer stream and hang there like a fish in the cold, seething current. As he tried to pull himself to the land he saw the inevitable rise and fall of hands and a blunt head drawing towards him through the black water.

Scrabbling, he found earth and mud under his hands at last and, feet scraping the sharp stones of the bank, got himself out of the water. Ducks, frightened off their night roosts, flurried around him, quacking loudly. Dan stood up and instantly collapsed, knee hot and agonizing as it doubled beneath him.

He vomited water and shivered. He realised his Pad was back on the bridge. The man was coming.

He was so bloody angry with himself. What a complete balls-up. What a total, pathetic, stupid, piss-poor waste of time he was. Probably he deserved it. Even so. He didn't give a shit for what he deserved or didn't deserve. Natalie deserved better and he should warn her about Shelagh Carter and her tech before it was all too late for that as well as for himself.

Turning onto his stomach he got up on hands and one knee and began to crawl towards the distant lights on Bishopthorpe Road.

He hadn't even reached the hard surface of the tarmac when he heard splashing and grunting behind him. The agent caught up with him easily and, with a stamp of his shoe to Dan's back, slammed him flat against the tough grass.

"I think you've caused me enough trouble for one night," said the dull voice, as though nothing could be less interesting.

Dan braced himself for a kicking but no final blow came. He heard calls being made to arrange for collection and then all the air was knocked out of him as the man sat down heavily on his back.

"Right fucking toerag," he said, almost amiably, and then sighed. "Shelagh wants to see you." It was the only phrase that carried any information over and above the content of its words.

Dan realized that this man was afraid of Shelagh, loathed her even, but he didn't answer. He was fighting to get even a tiny amount of breath. His ribs felt as though they were about to break. He'd lost. As he heard the roar of a van barrelling towards them and then the harsh shriek of its brakes he wished Natalie's system had been capable of creating telepathy.

Natalie had been sleeping a lot. Since the accident she had slept, she reckoned, at least twelve hours a day and much of it was deep, slow-wave sleep that she couldn't have woken out of if the house had exploded. It was her brain, catching up, she thought, with what the Selfware had done, doing a bit of smoothing work around the edges, tidying, getting used to the new plan. Whatever it was, each time she woke up she was new.

On the day she and her father were due to travel to America she woke at five in the morning, feeling alert. The old house was quiet and the street silent, but she had the sensation of her ears ringing in the aftermath of a sharp outcry—foxes or cats? A voice, she seemed to remember, a shout.

She got out of bed and went to the window, listening, looking out. Her room faced the garden. This was the wrong direction.

Sliding out of her nightshirt she found jeans and a T-shirt, socks and shoes, and padded downstairs. The hall night lights were on and the security guard by the outside door was asleep in his armchair, lightly snoring. Beneath her father's study door the light shone brightly and she heard his old keyboard tapping in fitful deathwatch rushes. She paused on the last step to tie her shoes and then quietly opened the door and went out.

She could smell grass and the river as the wind blew over her after its journey across the racecourse. The sound of cars was just audible from the major roads a mile away where trucks and cargo land-trains moved rapidly under the last of the night. At the gate a weary dark-suited figure came to meet her.

"Where are you going?"

"Out for a walk. If you're going to come you'd better stay quiet and at least twenty yards behind me," she informed him crisply. She had no doubt that he would obey her and so he did, trailing after her with all the enthusiastic spirit of a popped balloon.

The dying echoes of the dream sound were very faint. Natalie followed them without questioning how she knew that one turn was better than another when they came to a crossroads. They quickly covered the long grass of the Knavesmire and then moved through close-built terraces of red-brick housing to the main road where the tanker from the brewery was just pulling in to the Winning Post's parking lot with a stiff sound of hydraulic brakes. Natalie crossed it without hesitation, passed a laundry and a baker's, a Pad shop with its shutters down, and began to jog along the cycle track by the riverside. Here, where the path bent along the bankside, her intuition went dead on her, as abruptly as if its batteries had run out. The trees, the movement of a pair of lone ducks, and the trudge of bored walking as her minder arrived were the only sounds.

She saw that the grass here was wet and there was a muddy slide between it and the bank. Feet and hands had moved in it. There was a recent tire track. Nothing more. She glanced up at the bridge, some two hundred yards off, and saw a police van there, parked up, its lights dull.

She wondered what she was doing out here in the early hours and looked across at the opposite bank towards her old flat. Since she was so close she thought she might as well go further down to the footbridge and see if Dan was in. It would be her only chance, said the older section of her mind. A new part said that Dan wasn't even in York any more. The muddy grass was the closest she could get to him now.

Ignoring that intuition and the guard she turned downriver and carried on with her walk. She was still a way off from her own street when she saw police cars parked there in a thick cluster at the corner, with figures standing around. She wanted to go and ask questions but a strong feeling of unease made her avoid taking that turn at the last moment. Instead, she went along a parallel road and began making for home again, listening to her pursuer scamper each time she reached a corner and went out of sight.

She knew that Dan wasn't at the flat. She thought he might have gone to the shop and went to look there, but the only inhabitants were the clerk and the cleaner, sweeping listlessly along the magazine racks. They said hello and, knowing with certainty that she would never see them again, she found it hard to close the door after her and step outside.

So, she thought, *are you going to admit it at last? He's gone. Gone.* A shiver racked her from head to toe. If the police didn't have him, then where could he be?

Dawn was bright as she reached the house on the Mount. Natalie was puzzled, uncomfortable, and cold. She took her shoes off, left them in the hall, and walked up to her mother's old room, which had a bay window that overlooked the race course. The bay had a small, cushioned seat and Natalie took it, staring over the ground she had walked, trying to understand what was going on, wordless and trackless, in her own mind. She kept returning to the image of the black water and the mud-streaked ground, the smell of soaking earth and . . . floor cleaner. Yes, industrial soap, that's what it was. It had a clinging perfume, like sickly sweet flowers.

Where was Dan? She had no answer. She began to construct a reason to return to the Clinic before they departed. She would find a way to get a message to him and reassure him that whatever he'd done . . . but what was it?

If Dan had been in the river and was gone—but she didn't think he was dead. She didn't get that sick, gut-deep plunge she'd felt when she'd heard about her mother; even before the rest of the message had arrived, with the first word of it, she'd known then. The reasons had been trivia, nonsensical detail around a great, hard fact. Later, the reasons and the detail became the only important things; the final connections and explanations that capped a story told in full at last, the ending so unexpected and brief that anything to lift its sheer banality was something precious.

Natalie turned her attention away from the window and looked around the room, its grey softness just beginning to colour with warmth.

There was an ornate set of shelves, carved with mice and grapevines, which held an almost complete collection of *Tatlers* since 1980. *Vogue* was crated and stored in the loft space above. The journals that Charlotte wrote for—*Hello!* and *Abroad*—were not so privileged and lay in untidy heaps and cardboard boxes filmed with dust because the cleaner had been warned exactly by her father as to what should and should not be touched and had taken his strict advice absolutely to the letter.

Postcards from all over the world were stuck to the wallpaper with ancient Blu-tack. Natalie, as a child, had arranged them there as reminders, so that when her mother returned from her frequent trips she might see them and some of her restless spirit would be calmed and allow her to stay at home. It was a spell that hadn't worked.

Natalie pulled down a picture of New York and turned it over.

"Dear Nat, a tiring day touring the publisher's and then meeting all the special celebs. Very late now and am just writing this before I call through the copy; saw a great dress today and thought of you—am sending some shoes along by post for you but I'll probably see you before they do! All my love, Mum."

In between the shelves Charlotte's amateurish photographs of places sat in cheap frames. Natalie looked at a faded print of Reichenbach Falls, an ironic smile trying to rise to her face, and put herself there, behind the eyes that had taken the picture.

Did she know she was going to die when she boarded the airplane?

How could anyone in their right mind take a two-seater around the cape in those conditions? Did she love us? Why wasn't that enough?

Natalie listened to the clock in the kitchen softly chime six-thirty. Somewhere the answers lay, lost to her, hidden in a distant cranny of space-time. In their absence, she'd made up a story from the map of known events. But all maps are patchy and so all understanding is a story and no more. Natalie herself was a story, a construct of reasons and connections and ideas tethered together by narrative links she'd chosen to believe. What if none of those were right?

Natalie put the postcard back, but it wouldn't stick. She laid it on the desk. Everything she'd done from the moment of Charlotte's lightning-lit and fatal sea-ditch had been fashioned by that sudden voltage out of nowhere. It had fused her determination to find the Truth and set her out to do it. But her counsellor had told her this was only a sublimated wish to recover that lost love, and wasn't that the sad reality? A horrible, random event had shaped her dreams and here she was with a fresh headful of her own handmade denial, dreaming and wondering.

Playing the flirtatious woman with Jude was no more than a clinging reaching-out for love, wasn't it? And Dan was the reality—gone.

She emerged from her reverie in the blink of an eye.

Dan had tried to tell her something before the Bobby test. What was it?

He'd asked before about scanning. Why?

Natalie got up from the seat and went through into her study. She pulled up Jude's files from her disk and looked them over again.

Of course these programs certainly weren't going to be the only ones circulating now such things were possible. Why wait for perfection when a quick hack would serve your purpose? This was madness in a jar and no doubt there were other crude commands: listen and obey . . . forget . . . memory erasing would be easy if you didn't care whether the results left functioning minds or not. Add spoon and stir, like Jude said.

If Dan was the victim of this technology then that would explain why he'd done what he'd done. And she was even less safe than she'd thought, sitting around with a brainload of open gear. She had to plug that socket before someone plugged it for her. The trouble was, she didn't know how to do it. Any shutdown orders could probably be hacked open again.

She heard doors opening and closing downstairs. People changing shifts. Soon it would be time to leave. Her opportunities were already limited enough.

In her kit she had a prototype scanner. It was packed but she went to fetch it. As soon as she was ready she loaded it with the latest version of Selfware, typed a specific timed-run command line into it, pointed it at herself, and pressed the trigger. It should take her to a point just short of Bobby's fatal discontinuity.

Soon she'd be smart enough to figure out what to do or spaced out enough not to care. It was a Dan kind of solution. It made her smile with nostalgia, while inside she felt as bitter and angry as she'd ever felt in her life at the unfairness, the stupidity, the greed of it all.

Jude had an early call from Nell, the lab technician, that woke him up. She left him a message asking for him to meet her out on the Mall. It didn't surprise him unduly; she disliked talking about anything remotely unorthodox close to the Special Sciences building and he had no doubt that whatever Tetsuo had put in that vial was going to be that.

He lay in bed, looking at the clock, listening to the distant traffic noise, remembering with a grimace the scene in the Atlanta kitchen. He was good at keeping cool in a situation. Not so good a day after, when it reappeared with all its gruesome disgustingness intact. Not that he'd known Tetsuo personally, except as an associate spoken to very occasionally, paid out of the standard bribe funds, but he'd met him before. The sight of someone who had lived and breathed being reduced to a heap of meat amid their own personal surroundings—it made him nauseous. He didn't want to think about it, but he couldn't help it. And that cat—what a weird animal. But nothing more than an animal, so why did he find it the most repulsive thing he'd ever seen?

He had to get up and shower to stop the train of thought going any further.

By the time he was out, White Horse was already dressed and making coffee.

"Mary's going to find a good law firm for me," she said. "And a matching journalist."

"Mmn hmmn." He knew Mary could, if anyone could. It was kind of her to offer. He called her, but the answering service and the office detailer told him she'd gone for the day, on home-working retreat, and didn't want to be disturbed. It was okay. It gave him time to talk to Nell.

"What're you doing today?"

"Not much," White Horse said. "I got a videoconference link to the Deer Ridge community meeting this afternoon. I think I'll take a walk this morning."

"You should stay here," he said, uneasy at the idea of her moving about alone.

"Sure," she agreed, with the look that meant she had no intention of doing any such thing.

"Keep your Pad on all the time. Call me," he told her, sliding into his jacket and adjusting his gun holster. It pulled sometimes.

"You use that a lot?"

"No," he said.

"Keep it clean."

"I do."

"Good." She turned back to reading the papers. "It says here that some Micromedica trials in Britain have proved that the NervePath neural technology works *in vivo*." She glanced up at him as he paused there. "Think that's us?"

"Probably." The information only made him wonder what the hell was going on over there. There was no new message from Dan, or Natalie, or anyone. He didn't have a contact who would know. He was stuck. He shrugged. "I'll try to find out. Meantime, don't get into a mess."

She snorted as he left and called out, "By the way, Uncle Paul has sent you some more of that BIA peanut butter surplus. Eat smart, play hard." She laughed, quoting the Department of Agriculture line. "You won't have that in Washington, he says. I put it with the rest of the tins under the sink. When you gonna eat it? It's only good for another few years."

"I hate the stuff," he said, instantly feeling the sensation of gloop stuck to the roof of his mouth, tiny chunks wedged in his molars and gums. "You can find some charity to give it to."

"You're his charity. It's a care package. Washington has sophisticated food, not enough calories for you guppies." She sniggered. They both knew that Paul was tremendously fat due to his views on nutrition as insulation against most of the world's ills.

"I'm grateful, really." He gave her a cynical wink and closed the door, wondering what on Earth his family were on. He *was* grateful, but confused. Peanut butter. Paul sent a big tub of it every other month. Jude had enough to send on a third world rescue mission. He should find someone who liked it, but he always forgot to.

The newspaper article made him send out Nostromo to find all articles on the subject and get any translations necessary for him. He was just getting a list up when he arrived at the grassy area of the Korean War Memorial and started looking around for Nell. The oversize soldiers had a semidissolved look; they seemed to have emerged from the earth, mud creatures, and to be subsiding back into it at the same time. Close to the man with the radio pack Nell's small, neat figure was walking slowly, eating a Danish out of a paper bag. Jude touched her elbow as he drew alongside.

"Good morning."

"Jude." She swallowed quickly and dabbed at her mouth with a paper napkin. "Here, before anything else," and she pressed the vial, warm from her pocket, into his hand. As she met his gaze a look of fear and loathing flitted just under the surface of her good nature. "Don't ever bring that kind of stuff in again," she whispered. "Not near me. Christ, I didn't even know such a thing existed. Do you realize it took me until this morning to figure out what it does?"

Nell did look grey-faced and haggard, it was true. He apologized and offered to buy her a better breakfast but she declined. She made him put the vial in his jacket and said, "It's not hazardous as it is now, in that state. If you break the glass you won't die of anything." She threw the uneaten half of her pastry into a wastebin. "But if you combine it with just about anything else you've got a better plague than the Black Death going."

They began to walk up towards the Capitol. Jude waited for Nell to explain it in her own time.

"It's like Micromedica gear, right? But some sort of hybrid thing. It's not just a bit of inert engineering, it's almost alive. On the surface it looks like a small organism, say a kind of a virus, but this is much bigger. It has similar sorts of properties: invade cells, use the host body to replicate big numbers—and that would cause symptoms, just like a virus infection: sneezing, coughing, all that large-scale histamine production, et cetera. Okay, but it has another function. I think this is just like a jacket, you know, a coating to get something else inside the body."

"A delivery system?"

"Yeah, but a very clever one." She took a deep breath and let it out steadily. "This thing has an inside big enough to take several viral cells, or a bacterium of quite a size, or some drug molecules, or, you know, anything in that range. But, and here's the kicker—" she glanced up at him with worry lines etching her face "—whenever it replicates itself, it also replicates whatever it's carrying."

Jude snorted and shook his head. "No way," he said. "That's not possible. Did you test it?"

"Of course," Nell said shortly. "I tested quite a few things on it and stuck it in a tissue culture and in a bath of everything from acid to Jello and, believe me, impossible or not, when it has the resource it can make a perfect copy."

"What do you mean, resource?"

"Anything won't do. Water, saline—it has to have a variety of organic and inorganic components. It needs a bodily host, although it survived a good hour in weak acid. I don't know. It's tough." She was shaking her head now, digging her hands in her trouser pockets, scuffing the ground with her shoes. "Whoever designed it was like an Einstein of the biologicals. But don't you see the problem? Massive replication—carrying anything? There must be a trigger to release the contents—I don't know what. A certain population density. I don't know. But this way you can make ordinary bugs into killer infections; released into the body at supersaturation and the immune system has no time to defend. You could die of a cold."

"But if it was carrying some kind of drug," he said. "Wouldn't that be a rapid cure for something?"

"Could be," she agreed. "But you know what? Micromedica applications are small enough to fit inside it, and it replicates them, too."

They stopped, as one, on the path and stood to one side to let a couple of joggers go past. Jude had to think about it for a minute.

"Is it infectious?"

"You betcha. Droplet, skin contact, contaminated water—the whole range of chances."

"Is the reaction to it severe?"

She nodded. "You'll be coughing and sneezing hard enough to make a decent aerosol."

"Mmn. Does it ever die?"

"Jude, this thing has a Micromedica interface. It accepts command lines. It'll die when you tell it to."

"Programmable disease?"

"Programmable delivery system," she corrected him. "And think about it, Jude, there's even more. This stuff only targets human beings, nothing else in the animal world. It recognizes gene sequences. It can even tell you from me."

He stared at her. "You can't do all that with something that size."

"Biochemical engineering has come a long way since you studied it." But Nell's face was hard. "I don't know what they're going to use this for but I hope to God it's someone good who gets to decide. Is it ours?"

"I got it via the CDC," he admitted.

She nodded. "Okay. Okay. That's me done. I'm out. See ya around." She held up her hands and backed away. "And next time you find something, don't think of me first."

"Listen, Nell," he began, "I'm sorry . . ."

"No problem, man." She turned and started heading for home.

He watched her go and then moved to sit down on a bench not far away. It was still only warm out, but the sun was rising strongly into blue skies, heating the city into another sluggish, steaming day. No wonder they'd killed Tetsuo for interfering with that; but who? And come to think of it, had they really had to kill him? The vial hadn't been that hard to find. Perhaps Tetsuo was a bit of scheduled maintenance they'd been planning for a while already, so they didn't even know he'd taken anything, they'd just thought he was going to talk.

There was no way to know if he'd been rumbled or not. But the gene sequencing parts and the type of engineering sounded very like what Ivanov might have been doing in Florida, only a bigger operation. No wonder Mary had found nothing if the government had cleared him out prior to her arrival on the site. They really should do a better kind of liaison between departments—but then, nobody talked about this kind of thing. Ever. Was it illegal? Several international treaties said so, but here it was and Jude was pretty sure it was American. It might even have been the thing they'd been invited up to Dugway to preview, the United States' legitimate response system to a bioterrorist threat.

But it was a hell of a weapon. Nell must have felt like she was witnessing the first-ever nuclear fission test when she set eyes on it. More so. Potentially it had the finesse of a scalpel, compared to the hammer blows of conventional bombs and guns. The idea of genetic recognition, multiple payloads—Jude's head didn't feel big enough to handle it. He sat and stared at the people passing, watched the grass, thought nothing, then got up and walked in to work, the vial in his pocket so light he couldn't feel it.

Fourteen

Mikhail Guskov looked around him at the interior of the Sealed Environment where Mary and her associates in the military had prepared his centre of operations. Its small dimensions, tightly stacked efficiency, and walls painted with technical symbols and instructions resembled nothing so much as a series of Egyptian tombs. He well realized that this could be the last place on Earth he would see, and it was ugly.

His own office was the largest of all, but still a rat-trap of a place, the ergonomic chair and state-of-the-art computer systems consuming all the available space. In an attempt at humanizing the place a guest seat, barely functional in size, had been left in one corner and a wispy-looking plant with variegated leaves that seemed to enjoy artificial light squatted on the desk. He had one of the soldiers remove both.

Mary had sent him a note to let him know that the standard issue of Deliverance was going to be showcased to the National Command Authority this week at Dugway, and later to those agencies the DoD decided should know. That would leave precious little to the imagination of those who discovered it, inevitably, postleak.

Some lab in Asia could knock up a serviceable version within months, maybe even extend its capacity to the private version he'd created secretly, using his alternative laboratory contacts, in a few more.

Then everything would fall apart like a house of cards and his decades of work and effort would go for nothing in the storm that followed. The Mappaware technology would no doubt become nothing more than a tool for manipulating people, either singly or in vast populations, ideology doled out with the drinking water and social obedience to any dictat determined by the nearest passing breath of wind. It was exactly what he wanted to prevent.

As he sat down in the control seat and looked around him, again the vague doubt assailed him that what he had made was as much the cause as the effect of the particular drive to create technologies of mass control or destruction. In quieter moments he allowed himself to consider it in the cold light of his own intellect.

Guskov didn't feel responsible for their situation. That was a power well beyond his control. History held the reins that drove him. If a technology existed, someone would use it. If their need demanded, they'd do what they thought they had to. Everyone was a damaged article and power accelerated their decline, so anyone with access to a power like Mappa Mundi would be sure to employ it to further the replication of their own version of the truth. He'd known that from the outset. Understanding it was part and parcel of accepting the burden this knowledge put over him, why he'd risked everything to be here, in this tiny airless room, locked down with his team under the scrutiny of the Americans. Because he understood his own human nature and the relationship it had with technology itself, he considered he was worthy of taking on the role of world-maker. Of course, the logic determined that the fact he'd come to this very conclusion ruled him out as a worthy candidate.

A worn smile crossed his face and he began to activate his systems, bringing them online for first testing. It was far too late for the philosophical high ground. The first to succeed in engineering the Memecube was the one who had the best chance to forestall misuses of the same ability later, and that was the truth. He knew he was only a person, like every other. He knew he was going to fail to some greater or smaller degree. Only time could reveal the extent of it.

The AI subsystems began running their start-up procedures. He watched them interface with the automated, insensible circuitry and slide quickly into command. The first of their language systems painted him a message on the wall opposite, which acted as his screen.

READY.

Most of what worried him right now concerned Dr. Armstrong. He guessed that the Americans wouldn't want her to be on the team and would attempt to take control of her. He himself wasn't sure that she was fit to come here—she hadn't allowed anyone to treat her condition, and the initial readings were inconclusive without a lengthy series of tests and interviews to back them up. He needed to maintain an upper hand. He needed to be sure nothing happened to her. She might even know the truth of what had happened to Patient X.

His thinking was disrupted when the major in charge of the Environment showed him how he would communicate with the outside world: everything went through official channels. There were no external lines. This left him with the final problem that he needed Natalie Armstrong or her Selfware system to solve, if it were solvable.

It was too late to carry on with his air of mystery as far as she was concerned. As he had with her father, he was going to have to let her in on the game while he still had his networks outside this wretched bunker to help him. Thanks to the Deer Ridge test all his better plans had been thrown on the junk heap. Now it was going to be the fastest mover and the smartest manoeuvre that won the day.

Once the presentation was over he took the opportunity of his few remaining hours of freedom to take a car back into the one-dog town that passed for the closest civilization. Parking up out front of the single row of stores he made a few Pad calls, using an encryption and transmission sequence he'd been saving for this moment. As he imagined how much it would annoy Mary Delaney to know he was calling, but not whom, nor what he had to say, he found himself sighing through his smile. He wasn't a fool. He knew that the Americans would get him in the end.

Natalie had packed her small bag of personal items and was waiting for the airport car to arrive and take her away when she received an urgent signal vibration from her Pad. Thinking that it was Dan at last, she whipped it out of her jacket and flicked it on, walking away from her minders and into the relative privacy of the old wood-panelled living room. The boards creaked under her feet as she realized it wasn't from him at all, but that Guskov had got hold of her personal codes and was sending a ream of stuff she most likely didn't want to know about. Still, it was furled with urgency banners, so she glanced over it as her disappointment waned.

What he'd sent her was a series of alternative joining instructions. They included intricate plans for shrugging off her plainclothes police guard and allowing agents of another organization entirely, which she suspected must be essentially criminal, to shepherd her onto a set of private planes and automobiles to the final destination—an address in Virginia she didn't know anything about except that it sounded like the middle of nowhere in the Appalachians. She asked Erewhon to run a source-verification check to get confirmation that this was indeed from Guskov and as she waited she turned to read an attached document that he said would explain everything about this "hasty action."

"Are you ready?" one of the policemen asked, poking his head around the door.

Her father had departed two hours earlier. Such was the secrecy of their plans that confirmations of travel weren't issued to the staff on the ground until it was time to move. When Calum's joining instructions came they'd discovered that they were to be shipped separately. Natalie made an equivocal movement of her head, "In a minute."

She sat down in the deep velvet of an ancient armchair and began to read. Watching her quickly bored the detective, who looked very annoyed, but withdrew, tortoiselike, into the bustling efficiency that had taken over the hall as they checked and rechecked the contents of her luggage. Vaguely, Natalie thought this was what it would have been like in the old days when grand families had staff. A right pain.

When Natalie understood the scale, the ambition, and the sheer bloody arrogance of Guskov's plans she sucked in air through her teeth with a regular carpenter's whistle and shook her head.

"You'll never get away with that, mate," she whispered to herself in her best builder's voice. "You'll need more than a few two-be-fours and a nail gun."

The plan, for all its complex detail, was simple. Guskov was going to use the military superpowers to fund his personal crusade against the incursion of regulation into ordinary lives and the spread of global politics with its increasing trend towards dictator-like legal and social measures. Mappa Mundi was the culmination of years of his hard labour, a tool that he intended to use to empower individuals to choose their own destinies, their own personalities, and their own minds in the face of what he saw as an inevitable development of centralized control methods.

Natalie didn't get the whole picture in a single pass but she realized what it meant for her in the short term: either she was about to be recruited into the private army he was building to finish the dream, or she was going to be the lab rat who served the governments and she would also, potentially, be his victim. Her choice, and there was no third way. Unspoken laws of *omertà* permeated every suggestion in the document. Now she was in the game whether she liked it or not.

She put the Pad away and wondered instantly if Guskov had had a hand in Bobby's experiment—to such a person nothing was too extreme. And if he had, was his interest in her only as a subject for test? But there were too many questions and no answers: even if he succeeded and Mappa worked as he hoped, how would he disperse it?

How would he get his hands on enough NervePath? How would he get it past the authorities? How, how, how?

She decided Jude could forget his guilt for having involved her in this. She'd been involved a long time before. And there were others also implicated—her father, of course, who'd never bothered to inform her if he knew of the greater goals of the project, for one. And Dan, for another.

Where *was* Dan?

Natalie stepped out into the hall and marched between two dark-clothed armed officers, to their waiting car. She'd had enough of playing their tunes. If she was going to join Guskov, she was going to do it on her terms.

"Take me to the Clinic," she said. "I forgot something."

They began to protest but she was adamant that her oversight was vital—a data source file she'd forgotten to copy—and so they took her into her offices. As the officer with her looked around in a bored, frustrated fashion, she made a show of copying something off the Clinic system and meanwhile began to search her desk. Fooling him was child's play. He wasn't really paying her any attention.

She was looking for her second Pad, which she found easily. She wiped dust off it, checked its power, and then put it down opposite the new Pad, leaning on the transmit button as she moved to use the desk system, copying what she could of the new one onto it, omitting all her personal identification documents and auto-registrars. This Pad contained older codes that she was betting the Ministry wouldn't be monitoring, and instead of the Erewhon service it was programmed to auto-direct enquiries and calls through a different 'pilot.

Closing her clinic account took a few seconds. She held up her usual Pad in her right hand, waved it, grinning, and said, "Got it. Sorry." At the same time she slid the old Pad into her pocket, and added, "I'll just go to the loo and then we're off, okay?"

The toilet escape had to be the oldest trick in the book, but she knew it was the best chance she had. They thought she was a willing participant in this job, after all, and the man set to stand guard over her wasn't really thinking that he should be watching her for signs of deception.

"Okay," he said, shrugging. "But be quick. We're late already."

"Sure." She went directly to the Ladies' and had cause to be glad she worked on the ground floor.

The frosted glass of the toilet windows opened into the inner courtyard where the waste bins for everything that wasn't to be incinerated on site were managed. It was sealed to the outside world but there was a door leading to the furnace room that she could get through. As soon as the door had closed Natalie walked across, undid the window catches, got a hygiene bin out of one of the cubicles and upended it, so that she could step up easily onto the ledge. It was a narrow window, one that would have stopped most people, and the drop on the other side was a good five or six feet, but she could see immediately how to get through.

She put her head out first, ears scraped back and eyes bulging for a second, then wriggled her small, flexible frame until her chest and hips had cleared the gap. There she hung for a moment, stuck fast by her legs as they wedged tight, giving her time to stretch out her arms and walk them slowly down the wall in support of her weight, watching the brickwork closely as she tipped further and further upside down . . . With a few contortions she managed to hang by her feet until she was able to touch the gritty surface of the yard and then easily plucked one foot free after the other and up into a comfortable balance. She walked a few steps on her hands and then dropped back to her feet once more.

Never in her life had she done a thing like that. It was as easy as breathing.

She marvelled at it, even as she remained alert, passing into the shadow of the heavy rubbish skips and the service laundry's plastic containers where the furnace door stood open to allow a straight gangway into the yard itself for the orderlies' carts. The furnace itself was in constant use. Its gas supply made a low hissing noise that masked voices and the sound of shoes in the big room until you were within a few feet of someone. She was able to walk behind the caretaker without being noticed and let herself out into the corridor of an entirely different wing. Bargaining on the fact that none of the staff knew she shouldn't be here as usual, she walked out of the side door and along the staff entryway onto Huntington Road where the security system had no trouble opening the gate for her.

Despite the relative ease of this escape Natalie knew there was no time for a mistake and she didn't make one. Knowing what to do and then doing it was an easy, fluid flow that came unhurriedly to her.

She ran towards town and turned into Haley's Terrace by the old baths, using her old Pad to hail a taxi. As it drew up to the curb at her side a few moments later she paused only long enough to send it an instruction to get lost on the ring road and fling the more modern Pad, her friend until a few minutes ago, in through the door.

As her police minders came running around the side of the building looking for her she was already at the bus stop two roads away, getting on the first bus she caught sight of going anywhere. By the time they'd figured out that she wasn't in the taxi she was walking fast down Coppergate, heading directly for the King's Arms.

It had occurred to her that she did know one person who was capable of giving her a temporary change of identity and who wasn't a fussy feeder. He might even know where Dan was, and she might spare him an audience with the local police about it if he did.

The back bar was dim and smoky but she caught sight of Ray's form immediately, recognizing him from Dan's descriptions: thick coat, slick hair, self-satisfied, belly-out air of a man in complete control of the pond. Some small, bent-over person was hunched opposite him, caught between the rosy glow of the fringed lamp and the orange ripple light of the fake fire. They were pleading ineffectually about something. Ray was grinning and his forehead was sheened with a mix of sweat and hair oil.

Natalie knew that her hours of listening patiently to the area's psychotics had been well spent. She put her hand on the whiner's shoulder and told him to piss off in a kind but authoritative voice, which he did, without even looking at her. She heard his scuttling as he made the turn for the door and his cut-off cry as one of Ray's heavies cuffed him in passing.

"Who the fuck are you?" Ray said with an amiable smile, waving a hand to suggest she take the vacated seat; all the largesse of a rich man welcoming a friend in his body language, all the good intent of a rattlesnake in his blue eyes.

"I'm one of Dan Connor's friends," she said, turning the chair around and sitting astride it, glad she was wearing her leathers and not some work trousers that day.

"Oh aye?"

"You don't happen to know where he is?"

"What's it worth?" Ray dropped his friendly arm and signalled his man for drinks. "You want anything?"

"No." She got an eyeful of his thick fingers and triple gold signet rings, one of them a sovereign. No taste, but they probably hurt when he hit you. She knew that he had no more idea about Dan than she did. She didn't know if she should be relieved.

"And what *do* you want if you don't want a drink?" he said suddenly, leaning in on her, his beery breath hot and faintly tainted with onion.

Natalie had to struggle not to flinch back, but she held her ground. "I want a temporary six-hour identity change with full international pass documents and a plane ticket, first class, on the next parabolic out of Leeds to Washington, DC," she said.

Ray sat back with his grin restored.

"Don't want much, do yer?" His thought process had a stage that passed visibly across his face, very finely. She could see him calculating. Then he grunted and adjusted his position to something more comfortable. "You're that doctor bird aren't you? The one that Connor shacks up with when he's not lifting shirts. Work for the MoD. I bet there's good money for not sending you on your way. Better than—"

"Mister Innis," she said quietly, maintaining a pleasant smile and eye contact. "I have a perfect record, crime-free. I am also the most wanted woman in Europe at this moment. When I tell the police that you kidnapped me outside the Clinic and have been planning to hold me to ransom, they aren't going to be impressed with your long list of convictions, nor your attempts to set up lab staff to feed you with illegal medical technologies. The disappearance of Dan Connor, who owed you money, will look like something other than a coincidence. I can assure you also that the US and European governments are so keen to find me that anyone causing the slightest delay wouldn't be so much compensated as erased. I have fifteen thousand pounds. I want a six-hour pass and the flight. I know you have contacts who can provide them. Get them for me right now, or I will drop you in the shit when the military police arrive. You've got about five minutes, max."

She could see him struggling to believe her, not knowing if he could delay, wondering how to stall her. He badly didn't want to believe her, but she knew that her performance was convincing and with the extra force of personality that the Selfware seemed to have given her since she woke up that morning he wasn't able to stop himself, even though it must have seemed most like a bad joke to him.

After about ten seconds he nodded.

"Fifteen?" he said. "That'll get you four hours on the pass, should get it in a few minutes. There's a flight in one hour from now. Think you'll make it?" He sat and stared at her, the left side of his upper lip curled in a snarl that was almost comic, daring her to protest.

"Fine." She beamed the access code for the money across to his Pad before he had time to argue. "It'll clear as soon as I leave the ground."

As long as she could get past Immigration she didn't care when the damn' thing expired. This transaction would make her doubly vulnerable. It would also seal Ray's fate, although he wasn't fast enough on his feet to realize that yet; he still thought that the banks' encryption suites were as good as they claimed.

As he waited for someone else somewhere else who owed him favours to sort it out, Ray looked her over with a casual air, belly-confidence restored.

"So, you don't know where Connor is either, the lying tub of shite," he said. "Run away, has he? After that accident or whatever it was. Some poor bastard dead on the slab somewhere having his grey stuff poked at because of you, are they? Or did he die on the table and you're all covering it up? You make me sick, you know that? I'd rather stick you in the river with lead boots on than help you do whatever it is you're doing. It's a crime against human nature." His smile became a snarl. "And you can tell that cunt Connor that he'll get the same if he doesn't deliver soon." He sent her Pad the relevant files with a heavy slam of his index finger.

Ray's man arrived with his pint on a tray.

Natalie, standing up to go, picked up the glass and made to put it down for him. Then, making eye contact, she smiled with heartfelt hatred and poured the contents over Ray's head.

"Thanks for the lecture." She put the glass back on the tray as both men, stunned, watched her, their shoulders rigid with disbelief. Foam and ale dripped from Ray's chin. Globules ran, mouselike, through the stiffly waxed tufts of his hair.

"I'll see myself out."

She expected to have the tray smashed down over her skull forthwith, but she was a fast mover these days and they weren't quick enough. She made it to the public bar and the street unscathed.

Her exultant, teeny victory over sad-twat Ray didn't last, however, not least because he'd still got her money and it was all she'd had. As she joined the express train service to the airport she tried calling Dan again. And again his Pad told her he wasn't available and took the message of her long, uncomfortable silence.

Jude in the office was a very unproductive worker. He turned the vial over in his fingers but it wasn't helping him think. Despite the air-conditioning he was sweating under his arms and the cold patches where his shirt stuck to him felt like dead skin. He couldn't stop seeing Tetsuo's surprised face and the flat, happy whiskers of that wretched cat, big eyes like twin dishes able to pick up Jude's thoughts. Those eyes had seen the shooting, he'd bet on it. If only there was a way to stick cats in some kind of scanner and read their minds . . . They'd have found Jude's DNA lurking in the apartment by now, be readying themselves to come and talk to him, or kill him, one or the other.

He'd submitted his reports on Atlanta to Perez. She was reading them now. But it was the Mappa Mundi project that bugged him even more than the cat. He worried about White Horse and her sketchy assurances that the people who'd kidnapped her wanted an investigation. All he had to do to set that in motion was write another report and use the file as evidence, with White Horse as the witness. All he had to do . . .

Or he could hang fire until Mary got back and let her in on it. He'd feel better if she knew. Somebody had to know, or the whole lot was likely to get blown away when they sprayed his brains all over the sidewalk one of these fine days. Thinking of dying made him hungry. It was afternoon and he hadn't eaten yet today.

He was in the middle of paying for a street hot dog, mustard, no onion, when he got a call from Natalie Armstrong. Juggling the 'dog and the Pad he moved to a patch of grass where a ginkgo tree gave shade next to the sidewalk and sat there cross-legged.

He didn't recognize Natalie in the vidlink at all, except for the half-face beneath the big, dark glasses and baseball cap, showing a dark mouth which was sincere on one side with a slight cynical upcurl at the other.

"Give me your address," she said. "I'm coming to visit."

"What . . . never mind." He sent it. "When?"

"Real soon." She broke the line.

Jude ran a check on it, but even Nostromo couldn't get a trace.

Groaning, he raked through his hair, took a bite of the 'dog, and tasted nothing but the turmeric and vinegar of mustard exploding in his mouth, which was the way he wanted it so he didn't have to think of Tetsuo's cat and its rose-petal tongue.

He dumped the 'dog into the nearest trashcan and went back to the stand for coffee. The guy gave him a tired, seen-it-before look. Jude left him with the change and turned back to the steps leading into his building. His boldness felt like it was coming to an end.

He called in to Perez and said he was going to interview a witness, then went home.

When he got there White Horse had left him a note written on paper in her tough scrawl, "Gone to meet lawyer at office downtown. Back p.m. Will call you if needed." She gave the address, which he checked against the city listings. It looked okay. The firm had a history, financial reports, tax records, famous cases, all above board.

Jude sat down on a stool at the breakfast bar and wondered why he didn't feel so good. He figured it was the 'dog and went to watch TV for ten minutes while he thought about actually calling the lawyers to see if she'd arrived okay. He moved his thumb over the Pad controls and played back Natalie's message a couple of times.

There was no doubt, she was wearing a disguise. That didn't leave a lot of time.

He was thinking that there wasn't a lawyer in existence who could touch this one. He wouldn't have. Who could he tell?

Working fast on the Pad he put together a list of tantalizing clues and information, rushed off a quick analysis, and put it on standby in the "message send" waiting list, addressed to the premier investigative journalists he knew operating out of Independent Networks in Manhattan. They'd gone into China undercover, scraped out alive from Libya. They'd try.

But then, on the verge of sending it, he hesitated, not even sure whose surrogate finger was on his, ready to press the key. The dark faction of government topplers? White Horse's own brand of deception and deceit in the name of the People? His own fear, trying to get anyone to help out?

In the end he left it sitting there and went to look for the Pepto-Bismol. He thought he'd wait until Mary got back and then tell her all about it. For the time being he was going to sit tight and do nothing except use what he already had to try and link detail from the CDC vial and Ivanov's other lives.

In his mind Jude heard White Horse telling him the People would lose Deer Ridge if he didn't carry on. He wondered how deep a conspiracy went that involved officers at Fort Detrick and federal court judges. He felt his guts tighten uncomfortably.

He sat with the ghost file and the open bottle of pink medicine and started to try and decipher the tightly packed Russian notes. The message to the journalists sat on file. He looked up at it now and again, but as he read on the idea of casually sending such a time bomb to some unsuspecting guy or girl started to shrivel and falter. By the time he'd found out the extent of Mikhail Guskov's dealings he wasn't sure if he should be more afraid of him or the government. In their ways and their powers, they were a nearly inseparable tangle.

As for Natalie, that side of the conundrum would solve itself when she arrived. He read on and the level of pink in the bottle slowly went down.

White Horse knew from the minute she set eyes on Roger Fassmeyer that he was no lawyer. The offices, the staff, everything at Gutierrez, Fassmeyer, Pilkington seemed fine, from their smart downtown location, their expensive stationery, and their external glass-floored elevator. But Fassmeyer looked lawyerly only in the cut of his suit and the cold demeanour that sealed his face off from his brain. When he stepped in to meet her White Horse's entire body experienced that terrible plunging sensation of a sudden fall; it tightened, braced and closed in. Her heart almost failed. She prayed that it would, and spare her the rest, but it didn't.

Fassmeyer gave her some cordial bullshit she ignored. She watched him invite her to take a short trip with him, a drive, for the sake of security and no bugging and all that crap. She didn't want to leave the cool room and its mahogany chairs. But she did get up and leave and they walked out together. She stared hard at every secretary she passed, willing them to notice. They smiled at her, their pretty and made-up faces blank.

White Horse thought that Mary surely must have known. Mary might have set her up. But the idea didn't sit right. Mary was Jude's best friend. Mary was kind. White Horse had looked into her face and there'd been none of that badness in it. Nothing. She'd tried to help.

She sat with Fassmeyer in the back of a limo. It had everything. He opened the drinks cabinet and there was a bottle of champagne he told her was the best in the world. He opened it and laughed and she watched him pour it into the fine, delicate crystal of the glasses.

"I don't drink," she said, barely breathing in the smooth embrace of the seatbelt.

"Of course you do," he replied, smiling at her and holding out the narrow stem, nudging it against the tender skin of her burned hand. "Everybody drinks." The last words were a command.

Her hand took the glass. She stared at her bag, betraying herself. She didn't know what to do. Her Pad—she could call Jude—but it was out of reach. Fassmeyer saw her look at it involuntarily and reached over.

"Let me take that for you." He chinked his glass against hers as he secured the bag. "To the future."

She stared at him. He was laughing at her with his salutation. Even the whites of his eyes were brightening out of their African yellowed tinge at his own wit.

"Fuck you," she said but her hand was shaking too much to throw the glass at him. She saw herself smash it against his face, use the sharp edges to slash at his neck, staining his white collar with blood, but her hand wouldn't do it. Why not? Why not? Too afraid. Shame filled her. She tried to muster enough saliva to spit but her mouth was dry as sand.

Fassmeyer reached into his jacket and took out a gun. His smile remained, "This is nothing personal, I assure you. Look, even the drink is the finest money can buy. Spared no expense. Now, have a drink. It's good." He tasted his own and gave her a wink.

You enjoy this, she thought dimly and her spirit abandoned her. She felt it flee the car and rush out into the street. She took a sip. The champagne *was* good, even she could tell that. Her shaking arm made her spill it over her chin. She swiped at her face and the movement gave her some momentum. She jabbed the glass up towards him.

He caught her wrist, digging his fingers in between the bones to a nerve junction, causing her to gasp in pain.

"Careless," he said mildly, holding her hand there as he refilled the flute to the top. "I don't want to have to pour it down your throat like lye. What a waste that would be. Now, this time, with some grace, drink up." Casually, he released the safety catch of the gun and moved the barrel so that it pressed into the muscle of her thigh where the seam on her jeans ran.

White Horse gulped and the bubbles ran up her nose and made tears run into her eyes. The next hour passed in a blur of sights and sounds that didn't link up in her head. The fear between was too great.

They drove a way through the heavy traffic, down to somewhere called Columbia Island Marina. They got out of the car and onto a big, white motor launch. More champagne waited. They got to the third bottle. Fourth. Out on the waters. Brown, silty, filthy waters. A plastic bag floated by, white, crumpled, half submerged.

She thought of her life, because she knew she was incapable of doing anything by then. As the wine went down and her mind began softening she wished she'd been less serious and more funny. She wished she'd had a relationship that lasted and a child or two, maybe three, maybe more. They'd have been fine kids; the girls strong, the boys proud. And Jude; she'd tell him in time that she'd been an air-head about taking the politics so hard to heart that he got on the wrong side.

Her bag was back in that car.

Fassmeyer topped up her glass. "You're drinkin' the ship dry, honey," he said and his black face split with a white smile like a fruit bursting in ripeness under the sullen sun.

"I don' wan' to die," she said to him, her own face in a distorted shape that hurt.

"I know," he said. "Believe me. Neither do I. But one of us has to and it ain' gonna be me."

"Why?" she slurred, hardly able to keep her head up.

"Because this world's too big and too ugly," he said, not joking for once. "That's why."

He was right. She knew it. She drank her glass to its dregs.

"Not always," she said, thinking of home.

"What's that?"

"It isn't always so bad." She couldn't hold the flute any more. It fell out of her hand and broke on the boat's decking. "I remember . . ." But she didn't.

She hated herself. It was time to be ended. Vaguely she saw buildings pass on the shores, the white boat, the heavy water, the cloudy sky. She tried to love it all but it had no meaning. She tried to feel its presence but it rejected her. She stretched out her mind, hoping to touch something beyond herself, a spirit, a ghost.

She didn't notice when she passed out, realizing only that she must have when the cold water suddenly closed over her head.

White Horse was a good swimmer. She had learned to swim in the creek, with Jude, who stayed out in the deeper water treading it easily, teasing her that she couldn't take her foot off the bottom.

Now she could. There was no bottom.

She swam towards him, wanting to get there and push him under, fling water in his face. She saw him from her hiding place under the water. She would swim there secretly and duck him. He wouldn't see her.

She kicked. The air was lead-heavy and painful in her lungs. Her face and hands burned.

She saw Jude in the clear air. His hands were reaching towards her. She could nearly touch them. She saw her own hands, tight and painful, reaching, stretching to the light and his smile.

"Don't trust her!" White Horse shouted out to him but instead of the words coming out the water eagerly rushed in. Cold fire plunged into her chest, pushing her down, remembering the time she'd escaped it at the house.

She felt Jude's fingertips brush hers like feathers as she sank. She tried to leap up out of her body and escape, but it was a little while before it let her slip away.

Fifteen

Mary Delaney sat in the joint meeting of the Science Advisory Group and the secretary of defense with her Pentagon boss, Dix, and cursed the time they were taking to deliberate; muttering, scratching around in dead ends of idiotic and unscientific worry—*What if this doesn't work? What if Marburg isn't as deadly as it was last week? What if we all jumped off the top of the CN Tower, would we really all die after eighteen hundred feet of acceleration into the hardtop, or should we include a secondary plan for that?*—like a bunch of twittering Microsoft geeks in a retirement village.

She thought the idea of real-world tests on Deliverance, the biochemical carrier system, was stupid, but they'd got it into their heads that only a payload of a deadly disease and extensive animal research was going to convince them that its genetic-recognition capabilities and "maximum fatality density" were real. That wouldn't have been so bad, but because of the secrecy level they were getting ready to go ahead and test without telling any of the military people involved exactly what the risks were. And that, she felt certain, was dumb to the point where they were qualifying for a Darwin.

"The grunts won't treat it with the right care if they don't know," Rebecca Dix insisted in her last speech, tailoring the words into that bizarre cocktail of basic vocabulary and macho-shit that talking about arms investments and progression seemed to require. "You don't have to tell the truth. Tell them it's Ebola or some goddamn' hantavirus that's double deadly to humans. Flesh-eating. It doesn't matter."

"The facility is fully BSL-$_4$ equipped," Ramirez, from the secretary's office said. "It shouldn't make any difference."

"But people are people and it does," she insisted, trying not to grind her teeth. "The environments are only as secure as the most careless person in them. And nobody there really wants to be there. They act fast to finish early. They make mistakes. It's only natural. And they know that we aren't telling the truth. So they're resentful. And they're scared and that means their minds aren't all on the job."

"Then that will be enough of an incentive to take extra care."

Sometimes Mary wondered how these people around her got into the positions they were in. She wondered what their thoughts were before they fell asleep and what world they lived in that they could be so confident it would react exactly as they expected it to. They knew shit about ordinary people, so she didn't understand why they got to determine national policies on security that involved actual human beings. If it wasn't for the fact that she was going to get her butt into one of their seats soon she'd be tempted to blow the game on all of them. But that was just her temper talking and she'd learned to sit hard on it.

The decision got made despite Dix's vote against it. They were going to proceed.

Ramirez turned to Mary, shifting his bulk like a tanker turning, smarting at Dix's previous statement.

"You're getting careless. You need to turn the Feds right out of the park, not play half-measures. The Chinese already have a series of diseases that can target exact vectors in the population. The Pakistanis have put together prototype NP systems that are effectively religion-as-contagion and we don't have time to mess around. Your finer feelings aren't worth the country."

"Religion already is a contagion," she retorted, staring pointedly at his gold cross where it dangled over his tie and collar on a fine chain, "and it wasn't the failure of our people that let the Mappaware test contaminate the population. That was a leak from your end. Just like it won't be our fault when this gets out and kills whole states."

She stared him down, because they all knew that he was supposed to be controlling the efforts of the growing anti-Perfection element as it spread through levels of government, and he wasn't succeeding.

"No argument." Ekaterina Estevez, chair of the Joint Chiefs of Staff, sat back in her seat at the head of the table. "We aren't children. The tests must be done. Mary, you will remove the FBI's interests in Mappa Mundi. Juan, you will ensure that the Dark Faction are delayed on any anti-Perfection actions until the Mappa project is fully entombed. Everyone else, you will support and enable both projects. And then, we finally reach the point where we have working systems. The question then will be, to strike or not to strike. We all understand the ramifications. Let us put it off no longer. It's time to vote."

The silence that followed her words was tinged with an almost visible black edge, so much so that Mary found herself mentally shouting, *Gather, Darkness!* and wanting to giggle. She bit her tongue.

When Mappaware was up and working it could be used to remove the enemies of the United States by simply reinventing them as citizens.

Guskov had given them lengthy and exhausting seminars on the hows and whys, encompassing the theory of memetics, genetics, brain physiology, and thought-formation, not to mention the social psychology and all the other complex bits that had to be considered when you broke down a human personality into its components. None of them at this table understood the half of it, but they did understand that it was a tool that made people mentally into clay that could be endlessly remodelled into any shape desired.

This vote would determine whether or not the USA would take it upon itself to make this effort to unify the world.

Mary believed Guskov when he said that it was possible for a person to remain essentially "themselves" (and that was a minefield of definitional problems), whilst shifting the core of their identities to a sufficient extent that an Afghani Muslim could experience themself as a part of the United States' diaspora, loyal to the flag, espousing democracy, even tolerating libertarians on the same street, because of the stars and stripes flying overhead. It sounded crazy. It needed testing. But they all believed it, because they'd seen Mikhail Guskov achieve exactly that using only ordinary hypnosis upon one of their own—Sandy Piccirilli, Estevez's personal secretary.

Piccirilli had sat in this very room, at his usual chair, and become variously a Revolutionary Communist, a devout Hindu, a white supremacist, and the King of Siam, all within the space of a couple of hours. Guskov had explained each time that the change required total shifting of the core memeplexes that affected Sandy's entire Memecube; the ones through which he unconsciously filtered all his knowledge about the world. The results had been very funny. But even though he vowed with all his heart to smash the bourgeoisie or sacrifice to Shiva, the curious matter was that they could all see that it was still Sandy, just Sandy with some funny ideas.

Piccirilli's new ideas would, of course, have come under severe stress if they'd lasted. The dissonance between his views and the reality around him and as told to him by his friends would have disrupted the ideas eventually, or put him in a nut farm. But Guskov said that with NervePath in place this wouldn't happen. Because the system restructured the whole mind to prefer the new idea strongly its entry into the personality was achieved without internal conflicts arising.

The identity was the last sacrosanct piece of an individual that hadn't yet been interfered with by science at anything other than a conversational level. Now it was going to be open season.

Just as with the physical Perfection technologies, the determining of a "normal" standard and a "desirable" range of values was a subject nobody felt remotely happy about. But as long as they were only talking about making dangerous opponents into allies who could retain all their "essential" items of otherness ("their color," Mary thought), they didn't find the discomfort unbearable. In fact, the idea of the globe being peacefully allied under a gentle cloak of democratic congruence was just peachy, especially as the democracy in question would be their model. It looked goddamned ideal.

It reeked like a two-week-dead skunk as well, if you had any kind of ethics left.

Mary thought it was an incredible idea, utterly terrifying. She couldn't see what the point of the human race carrying on would be, once everyone was in agreement about everything that mattered. What kind of homogenized life-in-Stepford was that? What did it mean? Wasn't oppression of the ignorant still a mightily fucking awful oppression? Was it any different from swanning into some country with a big army and saying, "Do as we say or we'll kill you?" Only in the sense that there'd be no hint of resistance. You'd have killed them off already.

"It wouldn't be like that," Guskov had assured her. "Neighbours will still fight over where to put the fence. Inequalities will be everywhere, class divides, rich and poor. As the initial surge of loyalty passes, within hours people will begin to deviate from the standard set by the software. They'll think for themselves. They'll change. But the biggest differences, the nation-killer ideas of what life means and what's important—these will be brought into line by the NP system for long enough that whole populations will come to agree, broadly. Then dissent that tends towards serious violence can be controlled humanely with booster programs, minor adjustments." He didn't say what template of the world, or more important, whose, he was going to use for this trick. That was a matter for presidential and NSC discussion to come.

Well, yadda yadda, Mary thought, *easy to say that, harder to live it, and if the only test ever run is Deer Ridge then God help us all*. But despite her reservations (*ha ha*) how could she vote "No" when she and others in the CIA already used the prototypes of Mappaware to run their own unofficial people?

Mary knew it worked. They didn't like her instructions, sure, but they couldn't stop obeying. They were miserable, but they did their jobs and then, because of the natural quirk of a delay between an action and consciousness of it, they rationalized their reasons and thought it was all their own doing. It was quite brilliant.

She wouldn't want that for everyone, but it helped things go so much better than they had in the past. Nobody ratted when ratting wasn't possible. Besides, if anybody else got their hands on it she didn't want herself going all Japanese or Arabic in the depths of her grey matter, handing over the entire security plan for the state with a smile and a Have a Nice Day. No, it was no time to be squeamish.

She raised her hand with Dix's group among the "Ayes."

The action was voted in.

Nobody was against. Ramirez and a few others abstained. She knew they hated the existence of Guskov and all his engines, but they had too much political smarts to show a "Nay." She'd have to watch out for them. People with gigantic contradictions sitting happily in their heads were people who could successfully fragment their personalities for maximum efficiency. Like her. Like Mikhail. They could get anything done.

As they were breaking up the meeting and recovering their Pads from the offices outside—all such meetings took place in private with no records made—she found three new messages. One from Fassmeyer, blank. One from Jude.

She knew what it was going to say, poor guy. She didn't want to think about him right now. She hadn't felt any plunge of shame or guilt when she saw his name an instant ago. No, that was too much lettuce at lunch.

The last was an urgent flag from the Euro Defence contact.

As she read it her heart genuinely sank and a cold fury washed through her. Why was it her job to deal with all the shitty ends of all the sticks in this business?

"Dr. Natalie Armstrong defected. Contact lost. She may be en route to DC. Considered dangerous."

How could they have been so inept? One woman, on her own, head full of NP and no special assistance and they lost her. Dangerous? They must be kidding.

Mary would show her dangerous.

Dan was a long way from home. He didn't know where he was and it could have been almost anywhere; he'd been blindfolded and tied up for what he thought was about six or eight hours, moved from a van into another vehicle and then put in a trunk and taken through what sounded like an airport. He had flown and then there'd been another car, a long wait in silence, and finally a transfer into this room where he was allowed to walk around and where he sat and stared at the curtains drawn across the window.

He drank from a jug of water they'd left him. There was a TV, which didn't work. He'd tried it. There was no escape, he'd tried that and got a shouted warning from the heavy who'd nearly broken his back last night at the river. He sat, looked at the cheap, nasty surroundings, and picked at the mud on his hands and trousers. His Pad was gone. In its absence, he composed messages to Natalie: pleas for help amid apologies, because if he hadn't been such a hopeless git none of this would have happened. Probably.

His stomach growled with hunger and then knotted itself up again with fear. He sat down, paced three strides from one wall to the next, sat down. There was a bed but it was covered in such a tatty blue nylon cover, full of cigarette holes, that he didn't want to touch it. Pubic hairs, not a few, were stuck fast all over its surface. Smears of food or other things lay in crusted patches here and there. The chair was marked with a footprint, but at least it didn't smell or look like it had fleas. It was the end of places, the arse end, a hole where nobody expected anything good and they got it by the bucketful.

A pack of cigarettes and some HighFive chewing gum, full of dope and tranquillizers, was laid out for him on top of the TV. He took some of it, because there was nothing else to do. So, Shelagh Carter, huh? That bitch.

He shivered and looked around for the heating or a blanket. His clothes smelled rank from being damp with river water for so long.

The gum juice flowed sweetly over his tongue. He started to feel better.

Then the door opened and there she was, a person who'd never fit in a neighbourhood like this with her blue suit and her immaculate face and her shining hair. Civil Servant Barbie carrying a scanner in her hand as if she were starring in her own Manga cartoon, fingernails frosted pink on the trigger guards.

"You've been most helpful, Mr. Connor," she said politely in a British accent that suddenly sounded hammy, although that might have been the gum in Dan's brain. "I'm very sorry. This is nothing personal, you understand."

"Oh yeah?" he said but stopped there, because he couldn't think of anything witty or even the right line or voice to do it in. She was going to kill him and he didn't even know why. His legs started shaking. He thought, *I should have bought that bloody ticket at the travel place and gone to Rio. Oh fuck.*

"What is it, then?"

"Business," she said and pointed the machine at him.

He flinched but felt nothing. He swallowed the gum by accident and felt it slide in a lump down his throat and stick halfway. He looked around him and wondered where he was and how he'd got there, what it meant, and why he didn't understand.

"Where am I?" he asked her.

"Nowhere," she assured him.

He nodded: that made sense. "Who am I?"

"No one." She turned to the two hooded men who had followed her in. "Hold him up against the back wall," she said, "and turn the lights on."

She smiled at him. "Everything's okay. You're doing fine."

He smiled back at her, happy to be doing fine. He stood in the bright lights and looked into the screen of her Pad. They were sending someone a picture. You smiled in pictures. You gave them your best side.

Natalie's Pad thrummed in her bag for a few moments, trilled patiently a few more as she fumbled to get it out of her jacket, and then emitted a high-pitched baby-squeal of fear to get her attention.

As the expensively dressed couple on the other side of the aisle started tutting she silenced it with a deft move and the call arrived on-screen as she raised it to her face, wondering who could have located the number, hoping it was Dan but dreading the answer. Any security agency worth a damn could have probably found her by now.

Dan's face loomed into view, lurching forward towards the camera at his end of the call as though he was drunk. His hair was greasy and dishevelled and he looked terrible. He had a peculiar, zany smile on his face.

"Dan, you silly arse," Natalie began, whispering close to the mike inlet and grinning at him with delight. "Thank goodness you're—"

He looked puzzled and stumbled in saying her name, when suddenly he was yanked out of shot.

A great big fist of ice suddenly clamped around her throat and in her chest, making her breath lurch and stall. At the same moment she turned the Pad in her hand, trying to see around corners with it. But whoever was controlling the image was already letting her see more than she liked.

The view panned back to reveal a room with cheap floral wallpaper and a boarding-house air of too much nylon lace and yellowing white paint. Dan was held against a wall, pinned by two figures in dark clothes whose heads were covered in the reflective mylar bags that large circuit boards are shipped in to protect them from static and magnetic interference.

Natalie was trying to understand what she was seeing, had started to say, tentatively, "Dan?" when a woman's face appeared.

Natalie immediately thumbed the "record" command but it didn't work. She glanced down, trying to see if she had missed it, when a voice that was processed into a hoarse, throaty drawl came from the speaker.

"Dr. Armstrong. I suggest you stop trying to fix your machine and listen. You have two minutes. First, let me show you that I mean what I say."

Natalie looked closely at the face that filled the whole of shot for those few seconds, trying to extract every bit of information from it that she could.

It was youngish, thirty-five, she thought. The features were small and regular and the skin a smooth Celtic white, plump with rich cosmetics. A few freckles dashed over the nose and cheeks in palest ochre, so well-placed they might have been tattooed there for their light-hearted effect. The eyebrows were a natural redhead's auburn and the long, thick curly hair the same colour. The eyes themselves were blue, although they looked like fakes, contacts over another shade. Natalie saw naked ambition, wit, intelligence, and a will strong enough to ride roughshod over anything in its path. The combination was startlingly attractive, as this sudden new enemy turned her shoulder with an elegant twist, so that the rest of the scene came back into view.

With a graceful movement the woman raised her arm. Her hand held a gun of a sort Natalie had never seen before. It was grotesquely large and blunt in her grip, looked like it should be too heavy to lift but she never even shook a hair on her head with the effort of raising it. There was a soft, sibilant noise and a wide red circle appeared on the wall behind Dan's right thigh. Natalie heard his scream as the woman turned and blocked him from sight, looking into Natalie's face.

The screaming was a near-unbelievable noise, high and terrified and uncomprehending; the product of a pain that killed all awareness of anything else. It ripped out of the Pad's digitally perfected speaker at a distorting volume and tore through the first-class cabin of the aircraft with a force that made several people shriek with fear that they were undergoing explosive decompression. A nervous jolt and the shooting needles of horror in her chest made Natalie shake so badly that she dropped the Pad and had to scrabble around on the floor for it. It screeched and gibbered face down.

"Excuse me!" began the expensively dressed woman over the aisle, as loudly as possible. "I hardly think that horror—"

"Fuck off!" Natalie hissed at her, coming up from her crouch, the words so venomous that the woman went white and shrank away from her. Natalie didn't take her eyes from the Pad. Her heightened senses and the peculiar "aliveness" of her being since the last acceleration of the Selfware suddenly escalated. The plane and the other people ceased to exist.

"Listen and then answer me," the redhead said, calmly waiting for breaks in the sound of Dan screaming, and smiling at Natalie's difficulties, which no doubt she could hear very well. "If you don't, then I finish what's left of him." She turned again and raised her arm.

"Wait! Stop!" Natalie cried, pulling the Pad close to her face in the hope that they would hear her more clearly. "Stop! Please! Let him alone. What is it?" If they had intended to throw her off balance they had succeeded all too well. Some part of her that didn't require conscious attention informed her that a steward was coming towards her, and that people were looking and starting to point.

This time there was no gun. Natalie recognized the scanner instantly.

It was pointed at Dan. He stopped screaming and stood up straight, his face uncrumpling like a film played in reverse.

Blood pooled heavily around his right foot and there was a faint stain on his left leg, like an afterthought, where vaporized blood had finally sunk in, but now it was as though there was nothing wrong with him. He looked calm and attentive, even grinned a little in the old way as he said, easily, "Hey, Nat, what's cookin' ya?"

"Dan!" she said softly, touching the screen where his image moved, unsteadily balancing on its only good leg. She realized what they were using and that he must have been infected long before this blew up, long before Jude appeared. How had she not noticed before, when she'd had time to do something about it? Was that what he'd tried to ask her about when she'd told him to shove off, on Bobby's day?

The woman came back into full shot.

"Your friend is infected with a mind-system very similar to your own. But then, I expect you know all about that, Doctor, from Jude Westhorpe." No trace of an expression other than straightforward calm crossed her face. "We are ready to forgive your actions against us if you will return immediately to your US destination as planned. Otherwise I regret that we will have to employ our functional mindware on you, in order to ensure your cooperation with the project."

As she finished speaking she raised the scanner and keyed in a new command.

Natalie saw that it was a string sequence that would cause the NervePath in Dan's brain to shut down the synapses completely. If he had reached saturation it was certain death.

Natalie could hardly get her mouth to work. She watched the woman watching her. The pale face held no pity as Natalie tried to speak, and she knew then that Dan was dead, because she, Natalie, Brain of fucking Britain, didn't know what to do.

"Let him go," she whispered, pleading without shame. She tried to pour her emotion down into the lens of the Pad, into that blank statue's face.

"I agree. I'm en route to Washington anyway. I won't cause any trouble. Whatever you say. Let him go. Take him to hospital! Please."

The auburn woman nodded and her curls bobbed perkily against her neck. Then she turned and pointed the scan unit at Dan again as Natalie started to scream.

"No! Don't!" Natalie yelled in fury, shaking the Pad. "Let him go!"

But Dan was speaking, lightly conversational, in his English gent's voice, ever so, ever so, and what he was saying were words straight out of a report that Natalie had written, just twenty-four hours ago:

"The Selfware programme tested on Bobby X is a learning system that maximizes host cognitive abilities to their limits, within the parameters of the design view. The speed of change is determined by preexisting structures and potentials. With the alteration in place the NervePath system becomes symbiotic within the host central nervous system. Any attempt to interfere with, or remove, the NervePath nanytes will probably cause immediate and total cessation of all neural activity."

He grinned and waved weakly at her, back to his old self for the last moment. "Natalie, check it out, girl."

His body folded down, joints collapsing, and lay sprawled on the floor, his head turned away from her. The bloodstain spread on the squalid carpet underneath him; long shadow under set of sun. He was still.

The uninterested guards walked over him, as though he were a bag of rubbish.

The beautiful woman returned for the last time.

Natalie met her eyes through the link and thought—*I'll find you. And you'll wish I hadn't.* Inside her, a shift of Selfware or a shift of self caused everything uncertain in her to fuse. It became solid, absolute. She realized why Bobby was prepared to hang around to see some action.

"We'll send you a limousine." She was so cordial. Such a pro. She took pride in that, like it was a business thing, a clever thing, a trick she'd pulled off already. There was her weakness.

"Do that," Natalie replied, more cold and full of hate than she had ever felt in her life, a sensation inside her as though her skeleton was turning into metal, her insides coagulating into a kind of engine that could run and run until it found this woman and squeezed the life out of her one drop at a time. "You do that." She cut the transmission and sat on her seat edge, breathing slow, measured—*a deep breath is a . . .*

The steward was leaning pointedly at her, waiting for just that cue.

"There's a private cabin just ahead for intimate personal—" he began. Then Natalie looked up at him.

His mouth worked vacantly, trying to reel his words back in.

"Where are we?" she demanded.

"Uh, just beginning our descent . . . what are you doing? No, no, you can't get up now, madam, the plane is about to go into full re-entry and the turbulence . . . excuse me!"

Natalie pushed him out of her way and walked quickly towards the front of the plane. She passed two more crew in the last stages of strapping down the drinks trolley and put her hand on the entry to the cockpit.

"You can't go in there!"

It was locked anyway, with some numeric keypad combination, but as the steward came after her to try and pull her away Natalie looked carefully at the grease-dirtied marks on the keypad, the shininess of the numbers. Somewhere in flight she'd already heard them type it in. Her fingers moved before she knew what it was.

One Three Two One.

The door opened. With the steward hanging onto her jacket tails she clawed her way through and into the tiny space behind the navigator console. She saw the entire cabin in a flash and reached out instantly for the aerosol pepper spray the steward was trying to fumble out of its webbing in a quick recall of his hijack training.

She flicked off the lid and zapped him with a dose, kicking him backwards out of the way as he bent double, yowling, then reached around behind herself and ripped the keypad off the wall with a strength born of rage. The door buzzed unhappily and slammed shut: another antiterrorist tactic.

Natalie tossed the lump of wires and fascia on the floor and braced herself against the bulkhead as the two pilots stared at her, full of hostility. One was grappling around with his foot for the emergency stud, but slid in his seat as they started to brush against the atmosphere and the plane's body juddered.

Through the windows Natalie could just see the high curve of the Earth's blue sky, brilliant as sunlight shot through it, singing off white clouds and sparkling on the distant surface of the ocean. They were plunging towards it, and the first traces of reentry heat and compressed gas were beginning to flare over the nose. She wondered where Dan's body was and if it would ever be found.

"I've got a bomb," she said.

Firm. Loud. Insistent. Absolute.

I.

Have.

A.

Bomb.

Four words that fill and define a large space of unpleasant possibility.

She waited for the information to sink in.

"Don't send any signals."

She glared at the pilot, who took his foot back meekly and tucked the toe in behind his other ankle.

"I want you to divert this flight to JFK."

Natalie felt like she was living in someone else's life, a rider on a wave. She felt delirious, but this didn't make it out to her surface.

The copilot looked stupefied. "New York?" she said, frowning and wrinkling her forehead. "It's going to DC, and you want to divert it to . . . New York?"

"That's right," Natalie said.

"Hell, honey, you can drive from DC to New York," the copilot replied, the whites of her eyes stark and round in her dark face.

Natalie held firm.

The two pilots shared a glance of confusion.

"Bomb?" asked the pilot. "Where?"

Natalie patted her chest, "Right here. Body cavity specially made. One lung removed. Plastic explosive, enough to finish all three of us, and the nose. Triggered by a tooth switch."

She'd read that in a book and it sounded just plausible enough for her to risk it not being wrong. Her fury and grief over Dan gave her more than enough emotional conviction to pull it off.

"JFK."

The copilot sighed and nodded, "Okay, lady. It's your party."

The pilot said, "You know, you'll get a lighter sentence if you remove yourself voluntarily into arrest before we have to change course and notify the authorities."

"Oh, will I?" Natalie said lightly. "Okay then."

They stared at her.

"Is this some kind of practical joke?" the copilot said, starting to scowl.

"No," Natalie held out her hands for the cuffs. "This is serious. Call the local police and have them meet me on the runway. I changed my mind. But I can change it back." She grinned.

The pilot returned to flying and started calling instructions to the crew for Natalie's arrest. The copilot just shook her head.

"You're nuts," she told Natalie. "This is a five-to-ten stretch."

"On the runway," Natalie insisted. "With lots of armed officers and a big, bomb-proof truck."

Through the windscreens she watched the colour overhead change softly from black to blue.

Sixteen

Jude looked down at his sister's face and saw that he had been dragged into the wrong reality by the vicious twist of a timeline he hadn't really believed in.

All through the news that she'd been found stranded among tidefuls of junk at the Mean Low Water line alongside Rock Creek Parkway; all through the journey to the city morgue; all through the preamble and the coroner's assistant telling him to take his time—he hadn't believed for an instant that it would really be her. Even when he nodded in his ignorance and the assistant drew away the cover sheet from her head, he'd seen the grey pallor and magenta lips of an old drunk bag girl, her horrible flea-ridden hair matted into thick dreadlocks, her face distorted with an expression of self-hate. It wasn't White Horse, who had waist-length, shining black hair so smooth that not even a fleck of dust could stick to it.

Beneath her chin the weals of the fire marks had become a beige, age-spot brown. The wrinkled scar tissue looked healthy against the rest of it. Her eyes were closed. He wanted to look into them and be sure she wasn't there. What was under there? He waited for her to breathe.

The coroner's man laid the sheet down carefully, leaving her head exposed, "Would you like a moment alone?"

Jude nodded, but he didn't want to stay there another second. He turned away and said, "That's her," and then walked out of there as fast as he could and into the bright sunlight on the steps outside. He gulped at the soupy humidity and blew the cool, deadly vapour of the tiled room out of his nose and mouth. He stared vacantly at the street and then, with a weakness in his legs, sat down on the steps and put his head in his hands.

In his mind's eye he saw Tetsuo's cat, globular eyes shining. It opened its mouth into a rosy bloom and a trail of fine black hair was vanishing down its softly petalled throat. He stared at the cars passing to get rid of the image but its emotional scent lingered; a sweet stink of repulsion.

The assistant came out and offered him a cup of water. Jude drank it. He felt that he didn't know where he was. The soft membrane of the air against his skin had been pushed through and he was on its other side now, in a city that was at every turn just like his own, but whose meanings he couldn't read.

"Do you think you can come and fill out the arrangements? It'll only take a few moments. There's a counsellor on hand if you'd like to talk," the man said, awkward, with a tentativeness that made Jude want to shout at him.

"I'm fine," he said and got up. They went indoors and he answered the necessary questions that would release the body for burial.

"What did she, I mean, how did she die?" Jude asked finally, mustering the courage at the last moment. He didn't want to know, he just had to.

"Drowning," the assistant said, trying to make it sound less horrible by saying the word gently. "But her blood alcohol was high enough to kill her on its own."

"Blood alcohol?" Jude repeated stupidly, glancing around the calm, efficient room and then back at the neat collar and blond hair of the coroner's official. He was a clean-cut young man. Unconsciously he tried to pare the nails of one hand with those of the other as Jude watched him, removing an invisible filth.

"She didn't even drink."

The man checked the records, using his finger to trace across the charts and show Jude he was patient. "Blood alcohol level ten times the legal drink-drive limit. Champagne." He paused and blinked, surprised and unable to suppress it. "Champagne, and whiskey. I can even tell you the brand . . ."

"But she was alive when she went in the water?" Jude had to get it straight.

"Her lungs were full of water," the assistant agreed, nodding. "If they hadn't—"

"So, where's the homicide detective?"

"Excuse me?"

"My sister didn't drink. She didn't like swimming. She was afraid of deep . . ." Jude found his throat hurt. He started again, spreading his hands out on the desk, looking at them and not at the official. "Why isn't there a homicide investigation?"

"Um . . . according to my information she was a registered alcoholic street person . . ."

"That was ten years ago," Jude said, looking up from the spread of his fingers where his nails were starting to become white. "And in another state. She hasn't drunk in all that time. She didn't drink. How could she have a record here? Are you listening to me?"

"Please, there's no need to get agitated, Mr. Westhorpe. I can call a detective in, to take a statement. I'll do that right away." He got up and hurried out, closing the door after him.

Probably this guy'd had worse cases to deal with, much worse, but Jude didn't have any sympathy to spare. So, they were going to treat it as the accidental death of a bum? He shouldn't be surprised by this. He shouldn't be surprised by anything. Even if there was an investigation it would only end up inconsequential, or pinned on some worthless expendable who certainly hadn't done it. Whoever had put an end to White Horse's inquiries wasn't going to stumble over details like that and he knew already who they were, their office if not their name. Why bother?

He got up, put his jacket back on, and walked out, rubbing the centre of his chest where it felt like something sharp was trying to grind its way out from the inside.

The rest of the day he sat in a dark bar, on his own, one of those places that caters to lonely thinkers and doesn't try to make any efforts at creating a social scene. Amid its purple walls and dark green lighting, flaking paint and the smell of deeply entrenched dry rot he made the arrangements to send White Horse back home: coffin, carrier, delivery points. He called his Uncle Paul, the peanut butter king.

"Jude," Paul said, sitting down in the blue-and-white-check kitchen of his house on Deer Ridge, curtains blowing in the fine breezes of a sunny Montana afternoon.

Jude waited for Paul to see his expression and change, become ready for the thing that nobody was ever ready to hear. As the old man's face softened and the brows drew closer he said, "White Horse is dead."

Paul's face didn't change much. He nodded after a moment. "You okay?"

"I'll be fine," Jude said. "Here's the arrangements. I put you down as delivery address for the body. Nearest living relative out there."

Paul nodded as the files came through. "I'll see to everything this end, don't worry."

"Thank you."

"Will you be coming?"

To the funeral, he meant. Jude hesitated. "Yes. Let me know."

Paul nodded. "You looking out for her there?"

Was he investigating?

"Yeah."

"I'll tell the others. We'll pray for you."

They looked at each other for a few moments but Jude couldn't bear the lack of questions and the calmness; his finger pressed the End key and the Pad went dark.

Hadn't White Horse said that she'd gone to see some lawyer Mary recommended? He'd meant to call and check but he hadn't. Why not? It would have taken a minute. He had the numbers.

He called them now. The girl on the phone confirmed the name and appointment. She said White Horse had never showed up. He asked if Mary Delaney had referred her and the girl answered that she hadn't; White Horse had made her own appointment and would he like to reschedule for her? He said no. No appointment.

Leaving a twenty on the table for his Russian coffee Jude went home and reread the note she'd left for him, touching it this second time with the knowledge that it was the thing that had been closest to her most recently. Nothing about it suggested it had been written under duress. It was almost illegible.

He traced the lines of it with his finger and reminded himself of Natalie, touching her own writing in the back of the file. Dully he recalled that she was supposed to arrive soon. He looked at the clock. It was late, he had no food in. He walked through the apartment, blank, and for the first time ever noticed that it reflected exactly this blank state, as though he'd been expecting it and unconsciously prepared for it; the moment when personality breaks down and waits to reform in a new shape. White Horse had said he'd run off to the East to get made and find his skin. All this time was preparation. Now the flaying of the old. He shivered and thought he caught a scent of snow, but it was his imagination.

Later . . . later . . . but his thoughts wouldn't run any further.

White Horse had left a few clothes behind. Washed, they were hanging out to dry on the rack in the spare room. He began to take them off and fold them up. He got out the iron and pressed her shirts, breathing in the scent of hot steam and cotton. He put the iron away and placed the clothes in an overnight bag and went to strip the bed.

Her nightshirt was under the pillow. It said on it, "I've been to Yellowstone National Park," but, as far as he knew, she never had. Fragments of broken-off hair dusted it.

He held the shirt in his hands and put it to his face. Hours ago she wore this. Stayed here. Safe with him until he went away. He should have known better. He *had* known better. The fact became unbearable.

Jude opened his mouth and jammed the cloth into it and against his nose, into his eyes.

Mikhail Guskov sat with his feet up in the common lounge area of the Sealed Environment, talking with some of the other newly arrived members of his team. They were drinking tea and coffee and trying to make themselves comfortable in the functional room with its utilitarian furniture and breeze-block walls. Obviously there wasn't going to be much time for relaxing but it was hardly the kind of development environment that showed any forethought, particularly in these days of work-play crossover. It reminded Mikhail of the old days in Moscow more than he cared to remember but a part of him thought it was nonetheless fitting that they'd rather hole up alone in their own parts of the cage than come to this cheerless place in an effort to find company. It was what they deserved—purgatory.

Nikolai Kropotkin, neuropsychologist at the Moscow Brain Institute, and Isidore Goldfarb, the American programming developer who had worked on Mappaware from the outset, both seemed not to care about the environment very much: Kropotkin because he was used to practical economies and Goldfarb because he had Asperger's syndrome and didn't notice it.

They paused a moment in their discussion to listen to the sounds of others moving in—Lucy Desanto, Alicia Khan, Calum Armstrong.

"Gang's all here," Goldfarb stated. He gave a practised social smile and held it for precisely the number of seconds his training had instructed him to.

"Not quite," Guskov replied, blowing on his lemon tea. "Natalie Armstrong has yet to arrive. Her journey has taken a small detour."

Kropotkin, older, wiry-haired, grey, and small like an Arctic fox, peered through steaming-up spectacles. "I don't blame her. I, too, would take a detour." He drank his coffee at a scalding temperature that forced him to suck air in over it with a smack of his lips.

There was a moment's quiet. They were all aware of the lengths the US had promised to go to should it be necessary to persuade them to work harder. They knew what Guskov meant by a detour.

"She can't escape." Goldfarb stated that, too, as a fact.

"That depends," Guskov said, glancing down at their Pads on the table—they had been file sharing and discussing the case of Patient X—"on what she is."

Kropotkin finished his mug and stared into its empty depths as he spoke. "There is still no consensus on the fate of Patient X," he said. He put the mug down. "The camera footage seems impossible, yet there's no evidence that anyone has interfered with it. My assessment of the Selfware system of Dr. Armstrong's suggests, in simulation, that there may be a point at which the restriction of the NervePath to neural cells may be worked around by this programme, which regards all cells as capable of transmission of information.

"I believe that the redefinition would write back to the core NP code and override the distribution constraints, making the nanyte structures capable of invading the entire body, treating it like an extension of the brain. After that, the reorganization and prioritization involves not just the connections of the central nervous system, but all systems. This creates an information potential that would considerably outstrip the most advanced of our mechanical processing capabilities. Coupled with the verbal evidence of Patient X's behaviour in his last hours, we should face the possibility that some kind of understanding of fundamental particle physics has taken place at a direct level, and enabled him to interfere with his own atomic structure."

Kropotkin paused. "It sounds insane. Yet it must be an explanation we consider."

He met Guskov's stare, his own dark gaze deeply uncomfortable. "I can't tell you what an extreme difficulty I have with this supposition. Nothing in physics suggests that it is possible to influence directly the structure of hadrons without the application of gravitronic or electromagnetic forces, and to consider a human being becoming capable of enabling such forces by willpower or thought is simply absurd."

"Unless they are no longer human. Would that create less difficulty?" Guskov asked.

"No," Kropotkin said sharply. "Anything that is not a machine equipped and built specifically for the task is too great a leap of belief for me. People are animals that live on the classical Newtonian scale and all their senses and structures operate within an extremely small window of the Information Hypercube. They don't even have direct contact with reality at a conscious level: their entire map and perception of the world around them is a fabrication created by the brain to allow successful living in a complex world. This theory of yours that suggests that somehow this person has altered so greatly that their cells have become capable of direct quantum detection and manipulation is ridiculous. The fact I have no other explanation doesn't mean that I am any more inclined to believe yours."

"It doesn't have to be that strong," Goldfarb suggested, carefully modulating his voice so that it didn't appear too flat. "It's more likely that the quantum-state interactions between the patient and the universe take place at a subconscious level. Consciousness is the emergent product of a complex and discrete set of actions in the brain. It is the narrative story that comes a fraction of a second after the subconscious mind has already made its decisions and taken its actions. It is a macro-level event. But the quantum manipulation may be a very low-level event, taking place far beneath even the subconscious, with effects and awareness of it only occurring spasmodically, or maybe never, at the conscious level."

"And the effect of the will?" Guskov asked him, pleased with his response.

"A conscious desire to act," Goldfarb said, "which is really a late understanding of a subconscious decision, could conceivably have a downward filtering action, just as it does when we move physically. Like walking downstairs, all the patient would be aware of is that he wants to go down and his feet take him down—he doesn't have to work every muscle in his legs to do it. In this case Patient X may simply wish to vanish, and so he does, without understanding exactly how he is doing it."

"Nikolai?" Guskov turned back to his old friend and colleague. "Still too difficult?"

"Yes, yes," Kropotkin nodded. "I see your points. But I do not see how an organic creature can achieve interaction with fermions and bosons, as would be required to achieve this complete matter-transformation that you seem to think so easy.

"Fermions are the stuff of matter and bosons the stuff of fields, together forming the fabric of the universe. How could consciousness, a product of organic chemistry, reach down to that level and manipulate it? More, how could it do so without altering itself in the process? The changes you're talking of involve Patient X's entire structure and so, necessarily, his mind. How can the information of what he is, physically, survive that complete change? Where is it stored and how is he *re*stored? *Has* he been restored? That would go a long way to convince me, at least, but you have nothing, not a single cell remains. Even supposing you are right, the act of vanishing seems as though it would be a final act."

"Good afternoon," said a voice from the doorway, a light, female voice with the verve and authority that suggested it was used to facing interrogative panels and grant committees and getting its own way. "Wasting no time, I see."

"Doctor Khan." Guskov got up to introduce her to the others. "I hope you've settled in well."

"It's hardly the Ritz," she said and shook hands with Goldfarb and Kropotkin in turn as they stood up to greet her. "Alicia, please," she added, including them all in the sweep of her amber eyes. "I am your statistician and probability guru for the duration. I hope you won't all be too long about it, either. I've left a stew in the oven." She smiled, an infectious smile that Mikhail and Nikolai responded warmly to and Isidore copied faithfully back at her. Mikhail had never met her before but he formed an instant dislike for her in that moment.

There was a sound of footsteps at the door and Lucy Desanto walked in on Alicia's moment, hands in the pockets of her slacks, her eyebrows raised beneath the grey and brown sweep of her fringe. "I see the party's started without me," she said. She greeted them all with a single nod of recognition and a sardonic smile. "All the happy guests, thanks to your sweet invitations, Mikhail. So full of blandishments and pleasant words about my family. You must be pleased with everything you've achieved already." She sat down in a vacant chair that was just outside the line of the group and folded her hands in her lap. Her gaze was relentless.

"I sent no such letter." It was the truth.

"Your lackey, then. Ms. Delaney from the Department of Defense. What a charming girl. I'm sure she's destined for the top."

Her arrival had filmed the atmosphere with a slick of discomfort, as she had intended. Mikhail didn't make the mistake of attempting to disperse it. He waited for them all to accept the situation and to see what their reactions would be. They would have to get a lot more weight off their collective chests before any of them were capable of continuing Mappa Mundi, and the sooner it started, the sooner it would be over.

"Mary Delaney is one of those who stand directly in the way of achieving anything with this project," he said, keeping his attitude conversational although his eyes gazed firmly into Desanto's. "The Free State of Mind can never be brought into being as long as she and her compatriots exercise the control they do over us. We are not here to work for her. We are here to free ourselves."

"Ah, yes, your crusade," Desanto replied. "But here we are, locked in a bunker, no outside communications and no escape. We couldn't even get a letter out. I expect that is all in the plan, though, is it?"

"Is this place bugged?" Alicia was looking around at the walls and ceiling fitments. "And if not, why not?"

"It's riddled with bugs," Mikhail assured her, "which we've disabled in here over the course of the last few days. No doubt they will complain, but considering the situation, they will not be replacing the devices." He was glad that they could speak freely within the confines of the environment. "It was also a condition of my continued support for the United States."

"Why? Going to defect again?"

"Just once more," he assured her. "But we've run out of drinks. Let's get some more, shall we?"

The group broke up and went about finding things in the kitchen with shows of relief and small talk. Only Nikolai stayed behind, touching him on the arm.

"You're very certain of yourself," he said. "Why do you trust them? They can listen from anywhere."

"Because," he said, "they know that I have all the production facilities in place for a global-scale NervePath output and they don't. They like to believe their security here is faultless, but they know we're smart. I don't trust them, they don't trust me, but they won't come for us until they're certain the product is viable without us, and until then, whether they're listening or not, they can stuff it up their ass. They may as well know the whole plan, because it doesn't change the fact that they need us for now."

"Not up to the usual scope of your security and ideas," Nikolai said and smiled, patting Mikhail on the shoulder. "I see that at last you're like the rest of us."

Mikhail waited for him to finish. He'd worked a long time with Nikolai, longer than with anyone else. They'd first had the inklings of Mappa Mundi back in the early 1990s in Germany, working together in the same departments in Berlin. Now their ideas were slowly coming to life, and their lives, simultaneously, moving towards a conclusion. He was sure that Nikolai had an important statement, witty, precise.

He wasn't disappointed. "Like you?"

"Yes. Pissing in the wind." Nikolai laughed asthmatically and coughed once or twice. "At last the playing field is level. I like that. It will be interesting to see what happens, even if none of us ever forgive you."

"Forgiveness isn't necessary," Mikhail said. "Your gratitude will be my reward, the day all this secrecy and lying and deceit and unfairness comes to an end."

"Yes, of course it will," Nikolai said. "And I will paste my thanks to the rear end of a flying pig." He took his glasses off and wiped them on an optical cloth from his pocket, replacing them carefully afterwards. "You think all human nature is like yours. It isn't."

"It will be."

Nikolai ignored him. "You know, this Armstrong incident has changed everything. You have to find her before they do. You have to get her on our side."

Mikhail sighed heavily. "I think that's out of my hands now," he said.

"Pray, then," Nikolai said, watching through the hatchway that led to the kitchen and its shining stainless steel as the others moved cautiously around each other. "Because if you're right about her and Patient X then you haven't got the power you think in Mappa Mundi on its own."

Mikhail watched them, too, Isidore oblivious between the two women on either side of him. Kropotkin was right. Now the power structure had changed. Nothing was as he had planned. All he could do was wait and hope that the few cards still in his hand stayed secret a little longer. The death of TetsuoYamamoto might have bought him a few more weeks. It might not. Here there was no knowing what went on in the affairs of the living.

He made an excuse or two and retired to his own rooms to pour himself a single shot of scotch and stare at the simulation of a window overlooking the harsh Siberian steppe. Its windswept ice made him glad to be inside. For now.

Ian Detteridge swam in oceans of flux. A place, no name, a play but no game, a chance in a field of chances dancing on the surface of his mind. Nameless places passed through him on their way to somebody else.

His awareness flickered listlessly in and out of existence. The control he'd once had was gone. He'd thought it would, but that was no comfort now it had. It would and it had, it could and it did, it might—what was the word that would drag it back to his future?

Like an albatross, by instinct he followed Natalie Armstrong, true to his word, keeping in touch, beneath and above, through and between, sailing the wind of the world.

He tried to summon an effort of will. The chain of his trying to try stretched out in a yawning distance in every direction and he hung suspended in the zero-g of its centre point, becalmed. He thought he travelled. He thought of nothing, which was not the same as being nothing. He struggled to try, to remember to try, to search for the surface of things.

He made his way, jiggery, jaggery, uncertain as a child in the dark.

He decided to reach out.

He reached into the tough, rough, solid, the dense, loose, light, the hard fixed form.

He stepped into a truck with a curiously quiet engine and an almost silent, rail-smooth ride. Its walls were grey and fitted out with straps and clips and holding clamps of all kinds. In a soft chair, secured with seat-belt webbing to the floor of the truck, sat Natalie Armstrong like a queen, her flame hair in an explosive disarray, her jacket rumpled, her leather trousers shiny, her tough boots braced, and her long fingers drumming on the armrests, a mambo on the right and a march on the left.

"Bobby," she said, smiling a smile that made him feel suddenly good about being again. "I mean Ian. Thank God. You've got to help me get out of this thing before we get wherever we're going."

He recognized immediately that the NP system had spread inside her. She was almost completed, but she'd managed to halt it right before the fatal point where it changed, under its own rules, and became free. The results of its actions were still developing in their subtlety, and she was almost like him by now. Almost, but not enough to shift form.

Ian looked into the structure of the truck's sides and reached into the gaps with fingers that felt their way along the domain lines between the crystalline forms of the metal and separated the lattices at these faults so that he could lift out an entire circle of the wall and put it on the floor. He turned and Natalie was watching him, her face fearful but a smile lingering on it. He nodded and together they peered out for a few moments, faces into the wind.

They weren't going too fast and the land outside was barren-looking industrial sites, some disused and decaying, others apparently limping along, still in business. Nobody saw them and they saw no police escort. No point in alarming the public, Ian thought, or perhaps they assumed there'd be no escape from the vehicle.

"Can you jump?" He glanced at Natalie who was watching the paving and the road slide by. Fleetingly he felt anxiety, as though his body could be damaged by sudden contact at speed with the concrete, but then he realized it was Natalie's fear, not his own.

"Yes," she said with confidence. "But let's go out the back so they don't see us straightaway. With luck, we'll be able to hide before they know I'm gone."

"Okay." Ian replaced the panel and realigned it carefully until even the paint seemed as if it had been untouched.

Then he turned his focus to the rear doors and cut through them, avoiding the alarm and pressure sensors. It was tricky. Their wires ran everywhere, but at last he had a narrow gap she would be able to squeeze through. The bed of the vehicle was high, but he thought it looked easy enough, so long as you knew how to fall.

"Don't forget to roll," he said as she balanced in the hole, her hair jiving in the wind, jacket tails rippling.

She turned to him, an exultant look on her face. "This is madness."

He nodded. "Maybe you'll enjoy it more than I have."

They slowed and came to a kind of junction at a corner.

Natalie stepped down silently to the blacktop and said, "Come on. Put that back."

"You go. I'll catch up with you," he said and started to fix up the panels.

As the bomb truck wound its way through the old industrial estate and carried on with its slow route to the safe area, avoiding housing, Natalie walked the other way, towards the airport, concealing herself with buildings and walls as she went, eventually finding a highway that led into and out of the city.

She hitched a lift with a salesman, coming home after a tour of the state, and Ian followed her at a distance, several levels below, waiting, conserving what he could for the moment when he would get his chance to do something that mattered.

Seventeen

Natalie made straight for Jude's address in Eastern Market, surprised to find him within a stone's throw of the Capitol itself, amid handsome streets where mature trees had buckled the paving around them into hills and fissures with their roots. In a pale stone apartment building, on the top floor, his windows had a view of the old city heart. Dusk was coming on and the white buildings shone, with lights illuminating them from the ground. Importance and power were written deep in their architecture. In the homes and rooms close to her Natalie felt other energies moving: the blurred, vague impressions of people shone weakly like reflections in running water.

She shivered as she stood on the curb and calculated how long it would take them to find her by tracing her taxi-payment transaction. She'd used the best encryption, but there was always a way. She estimated a few hours at the outside and if they'd any brains they might already be here, waiting for her to make an appearance.

The heat and the smells were exotic. They almost nullified the nightmare of Dan's death with their newness to her. She lingered in the shadow of a ginkgo tree whose leaves trembled on an unfelt breeze, and absorbed the calm of change for an instant, looking unobtrusively around her for spies. There was no one loitering, apart from herself. Without waiting any longer she trotted up the steps to the foyer entrance and buzzed the doorman's attention.

Her false ID worked on the building AI and she was admitted without any of the simpering interference she'd half dreaded from a place like this—but the doorman didn't believe in snobbery. He liked the idea that human beings could come and go without the third degree. He liked the look of her, even if she was a touch on the goofy side. She smiled at him politely through her exhaustion. Polite he liked, and he opened the lift doors for her and sent her on her way.

The white corridor was hospital stark, Natalie thought as she stepped out and made for the fourth door along. All it was missing were some tiles, a lino floor, and the eternal stink of urine and it would have been a dead ringer for her psychiatric ward. Apart from its doors and lights it was featureless. It said to anyone—you are in a dead zone between lives, take a door at your peril, but for the sake of sanity, take one. She hadn't come for peril, although she knew now that Jude was certainly deeply in it if he was still here.

His door had a touchpad service on the jamb and she brushed it with one finger. A beam scanned her face and she heard a chime sound inside.

She waited almost a minute. Then the door opened and she was about to fall in with relief and anguish and the desperate need to collapse somewhere secure when she saw Jude.

Although he was trying to appear normal as he held the door it was obvious he was in deep shock. His gaze was slow to fix on her, it wavered erratically and the hand in his hair had stopped midbrush through and seemed to be supporting his skull. His face was haggard his eyes looked sticky and red. More than that, inside his mind she didn't see Jude the competent detective but two other people: a man who was full of rage and despair, and someone who wanted to curl up in a corner and regress to the point where he didn't even know his own name.

Whatever had happened to him in the days since they'd parted, it must be as bad or worse than what had happened to her. She knew it. Much as she wanted to, now was not her time to unlock her feelings about Dan and Selfware. She was the stronger one and she had to take this on the chin for longer.

"Come in," he said, blinking as though the light hurt his eyes.

When the door was shut she put her hand out to his arm and held it as he was turning away from her, slumping with shoulders forward in a semiprotective posture. He rotated towards her, still closed up, and she said, quietly, "What happened?"

"My sister . . ." he began, but then forgot how to continue and simply stared at her with the flat dullness of imbecility.

If she hadn't known otherwise from his breath and the absence of any giveaway smell she would have thought he'd been drinking heavily. She realized she had to help him.

"Come on, let's sit down." After the entryway the apartment branched out into a big white room with what looked like comfortable furniture. Jude let her guide him and sat passively on the edge of a couch, resting his elbows on his knees.

He rallied to say, "I should be asking you, shouldn't I? I heard about something. An accident at the Clinic. Was that you?"

She was gratified for the instant that he searched her face with real sensitivity, trying to listen for her answer.

"It was, but that's not important right this minute. I'm still here, see?" She spoke in her professional voice, the calm, warm tone she used to use for trauma patients and victims of violent crime. His whole behaviour suggested that he'd seen or been involved in something like that very recently. She thought about what he'd said—his sister—and became convinced that there was a horrible and fatal story in the offing.

"Can I get you a drink?" she asked, crouching down at his side, all the time assessing him. He took a moment to answer.

"Tea," he said and made an effort to smile. "That's what the English do, right? Tea for all problems."

"Universal cure," she agreed. "I'll be right back."

The white lounge, vast and airy, studded with diamond energysaver lights, narrowed on one side and became a small kitchen, again full of white marble, shiny metal, and brilliance. The effect was like living inside Tiffany's front window, she thought, and shivered—how very odd to find him in a place like this. It didn't fit him. It was a show home, a designer "poof's palace" as Dan would have called it. But then, she wasn't thinking about Dan.

She opened and shut cupboards until she'd located cups and the red pack of Twining's English Breakfast tea bags. It was very light and when she looked inside only tea dust remained. There were no other boxes in sight.

"Shit," she said, "you're all out of tea."

"No, there was one left," he said and, exhausted, got up to show her.

He took the box and confidently turned it, only to stop dead as he saw the inside.

"That's odd," he said. "I could have sworn I had . . . I must have." He paused and swayed so suddenly that Natalie grabbed his arm to stop him falling. She thought he was fainting but he shot a hand out to the breakfast bar and steadied himself.

"What is it? Don't worry. We can have something else."

"No," he said, forcefully. He pushed himself off from the bar and staggered into the lounge, the box still in his hand. She didn't understand why he was fixated on it, but he didn't seem to have lost the plot entirely, so he probably wasn't suffering a paranoid delusion.

He turned and balanced, speaking carefully, in control again, "White Horse doesn't drink anything except tarpit coffee and herbal tea. I don't drink tea. You do. Mary does. Last time that Mary was here she made herself a cup and said there was only one left and not to forget it next time I went to the store."

Natalie waited for him to conclude. Her own desperation and tiredness threatened to fight her to the floor but she stood nonchalantly and looked interested.

Jude looked around him and Natalie followed his gaze that lingered on a handsomely mounted piece of Native American art and some kind of jewellery or beaded shirt display. "Mary must have been here when I wasn't. White Horse said she'd spoken to her and that Mary had told her about a lawyer. But I thought . . . I thought she meant they'd spoken on the phone, I don't know why. But she was here, and she didn't mention it."

"Who's Mary?" Natalie asked. Behind her the kettle chimed and switched itself off.

"Mary, my partner," Jude said, distracted. He sat down and turned the cardboard tea box in his hands, letting the dust sift out onto the immaculate carpet. "We've worked together four, five years."

"Friends?" She had the strangest impression, in what she was coming to recognize as the true Selfware style of magical knowledge from nowhere, that the person he was talking about was someone she'd met. But that was ridiculous.

"Yeah. The best." But he didn't sound certain.

Natalie tried not to wonder why he'd chosen never to mention her before, but she did wonder. Yes, his trip to England had been covert, but even so. Wouldn't this friend be helping him to investigate this? Natalie tried to shake off the feeling that Jude was rapidly becoming more of an enigma as her knowledge about him increased.

"You mean, you were friends, and now you're not?" She tried to get him to clarify.

"I don't know." He looked across at her and just like a switch being flicked the Jude she did remember seemed to come back on. "Sorry. This must sound like a crock to you, but this box . . ." He held it in his hand and then, without warning, grimaced and crushed it up into a small grey and red ball. Then, when he turned back to her, his face was calm.

"A lot's happened."

"To me, too," she said, and then her decision was made about whether she could or should trust him, could or should involve him further. "Come on. We can't stay here. Get whatever you need and let's go." But it was hard to say it. All she wanted to do was sink down on one of those couches and curl up and sleep, not go out into a country and city she didn't know with nowhere to hide.

He stared blankly at her as though he didn't understand a word of it but then got to his feet. Back to dull again, hesitant and pained, he nodded.

"Give me a minute or two."

He disappeared into one of the other rooms and she heard the sound of wardrobes opening. She poured herself a cup of hot water and sipped it as she made a closer inspection of the room. Its neatness and order made her feel even more ravaged and helpless.

"What did she do with the machine?" Natalie called through, without really thinking about the question.

"It was taken off her," he said, grim-faced as he returned. He took the beaded thing off the wall and removed the back of it, taking the necklaces and other things out from their pinnings and packing them carefully in rolled T-shirts, which he placed in a briefcase. He explained, in clipped terms, what had happened, the kidnap and the threats.

"Your cornflakes packet is all chopped up," she said, not sure herself why it was important, only that nobody here looked like they had the time or inclination to play with cardboard and glue for fun.

Jude looked blank. He obviously wasn't someone who ate at home very much. It seemed like news to him.

"You said she was determined to find hard evidence. The scanner was it. But she carried it round in her bag all the time, you said, even after you warned her. She must have thought it would expose her to danger. Wouldn't it have been better to put it in a safety deposit?"

Jude shrugged, but his expression showed that his thinking was suddenly starting to follow hers. "She didn't trust big institutions, banks included."

"Do you think she might have left it here?"

"What, and made a convincing replica out of that?"

"No. But it's like any other device. It's got a fancy outside and working insides. The outside isn't important, and, more to the point, it's the kind of thing that you couldn't tell didn't work unless you had some active NervePath to test it on. She didn't. She may have realized that and taken the case with her in case she was caught, to use as a bargaining chip for her safety. Others would have no reason not to believe it was the real thing and she got to protect her evidence." Natalie knew she was right.

"She might not have told you, so you wouldn't be able to give it away if you were questioned. You've got to expect that whoever did this to her isn't going to stop at raiding this place and—"

"Did what to her?" He was cold and direct as his stare arrowed at her across the room.

"Drowned her in the—"

"I didn't say anything about that."

The temperature in the room seemed to drop to absolute zero. Natalie at once realized that she had no idea how she knew the details of what had happened to Jude's sister, except that she did, and he was now looking at her with piercing suspicion and a simmering, violent hostility. She was glad the breakfast bar was between them again.

"No," she said, reaching for her treatment voice and letting her own shock show with it. "You didn't. But she did drown in the Potomac, didn't she? And—" she didn't understand what came into her mind next, but she said it aloud "—she was drunk on champagne."

Jude left his briefcase and stalked across until their faces were only a foot apart, the bar between them. He leaned closer, his dark eyes scrutinizing hers and brimming with the beginnings of tears that she could see were due more to anger than to grief at this moment. His voice was quiet and more controlled than she expected.

"You'd better tell me what the hell happened to you in that accident or we are going our very separate ways."

In as few words as she could, keeping it simple, she told him what had happened and how she believed she was changing.

"I've never had this before," she insisted, not giving an inch. "I don't even have a theory for it. On the plane, in the taxi—it was like I could read people's body language and get information out of everything they did. I knew their real feelings. That was like seeing their mind. But I don't know how I know about White Horse. I just know. It must be from you. I don't know how. How could that kind of thing be in your behaviour? It couldn't." She held her hands out in the universal gesture of supplication and he looked down at them, unable to stop his suspicion, his natural dislike and distrust of someone with an apparent ability that was out of his understanding and that violated the privacy of his own mind.

Natalie would have felt the same. She *did* feel the same. She didn't want to acquire the contents of other heads without asking. She'd been through lots of minds, many deviant and damaged, some banal, some wretched. Imagining them as her own was bad enough. This was frightening.

She put her hands down on the cold marble top and took a long breath as Jude leaned on the bar, head down, thinking hard.

"Actually, that's not quite right," she said. "I have heard a thought before, but I didn't know what it was."

He looked up reluctantly through his long fringe, face still swollen with emotions he wasn't ready or able to express.

"It was yesterday now. It woke me up. I went out to find where it had come from and I thought it must be Dan, even though that's ridiculous. He was miles away. But I'd been under house arrest and they wouldn't even let us call each other. I didn't know if he was still at the police station—they thought he'd sabotaged the experiment, you see, at first.

"So I thought, here's my chance, I'll go and see him. But there were police all over the flat and there was nobody where I thought I should go, so I ran back home. I didn't know what was going on, but I decided I couldn't stay and obey any more—the Ministry had something to do with the sabotage or, at least, they allowed it to run on once it'd started. I skipped the flight I was meant to take and came here instead. On the way—" She paused and looked around the place for assistance, a way to protect herself from what she had to say.

She looked at Jude's face and clung on to its mistrust and its misery.

"I got a call from someone on this side, the American side, I think. Her accent was all wrong. She had Dan. She told me that if I didn't go straight back and start cooperating that they'd send someone who would—" she made a gun shape out of her hand and pointed it at her head, "—zap me with something that would make me comply. And in case I didn't want to believe that she could, she used it to kill Dan, right there. She switched him off. He's dead."

Jude immediately closed his eyes and squeezed them shut. He straightened his back and sighed, "I'm sorry." But there were too many emotions seething in him for him to be able to say any more.

Natalie walked around the end of the bar and put her arms around him. He turned and they held each other tightly for a while. By mutual but unacknowledged agreement they drew apart after a short time and Jude went back to his briefcase, checking his Pad was in his pocket. Natalie kept her hands inside hers, the old Pad under her left palm. She watched him take a last look around. His gaze fell on the grey and red ball of the tea box and stayed there, transfixed.

He looked at it for almost a minute.

"What does it mean?" she asked quietly, as he finally turned away and picked up his case.

His face was grim and he looked like he was pushing fifty in that moment.

"It means I think I may have been a fool," he said. "I can't quite tell you why. Maybe it means nothing." He went into another wandering moment in which he seemed completely lost, and then the marine in him, or the detective, took over and said, "If White Horse did leave that scanner here, I haven't seen it. Do you need it?"

"Yes," she said. "I've got nothing with me. It could help, if someone comes who's already under the influence, or if I need to switch it on again."

"Again?" He stared at her, uncomprehending. "I thought it'd be more use for taking out whatever they throw at you."

"Maybe," she could see he wasn't ready for her line of thinking—that Selfware accelerated even further could enable her to get around almost any kind of trouble. At a cost. She let it go. "There isn't time for a long search. Is there anywhere that she was likely to hide it?"

He shook his head. "She hadn't been here long."

"What kinds of places does she usually hide things?"

"Hide? I . . ."

Natalie could see him thinking way back, to their childhood. "Places like, kind of obvious but not obvious. Somewhere you'd have to try and find it, not immediately see it. She had this bangle once, turquoise and silver, cheap but she thought it was good. She hid it one time, too well, and never rememebred where she put it. Still lost. Ever since then she always used to pick a place that she'd come to for another reason . . ."

"Do you think she'd put it somewhere you might stumble over it, in case something happened to her?" Natalie had a headache coming on but she tried to stay calm and persist. The chance of finding a working scanner was too good to miss. It could mean the difference between freedom and slavery. "Someplace only you were likely to go? Maybe something you had in common might mark it out? Or, if both of you were compromised, something that could be sent home to your family as a personal item?"

He looked in the direction of each room of the apartment in turn, progressing mentally through each one and its objects, its angles. "I can't . . ." He hesitated, looking at the kitchen. "Wait."

Natalie watched him as he strode suddenly to the cupboard under the sink and began hauling out large silvery tins, reaching behind to put them on the bar near her. She read the side and its utilitarian writing—*Peanut Butter. Be sure to eat something from the four food groups every day.*

Jude reached into a drawer and passed her a knife. He began to open the first can, which seemed lighter, using the knife as a lever for the pressure-fitting lid.

Natalie couldn't believe anybody bought peanut butter in such huge quantities. She opened hers and was faced with a paper seal and then a solid mass of light brown sludge. She weighed the can in her hand. It said on the side it held three pounds. American pounds—what was that in real weight? She was distracted by Jude, who had plunged his hand straight into the opened tin and was feeling around in the bottom.

Natalie turned hers over and looked at the lower ring seal. It did seem a little bent in places.

"There's something," he said, a second of excitement lifting his tone to near normal.

Natalie started to scoop the thick, cakelike, oily stuff out and put it on the tin lid. As Jude pulled out a plastic bag from his and peered at the microchips it held she grabbed a second one, larger, and extracted it from the base of her tin. The smell made her realize how hungry she was. Starving. She picked up a lump and started eating it as she saw that her bag held the projection board and cooling system. The third tin they wrenched the base off completed the whole scanner.

"She was a good engineer," Natalie said, licking her fingers and hand clean. "They look fine."

Jude vanished for a minute as she shoved another handful of the goop in her mouth and then reappeared with a small toolkit box that he slid into her right pocket.

"We have to go now," she said, ripping a section of paper towel out of the dispenser and cleaning her hands.

"Agreed." He collected his case. "The only question is, where to?"

"Anywhere," she said, following him to the door. "Anywhere we can talk and not be overheard."

He turned to her in the confined space, looking down at her. "I really am sorry."

"I know." She leaned past him and opened the door, trying to ignore the sudden uprush of tears in her eyes at what she could see inside him, inside herself. "Let's go."

Mary discovered the facts of Natalie's second escape late. The cops called out to the airport had taken FBI officers with them, but since none of them knew anything about the Mappa Mundi project or Natalie Armstrong's special status they treated her as an ordinary crazy bomb suspect and put her in a truck to take her to the explosives and detonation site out of town. The personnel that Mary had sent to the airport herself hadn't been filled in on the developments during the flight because that got relayed to the local team, who weren't her familiars. They'd stayed on in the arrivals hall as the police shot out in force onto the apron in a far distant corner of the airfield.

Alarms had only spread wider once the truck arrived and was opened to reveal an empty space with no sign of Dr. Armstrong's presence save a couple of red hairs and some clothing fibres stuck to the chair inside that matched those on her airplane seat. By the time the Feds had called in a TV magic expert to help them figure out how she'd gotten out of a high-security vehicle without appearing to touch it Mary was settling down in the tub for a long, hot soak, thinking that her day had already been more than sufficiently filled with stress and degradation.

The news made her haul herself out again five minutes later and start getting dressed, cursing loudly with every Irish insult she could think of. Armstrong had got her message but wasn't going to play? Or maybe that stuff in her head had given her access to a whole new world of genius that Mary wasn't able to react to fast enough. *But let's not think that*, she decided, towelling her legs until they were an angry red. *Let's not get ahead of the game.*

She made herself comb her hair slowly, picking out the tangles, and read Jude's message, the one she'd ignored at the Pentagon.

"Mary—White Horse never arrived at your legal office. She's been found in the river, they say. I'm going to ID. Can you meet me? Just in case. I've tried her numbers, but no answer. It's like the Pad's vanished, even using MaxTrace. Or catch up with me at home. Or call ASAP. Jude."

It didn't sound as though he suspected her at all, even though he knew about her connection to the law office concerned. Even so, this had been a couple of hours ago. She called him. There was no reply and the rebound said that his Pad was out of service. Probably he was at home with everything switched off. She'd have to go there.

She pulled on jeans and a sweater over her underwear and put some cowboy boots on her feet. She tied back her hair with a bolero tie. Looking at her face in the mirror she put on only a trace of makeup. Lots wouldn't look sympathetic. Even thinking about what she'd ordered done and what she'd done herself made her feel giddy and out of kilter. She hadn't been sure she was capable of it, not even fixing Guskov's scientists up, but she'd done it and the triumph over herself was tainted with disgust. The face in the mirror hardly seemed like her own. The blush and the foundation couldn't make it so, but when she put on her perfume and picked up her bag she felt absolutely ordinary again. So this was what it was like to be a ruthless, dedicated careerist—it had its moments of twisted exhilaration and its vast flat acres of plain, boring, ordinary life. She couldn't decide if that was disappointing. Maybe she'd have been happier if she'd grown another head. The thought made her laugh.

Jude's apartment was only five blocks from hers. She walked, gathering her thoughts, stopping at the Seven Eleven on his corner to pick up a care pack of basic groceries: milk, coffee, fruit, his favourite ice cream. More out of habit than judgement she took the back stairs to his building, using her own key set—she'd done it deliberately when she came to see White Horse in case that nosy doorman took it into his head to start talking about her visits and now it seemed prudent even though there was no real need.

When she cued the presspad on the door she felt genuine trepidation: she'd never seen Jude in deep stress and she didn't know what she'd find. Her curiosity faded as the moments passed, however, and she realized that either he wasn't answering or he wasn't there.

She took out her Pad and overrode the door system, sure he wouldn't mind if he was just slow in moving: they had passes to each other's places as a matter of routine. Once it opened she called out,

"Jude? It's Mary. Sorry I'm so late!"

But there was no answer.

Mary walked slowly in and took a look around, putting the grocery bag on the breakfast bar. She saw the open tins and stared at them. He'd had a real go at those for some reason. Maybe because they were BIA? He hated peanut butter, she knew that, and the BIA connection could have set off a rage against the perceived injustices of his sister's life, the all too real outrage of her death. People did strange things in their grief.

Then she noticed the pictures that had been taken down and torn apart. The beaded pieces were family heirlooms, deeply connected to everything he shared with White Horse.

She was looking at them in more detail when she noticed the balled-up cardboard on the floor and a little chill ran down her back. She picked it up and it was, as she'd thought, an empty tea-bag container. Fair enough, you rip down your pictures and drag out what's dear and important, maybe you take it away to hide or send home or do something else with it that eases your pain, but Jude was a neat freak. He didn't throw trash. He wouldn't leave this here.

She put it down and walked through the other rooms quickly. There was nothing, but again she noticed the extreme tidiness. Even the room his sister had used was cleaned up—had he already packed her away? The idea of his being so practical chilled her. She tried calling him again, but no answer.

"Shit," she said quietly and sat down on the big, white sofa. It was then that she wondered if he'd been alone. Natalie Armstrong—he'd contacted her before. Had she been here? Finding out would take her a few hours and could provoke a big ugly scene if he came back and caught her forensic team messing about. But the idea lingered.

Mary stared at the remains of the tea box. Vaguely she had an idea that last time she'd been here with him, curled up on this very spot, drinking tea, Jude rubbing her feet, she'd said something about being down to the last bag. Jude didn't drink it. He wouldn't have remembered because he was a hopeless shopper like that, all impulse and no organization—quite the contrary of his at-home habits. One reason they rarely ate here was because the cupboards held cereal, cocktail olives, tinned tuna, truffle oil, cheese crackers, and precious little else.

Did this ball mean he was angry at her? But why?

She checked with the police records and confirmed that White Horse had been identified more than two hours ago. Jude had left the morgue abruptly, the clerk noted, after asking for a homicide detective to take a statement.

He must have realized the pointlessness of that. Which meant he had a good idea of the scale of what they were both getting mixed up in. So he knew more than he'd told her. For sure. But how much?

Mary ground her teeth in frustration and made an office check with Special Sciences to see what he'd reported from the day before, when he'd gone to Atlanta on that mission for Perez. His entry in the form read, "The contact failed to report at the stated time. His address was located using datapilot service Nostromo. The contact was discovered dead [see CrimeRef 1HX8897] and the body reported to local police, investigation to be continued by FBI and regional. No messages or other evidence related to the contact message [CE9Y7] were found. Awaiting forensic reports."

Which was nine-tenths jack shit.

Unless Jude was lying, of course.

But she had no way of finding out whether he was or not. To her knowledge he'd never lied before, but as a practised deceiver herself she knew that meant nothing. To get away with a successful secret it was better to be regularly truthful and so never incur suspicion. And he might have thought he had good reasons not to talk—when she'd tried to open him up in the bar his discomfort had been obvious. He might even have thought he was protecting her.

Whatever Jude was doing, as long as it didn't involve Natalie Armstrong she could stand it. But Armstrong was the problem she had to solve right away. Find her and get her back on track. The truck evidence, preposterous as it seemed, had struck a chord—hadn't the other Patient X done something like that? Maybe the video evidence was spot on and he *had* disappeared. If she'd disappeared she might even be dead, or never coming back.

That would almost be the best possible result, Mary thought, and got up. She put the groceries away in the refrigerator and left a note written on the bag: "Jude. Came to see you but you weren't in—obviously! Left you some milk etc. Going to the Beer House down the street to watch the cable sport and wait. If you don't show in an hour or two I'll be at home. Love, Mary. PS Your Pad is in Off mode, did you know?"

Jude and Natalie had hired a car under one of Jude's false identities and driven a short way out of DC to a cheap motel in a small town that looked like it wasn't used for anything except middle-level business conferences and the raising of low-rise suburban children. At Three Pines Lodge there were no AI security systems and no surveillance cameras. The security was entirely human or canine.

Jude had never felt so empty in his life, or so lacking in knowledge of what to say or do. He went through the motions of driving, paying for the room, getting the keys, walking up the outside steps and along the verandah to the door on automatic, as though the link that kept him attached to a motive had been disconnected. He didn't even know if he wanted to be there. The things she'd told him . . . he couldn't believe them. There was so much he couldn't come to grips with.

He fumbled the key and stabbed it angrily in the lock. Even his hands didn't work right now.

Natalie's shadow, cast by the glitzy neon rimlights of the hotel sign, flickered over him. It shuddered, although she stayed quite still. He stared inside at the small room and its double bed and was turning to apologize and say he'd asked for two and there must have been a mistake when, before he could turn the lights on, her small but powerful hand had grabbed him by the shirt-front and she was pressed up against him, kissing him on the mouth with frantic urgency, her other hand pulling down the zipper of his trousers.

Her touch was like a flame on a fuse. Before he could think or react he found his hands were all over her, tearing at her clothing, his mouth welded to hers. He picked her up and then they were both on the bed. As he fell back he saw over her shoulder the clear night sky through the open doorway, the dim glow of Washington and the tiny stars, the black claws of the trees that overhung the yard below. The fierce grunt of her triumph as she wriggled out of her leather jeans and kicked her boots into the dark sounded sharply against his ear. She bit it.

The pain was fantastic, amazing. It was real and it hurt. He dug his fingers into the flesh of her bare buttocks and thrashed out of the remains of his own clothing. Then, for several minutes, he had no thoughts, only the sharp, bright, darting awareness of one sensation after another in a huge cascade that primed his hunger ever more as they fed it.

Biting and licking, thrusting like an animal, wrestling, groaning, sliding in sweat he flung himself at her and, as she lay beneath him in one instant and the neon lights lit her, he saw his own savage face reflected back at him, his own desperation in the wild thrashing of her head and her body as it bucked.

When he came it was like a ferocious electricity that ran in every bone and so powerful that something fragile in him burst. He shouted out. He felt Natalie's fingernails tear his back open and for a second he thought he felt two black and hideous wings of bony hide leap out of the gaps and arch over him in thrumming tension like high wires poised beneath a storm.

They lay, a sludge of human flesh on the tough and unpleasant nylon cover of the bed. Through the door the breeze came in to explore their wet skin. A siren wailed and faded far away, lost forever.

He looked down, suddenly quieted, and saw Natalie crying silently, her face turned away from him, a flat mask. He put his head back down on her limp chest and opened his mouth. He retched drily. Now he'd finally felt something it wouldn't come out. It twisted itself inside his heart, dislodged for sure, but it stayed there, a faint vibration running all the way up to his skin.

They lay until they heard someone come along the verandah walkway, a man and a woman, talking loud, sounding a bit drunk.

Jude became aware of Natalie listening. She held her breath.

"Small-town affair," she whispered and giggled, sniffing and giggling even harder when her laugh made him finally slip out and a hot rush followed him to stain the cover. "Seedy."

They heard the man and woman stop at their door, which stood ajar.

"What the . . . ? Are you okay in there, lady?" the man said, a mixture of alarm and confusion and humour in his voice.

"Tyrone!" The woman was much less impressed. Jude thought it was her hand that grabbed the doorknob and yanked the door shut. "Some people jus' like animals. Can't even wait to git alone!" Her outrages faded away and the man went with her, chuckling and muttering childishly, "Well, Nora, what've we come here for if it ain't a bit of fast and dirty—"

"Tyrone," she said, friendlier now, as their door closed them off from the rest of the universe.

Jude and Natalie moved apart, but not far. They left their legs entwined. He moved so that she could lie and rest her head on his arm. She toyed with his hair.

"Look at your bangs here," she said. "Nearly as long as Dan's."

They slept a few hours, so deep in exhaustion that when he woke again and saw dawn they hadn't moved to ease their aching limbs. Jude's legs and hips hurt but he saw that Natalie was still asleep. She was warm. He heard her heart beating, very slow and very even, its rhythm counting down the seconds of her life.

He looked at the rays of the new day and knew that White Horse was gone forever and his last blood connection to that half of the universe with her. He was free.

He saw himself sailing high in the sky on black and white wings. Below him the houses and hills of Montana were so far away. He could only imagine them over the horizon.

Without her, how would he come to fit this skin?

Eighteen

Jude woke up the second time with a crick in his neck and an ache in his chest that no amount of anything was going to cure soon. He shifted and felt with a shock of real physical pain the raw areas on his back as the harsh nylon sheet underneath rubbed them.

Natalie was awake, staring at the ceiling, or so he thought, but she didn't look his way. Her eyes seemed to be part glazed, blinkless.

As he was watching her she lifted her left eyebrow into a half-moon.

"People used to think Dan and I were an item," Natalie said. "They didn't notice that he'd got none of that reaction towards me or any other woman that would have made it possible. People are blind as bats, but it's all there, right under their noses."

She turned and faced him, tucking her lower arm under her head before she continued. Jude looked down cautiously at her body, hoping not to see signs of violence on it. The night before was dreamlike, but strong enough that he hadn't forgotten any of it. Guiltily he saw hand marks on her arms, fingers clearly delineated. Her right breast was almost blackened with a huge suction mark. She went on, oblivious.

"He was in trouble and I didn't notice because I was so distracted by Bobby and the stuff that happened with you. That file." Her face was wretched and he could see she was making an effort not to cry and be self-pitying.

"Oh, that." Jude glanced involuntarily towards the TV unit where he'd left his briefcase. It was still there, the Russian's file in it, and the vial from the CDC.

He cleared his throat. "It's funny. I'd nearly stopped being freaked out by that. I'd forgotten it. So many things . . ." But he wasn't sure even now that he could talk about those. He didn't want to think about them. As soon as his mind touched on them they slid out of his grasp with fishtail flicks of icy loathing. Tetsuo. The vial.

"We have to decide what to do," Natalie said, as much to herself as to him. She sighed and curled herself into more of a ball. "Tough but practical if we want to survive. We have to decide if there's anything we can do about any of what's going on except save our own skins. That means sharing what we know."

"We may not end up with the same goals," he said warily. "Just because we have dead people and the opposite edges of a conspiracy in common doesn't mean we're on the same side."

She pulled a few faces thinking about it. But he could tell that she wasn't convinced by his caution.

"Maybe. Although I don't see what good the results of this research will do either of us and there's every reason under the sun to think that two people against a military superpower and some tough-minded revolutionaries won't be up to much. But we're probably the only people who know enough to make any kind of a difference at all. You still have a chance to go back," Natalie pointed out. She shivered. "But I think all I can do is go on."

"Because of the—accident?" He didn't know what to call it. He saw the edge of his shirt and pulled it out, put it over her.

"Yes. And I couldn't go back to York, not now that Dan's gone. Even if I could, Guskov is continuing Mappa Mundi in a sealed environment under US government control, and I know all about what he's doing. If I join it as a working scientist I still have a chance to act, both to affect its outcome and maybe to determine what happens to it when it's complete. I don't trust the Ministry or your people, and I don't think I trust Guskov either.

"If it weren't for the Selfware they'd probably get rid of me, but at the moment it's an unknown, and when they find out how I got out of the airport it's going to be an unknown they want to get to the bottom of quickly. But if you go AWOL, Jude, then whoever is tailing you will know you've changed sides. You've got no chance once that happens."

He smiled, trying to show a bit of spirit, and it hurt deep inside. "Oh yeah?"

"You could try recruiting, of course," Natalie said, her wide, handsome gaze becoming gentler in response to his expression. "But that will only get others killed as well. This is far too hot for mistakes.

"Those people who tried to co-opt your sister were idiots. They want to topple the Democrats with this, that's their whole game—using the Perfection Bill and its global unpopularity to start a moral crusade—but they don't even understand what the stakes are; that they're not even about domestic politics on any scale. It's about all our futures, and whether or not the ideas we have will be our own or someone else's.

"Maybe White Horse could've started a publicity campaign that would ruin the election chances of the party, but this entire technology stream is secretive and badly understood. To inform the public about it and try to get them behind an anti-Perfection camp means blowing everything the civil service and the military have been working for, way above elected goons. They'll never let that happen. They'd use a bad first version of Mappaware on the whole country before that. The attempt to go public will only cause the social-suppression function to be slapped on hard, when that's the last thing it should be used for, and once it's started, there's no getting back. Ergo—" she smiled "—it's a stupid plan that will almost certainly achieve the opposite of what they want. You could talk to them, tell them what you know, maybe even get them to back off for a while."

"Yeah, that'll work," Jude said, the sarcasm in his own voice making him angry at himself.

"Or you can stick where you are and see what else you can find out," Natalie said.

"But as soon as I admit to knowing anything I get my head blown off," he pointed out. The more he thought it through the more he felt like he could sense the damage the bullet or the knife was going to do when it came for him. His heart was skipping beats.

"So don't admit it. They aren't telepathic." She sounded like she believed he could pull it off. She smiled at him.

"But if I keep it all to myself, what's the use of it? And what can I do, on my own?" He'd been wondering that a long time. White Horse's dead face came to his mind as an answer—you can get people killed. He should have told Mary days ago, got her to help. He still could.

"I wouldn't," Natalie said, staring directly into the centre of his mind, just as he'd once imagined she could.

He returned her look, trying for the same, but he didn't see anything except her grey-green eyes, pretty irises almost emerald in places, smoky in others, like marbled paper.

"Don't bullshit yourself about letting her in on it just because you get tired," she added, yawning widely. "You can't trust anyone."

Jude saw the empty box of tea, the drift of black dust on his white floor. He couldn't believe that Mary was responsible, not just because of the referral. She wasn't like that.

"She'll have tried to find me there," he said, moving carefully to try and find a scrap of comfort, but the bed was lumpy and rough as a wild dog. "She's not stupid. Fact, she's about the most devious-minded, suspicious woman I know. Usually right about people, too. At least, the kind of people we end up dealing with."

"And your closest friend," Natalie said with a curious expression between envy and caution that he couldn't place. "So you don't want to get her involved."

She paused and then seemed to give herself permission to say, "You love her."

"Get out of my head," he said abruptly but without anger, rolling onto his back and putting his forearm over his face. Thinking about it made him feel guilty, of all things, like he'd betrayed Natalie, even though this nonexistent relationship with Mary would have been in the past.

"I was only asking." She seemed about to say something else, but didn't.

Jude looked through a slit in his eyelids and saw Natalie taking him all in. She seemed pleased with what she saw—God only knew what that was.

"It's none of your business," he said primly. *Shut the door, Jude. Well done. Just the action advised in the book of Post–Grief Fuck Etiquette. Why, it's like you don't almost feel that way yourself.*

"It is," she said. "You're the only person apart from Dan who ever let me talk a lot of self-pitying crap and then sent me up for it. And I may be rebounding so hard from Dan this is just rubberized desperation talking, but I consider you more than a friend, so you don't get off the hook."

Jude turned his head and examined her face minutely, looking for mockery or an effort to control him. He saw her face, elfin and a little wild-looking. The darting elusiveness that had once been its common occupant was now replaced with a strong, direct force that was confident enough not to need to lie.

Jude put his hand out and touched her face, a kind of thanks. He realized why she'd talked about Dan, seemingly apropos of nothing—because she had to tell him something. He had something to tell himself.

"My sister thought of herself, deep down, as a Cheyenne dog soldier," he said, making an ambivalent face and shaking his head as he recalled just how that serious side of her had eaten away the happier girl she used to be.

"Tough. Hard. Fierce. Everything for the People. She had a strong sense of justice and she got stuck in nostalgia. She did the Sundance on her twenty-first birthday; hung her whole bodyweight off two hooks in her chest for twelve hours, until the skin broke free. I thought she'd totally lost it. I'd just joined the marines at the time. It was like—I didn't even write to her for months. I didn't know what to say. She was so extreme. It was like she was another person."

The scars would be there even now, on the slab; those skewers truly embedded, dragging her to her death . . .

Jude shook his head. "She understood what she wanted to be, even if it was going to cost a lot. Stayed at home. Lived every minute in the right way, according to her rules. I never knew what I wanted to be, except that it had to be as good as that, so that I could show her she wasn't the only one who could do right. She didn't have any business thinking of me as second-class because I didn't want the same things as she did."

"You felt that she showed you up," Natalie said, guessing.

Jude sighed and screwed his face up because it was painful to admit. "I talked to her about what a great multicultural world it was and how I was having a fine time; white and red in one body, hell, not even caring about what skin or background meant. But all the time her passion was this mark she'd set that I was trying to match; her ideas I was living in. She was definite and I'm . . . not yet defined. I don't commit to anything. I never liked the idea of being identified with something as random as my genes." He paused, aware that he was talking around what he wanted to say.

"If I'd been less of a control asshole who wanted to be right and told her more of what I knew she might not have gone out alone to die."

Said it. It sounded like a movie line. It was there in his mouth because he'd heard it said before by a tough guy doing remorse, when instead Jude had this sensation of a wave poised always overhead, not knowing when or who it would choose to fall on, or why. It had crashed on her and he felt it should have been him.

"Don't worry about your survivor guilt, you won't live long enough to enjoy it," Natalie said suddenly, imitating exactly the voice of the movie hard man he'd been thinking about. She risked a smile, tentatively.

Jude laughed soundlessly and found that his ribs hurt as well.

Natalie brushed his hair out of his face carefully and then pushed herself up with purpose. "I'm going to take a shower. In the meantime you might like to read this." She picked up her Pad from the side table and cued a file.

Jude watched her go, a momentary retreat from the field. She was so small, he thought. But perfectly made. He wondered how much of her had really gone with Dan—the man who'd nearly knocked him over outside the Clinic that day. Jude couldn't even remember what he'd looked like.

He got up and went to the window, tugging back the net to look out over the courtyard and the road. Pickup trucks moved slowly around the diner across the way, like heavy beetles. He listened to the water running in the bathroom.

Life did go on. That was the worst and best of it. Parts dropped off, but it kept on going. If it had a larger meaning then Jude didn't see it now, any more than he ever had. He was glad about that. It was a validation of a kind and it meant that whatever influence he had was small and mostly unimportant, which was a good thing.

He decided to look at Natalie's file and get some relief from being himself. He threw the bedcovers back so he could at least rest on something softer than the coverlet, picked up the Pad, and read.

> The Mappa Mundi project has only recently become a unified enterprise. It rests on two sets of theories.
>
> The first concerns the physiology of the brain, the physics of thought.
>
> The second concerns the nature of consciousness and the structure of the mind.
>
> The first one is empirical—you can poke it and see if you're right. You

can make maps and pictures of what actually happens in a brain and analyse the data. It's firmly fixed in the real world.

The second, until the development of Micromedica's NervePath™ system, has been purely theoretical. It was a mental construct, an idea, of how an experience of Self could be analysed.

In order to get a map of the mind, in order to have a chance of fitting it onto the physical map of the brain, the concept of the *meme* was adopted as a primary tool.

The meme is the basic unit of ideas, like the gene is the basic unit of a DNA strand. All ideas are memes, or are made up of combinations of memes, in which case they are called a *memeplex*. Each meme activates specific neural patterns in the brain. This relationship is consistent. You can relate a meme directly to a physical pattern of neuron activity. Therefore we can use memetic theory to model the mind and brain.

In the ordinary world a map is a two-dimensional representation of a three-dimensional reality. In a mind map there are many more than three dimensions to account for.

The human mind organizes its ideas around a cluster of scaled axes in a theoretical *n*-dimensional space called the *Memecube*. All the axes are bipolar, such as the scale of Size, which has two opposite extremes: Little and Big. Other Primaries are Good/Bad, Hard/Soft, Warm/Cold, Alive/Inanimate.

The axes themselves are not memes, but fundamental concepts, drawn from sensory information about the real world; they are cross-cultural. Each meme occupies a single, unique location within the mind's structure and its position can be mapped by referring to its coordinates on these axes.

Other definitions you will come across:

Information Hypercube: the theoretical space containing all the information in the universe.

Global Common Cube: the theoretical space containing all memes that are shared by human beings alive today.

Every individual has a unique Memecube; the total of their knowledge accumulated through experience. This includes, as a large subset of that knowledge, the Selfplex. An individual's Selfplex contains all of their beliefs about themselves and the world. The Selfplex is the identity of the individual and the master map by which they navigate their lives.

When the project, Mappa Mundi, is completed, it will be possible to use Micromedica technology to map individual Selfplexes. Micromedica NervePath™ has provided the technical ability to detect meme-patterns, composites of information, and emotional assignment. NervePath also has the capability to alter memetic patterning. It can "install" new knowledge by predicting the meme-pattern and setting it in place. It can alter attitudes, by tweaking the emotional triggers within preexisting memes.

Mappa Mundi will thus be a tremendous power enabling instant "learning," the controlled modelling of a personality by careful grooming of its components, the eradication of certain memeplexes from the Global Common Cube (example, racism, a conditioned social reaction, but not something such as hate, which is an emotional response), the manipulation of individuals to prefer particular products or political ideals, and so on, *ad infinitum*.

You can see the potential is vast, for good and for worse.

Jude read further into the links on the file, slowly capturing the extent of Natalie's knowledge of Mappa Mundi, the way the systems worked and what had happened to her Selfware programme when it had been sabotaged and illegally tested.

Jude's body temperature cooled and he became stiff and tense as he read it. Infinite organization and adaptation taking over every cell? But she looked so—normal. How could it be? When he got to the part that said Patient X was still alive and "out there" he felt his whole body waver with a pulse of deep physical and intellectual unease. He was tired and his mind was at the edge of comprehension. Despite this, its appetite for facts and figures didn't abate, but he became more strung out, doped on the information. As he read, his instincts started to tell him he should get the hell out of Washington, DC, find a new identity in another state, preferably another country, and reinvent himself in a profession more suited to living.

The file also told him that Ivanov/Guskov, his Russian, had been playing the whole of the Western military for fools, using their money and their anxieties to put himself in a position of power, running "black" projects whose yield was going to be entirely in his own service.

Jude couldn't believe her theory here: could a person have that much barefaced gall? But there it was. Guskov had foreseen the development of something like Mappa Mundi from a long way off and had realized its dangers. In return, he was determined that the technology was going to be used for freedom and not repression. But Jude didn't see that forcing it on the world was anything but oppression.

Natalie pointed out in her text that there was no future in arguing this one, because the stuff was all but built, and he supposed that was true—so who was to blame? Did the arms race reach all the way back to the first wheel?

As the file came to an end with cold predictions about Bobby X's impending fate Jude began just keying up files at random, to look at anything less distressing. He came across some hastily jotted notes and doodles. One of the pictures was particularly odd, a scatter of curlicues and flowers and twisting vines interspersed with fractal-like arrays of lines. There was only one word. It sat in the middle of a briar patch where small animals lay dead on the long thorns of the vine. It said: *Distribution???*

Jude put the pad down and closed his eyes. Distribution was the problem with it, no question. NervePath was highly regulated and production was very limited. A global assault couldn't take place unless that changed. Not even the US would have the stockpile to do it.

He lay back on the bed and stared at the blank and featureless ceiling. A slow, nasty, insidious thought, like the tail of a big bluepoint cat, was sliding through his mind.

Natalie scrubbed hard in the shower. She had changed and it wasn't all due to the Selfware. Now, when it was quiet, she heard in the running water the sound of a distant storm coming, a thousand blades of water being honed in the wind. Despite the heat of the jets on her skin, she shivered convulsively. When Jude had spoken about Mary, that was when it had begun. She'd been trying to find out why, but out of respect had made herself stop trying to see what he saw. Now she wished she hadn't been so polite.

As she dried herself later she glanced at her face in the mirror, wondering if she looked as on-the-edge as she felt. Her hair was flat.

Jude was lying where she'd left him. "I did my thinking," he said. "You're right. We have to trust each other." He flicked a finger towards her Pad where it lay on the carpet. "Disturbing reading. Guskov sounds like he's more than halfway to crazy already. Kinda makes sense, though, all those different bits of research I could never fit together and his protection coming from both the mafia and the government. He must be the most protected man on the planet."

"Only because he has so many people partially informed who think they're better off helping him than not," she said. But Jude was right. Guskov was untouchable.

Jude didn't move. "That stuff you know, about the distribution still being out of whack with the rest of it—Guskov not having NervePath production capacity and no means of getting a global strike . . . ?"

"Mmmn." She was looking at her shirt and underwear with some dismay.

"Does he have any Micromedica capacity anywhere you know of?"

"No," Natalie replied, staying wrapped in her towels. "It's all under government licences and at particular sites. Unless there's already a black market set up, and you've got any evidence of machinery going out of the country under false papers?"

"But I bet there's a lot of genetic capacity out there." He was almost talking to himself. "In this country alone there's at least four or five labs running who're doing unlicensed and black-market work—mostly run under hard protection from organized crime rackets. In other parts of the world, less famously regulated, that must be much easier."

"Genetic?" She glanced at him and sat down, wearily, on the edge of the bed, scrunching the nasty carpet between her toes. "Yes. There must be quite a lot. That's why there's so much fuss about tailored diseases . . ."

"Tailored viruses and bacteria," he said. "Caused the government here to start a counterterrorist programme, very late in the day, based at the CDC, using Mikhail Guskov on advisory because he had excellent contacts with leading Russian scientists and Chinese labs doing the best work—they're just about to test it at Dugway in a couple days' time."

"But that's a biological-based operation," she said, seeing by his expression that it was more than that and dreading the revelation.

"Yeah," he said. "Designed to disperse counteragents over huge areas of population as fast as possible, working from relatively small release quantities that are set loose in densely populated centres. A disease that is maximally infectious and carries antigens—or any other payload—using its own virulence to replicate both itself and its cargo."

It took a moment for Natalie to realize what he was saying. "It can carry Micromedica as cargo? Replicate it?"

"Well," Jude said, pushing himself upright and taking a long, slow breath. "The version I got out of a dead man's hands can. But something tells me that this isn't what I'm going to see at Dugway."

He looked up at her and his eyebrows were raised quizzically, too, as though he was surprised at his own capacity for conclusions. "Mary and I are to witness the trials, make sure we know all about it so that we can stop any thieves stealing the ideas. She didn't mention anything but antigen dispersal, though. And the thing I've got does a lot more than that. Looks like our man's got around his troubles that way. If he has labs across the world producing even tiny amounts of this Deliverance thing, then he only needs a sample of NervePath as big as a pinhead, plus his programs, and he's free and ready to rock."

Natalie shuddered—it seemed like her whole body wanted to spasm. She dragged back the orange and brown coverlet and got into the cleaner sheets, hoping to stay warm.

"Are you okay?"

"Yeah," she said, drawing the blanket up to her chin. "Your turn."

As Jude went into the bathroom and closed the door she lay back on the pillows and tried to ignore the fizzing sensation in her nerve ends, like every nerve was a wire and every wire was in a magnetic field and jumping like a flea. She assumed it was some effect of Selfware. Everything had happened so fast, there'd been no time to assimilate it. She hadn't believed Mappa Mundi could be so advanced, nor that all the assumptions it made about people, their brains and minds, could be right. Did the government really imagine it could broadcast ideas like TV programmes and have everyone fall neatly into a big, organized group? Control of that kind wasn't possible and it wouldn't last. When the reset ideas started to break up or caused other parts of people's meaning structures to dissolve, what would the results be?

In Dan it had caused confusion and loss of motivation. In others—there must be others, of course. People who didn't know what was wrong with them, like the Deer Ridge population, some becoming depressed, some losing a little memory, some becoming psychologically so disturbed that they were entirely unpredictable and dangerous. Get a large population as destabilized as that and a few dissenters or even organized opposition would be the last of your worries.

She wondered what her father would say. So much potential, he'd probably tell her, for saving and fixing these poor bastards on the mental wards . . . all used up by idiots in making everyone else an idiot, too. And yet, he was in on it from the start.

Natalie looked at the briefcase. Inside it were the pieces of White Horse's scanner system.

She got up and brought it back to the bed with her. As she heard the people next door getting up and talking about breakfast through the paper-thin walls, Natalie extracted the components and the toolkit and began to rebuild it.

When Jude came out of the bathroom she pointed it at herself and depressed the Send key. The LCD screen readout—a long grey strip that sat loosely out of place on top of the massed circuitry—flickered and fussed, but the readout of the saturation levels was accurate. She then searched for Any Other Systems, besides the NervePath type she'd already known about. The readout confirmed her suspicion.

"Look at this," she said. "My latest version NP has just cleaned out the last of a bunch of older-style material, introduced yesterday and trying to follow its instructions to colonize my nervous system."

Jude stared at her. "What?"

"When you go home," she said, "you should bag that peanut butter and try to get some from the same batch that went out to the reservation. I'll bet you folding money it's all contaminated."

"What?" he said again.

"Did you eat any?"

"No, I hate the stuff."

"And yesterday, did you handle any?"

"Handle?"

"When you pulled out the bag you had your hand in the can," she said. "Did you wash it?

"I wiped it on the—shit, what're you doing?"

Natalie looked down at the readouts taken from him.

"Eight percent," she said as despair and fury washed through her. "Oh shit, shit, shit!" She flung the fragile machine down on the mattress. "Can *any* of this get any fucking worse?"

Jude sat opposite her in the roadside diner and listened to her talk comfortingly about what he could expect. He was numb with the new shock.

"You won't feel anything," she said, examining the salt shaker and looking anxiously out of the windows, one and then the other. "As long as nobody zaps you with some half-baked software, you won't notice any difference and there won't *be* any difference."

"Couldn't you write something to stop it?"

She shook her head. "Its replication and occupation controls are preset in its hardware. I've got no access to that. Even if I did, I don't write in nanolanguages—they're supercompressed, no more than fundamental switching systems expressed as single electron jumps . . .

maybe if I read up really fast . . ." She glanced up at him with deep sympathy and sorrow. "Maybe I could. But there's no time. We've got to go along with what we decided, and even then . . ."

"Yeah, I know." He reached out and squeezed her hands around the plastic shaker. They didn't need to talk about it any more. It was decided.

The waitress came and took their order. Natalie drank all her water. Jude tried in vain to detect anything untoward going on in his head.

"Would this version of it carry what you've got?" he asked.

She put the salt down and pushed all the table salad out of the way, to stop herself fiddling, but immediately her fingers tapped an almost inaudible soft rhythm on the plastic top. "No," she said, after a minute's thought. "It hasn't got the processing power. This version—" she brushed her fingertips along the line of her right temple "—is about a thousand times more powerful and sophisticated. Yours can't do it."

He smiled weakly. "I don't know whether to be glad or sad."

"Be glad," she said. "Yours is unlikely to kill you."

"Unless someone hits me with what they used on Dan."

"Yeah, well, they want to hit me with that, too, and if they're working on your version they won't get me and if they're working on my version they won't get you." She leaned back as their breakfasts arrived, steaming and gigantic. "That'll give one of us about ten seconds to get revenge."

"I'll remember that."

Natalie stared at her stack of pancakes and Jude's mountain of eggs and hash browns with anticipation, picking up her knife and fork.

"You learn to eat like this in the army?"

"Nah," he said. "These days the army is all health food and computer-guided nutritional balance. This is strictly home."

She looked at her watch. "It's getting late."

"Time enough," he said.

Natalie looked out at the ordinary day, the road full of cars and trucks moving slow. She smiled at a kid who was trying to find some distraction from the boring conversation of his mother and grandma at the next table. She wanted to tell him to enjoy it while it lasted.

He cast her a look of sullen mistrust and went back to kicking his chair legs.

Jude hesitated, still not eating, although Natalie already had her mouth full. She gave the sullen kid a nasty scowl next time he looked over.

"Will they be able to read my mind with this?" he said.

Natalie stopped chewing. She swallowed and blinked and looked him in the eye, "As I said. Not if they don't know it's there."

"Fuckin' A," he said and began to work on the hill.

Nineteen

No one was more surprised than Mary Delaney when she heard that Natalie Armstrong had surrendered voluntarily at a police station near the Capitol. The message arrived as a regulated alert from one of her Net pilots and she moved quickly to ensure that Dr. Armstrong was immediately escorted to Fort Detrick, there to await transfer to the Sealed Environment site.

Mary finally got through to Jude.

"I'm so sorry," she said when he answered and she saw that he was at home. "What did you do? Go to ground somewhere? I came looking but you weren't there."

He sighed. "Yeah, I went out to the coast and sat looking at the sea, got some air and out of this goddamned place."

"When's the funeral?"

"Next week. I'm going to take a few days' leave, go back. I'll fill you in on that Atlanta stuff and you can take it over, if that's okay." He seemed completely uninterested in it, despite his enthusiasm two days before.

Mary asked gently, hoping the answer would be no, "Are you going to take up where White Horse left off?"

"Investigating the Deer Ridge thing?" Jude rubbed his face with both hands, in a washing action. "I don't know. If she had any hard evidence it's been taken or gone. Without that, all that exists are the doctor's reports and the witness statements, all of which will no doubt be shredded by government lawyers unless I can find some people willing to testify who won't break down under cross-examination. Maybe I could. But then there's all this stuff about the minerals rights on the land and that'll get dragged up. I can see the government and the res both claiming the actions are purely some kind of trouble stirred up to confuse the issues there. It could take years to make a case and get it to trial, and meanwhile—" he glanced dolefully at her "—the secretive elements of the technology could land us in some deep shit. I don't know. I'd like to, but I can't think about that just yet. You know?"

Mary smiled and nodded. She touched the screen where Jude's face was, running her finger down one side of it. "You take care now. I'll come over as soon as I've checked in at the office."

"No need," he said. "I'm coming in. I'll see you there."

She felt so much better after the call; now he was going to tell her what he knew and she could parcel him safely out of the way of the Mappa fallout. The only thing she was falling down at now was her FBI job and she had the whole day to devote to creating enough reports to satisfy Perez that she'd been doing serious homework. That left her no time to see Dr. Armstrong in person, but that was no doubt just as well. She could leave the briefings to Bragg, the general in command of the Environment area, and then Guskov would handle the rest.

It was as Mary was walking to work across the long lawns that separated their building from the labs that she felt the unmistakable sensation of being watched. It was so strong that she turned around to see who was behind her.

Over the manicured, short grass all she could see was the faint shimmer of rising warm air. The trees to her right were still, and the computer-centre windows were blacked out with heat-reflecting cool glass. Nobody was in the quad with her. But the sensation only grew, an invisible itch between her shoulders. She cued her Pad to check the area but it came up with nothing more than a few security cameras on auto.

Shaking herself down, she turned and resumed walking. Without warning she was suddenly enveloped in a cold pocket that made her breath mist and turned the warm air around her into a penetrating damp like an early morning New England fall. She gasped with surprise and stopped dead, looking in all directions, but, again, there was no sign of anything untoward. In a few seconds the air was as hot as ever and she had begun to perspire freely.

Mary thought it must just be to do with the ground, even though she was out in the full light of the sun. Trapped underground air venting up through some small holes. It was possible, wasn't it? She'd seen that happen in Centralia, where the underground coal was on fire.

She walked on, slower and more cautiously, speeding up as she neared the path.

A figure made out of air and bent light shot past her nose. She caught the impression of a human body, but streaked in long lines, as though it was moving so fast it was trailing light. In its wake she heard voices, quite a few of them, hostile and hissing. In the midst of them, unquestionably, was the sound of Daniel Connor's last speech—"Check it out!"—followed by a volley of ringing laughter that distorted rapidly into a screeching squeak that hurt her ears.

Silence followed as cool tendrils of backwash furled close against the skin of Mary's face. She tensed, bolt upright, muscles rigid.

The sense of a watcher was gone. The day around her bloomed hotter again, stifling as an oven. From the corner of her eye she saw a woman in a red suit begin to cross the quadrangle, a heavy briefcase swinging in her hand.

Mary ran the rest of the way, up the steps and through the doors of the Sciences block, and ignored the security guard's remarks about being hot and bothered as she swept into the air-conditioned factory coolness of the atrium. There, clutching the side of the marble fountain, she caught her breath and pushed her emotions to "Hold" until she was calm enough to review events without reacting.

"All right, Mary?" It was David from the next floor.

She straightened her back and turned.

"Just gathering my thoughts." She grinned and walked with him towards the elevators, but her heart continued beating out of time until long after she had sat down at her desk and begun pretending to type.

Bobby X, who had forgotten his own name—was it Ian something and then a word like "ridge" . . . ah, Derridge, yes—followed Mary, easily tracking her unique event-wake in the continuum like a hunting dog. He had no name for the senses he used, and didn't care to give them one. There was no need for words and their slow limits.

He was furled like a series of whirlpool eddies, and in each curl was the brief, human pleasure of having given her a good scare. Along the outer edges of the waves his anger and resentment shimmered. He'd been back to see Dan Connor and the manner of his death. The going and return had weakened him much more than he'd expected. He felt himself on the point of dissolving. One more appearance, one more return to the slow processes of biology, if he could manage that—if not, the illusion would do.

Meanwhile, he had his revenges.

It was a petty thing. Tiny. Insignificant. Ultimately, pointless on any scale other than that of the mediocre human being he had been.

He watched Mary sit at her desk, try to understand—and fail.

He saw the flow of energies and their states that made her and wondered how it was that something so beautiful could be so banal and bollock-awful. Her and him both.

Give them the universe and it meant nothing without a dream or a motive, without a framework of limits to set it in. He'd expected the wonder. He'd maybe anticipated a meeting with God or, at any rate, something more than a bog-standard life-form wandering lost in an unremarkable galaxy. But there was nothing of that sort and to look back and understand exactly how much of their world was made up solely from pitiful dregs of information, misunderstood, badly processed, and then sewn together with comforting delusion into a tissue of fictions . . . He would have cried if he'd had the organs to do it with. A small, planet-bound animal in a vast, vast—no words for any of that either. If he'd been a poet maybe he'd have found the way, but his transformation had made him aware, not talented.

Words. He wished for direct experience to be made words, but wishing didn't make it so. He'd send Mary a thought for the day, however. Minds took information out of many more things than words, and all paths were useful.

He showed her the Universe.

Natalie found it a relief to have all decision making taken away from her for the hours she had to sit in the army jeep and then in the holding areas at the base. Around her uniformed officers did their duties and she followed. Since her surrender to the police life had been a holiday from stress. The only down note had sounded when she'd said goodbye to Jude for what was possibly the last time, standing on the platform at the station and watching him walk away, tall and strong, into a life that was now balanced on a knife-edge.

Hers was arguably no better, but she felt more able to deal with that. In her pocket the old Pad was programmed for encrypted transactions with his, using secured lines and series of faithful datapilots they trusted. But this wasn't watertight and it might not have survived the army's search strategies when they inspected it. She'd said, "Send me your thoughts and I'll know." Sort of joking.

"I will." He was serious.

She had no idea if that was possible, but already, sitting in her cell and looking at the mirrored window, she knew that behind it sat three curious officers, one who knew about her situation and the others who didn't.

Natalie used her time to rest and consider that fact, which was curious.

She was disturbed thirty minutes after arriving by the door opening.

Mikhail Guskov, accompanied by an aide, stepped into the room.

He looked much broader and more powerful in real life than on any screen. Natalie was impressed immediately by his physical presence and its vigour, expressed in his thick, greying beard and intense, direct gaze. He offered her his hand.

"Doctor Armstrong."

"Professor," she said and they shook. There were layers and layers of carefully accumulated cautions in him that made him very difficult to assess. The strength with which he projected the persona he wanted to was so powerful that she felt it was an almost physical rebuff to her involuntary attempt to see the truth of him.

"I was so sorry to hear of the events at York," he said, his voice loud and deep in the confined space, as though he didn't care who heard him. "Are you well?"

"I'm fine." She took her hand back from his solicitous grip and nodded.

He produced a scanner in his hand, the sort she was familiar with. "I trust you will not mind if I . . ."

"Carry on." She shrugged. "It won't be the last." She watched with amusement as his face reflected his concern and disbelief at the read-outs, although he must have received data from the Clinic.

"Forgive me," he said after a moment had passed. "I hadn't entirely believed the scale of it, until now." He switched the machine off and passed it back to his aide without a glance, reserving his attention for Natalie. "Do you know what happened to the other man? Patient X?"

"Ian Detteridge," she corrected gently. "Yes, I do." She glanced at the mirror wall and then back at Guskov, who gave a minute nod. His thick hair moved like a lion's mane. She was convinced that every strand of it was exactly managed for effect. Every piece of his skin, every article of clothing, every nod, blink, and smile. He was an expert.

"Excellent. Then we have much to discuss and to learn. You will come?" Asking as though she had a real choice. She rather liked that.

"Yes."

"Let's go, then." He gestured for her to precede him and she followed his aide into the corridor.

During the formalities of her discharge and briefing for the BSL-$_4$ secure environment she paid no attention to the surfaces of what was going on, but watched the individuals around her instead. There was no doubt. Since her last Selfware run, something beyond "mere" enhancement of the ordinary had happened.

The general for instance, General Bragg. Below his professional manner and the sound knowledge he was giving to her about air exchangers and the emergency exit routines and the scrub-down facilities he was deeply disturbed by Natalie's own presence. He knew that she had been changed in some way and was fascinated and repulsed, partly because of his religious convictions—a general Christian devotion that wasn't to any particular church, but sincere nonetheless—and partly because he knew about Mappa Mundi. His convictions aside, he was about as keen on the idea of having some enemy walking through his mind as he was about having them overrun the country. Less so, in fact.

Natalie sympathized, but she knew that Bragg's loathing had gone further than personal feelings. He was remembering as he spoke, seeing brief flickers of a past moment when another woman had been here and they had dealt with this matter. And he was also mindful of pressure from his superiors and this made his anxieties very complex. As he flicked steadily through the presentation slides, showing her layouts and access and maintenance and the rest, Natalie knew that he was himself thinking of ways that control of the Environment could be subverted by those within it and of ways in which he could prevent that happening. He wondered how easy it would be to kill them all. He was wondering if he should, and immediately overriding that thought with less terrifying ones in which the colleagues who shared his conspiracy to stop the technology being used or disseminated would take a share of the action and the consequences.

A chill ran over her body as she sat dutifully listening and she shivered. Guskov looked across at her from his seat, wondering if the Selfware was causing her distress. She had to wait for him to ask, "Are you all right?"

And only then did she let herself say, "I'm fine. Just cold."

"Fetch Doctor Armstrong a fleece," Guskov ordered, signalling to one of the privates with an imperious flick of one hand. The man glanced at his general and then went to obey. To Natalie's pleasant surprise he returned with a piece of her own clothing. Her luggage had obviously made it here as planned. She took off her jacket, ignoring their stares at the holes in her shirt, and put the thin top on, zipping it to the chin. Better. A taste of the normal in the midst of madness.

She wondered if Guskov knew that there was an organization opposed to Mappa Mundi's existence that was operating within the armed forces and wider political arenas, but she guessed he did at least suspect it. It was almost a necessity, and what did it matter if Bragg or someone else was in the thick of it? Inside this high-security prison that didn't even let microbes in or out the science team were sitting ducks. What a good job they knew nothing about Bobby X yet. But there she had a kernel of doubt. She hadn't heard or seen Ian since the truck business and he might well never be coming back, despite his intentions. He would be the first thing Guskov asked her about and the last thing she wanted to explain fully. Without having an exact reason, she knew that he could be valuable in what was coming; and wasn't that nice, using him this way? She scowled and tucked her chin into the circle of collar beneath it.

When the briefing and documentation of her arrival was done Natalie and Guskov were escorted to a closed vehicle and another journey began. She wouldn't have known the site of the Environment at all were it not for the fact that the driver knew the way very well and liked to describe the scenery vividly as he drove. Natalie knew the places as names from a tourist column her mother had once written for one of the glossy magazines, pretending to be a glamorous city girl roughing it across North America's scenic territories.

They headed into Virginia, up along the Skyline Drive where the road ran along the ridgelines of the Appalachian Mountains, and finally arrived at a little town that was no more than a few houses, a bar/diner, and a gas station. Its name was Stone Spring and it had some mildly interesting caverns that weren't much of a match for the larger tours down at Luray a few miles away. But the caverns here had been quietly acquired and put to a better use as a military installation of which no residents were aware. It had once been a secondary site when Mount Cheyenne was being developed, but had then been left to go dusty awhile until the need for more biosafety research centres arose out of Pentagon plans.

The truck parked up in the driveway of the house on Lot #22 and they all got out. It was a long way from the road, isolated by a winding, potholed dirt track that felt to Natalie's sore spine like it must mud-out every time there was any serious rain. Around the scrappy building's grey-painted boards mature trees and heavy brush loomed and cut off most of the bright daylight as afternoon shifted into early evening. Insects spun in the warm air and, apart from the scrunch of boots on gravel and the sound of voices, there was a deep hush in the place as though it was a long way from civilization, despite being only a short drive from several popular resort hotels.

Natalie was sorry she wasn't going to be staying at the house itself—it would have been just what she needed, some solitary peace—but Guskov led the way into the garage and there all pretence of normality and old-style America vanished.

The elevator was waiting for them at the top of its smoothly channelled shaft. She and Guskov stepped inside the car and their escort saluted as the doors closed.

He turned to her. "A tedious journey. I apologize. But we were all most surprised by your . . . detour."

Natalie raised her eyebrows. Let them be surprised. It was none of their business.

"I'm here now," she said. "That's what matters."

The elevator car dropped them a hundred feet into the antechambers and they passed through the airlock systems without talking. Another elevator skimmed them deeper into the rock and then sideways on tracks that she estimated took them about a quarter-mile north of the actual town overhead. The underground redoubt wasn't a walk-out. A power cut would trap them effectively. She tried not to think too much about that and the fact that she might not stand out in the sun again, but it was difficult. She concentrated on Guskov instead and found that he was worried about her, and not in an entirely scientific and selfish way.

"You read my messages?" he asked then, as though her attention had prompted him. Perhaps it had: she would have to get to the bottom of what was going on.

"Yes, thank you." She was polite. "The Free State of Mind. I read them. Is everyone else here of the same opinion as you are?"

"No. Some are here under duress. I regret that, but there are times when it is necessary to get a thing done."

"And there was I, thinking you had human welfare so much at heart," she said, meeting his gaze. "But it sounds like utilitarian practicality when you get closer to it."

He smiled, wolfish. "Do actions carry with them into the real world the burdens of morality and intention?"

They stepped out of the second elevator car and into a corridor, as the plans had stated. Like the one running to Jude's apartment it was functional and no more. There was still a smell of carpet glue and paint about it.

Natalie matched Guskov's look and answered, "Where is the real world, Mika? Answer that and I'll answer your question."

He froze on the spot and his face became heavy, eyes glittering with a combination of ego and the intelligent understanding of power that would be extremely dangerous to try and cross. But she wasn't upset.

"Only my closest friends call me that," he said.

"And you didn't ask me in that close. And even they aren't really that close, those who are still alive," she said and smiled, enjoying her own power as she realized it for that moment. "Yes, I know."

Jude walked into the offices at ten past ten. He'd gone home, tidied up, packed the peanut butter cans in thick plastic, boxed them, and taken them to a U-Stor-It, the keys to the room taped underneath the passenger seat of his car. After minor attention to his back with antiseptic he'd changed his clothes and thrown the whole set he'd worn the day before into a Dumpster two alleys down from the U-Stor-It. He felt tired, sore, and his chest physically hurt with a dull ache that persisted no matter how much breath-practice he tried to use to calm down. In the end he bought a can of Gatorade and one of SlimFast and drank them both on the steps outside the Sciences building before getting up and heading in.

He looked at his watch and then out of his window and across town to the south. He wondered how Natalie was and then made himself sit down and think. That lasted about a minute before Perez herself appeared in the doorway.

"*Hola*, Jude," she said in her preoccupied style, "*¿Como estás?*"

"*Vale*," he said. They continued to speak in East Coast Spanish.

"Is it true?" She closed the door behind her and crossed to his desk, touching his elbow. "Your sister?"

"Yes, it's true." He looked at his case and its open contents. The file. It was right there if he wanted to spill it all to her and have it lifted out of his hands. The temptation was so strong that he actually took the breath to start—and then let it go in a big sigh.

"It has something to do with your absence, with your trip home," she said, not asking. "I thought it would. But if it concerns the department, you can talk to me about it." Her softly pouched face with its heavy care lines and her white-streaked braids of hair were good for motherly expressions and they held one now—canny but sympathetic. "I will help you." She squeezed his arm and then let him go.

"Thank you." He lifted the file out, set the bags containing the scanner's electronics down on it, and placed his Pad beside them before raising his eyes to meet hers. "But I think that would be a mistake for both of us. I don't have enough evidence for a case, only a lot of disconnected lines. Which is what we've always had on the Russian and I don't expect to tie them up without treading on a government tail. It's hard to say whether it would be worth involving the department."

"But if you won't, then I can't give you more time and more money," she said simply. "Either you and Mary start to show me what we can deal with or you can find another case. I mean it, Jude. It's a waste of your life and talent to pursue this one man and his problems."

"But—"

"But no more buts. I'm telling you. I want to help you. You can take leave. You can take a sabbatical. Ask me for what you need. But don't keep chasing tails if you don't mean to tread on them with the full weight of the law." She was at his pinboard, looking at his large array of photographs, pictures, and displays. "That I can't sanction, for your own sake, and I can't pay for. I won't be able to fish you out of it if you get into trouble. Do you hear what I'm saying?" She shot him a look from her deep brown eyes that was flinty. Then she softened.

"I guess your sister is a part of this. But think first, Jude. Be careful. Don't drag us in. It's face first or not at all."

He nodded.

She poked at a colourful sheet of paper. "What is this?"

"It's a scan of Martha Johnson's brain," he said. "The storekeeper who tried to burn White Horse to death."

Perez smiled and flicked the corner with her poppy-red fingernail.

She turned to him with a wry, sad smile, "I was going to say how pretty." She took in his expression. "You won't always feel like this. It's a dangerous time."

He knew she wasn't bluffing him. Her husband had been shot in a drive-by three years ago when he was on his way to the post office. She'd been angry since then, but it had mellowed and changed, hardened into a stubborn refusal to give in.

"Keep talking to me, Jude," she ordered him. "But get out of here now. Go and do something else for a while."

"I'm just sorting out some things," he assured her, knowing his vagueness was only annoying. "I'll go to Dugway tomorrow with Mary and then I might take some days and go home, to Montana I mean. To Deer Ridge."

"Can she go with you? You should have someone."

"I'll be fine," he said. "I'd rather go alone."

"She was on her own in Florida when the lab was closed," Perez said, without changing the tone of her voice. "Isn't that right?"

"Yes."

"Yes?"

"Is something the matter?"

"No, yes," she said, shrugging in an elaborate way. "No. You endorsed her reports. Did you read them?"

"Yes."

"Did you know that Tetsuo Yamamoto used to work for Gentrex Labs before the CDC?"

Jude's mind stalled and then started again, bumpily. Gentrex was a sweet little bulk-sequencing company that contracted to larger investors as basic number crunchers. They'd had a sideline for Ivanov in cross-matching and grading athletes' DNA in a scam to pick and train potential gold-mine pro basketballers, picking them up almost by random sampling from poor and disadvantaged areas of Asia and the eastern republics. It was a moneymaking venture and the science had been pretty basic, but some teams had paid millions of dollars for the information.

"I didn't know that," he said. Worked for Ivanov? Then it made it almost certain that Tetsuo had a good idea of what he was handling when he'd brought that vial for Jude—something illicit that Ivanov/Guskov was now making. Something to do with the mafia side and not the legitimate edge of his dealings. Not that one was ever really detached from the other.

Jude nodded slowly as he took it in.

"Okay," Perez nodded. "Okay. Go and rest."

He watched her leave and sat in his chair, mind churning slowly over what she'd said about Mary. Had there been something wrong in the reports? He had read them, that much was true, but he didn't remember the details, he'd already been tangled up in Mappa Mundi by then.

A familiar hand knocked on the door and pushed it all the way open.

Mary put her head around and smiled. "Hey," she said, walking in and moving around his desk, bending down to give him a hug. "Hey, you. Haven't seen you in forever."

He hugged her back, feeling how stiff she was, brittle and tense. She stood up and leaned on the edge of his desk, her arms crossed firmly, hands tucked into her armpits. Her normally pale skin was dead white.

"Are you okay?" When she spoke he knew she was upset because of the breezy way she asked.

"No," he said, truthful. "You neither, by the look of it. *¿Qué pasa?*"

She looked down at her feet and worked the toe of one shoe into the carpet, not answering, her arms becoming more rigid. It was so unlike her that a trickle of foreboding started to spread out beneath his ribs. Her gaze wandered up to the top of his desk. She turned and began to prod listlessly at the bags of circuitry, flicking the edge of the file case with her finger before pushing it aside. She cleared her throat and a convulsive twist made her shoulders strain against the seams of her jacket before she forced herself to speak.

"A couple of weird things happened to me this morning." Mary glanced at the desk again and added, trying and failing to smile, "I sorta thought someone here might be spiking the drinks, y'know." Her Charlottesville accent had started to show up, too. She coughed again and tried to meet his gaze, looking suddenly away to the wall behind him. "I was walking here from the computer block and there was this cold spot."

She dared a glance at him to see how he was taking the news. "And then I was at my desk, sitting, thinking about whether we should drop this whole Russian thing, when I had a kind of a . . . blackout." Her arms flew back to their defensive position as if of their own accord. She shuffled her shoulders and they settled into a higher hunch. "It sounds ridiculous but I wondered if there was some kind of new weapon that could make you unconscious. Or some kind of magnetic effect from all the power cables under the grass that could . . . God, listen to me." She rolled her eyes and smiled but the smile died back and was replaced by uncertainty.

"It's so cold in here." She walked quickly to the air-flow grille on the far wall and touched the pad next to it. "You don't mind if I turn this down?"

Jude decided she was serious, even though he felt warm. She was shivering. "This blackout. What was it like?"

"Well, I didn't fall asleep, I wasn't exactly out. It was more like . . ." She searched the air above her forehead for the right words, looking left and right. "Like this wave of total black nothing, this enormous emptiness, this sense of great, big, huge space and there were sort of two things in this space but the gap between them was so big that—" she held her hands in front of her, palm to palm, and mimed trying to push them together "—they'll never meet."

He nodded. He didn't know what to think.

"Oh, J, I'm sorry." She shook herself. "Bad timing. You must feel miserable."

"I was going to say it sounds like depression," he said and decided to brazen it out. "You've been working too hard. You need a vacation in Costa Rica. Some sun. A nice beach. A few cocktails. A new boyfriend."

"Are you offering?"

Jude was surprised at the come-on and at his reaction to it—anger. He smiled against his will, pretending she wasn't serious.

"Not this week," he said. "I've got to get back for the funeral." Now he felt angry with himself. What was the matter? A few bits of circumstantial and he was flipping out all over, suspecting everyone.

"The dead guy in Atlanta." He drew the conversation back to work, where it was safer for the moment. "He had some information about a viral engineering project. I think it may be related to the stuff at Dugway. I'll send you the files and you see what you think."

"Sure." She stood back and reached down to the papers on his desk, her hand loose and shaky. "Is that—?"

"White Horse's paperwork," he said, putting his hand on top of the brown folder before she could open it and see the top page. "Gotta fill it in this morning. Insurance stuff."

Mary moved back and looked at him in apology. "Oh. Listen, you want coffee? Anything like that? I need sugar."

"Sure, double latte," he said, giving her the apology-accepted smile.

She walked out, back straight and taut with what he thought was embarrassment.

Jude let his hand move from its protective position and picked the file up, sliding it into a drawer. He stared at his desk and reread the outlines of what he'd written on the vial analysis. If it showed up at Dugway tomorrow but without the capacity to replicate Micromedica internally, then Tetsuo was a much weaker choice of servant than Guskov usually made.

Jude checked on the local investigation into Tetsuo's murder and wasn't surprised to find the case open, pending further enquiry. If he'd been a government hit, like White Horse, then Jude didn't know if holding the story back from public attention was worth waiting on any longer, despite what Natalie'd said. She might have the ability to change things, but he doubted he was going to get anywhere other than six feet under. He felt beyond tired. He knew he was going to make a mistake soon, if he hadn't already.

Mary, in her own office, leaned against the shut door and tried to get her wits together. She was sure, just by its weight and shape and the colours of the pages in it, that the thing on Jude's desk was her goddamned Pentagon file on Mikhail Guskov. If it was, then Jude was all the way in there and she was up to her neck in trouble—he hadn't got it on his own, he must have contacts close to her. He must know about her. He must. But if he did he was a way better actor than she'd ever have believed. And who were his allies? Who was with him on it? God, she didn't want it to be true.

And then again, she'd been on this road before and baulked it. That had to change.

Her mind was still shocked by the event of the morning. She'd told him about it, just to get some relief and have another opinion. She hadn't told him how scared and helpless she'd felt as it was happening, as she was losing control of herself. Maybe it was stress. Could that make you crazy this way? The irony of it happening to her, who'd done similar things to others, wasn't lost on her.

She opened her eyes and stared through her windows, seeing nothing.

I won't kill him, she thought, flattening the part of her that told her she was being weak. *I'll watch him closely. If it* is *the Pentagon file then I need to know who he's with, don't I? Any rash moves and I might miss the rest of the conspiracy.*

She found herself gasping for air, almost like laughing although nothing was funny. The decision felt like a punch to the gut. Disappointment welled up in her, at her own weakness and how easily she gave in to it.

Why did it have to be him? Why did it have to be Deer Ridge, of all forsaken places? Why? She wanted, needed, to answer those questions—chance was not enough.

Twenty

The Sealed Environment was exactly as dull and uninspiring as Natalie had dreaded. She assumed, judging by the constant appearances of shoddily finished edges, splashed paint, and the smells of solvents, that most of it had been kitted out in a great rush. Certain zones, including the test areas, were beautifully done, with no detail spared. They must have been completed when the work was still going to schedule. But then some event had forced everything to be brought forward. It could have been many things, of course, but she was prepared to bet that it was the work at Deer Ridge and the actions of White Horse that had started this rush.

Fundamentally she was not happy or confident that the whole unit was sealed and conditioned as it should be. But that was not her problem.

She had ten minutes to settle into her room—a cube that wouldn't have disgraced some 1990s programming shed with a bed instead of a desk—but it had all mod cons including workstation, wallscreen, and even running water. She took five minutes, and that was spent wrestling with nostalgia as she unpacked her bags and saw things that, in all innocence, with Dan still alive and her mind more her own, she'd packed days ago. Natalie smothered her face in them and for an instant smelled home.

She was caught up in examining the stress points on the threads that made up a jersey T-shirt when her alarm sounded to tell her to go and meet her workmates. Head still fascinated by the shear-stress variations in the filaments that had been caused by the knitting process, she almost fell over her own feet. She had to shake like a dog to get back into a kind of normality and realize, late, that she'd no memory or awareness of the transition between ordinary thinking and that peculiar, total absorption in something she'd never even noticed before. *Couldn't* have noticed before.

When she saw the others and shook their hands, the talent seemed to have stuck.

Her father was first to greet her with a stiff hug, embarrassed by the fact they were watched as he showed her affection but genuinely delighted to see her alive and well. As he pressed her close and she closed her eyes she saw a clear image of a boy trapped inside a huge wall of rocks that left him only enough space to exist and barely room for the smallest of frequent, tiny breaths. She was still reeling from the impact of this as she shook hands with Nikolai Kropotkin, the Russian psychologist she knew only as a name in respected journals.

He was older than her father but he had a face that looked kind and, like her own, a touch impish. His handgrip was full of anxiety, however, and Natalie noticed as they said their hellos that he was more curious about her state than about her. She thought of a series of insects in amber, the stone polished to a jewel-like smoothness and shine, and in that shine Kropotkin's eyes reflected through a kaleidoscope of lenses; she was the mosquito and he the discoverer.

Isidore Goldfarb the programmer was a bigger shock. His Asperger's she recognized instantly by his peculiar fixity of eye contact and attention. The quality of the muscles in his hands told her nervous system how he felt at making such a bold and peculiar gesture—he had to struggle with his own instinct telling him not to do it as he fell into a set routine of movement and words as fixed and inherently meaningless to him as sets of programming code were to the machines that ran them. Beneath his veneer of procedure, however, he was bright-eyed; a fox curled in a private, dark den, watching the world through screens of shadow—Natalie saw herself through these veils. Her own state of hyperalertness was a fierce burn in the stare and her hand's touch was offensively warm as it flickered in a rhythm that upset him because he could not follow. He recognized her as a fellow defective, a curio, a broken drum.

Alicia Khan was a sheen of ebony over a cat's softness and sly grace. Natalie perceived her through what was almost an hallucination, symbolic in quality, which distilled into a few images all the information about her that she needed to know: a girl (Alicia in the past) sat alone in her room, working by the light of a candle whose wax was nearly burned away. When it burned out the girl's spirit would rise with the smoke. Her life would be gone.

But she had no time to do more than remark this bizarre new facility for seeing because Lucy Desanto was now in front of her, gripping her hand and holding her captive to a vision far more shocking than Alicia's. Her fury was barely disguised, and in the flat grey plain of her resentful stare lay a dead boy sprawled on a city street, eyes staring and purple lips open in an eternal scream.

Natalie involuntarily recoiled and felt shock numb her face. Lucy Desanto's annoyance became hurt and suspicion. Natalie looked down at the floor and concentrated on the tiles: green and black, count them, one, two . . . this was as bad as being on the ward. Hell, it was like being everyone on the damn' ward. *A deep breath* now.

She'd used to think how much time could be saved if only therapists could see straight into the minds of patients and get directly to what was bothering them without the gloopy, fretful world of language to bugger up understanding. Now she wished she knew far less.

"Are you all right?" Her father was at her elbow, holding on to her and shielding her from the rest of them.

"I'm fine." She made herself stand up properly. "I'm experiencing a few odd effects of the accident, that's all. It's nothing. Really." There, her own talk-to-the-mad voice was back and it calmed her down. She blinked and the composite images she'd been picking up from them all vanished into memory, leaving the present clear.

"Sorry," she apologized to them all, for violating their personal, unknowing space. She was only grateful that they couldn't see into hers.

Natalie looked up into her father's face and saw, with a sick plunge of her heart, that it was anguished. "Thank you for stopping it when you did."

He knew she meant the Selfware, when the Ministry would have let it run. "Not soon enough," he said in a hoarse whisper and almost crushed her hands where he held them. "And it wasn't me that did it. It was Dan. You must thank him . . ."

"Oh God, Dad. He's dead," she said and closed her eyes for a second.

"What?"

Slowly and with sadness Natalie explained to all of them the circumstances of her journey, from the Clinic to her arrival at Fort Detrick, leaving out, for the time being, Bobby and Jude.

The room was quiet for a minute or two after as they all absorbed the information. Only the sound of the cooling motors from the kitchen and the air vents hummed through the narrow lounge. Natalie sat down with Calum. They were facing Kropotkin, who spoke first.

"So, they are using it already."

"The versions are badly produced, badly written and run on low-percentage, old-version NervePath," Natalie said. "I don't know where they were made or anything like that. I can show you a sample of one system."

She activated her Pad and Kropotkin switched on the display systems in the lounge—no area was without its opportunities for constructive thought. All of them looked through the code intently, although Khan and Desanto had no training in it. Kropotkin used his own Pad to work the central computer system by remote and rendered it as a display: an engineering diagram of an active simulated brain.

The colour-coded picture fragmented and separated into three-dimensional segments, so that all the deeper structures came into view.

"This is the Deer Ridge phenomenon?" Khan asked.

Natalie didn't know that the news of it had broken, but Guskov obviously knew all about it.

"Yes. I wrote an erasure routine and that was used to remove the programming from those people under the effects last week."

"How many survived it?" Natalie didn't see any trace of foreknowledge that would suggest he'd been consulted about the original test idea. In that at least he was telling the truth.

"Fourteen out of twenty-one. Not bad, considering."

"Thirteen," Natalie said.

They all looked at her.

"The woman whose house was burned down by Martha Johnson, the storekeeper. She died as a result. So that makes it thirteen survived, even though she may not have been directly infected."

Guskov nodded. "In that case we should include the other two who were murdered by those under the effect."

"What was the programme supposed to do?" Lucy Desanto was sitting right on the edge of her seat, twisting the two rings on her right hand. Natalie felt her anxiety and horror without having to try.

Kropotkin glanced around to check whether anyone else was going to volunteer information and replied, "It was meant to disturb and disable coordinated civil action." He said the words in a lofty way and laughed ruefully. Natalie's own smile was twisted.

Lucy and Alicia looked momentarily baffled by their humour. Natalie explained. "It's far too abstract a goal—disable coordinated civil action. The programmers, who weren't really experts, and the other people on the team had to translate that into something that can be done in a living mind by a bunch of switches . . . they failed. It isn't possible to use NervePath and Mappaware to perform a wide-ranging social task. You can only use it to work within the individual's worldview and their own experience. This program is a monster. All it does, once you initiate your cooperation and friendly allegiance patterns, is send a huge shunt through your amygdala, punching you with anger and fear. Depending on how well those patterns were recognized or how much they filtered into the rest of your understanding—it's an emotional nuke. Way too big for the job. Way too stupid."

"And in about fifteen minutes it would turn you into a barbarian," Lucy said, nodding.

"Irreversible psychosis," Kropotkin agreed. He glanced at Guskov and in that brief second of eye contact the many long years of knowing each other was vivid. "Isn't that so?"

"You forget, Nikolai, that the British experiment prior to the Selfware test was a success. There are treatments that can restore these people within a matter of hours. It is anything but irreversible. That is the essence of the entire State of Mind—unlimited freedom of choice."

"These choices." Desanto interrupted him, her voice guttural. "What and who will make them? Supposing you are infected by a system that is a dogma, offers no choices—what would induce you to use anything that would change your world then? It would go against all you believed. It would be unthinkable. In that single step you would be imprisoned, your own jail and jailer."

"You should know the answer," Guskov returned, smoothly grinning at her discomfort, enjoying it. "You have just such a memeplex as the foundation of your identity, Lucy. And have you the will, the inclination, or the ability to contemplate renouncing it? Can you imagine other people's minds that are not fettered in this way?"

Natalie was surprised at such an instant and open confrontation. The emotional atmosphere in the room dropped a degree. Goldfarb had to sit on his hands to prevent them twitching in discomfort. Her father cleared his throat.

"We all have our delusions," Calum said sternly. "There's no need to victimize one Catholic and think the rest of us aren't as stuck in our ways. But her question is a good one, and your answer is not as good. In a natural environment ideas come and go from the Selfplex in a way you could speak of as though it was natural selection—strong contenders that find themselves acceptable to the existing structures are promoted, weak ones that find no support in the architecture fade and are forgotten. It is the Selfplex that determines value and acceptability. But Mappaware is much more radical in the way it manipulates the patterns of thoughts. It is possible to remove all awareness of choice and never to have it re-emerge. Mappaware can close some gates forever."

Natalie found she was staring at her father in surprise. She'd always seen him as so fixed, and here he was, talking about freedom.

Guskov tipped his chin down in a nod of agreement. "Mmn, you're right. Now we are getting to the heart of the matter. I know you're not here because you all agree with my views on this Free State or about the Mappaware itself. We should clear the air before we attempt to work together. The project depends on it."

"Yes, but what's the point when we all know you'll have your way?" Lucy said. "Far from being any kind of a free choice, it's your work all these years that's led to us being here, with no choice but to go forward and try to use this abomination of a tool to do some good. Even your decision that the world needs this kind of freedom is something you took on your own. How democratic is that?"

"I've explained this before," Guskov sighed. "The technology was never in doubt. Its existence was determined as soon as Micromedica proved that it could function intersynaptically without disrupting normal process—it was only ever going to be a matter of time."

"But you'd planned long before that," Alicia Khan said. "You and Nikolai together had ideas on this subject in the 1990s."

"Theories," Kropotkin said. "Nothing more. There was never a way that was delicate or discreet enough to put them into practice. And governments, especially this one, had a long history of attempted uses of all kinds of mind control and propaganda devices."

"Far seers." Natalie nodded. "The MK-Ultra project." She'd studied what she knew of the projects that the USA had run during the Cold War but all of her material had been anecdotal. She'd seen no proofs in which she couldn't poke a hole some way, just as with all the other paranormal claims she'd investigated. "They may have been able to do something. It's hard to say definitely either way."

"It's impossible," her father snorted. "Easy to claim, never proven in a controlled test."

Guskov turned to Natalie. "But you're in a different position now, Doctor Armstrong. You can read minds, isn't that right?"

Natalie hesitated, aware of all the attention in the room fixed on her and an undercurrent of wary and instinctive dislike, exactly the same reaction as Jude had first shown.

"It seems to be so," she said carefully. "But it's a result of the Self-ware process, the altered program. I don't know what it is." Their faces were wide-eyed. They wanted to believe her. They were frightened, too. "Why don't we put it to the test?"

Her challenge surprised them.

"Wait, I thought there was another test subject, I mean, a person—before you," Lucy said. "What was the outcome of that?"

Natalie looked at Guskov and her father, one at a time. "You know. Why haven't you told them?"

Kropotkin answered for them. "Because we would not believe it."

"I don't believe it, either," she said. "But now we can find out beyond a shadow of doubt. Your patient, Bobby X, as he was known on the list, is still alive. Unless he's reached a critical point, he may still be able to come here. He's volunteered to be our subject."

"Excuse me, but what are we talking about here?" Khan shook her head in confusion, both hands open to the air. "May be able to? We're a hundred and fifty feet underground in a sealed container. How is he going to get in?"

Natalie met her incredulous gaze calmly and smiled, "That's the most interesting question of all. Shall we go into the Test Centre and find out?"

As they got up, Isidore spoke for the first time. "This changes everything," he said, looking straight at Guskov. "You didn't foresee this. Whatever it is, it's obviously extremely powerful and dangerous. It doesn't fit the plan."

"We'll see." Guskov smiled and waved them out of the door ahead of him.

Natalie caught up with her father in the corridor. He glanced down at her and whispered, "Bobby X is still *alive?*"

"I think so." She felt his hand reach for hers and hold it, tenderly.

"Good," he said, squeezing her fingers.

She had to fight to breathe against the tough pain in her throat all the way to the control centre. Calum hadn't thought Bobby would survive. He didn't think she would.

Utah from the plane's window was orange, broad, and arid beneath the cloudless sky of the day. They flew in low to Dugway's tough little strip and Jude watched their shadow racing, getting larger and larger. Two jackrabbits broke cover and went dodging and leaping away as they touched down. Their frantic paws left fan-trails of dust that spread on the wind and then quickly settled. In the distance, mirage lakes shivered. The plane turned and taxied towards the huts at the edge of the airfield.

Jude turned away from the view unwillingly and looked at Mary as she put her jacket on in the seat across from his, smiling unconsciously as he did. She'd been such a good friend for so long, he couldn't think of her as a devious barefaced liar. The ghost wings in his back fluttered. His smile faded.

"Penny for them?" she asked.

"If it turned out that we'd already run into this project, in Florida, say. The procedure would be to hand over our materials to the project team leader and bury any subsidiary investigations, right?"

Mary's coral mouth, glossed and perfect, smiled as she tipped her forehead down, confirming that.

"But if this looks like an international—"

"Then we have the option to hand it over to the International Committee," she said. "You're not really thinking of doing that?"

"I'm sure it's in violation of a number of nonproliferation agreements and conventions, without even looking." He undid his seat belt and stretched his legs. His body felt old.

"We need a reliable deterrent."

"We need to keep everyone behind the line if any treaty is going to work," he said. "That's going to last about two seconds when they find out about this."

"You don't honestly believe that other nations haven't pursued this?"

He yawned. "I don't know what to believe."

She nudged his shin with her foot and uncrossed her legs. "Wait and see."

Outside, the sun had turned the morning into a baking oven. Heat radiated from every surface and the dryness of the air made Jude cough. He and Mary walked between their military escorts and took two cars to the Proving Grounds, the shift from hot blast to cold air-conditioning a shock plunge that Jude resented like a hole in the head. He was shivering when he got out and then within seconds they were through another wall of red heat and into a cold room that felt like an icebox.

"Who needs Swedish saunas?" he muttered to Mary and she grinned.

Despite his initiation into the marines Jude had never entirely liked army ways. Now the formalities irritated him. His head felt scratchy on the inside, but that was most likely his imagination rather than the actual NervePath spreading. Knowing that didn't help.

The Proving Grounds were an enormous lot of sixty-four square miles. Uninhabited except by lizards, rodents, rabbits, and the occasional deer they had been the test area for the USA's biological and chemical programmes for over sixty years. Out here there were animals that had become resistant to diseases that had been used in tests, including Q-Fever and equine encephalitis. The fact that, even under this torment, life could scratch out an existence and had adapted gave Jude hope in the face of what Natalie had told him of Guskov's plans. Things were never as hopeless as they looked. Then again, it was the animal migration here that worried him the most intensely, too. Local domestic animals and humans had been infected with germs from bomb tests on this land before.

Their contact here, Lieutenant Colonel Sharrock of the army's Medical Research, Development, Acquisition, and Logistics Command, met them in the bunker confines of the viewing station they had been ushered into. He shook hands with them and showed them to seats. In front of them screens were blank, except for the names and locations of their camera feeds set out in plain type. Sharrock, a heavyset man with greying hair and a face that was lean even down to the almost lipless economy of his mouth, had a cultured, authoritative voice that had long since lost specifics of local accent—although, as they went through introductions, he admitted to being a Texan.

Jude's first question was, "How does this fit in with the Comprehensive Test Ban Treaty, Colonel?"

The colonel blinked. He wasn't used to answering to civilians but he said, "As stated in our documentation, Agent Westhorpe, the Deliverance system is a defensive technology, designed to counteract the effects of terrorist attacks using biological and chemical weapons. Although we signed up not to test offensive weapons of this nature or with nuclear capacity there is no law that says we can't test countermeasures."

"Your countermeasures read to me like they have one hell of an offensive capability," Jude said, conversationally. He didn't have any quarrel with the man and didn't want to anger him, but the anger in himself wasn't going to let this situation slip past without extracting every chance to square off. As he sat back in the comfortable leather of the chair the grazes on his back fired into life. He twitched his lip in a suppressed curse and hoped he hadn't started to leak blood on his shirt.

Mary smiled, flirting by flashing a glance of mutual Jude-tolerance in Sharrock's direction. "What my very direct partner means is that we're very anxious to understand the full implications of your technology."

"I'm glad to be able to answer," the colonel said, his eyes showing no signs of annoyance. He must have been well used to being worked over by all kinds of interrogation strategies, including the nice-and-nasty technique, and if he thought they were doing it deliberately he didn't seem to care. "But first, let's look at this." He used a remote to cue one of the cameras.

"What are we looking at?" Mary asked.

The picture that appeared showed a strip of unremarkable desert. From the camera's high angle they could see the fence line of a small paddock. As the picture zoomed closer a selection of sick-looking animals came into sharper focus.

"This is a range of species." Sharrock pointed out the individuals with a laser pointer. "They're in a pen about ten miles north of this spot. They've been infected with anthrax. These steers and the sheep are just about on their last day. These others—caged off in the shade there—monkeys and coyotes, are rabid with the racing variant of that disease and hydrophobia has taken hold."

Jude's stomach clenched as the shots became close studies of suffering. A marmoset, flecks of foam around its mouth, was leaping and shrieking around its bars, tiny fingers bloody, eyes mad. Beneath it a coyote panted frantically and at its side another lay inert, flanks heaving. The larger animals stood or lay in laboured positions, struggling to breathe, shifting with their constant but futile efforts to obtain relief from ceaseless pain.

"They're beyond ordinary help now," Sharrock said and sent the picture up to the top left of the projection area. The main view now showed a microscope slide, dyed and highlighted in glorious colours.

"This is a sample of the anthrax-infected sheep's blood. These here are the disease marked out in red." His pointer skated over a set of bacilli that were rod-shaped and loosely linked together several at a time like chains of sausages, "And this is our product, Deliverance."

Jude looked at the green spheres suspiciously. "They're huge."

"About as big as you can get in the microscopic world, uh-huh," Sharrock confirmed. "Still just able to cross the tissue barriers into the bloodstream and that's the main point. Now watch. This sample is set to show you what happens when the release of the payload is triggered."

"How does that work?" Mary had her Pad out and was comparing what he said with her information.

"We set the shell to open when the immune response in the body has peaked in reaction to the initial infection."

"So, after you've sneezed and coughed all over?" Jude said.

"Exactly. Ensuring maximum spread." Sharrock darted his pointer at a green planet circling idly. They could see a shady coloration inside it, purplish. The histamine inrush was signalled by a surge of pink and, amid the flood, the cell wall of the planet suddenly thinned and separated, snapping back on itself like a broken elastic band. The purple and indigo colour of its payload spread out, revealing itself to be a pair of cells.

"That's the antigen—engineered T-cells that destroy the anthrax."

The purple cell's long tendrils caught and wrapped around the red invader. Within a minute they had infiltrated and destroyed it. As its wrecked parts joined those of the ruined Deliverance spore the indigo shapes, like jellyfish, floated off, tasting their way towards another red bar.

"Is this time-lapse?"

"No, real-time," Sharrock said and turned to grin at Jude.

Jude had to admit he was impressed.

"Now, let's see what that looks like in real life." Sharrock switched back to the pitiful animals.

"But isn't this shock against Deliverance going to combine with their original symptoms and, you know, kill them before the cure can take any effect?" Mary peered at the cattle now on screen with her nose part-wrinkled in disgust. Like Jude, she was semisquinting in an effort not to really see what she had to see.

"These animals went through their histamine shock about thirty minutes ago." Sharrock pointed to one steer that was coughing, a runny discharge splaying from its nostrils and mouth. Its eyes were watery and surrounded by clouds of flies. "The Deliverance should kick in any time now, as the levels start to decline."

"This won't be so much use against chemical warfare unless it's a slow-acting attack," Jude said. "But against biologicals it might do some good. Do you think the infection rate and transmission vectors would be strong enough?"

"We've predicted by modelling at the CDC that we could cover an area like downtown Washington within twenty-four hours, pretty much at saturation, working from just a few fixed-point releases."

"And if you're not infected with the disease or toxin?" Mary asked.

"Then it won't do you any harm, except for the sneezing and coughing," Sharrock said. "Although those can be pretty strenuous." He flicked a switch and the picture changed cameras. They found themselves looking at a test room full of soldiers in fatigues, sitting around. All of them had streaming eyes, running noses, and a miserable look. Those who weren't involved in a fit of explosive sneezing were very still. They looked exhausted and pissed-off.

"Volunteers," Sharrock said, grinning. "Testing an empty version. Only one man went in there with it two hours before this was shot. The rest were uninfected then. And we've done the same tests using water dispersal, food, and air contamination . . ."

"Prevailing wind tests?"

"Downwind testing, yeah. Right out here in front of this building."

"And where were the furthest cases found?" Jude asked, trying to gauge how far it would carry before settling into the ground.

"A hundred miles away there was a flu outbreak," Sharrock said. "We tested some samples of sputum swabs taken for the CDC and it was confirmed." He nodded with satisfaction, "Harmless when empty, though. Everyone made a rapid and full recovery."

"Nobody exploded," Jude was amazed, looking at the rib-shaking, nose-bursting scale of the hacking going on among the soldiers.

"We had to make it a strong enough reaction to fully aerosolize," Sharrock said mildly and flipped back to the animal screen. "And here what you've got are individually engineered packages. Not only is the payload an improved antigen but the spores are specific to each species, and they can get as specific as you like, right down to dominant genes for markings on the body, hair type and sex."

Mary glanced at Jude and they shared a look of caution and discomfort.

"So, if for some reason you decided to put the anthrax inside Deliverance, instead of the antigen, then what?" Jude asked. "Doesn't the body start to produce cells to fight the Deliverance infection?"

"Oh, sure it does." Sharrock nodded. "Sure enough. But the system is too virulent for that to take effect in time. Put anthrax in it and—" he shrugged. "No chance."

"How about putting in anthrax and tailoring it to kill only wealthy white men older than forty?"

"We can do everything except the rich part, unless there's some study somewhere that shows that money has a chemical effect on the body."

Jude nodded. "And your empty version, engineered for—what, generic humans?—is out there now, in the wild?"

Sharrock put his head on one side and adopted a patient expression. "I know what you're getting at, Agent. Isn't it going to mutate? Isn't it going to blend in with wild diseases? Isn't it going to start an immune reaction that will forestall using Deliverance in the future? No."

"Well, how can you be so sure?" Even Mary, advocate of this stuff, didn't sound a hundred percent confident now.

"That test batch had a half-life built in. By now it's all dust. Two, three transmissions and it dies within half an hour. If it made one more—the cell wouldn't be viable."

"I hate to get all Jurassic Park-y on you," Jude sighed. "But that sounds better than it runs in my paranoia. If bacteria had a constant behavior that never allowed any of them to conjoin, then we wouldn't be here talking about this. And we know that mutations can occur at any time. All it takes is one change that allows your Delivery boy to live beyond the expected span, maybe one environmental factor, and that's it."

"The empty test is contained," Sharrock said, with a direct stare that Jude absorbed without flinching. "There have been no cases in two days. It's gone."

"Okay." Jude could see he wasn't going to get any further with that. "What about a real release—when you have your baby and all its engineered immune responses out there in the big microecology, then what?"

"Then we'll have populations with long-lasting resistance to whatever the plague was in the first place," Sharrock said, going back to the PR.

"Jude." Mary was nudging his elbow with hers. "Look."

In the barren field one of the steers had moved across to the feed trough and was slowly eating something, its jaws stop-starting as they eased back into the long rhythm of feeding. As Jude looked it shook its head at the flies. But beneath the awning's dark shadow the marmoset lay dead in the bottom of the cage, its back arched in a rictus, its mouth open, and its eyes staring, spasmed stiff by its last fit.

"Why is it dead?" she asked.

"In the test, as I said, we used engineered versions of Deliverance. Some animals were given a match and some weren't. The monkey was a no-match. The payload was never released."

"So it did its share of spreading it about, but that's it?" Jude watched Sharrock turning off the picture show.

"That's it."

"And what was the use of putting that element into this?" he asked. "So you could let some die and not others?"

"So that animals could be carriers but not recipients," the older man said, sitting back in his chair. "So that if we need to we can be specific—we can make the spores unreactive altogether, unless they're exposed to the right markers. Animals can carry the Deliverance without being in any way affected, and if it's a human-active version, then they can infect humans. It's part of the infection vector."

"Okay." Jude decided to drop it.

"What happens to the animals out there now? Aren't they an infection risk?" Mary was still filling out her checklist for Perez.

"The animals will be destroyed and autopsies performed as usual," the lieutenant colonel said. "Speaking of which, we have some forensics for your inspection and some witness testimony and some medical experts waiting. I'm sure you'll be convinced by the end of the morning that this is the best system we've got for reacting to terrorism. The threat's very real, I can assure you."

Jude had seen information passed down by the CIA and he was sure it was, too, with India, Pakistan, and the Middle East proud of their advanced-technology status and as riddled as any other nation with opportunist weapons-dealers. He had no doubt either that the US wasn't going to hesitate if it thought this could work as an effective deterrent in the same way that intercontinental ballistic missiles and nuclear warheads did. If Deliverance could attack precise targets then it also had potential—massive potential. It was hard in the end to say which he liked the idea of less, Deliverance or Mappaware.

"Colonel," he said as they were getting up to leave the room. "Does the list of these microbes and antigens that you've provided give the only payloads that have successfully been reproduced by the system?"

"Not long enough for you?" Sharrock asked, eyebrow cocked.

Mary was listening quietly at Jude's shoulder. It was her reaction he was tuned to, far more keenly than the colonel's, as he added, "I mean, is it large enough to carry Micromedica, for example, or other nanotechnology? Can it reproduce them *in vivo*?"

Sharrock looked at him for a long moment, the question clearly unexpected.

At his side Jude didn't detect any change in Mary. He'd liked to think he knew her moods and responses and this wasn't how she'd have reacted if he'd mentioned something she already knew about and thought he shouldn't know. He *liked* to think that. But then, maybe he didn't know her that well. He turned his head and glanced at her.

She rolled her eyes. "Good question," she said and gave him a grin.

Maybe. He wasn't decided.

"It *is* a good question," the colonel said, "and one to which I don't know the answer. Let's go see the team that worked on it. They'll get you an answer, I'm sure."

Out in the proving fire of midday they crossed the compound and descended into the levels and protection of a new laboratory. Jude watched Mary all the way, but she was herself—calm, efficient, and flirtatious. That was all, until they were on the plane back to the hub at Salt Lake City.

Then she sat next to him when they were alone in the cabin and rested her head and its heavy load of bronze ringlets on his shoulder.

"Those animals," she said, fear and loathing in her voice. She rubbed her cheek against his collarbone and settled down. On her lap she was flicking through the information. "So, defensive or disguise?"

"Disguise," he said. "But a good try. Just think about it, with the weapon and the shield in your hand you can lord it over anyone with something as Doomsday as this. Protect your own population, nix the rest of the world. What a shame nobody's found a way of doing that without so much killing everywhere."

Jude put his arm around Mary's shoulders. Her fingers on the Pad keys had paused, French manicure shining in the cabin lights as the plane taxied out to the runway. The smell of her shampoo, expensive, filled his nostrils instead of the stink of dust. Natalie's mind-reading ability would have been good. As it was, he felt Mary pause and seem to think. When she spoke she was casual.

"Yeah," she said on an outbreath, musing. "It really is." She leaned on his thigh and drew up the file of the battling bacteria again, watching the gates open and the invaders rush in and envelop the anthrax. "Trojan horse," she said.

"Don't look it in the mouth."

She sat up and looked into his face. "Jude?"

He let his arm slide down, empty, to his side. "Mmn?"

She was staring very intently into his eyes. Then, of a sudden, she shook her head, "Nothing. Never mind. You've got too much to think about."

"What?"

"I never really said—about your sister, about White Horse. I'm so sorry. If there's anything I can do."

He nodded. "There's nothing."

"Do you want me to come with you?"

"No, thanks, it's okay. You didn't know her. I'll be back soon."

"Yeah." She leaned against him for a second and then sat back in her own seat, looking at him now and again with the sympathy he didn't want to see.

Jude watched their shadow rise and skate away from them, darting over the Proving Grounds' cursed earth and its programmed suffering. He closed his eyes.

He could feel her watching him until he fell asleep.

Twenty-One

Natalie sat in the hot seat inside the test room and looked through the glass partitions to the control centre. It was set up much the same as at the Clinic and was where the rest of the research team were arrayed, working on her readouts. Around her head the huge arms of the super-sensitive scan system were silent and dark. She was always disappointed in them. You would have expected them at least to hum or sizzle or have flashing lights but instead, like their handheld counterparts, they were silent to the last.

She hoped that Ian was going to turn up soon, but she didn't know if he would or how to contact him. In the meantime, the Selfware had been doing more to her than she thought. The way it had been altered before its use on Ian had radically changed its theatre of operations.

Way back in a dim past Natalie only knew was hers by the fact that it was all that was in her memory, she'd intended to create a tool for checking the activity states of the minds of people such as her yogis and martial-arts instructors—of anybody who claimed or had reason to think themselves capable of types of thinking and perception that were beyond the ordinary. She had hoped to find a significant difference between these samples and the general population that might be a clue towards a theory of paranormal abilities such as clairvoyance.

Her interest in this area had started the night she and Karen got home from the woods. Only two weeks later her mother was dead and, despite knowing that it couldn't possibly be true, a part of Natalie's mind had become convinced that her mother's life was the payment for that ill-made contract between herself and twilight. After all, she'd never specified a price for its control of the dark, so it was free to take whatever it could.

It was completely irrational, which made it all the more compelling. Her counsellor would say, "So, is it that you *want* it to be true?"

Natalie had always said, "No!"

Of course she did. Who wants to be responsible for killing her own mother in a stupid deal with the ancient gods of darkness? But deep down she did want it to exist, this kind of power that could be hers to wield, because if she had it then she wouldn't have to be weak and afraid. A thousand kids think the same thing. They grow out of it eventually. Natalie was prepared to see herself as a slow developer if that meant Charlotte's departure wasn't her fault.

"It's a classic overcompensation," she said to the counsellor. "I know that. I want supernatural powers to exist both so that I can have control over things I've no control of and so that I can dump the blame on it when something goes wrong. I know. I know. It's an identity-survival strategy that doesn't pay out as well as it promises." And she ground her teeth.

She developed Selfware to discover the truth about it once and for all.

Natalie had tested hundreds of claimants, and hundreds more controls. After summing up brainwave energies, crossmatching thought patterns, and analysing the deep structure of the connections between various centres where thought, imagery, and language were processed she had done her tests on the data and come up with no conclusion whatsoever. It could have been random noise. The only feature of interest was that some individuals exhibited larger-than-chance correct scores on sealed-card tests and far-viewing, and some individuals exhibited a larger-than-chance failure on the same—a negative psychic state.

Were they genuine psychics who counteracted their own intuition? Did they have reverse intuition? Were white cats unlucky for them? Had the high-scoring psychics stolen their unaccountable accuracy from these poor bastards who always got it wrong? She never found out.

The man who was her deepest meditator, a calm Zen guy from Newcastle, looked like he would be a perfect candidate for consciousness studies because he could remain aware and alert with almost no meaningful activity going on in his higher centres at all; a silent human machine, he just sat for hours and could switch that state on and off like a tap. He made no paranormal claims, however. She asked eagerly what use this ability was. He said it kept him grounded and calm, emotionally responsive but intellectually accepting—he had a huge tolerance and patience for everyone, and he liked it that way.

Natalie mapped his brain and studied it assiduously. She formed her first version of Selfware on its model. Selfware became interactive once NervePath was licensed and she could simulate its use in bits of cyberspace. From the people who had scored above and below chance on her tests she attempted to isolate common patterns. Little was common. But this forced her to develop the software to assess and adapt itself to what it found in individual mind structures.

Instead of assuming a generic format it would go through a period of testing for connectivity "fit," as it was known, and then send back its own map of the person's mind. By extracting information from these maps and matching them across a scaled environment based on crossmatching individual Memecubes, Natalie finally found a feature that did test strongly above chance.

The next version of Selfware worked to enhance that feature, for which she had no name. It was a level of connectivity and communication, with a strong hippocampal bridge component in all subjects that allowed both hemispheres of the brain to communicate more widely than the norm. She had no one to test this on, including herself at the time, since she was only licensed for read-only NervePath systems. So she simulated the results, leasing hours and hours of time on the University's virtual environment at fifty quid an hour, almost using up her whole year's budget.

That was the way she'd continued to work on Selfware until she'd been refused her licence yet again at the Clinic. By then it was able to work within individuals, assess their success rates in terms of cross-centre communication, enhance these, and then test patterns against each other, strengthening links that improved efficiency and reducing the strength of those that caused mistakes. So it had been in that form when they'd thoughtfully altered it and its limits.

Now it had become something else, and the NervePath system it was running on had changed in its capabilities since she'd designed it. Not only that but, from her understanding of Bobby's situation, the software and the hardware had fused as their instruction sets and capacities permitted. This was what the rest of the team were trying to work on, using her real-time information as a base, but she was sure in her own mind that she hadn't gone nearly as far. She'd been careful about the run time.

It was a shock, then, when she saw her own results.

Nikolai Kropotkin and her father talked her through them. They gathered in Kropotkin's office and watched the holographic representations flux and whirl.

"What you have to realize is that when you were infected with this system, it was already a fusion of the hardware and software—because in Bobby X it had run on for hours," Kropotkin said to her.

Natalie was staring at the diagrammatic outputs, which were telling her that not only her brain and central nervous system but her entire body had been co-opted into working for the ends of the Selfware programme. She kept turning her attention inwards, trying to feel the difference, but there seemed to be no change and that was disturbing.

"I still don't like your explanation of that," Calum broke in, almost barking in his dislike of the facts. "How can Selfware communicate with the NervePath in this way? It shouldn't be possible."

"On the contrary, the only requirement for the command code to trigger the NervePath to create physical changes in nonneural cells was that it redefine all cells as potential information exchangers. Once the brain had been adapted to optimal functioning Bobby was able to perceive the wider truth that, in fact, all our cells do communicate with each other all the time."

"But that was a change in his mind, not in the systems," Calum insisted.

"Yes, and by that point his mind and the systems were integrated. The adapted version was allowed to write back to the original NP code. I'd like to know who it was wrote in those additions." The expression on Kropotkin's wrinkled face darkened as he grew thoughtful, and Natalie saw that he was thinking about Guskov.

"Is he capable of that?" she asked directly. "Writing and testing material like this on unsuspecting people?"

Nikolai shrugged. "Of course he is. You experimented on yourself in earlier days, didn't you, with the Read-Only NP systems?"

"This is different," she insisted, feeling sick.

"Not when you have a world to save," Kropotkin said quietly. "Not when you have spent your life, and the payoff is hanging in the balance. Waste it for the sake of an unknown man's life, one life, against so many possibilities?"

"Not his life."

"His against another's. Yours against mine. This was your life's passion, this work, wasn't it? And would you have given up?"

"My work wasn't in this league."

"But it was. You just didn't know it."

Natalie turned to her father. His face was heavy with the weight of worry and anger.

"You knew," she said. "You knew what he'd done and you didn't tell me."

His florid face flushed an even deeper red. "It wasn't meant to touch you!" he said, through teeth that clenched and ground against each other. "I wanted you to stay in York and keep out of this whole . . . mess."

"But you knew what Selfware meant to me. Or wasn't it you who said, 'This work is unscientific, moronic'—wasn't that you? Or did my hearing play up? Hmm?" Her anger was only now boiling to the surface. She hated the hurt in him and the way it made her feel pity for him. "And you knew about this Free State idea and you kept *that* quiet."

He glanced at her, wounded and cautious, his pale blue eyes deep in their sockets and shrouded beneath lids that tried to protect him from her. She saw herself in that second as he saw her: Natalie, so like her mother, full of the dippiness that Charlotte had had, that kind of violet viewpoint that pushed romance and mystery into every cranny of an orderly and plain world, mucking it up with the dripping lace of imagination when even its ordinariness was a marvel she belittled with her furbelows. Natalie was a fragile flower, unable to cope with the grief of losing her mother, who had been deluded, insane with despair and caught in depression, the ideas that saved her spawning ridiculous fantasies of the mind's workings: beliefs in shamen and shadows. Natalie was his and must be protected. Natalie was his fault and must be fixed. He had thought, *If only NervePath had been working this well years ago when she was fourteen, I'd have sorted her out then, set her straight.*

"Good God!" She got up, almost staggered over her own chair, and found herself groping for the door. She glanced back, saw Kropotkin puzzled, her father agonized, and then she was out into the corridor and running down it for the isolation of her own room where there were doors she could slam to shut out this awful source of endless, wretched information and the leaking old vessels that contained it.

Payoff, was that what Kropotkin had said? Maybe there was a price for everything and Ian was right to exact his dues before he left them behind.

Jude woke and found his head resting on Mary's lap. They were still in the plane from Dugway. The cabin lights were low and unmistakably, although very slowly and softly, her hand on his head was stroking his hair. He pretended to be still asleep.

So, the army did not have the version of Deliverance he had possession of, which meant to him that the Russian was going to use it himself as the obvious method of mass-distributing the Mappaware—he was going to double-cross the government.

Jude wondered what program he was going to give out. The answer must lie in the file, back in his apartment. He would have to go through it in the fine detail he hadn't tried before, to piece together the whole story. Meanwhile, he had to bury his sister and prevaricate here, putting on a show to someone his doubts wouldn't let him trust but whom his loyalties wouldn't let him betray. He'd had less committed love matches than the unconscious faith he'd had in Mary. Maybe Natalie was right when she'd pointed it out. But what was this all about, now? If she were a liar, was this a plan to keep him sweet? If she were honest, was it a show of real tender affection?

The soft brush of her fingertips gave no clue. For no reason he could think of he was suddenly aware of them being alone together in this private cabin; him lying down, her possessive touch. Through the impeccable serge of her skirt he could smell her and it was an arousing scent that, once he'd identified it, stiffened his cock and made his heart start to beat faster.

He made himself lie still on the seats. He counted seconds. He longed to sit up and kiss her and get lost in a moment's stupid desire.

He breathed with the control of a hiding animal, trying not to give itself away.

Ian remembered himself as best he could and composed his physical form into its old shape. It took time and it was difficult. It cost energy he would rather not have used, because his store of it was finite—the only energy he'd ever had—and with each use the store diminished. Soon it would be all gone and he would cease. But his sense of outrage was still good and strong. There wasn't a poetic set of the scales of justice operating in any universe he'd seen, but as long as he was around he had a mind to put that right—after all, what was a mind for if it wasn't to get things in their proper place?

Now the last thing he had to fulfil was his duty to pay back the bastards who'd made him into this omnipotent, short-lived wonder. Knowledge hadn't enlightened him to the point where he was so ready to forgive. Human weakness, sure, he could've gone for that, maybe, had the individuals concerned not been so blind to their own motives; a simple show of doubt or remorse might have softened his resolve towards them. But their commitment had convinced him that there were no mistakes in the accountancy of their ethics; they'd screwed him over for the bottom line. His death was to their profit. He knew their sort.

Natalie's state called to him. He could read her signature on the energy face and it was like no other. He surfaced close by. They were alone together in an office; small, cramped, the air unusually full of volatile chemicals, unusually barren of organic particles.

"You shouldn't have run it so long," he said, launching straight in with helpful advice. She needed to get her head straight if she was going to be useful.

Natalie turned and at first her face was shocked. But then it became thoughtful. "Ian," she said. "We need to scan you. It's important. Will you come?"

"'S why I came." He was impressed by her self-control. She'd always been a much more complicated person, a smarter one. No surprises that she could move directly when needed. It was admirable, but he felt lonely because of it.

"You're right." She was responding to his loneliness, accepting his advice, including him. "I was stupid, but it seemed like a good idea at the time." She took a jumper out of her bag and put it on. "Have you seen them here?"

"Oh yes. That one whose son was killed. She's got an outside line. Waiting for her moment."

"The others will all go along with Guskov in the end," she said, waiting for him to confirm.

"Even your father," he said. "Got to now. Gone too far."

The right side of her mouth dragged down in misery. "Of all the people in the world—he was the one who believed in being rational, and here he is like all the rest of us, dragged along in the undertow of their lives, making it up after the fact, doing everything according to the map." She tapped her head. "And you, too. And me. No bloody escape, even when you can see it happening."

"It's not the end yet," he said.

"Soon." She walked across to the door and opened it for him with the touch of her hand on its sensor. As he passed her she said, "Does it get worse than this?"

"Not much," he lied. He didn't know how to talk about what it became. He didn't know what it meant, only what it made him understand; he did not matter.

She touched his arm as they stepped out into the corridor. "Did you ever . . . move anything with you, through space?"

"What, carry something? You mean when I'm—"

"Yes."

"Once." He nodded. He looked into her face, careful that she didn't see what it was he'd done. "Part of my payback."

"Payback!" she repeated and laughed, cynical and disappointed with herself. "Does it all come to that?"

"You tell me, love," Ian replied. "What else is there?"

"Forgiveness," she said, but in her heart she didn't feel it. She remembered Dan's death as if it had happened a moment ago.

Ian's stubble-covered jaw toughened. "Not from me."

Natalie nodded and beckoned for him to follow her. You had it in you, or you didn't. To forgive was to let go, and she and he had a lot to hold on to.

After their arrival in Washington Mary and Jude spent a couple of hours collaborating on a report for Perez and the rest of the Sciences Unit, detailing the significant points of the Deliverance system, how to identify it, what the lab might see in attempts at copies, and who they thought was most likely to try and obtain samples of it. Mary enjoyed their efforts—it was like old times. Except for Jude's undercurrent of sadness it was like any other case she'd written up with him—but this time there was no scrap-paper soccer under the table, no pizza take-outs and surreptitious listening-in to the baseball commentaries. When they were done it was almost midnight.

"Drink?" she suggested.

He nodded and looked at his Pad. "It's late, though, and I've got to get the early flight to Montana."

"We don't have to go."

"No, it's okay." He slipped his jacket on and switched down the systems for the night. "I've got something I want to talk to you about."

Mary pricked her ears up but didn't inquire any further. They walked a few blocks and caught the Metrorail, watching the late police stalk up and down the cars in their full body armour, like robots. They got off near his apartment and then turned south and through the doors of Mulrooney's, a bar where they'd once used to meet a snitch from the Russian mafia underground, Posey Tavorian. She'd been a mine of information about technology leaks until they found her face down in an abattoir's pile of ready-to-process cattle innards. Out of deference to her memory they'd avoided the place for a few months and staying away had become a habit. Mary wondered if Jude had a special reason to come back.

They ordered beers and got a corner of the bar to themselves. In the pleasant glow and the soft shushing sounds of the country songs Mulrooney's was famous for she almost couldn't believe it when he took the buff folder out of his case and slapped it onto the mahogany counter between them.

"Someone gave me this," he said, keeping his fingertips on it for a moment longer. "I don't know who, and I don't know how. One moment it wasn't there and then it was." He glanced at her and sighed, taking his hand off the folder and letting her touch it.

She had to focus so her hands didn't shake. She'd been right about it. Through a burst of relief and puzzlement she looked blankly at its old, dog-eared pages.

"Where—? You don't know?" She leafed through and made herself say, "It's all about our Russian."

"Yes," he said. "All of it."

She glanced at him through a curtain of hanging ringlets and saw he must have pored over it a long time, figuring that out. "What, even these Bulgarian papers?"

"A man of many identities." He drank half his beer and swiftly signalled the barman for another one. "A long story."

"God!" She turned over the familiar cards, the Kodeks entry—Jude read Russian, of course, and she didn't. He must know what it was. "What's this?"

"Admittance to prison," he said. "A life stretch, but he was out in three years."

"Why?"

"It's where he met his mafia master and got into the company. Within eighteen months of getting onto the streets they were both dead."

"Excuse me?"

"He took on another persona and took up science. Ask me why."

"Why?"

"Don't know. I was hoping you and I might figure that out."

"Well, why didn't you tell me about this before?"

"I wanted to be sure of a few things first." He shifted on the high stool to a better position, leaning low on the bar top, contemplating his drink. "Like, was it real? Was it connected with White Horse? Was it going to count?"

Mary closed up the cover and took a drink, tapping the tough ends of her nails against the glass and watching the bubbles rise. "Where's it from?"

Jude flicked open the top sheet and looked at the stamps. "Pentagon. Somewhere. Think we should take it straight back? I could drop it in the post box, plain envelope."

"Your prints are all over it."

"Then I can take it back in person and explain."

"Saying what?"

"Well, now, that's a good question." He closed the folder and grinned at her without humour, although his eyes glittered in a strange way beneath the low blue glow of the Labatt sign's neon.

"It's probably not going to yield any evidence except changes of identity and movements," she said, making it sound like a guess. "That won't get us a case."

"Was he on the team for Deliverance?" Jude pondered. "I'll bet he was. Think about it. Florida, Atlanta . . . not so far for a commute or a cover-up. And he is the contact man."

"So what you're saying?"

"It's a big leap." He finished his first beer and hauled the second closer. "But maybe he wants to ship samples out of the country, using his old network of friends. It'd be worth the gross national product to whoever buys it and gets it working first, specially if they're not keen on us."

"Ivanov—" she began.

"Guskov, his name is now," Jude corrected her, looking into the infinities of the bourbon optics.

"Guskov," Mary repeated, careful, "wouldn't be used here if he had this kind of leakiness. You think the NSC's stupid?"

"No." Jude reached over and with his fingers pushed her beer on its mat towards her. He smiled. She recognized that self-destructiveness: it wanted company. "I think it's full of players, and this stack of paper says they're playing with the wrong guy. He is too many people."

She didn't know whether to be relieved or not that he hadn't made the right connection and linked everything to point at Mappa Mundi.

"So, what do you say? Pursue or drop? Your call."

Steel-guitar music was playing. Its lonely plains sound rang against her teeth as Mary tried to see which way to go.

"It's not linked to your sister's case?" she asked, stalling.

"I don't think so." He shook his head and his hair, inky and blue-black in the dimness, fell softly along his jaw and against his shoulder. She noticed he hadn't had it cut in a while.

"The stuff she had, when she had it, was another kind of tech—Micromedica-based. Different. He couldn't be on both those projects."

The steel chords slid into one another on the airwaves. Jude had never looked more handsome than now when he was so beat. She could eat him. Mary didn't know what to do about it. Her mind was skimming, planning, fixing, but she couldn't stop looking at him and feeling that hunger she'd often had. Jude had always been unobtainable, but now? And she was an idiot for thinking that.

She straightened up on her stool and took a sip of her drink, putting it down further from her. She should have kept her idle thoughts in shape on that plane and not given in. What was the point in it? Nothing he'd said so far made him any less of a threat.

"I think we should take everything we have and hand it across to the CIA," she said. "He's their boy. They can worry about him." Watching his nodding, resigned reaction she felt suddenly grateful to him for cooperating his way out of his own death. If he was going to be biddable she might be able to preserve everything here for later, when Guskov was out of the frame and the entire wretched project was wrapped. Her whole never-have-anything-you-can't-walk-away-from attitude was faltering and it made her angry. She was going to lose it if she wasn't careful.

"And the Micromedica thing?" she asked. Was he going to admit going to England?

"I had someone look at it." He finished his second drink. "She said it was some kind of attempt at an emotional control device. Not a good one. She wanted to report it but I said it was something I'd found on investigation, criminal, better keep it all quiet until we'd made our arrests first. We left it at that."

"Who?" Which was really pushing it.

"A Doctor Armstrong. A Brit. She was listed by Nostromo as an expert. I sent it to her."

Sent, didn't go. Was that important? It was a lie of a kind.

"Uh-huh, well, if you don't have it now . . ."

"I have a copy. But since it's not an original and there's no identification on it, it doesn't mean anything yet," he admitted.

"Can I have a copy?"

He sent it across to her Pad, just like that.

"And can I take this home tonight, if you get some rest?" She reached out for the file.

"Sure, be my guest." He called the barman over again. "Chaser?"

"No, thanks." She watched him order Wild Turkey, a double shot, and, when it came, knock the whole thing back in one go. Even his movements were becoming more reckless. Concern made her say, "Take it easy. Early start, remember?"

"I just want to sleep," he said and stood up to go.

On the street she decided to walk with him as far as the main street they had to cross, where she could get a cab. Her shoes were smart and they'd started to hurt. On the corner, in the street light made dappled by the trees they paused to say goodbye. The pavement was uneven and Jude was unsteady. He slipped slightly and Mary found them both suddenly much closer than they had intended, but he didn't move back and neither did she. Since she was tall and in heels, they were at eye level with each other.

"Em," he said quietly—she couldn't see his face properly. The nickname was one he hadn't used in a while. She could feel his breath on her face. It was laced with bourbon, fiery. He put his hands out onto her arms, as if he was going to kiss her on the cheek as he often had, but instead he hesitated. Then he was kissing her on the mouth instead.

Before she knew what she was doing she'd responded, touching his tongue with hers and pressing up against him. He was that mixture of hard and soft, pushy and reactive that she liked the best. The traces of bourbon still in his mouth tasted divine. She was only just wondering what the hell she was doing when abruptly he pushed her away and held her at arm's length.

"I'm sorry!" he said, backing away another step. "Sorry, Em. I didn't mean to . . . that was a mistake. The drink. Stupid."

"No, no," she replied, light, silly. "That's fine. It's okay. Really. You're upset and—I know. It's fine. Don't worry about it." She took a step back. Her heart was racing. Between her legs she felt a burning heat more fierce than she'd known in a long time. She stepped back again. "Forget it."

"Shit. Sorry, really." He raised his hand in a half-wave goodbye, still backing off awkwardly, embarrassment and vulnerability in every step. "I'll see you. Yeah?"

"Yeah," she said quietly, watching him turn his back quickly and walk away from her, head down and shoulders hunched.

Mary waited until she felt cooler and then she walked home, dazed and feeling foolish. *What was that all about?* Her thoughts were telling her she was a moron but her heart was singing. She wanted him more than she thought she'd wanted anything.

It'll pass, you idiot, she told herself.

Then she opened the door of her apartment and a faint, sickly smell made her hesitate on the threshold. She sniffed the street but in its smell of gasoline and humid earth there was nothing unusual.

The sensor pads showed that nobody had tried to break in. She assumed she must have left something in the refrigerator that was going off, or maybe one of her flower arrangements was wilting early. She left her shoes in the hall and padded around to look, but they all seemed fine. There was an old tub of half-eaten ricotta cheese in her butter box that she threw out, but it had only just started to green.

The smell persisted and it seemed stronger and more . . . wet . . . the further into the apartment she got.

When she turned on the lights in the bedroom she was so fast to jump backwards in shock that she hit her head hard on the edge of the door and almost knocked herself out.

From her hands and knees, mouth open in shock, she could still see the decaying pieces of Dan Connor's body soaking into the hand-embroidered lace coverlet of her bed. Whoever had put him there had reassembled him thoughtfully, and shaped him in a star that looked like a welcoming embrace.

Jude stood in the white purity of his own shower, with the jets on full, feeling the water sluice and foam against his skin. With his hand on himself he masturbated, eyes closed, leaning on the tiles, feet braced. When his moment came he let go and sank down into a crouch on the floor, watching the swirl of water catch his semen and swirl it down the drain. He leaned on his hands with his head down and cried soundlessly as the flood poured onto his head and back, hot and raw on the gashes that lined his shoulders and ribs. He opened his mouth and silently screamed. He hadn't got any other way to try and keep feeling and he hadn't got any way to let it out.

He'd never felt more wretched and now he was afraid. It was a relief. Fear. At last, there it was. The knee-buckling terror that drains all purpose and will. Mary had recognized that fucking file. He'd sort of suspected it the other day when she was uninterested in it, and this evening—her face had been so studied.

He huddled with his arms around his knees and drew his legs in tight. He sat under the water and rocked back and forth. He'd made his bid. He'd decided to see what he could achieve by telling instead of keeping secrets. Tomorrow and tomorrow it would have to keep going until at last . . .

Seventy-three percent he was now. What did it mean?

He sent his thoughts out to Natalie, but he didn't even know where she was.

One more second and he'd have begged Em to come back with him, and she would have. He wished she was there. He wished he knew for sure if she was the real Em or not. He wanted White Horse back. He wanted all the things he would never have.

Twenty-Two

Mikhail Guskov looked at the information spiralling down the lines from Bobby X and knew there and then that his problems with Mappa Mundi were solved. This fusion of the NervePath and Selfware could be used in others the same way—transforming the existing mind into a programmable structure, opening it up for improvements without compromising any of its unique adaptations. It was perfect.

Natalie Armstrong, working alongside him in the lab, turned around and her flat, unsettling gaze made him stop in the midst of transferring his thoughts to the Pad in his hand.

"How convenient," she said quietly, glancing at what he'd written with the stylus. "You'll have the means in your hand before long. The only question that then remains is, what is this master program you're going to distribute to the waiting world?" Her left eyebrow hooked up into a question mark. "Or haven't you decided yet?"

He glanced along the line of equipment but Isidore and Calum were intent on their work. They hadn't heard her. In the glass chamber, inside the scan system's loose clutch, Bobby X sat, as solid as anyone Guskov had ever seen.

"Sarcasm doesn't suit you," he said cordially.

"I'll be the judge of that." She turned and some communication seemed to flash between her and the slumping bulk of Bobby. "I'm betting it won't be a lock-out. You could write one, you know. A mental immunizer. *I* could write it."

"It's already on the list." He grinned at her. "Along with many other off-the-shelf concepts which will be freely available—"

"Ah, when are you going to cut this bullshit?" she whispered, smiling with a real streak of acid in the long line of her mouth. "You know it isn't going to work out in perfect conditions. Most people are going to end up worse than they started. Or do you believe in yourself so much that you've forgotten why you started this in the first place?"

"You'd rather the Americans had their way?"

"I'd rather none of this had ever happened, but so what? As you claim, the technology demands a response. I say you should nip it in the bud and seal everyone shut against it. You can't control it once it's finished. Even if you did get it distributed and the stuff was free there'd be ten people in as many minutes writing programs for it. They'd learn. Meanwhile you have to play catch-up and race ahead at the same time. No way you can. In a few years everything we know of as our cultural life could have ground to a halt, people shifting in their understanding as the wind changes to different points of the compass. Identity will be written in water. Ideas will invade or leave without your choosing. People will be puppets with no master. It's a travesty, and you know it."

"You have a bleak imagination," he said. The direct force of her words and her stare was unnerving him, and he hadn't felt that way since he couldn't remember when. He liked it. She was a challenge.

Natalie snorted and glanced down at some of the data from Bobby. "I don't have an imagination any more," she said to the desk and then turned on her heel and walked away from him, down to the far end of the control centre where she sat down to use another terminal next to the high-shouldered shape of Lucy Desanto.

Desanto, Guskov thought, she was another problem, and Natalie knew about that as well. He suspected Desanto was here to spy for the US government and had a way he hadn't found out about that would allow her to transmit information freely out of the Environment to them. They'd wait until he was ready and then—what? Probably close in with an army group, threaten to kill them all, or their loved ones, if they didn't cooperate. And meanwhile, on the evidence of that piece of shit from Deer Ridge that Mary'd managed to keep a lid on, they were training their own programmers to use the languages and try out some ideas.

Natalie's words had bitten home, however. There was no question that she was now the most intelligent person in the room, although what that amounted to was hard to define. She thought faster, she had access to knowledge that eluded the rest of them, and she'd started out as one of the few NervePath programmers he respected. He didn't know what that made her, but for the first time he felt old. If Selfware had made this out of her, what could a more sophisticated version do for him? And the rest of the world?

Enlightenment wasn't that far from his ultimate goal.

But she was right in that maybe his original ideas had been far too grand and immature. At the outset he'd thought that Mappaware would make it possible to remove selected memes from the ecosystem of the Global Common Cube. But there had been the problem of language as a first hurdle—ideas being defined in the terms and limits of specific natural language forms—and although a solution to that looked possible with this new evolution of Bobby X, there was still the certain and proven fact that even if he had managed to erase, say, all beliefs in any form of God, given time this meme would reemerge in the population.

All memes were recombinations of older memes. As long as the roots of possibility existed within the Global Cube, any idea that could be constructed from their multiple combinations and subtle explorations would surface again. The more attractive and powerful it seemed, the faster it would spread, and the more deeply entrenched it would become in the minds it inhabited. He didn't believe now that it was possible actually to get rid of any ideas by this method. Nor would he want to. It was this cross-pollinating richness that allowed thought to move on from one generation to the next, developing technologies and amassing knowledge as it went. It was this phenomenon that produced the common experience of the zeitgeist and the synchronous evolution of the same new memes at isolated places, but within very brief periods of time. The more that people had free access to the Global Cube, the more frequently this occurred.

In latter days the more virulent religions and cultures had propagated their particular versions of the GC-Cube very successfully; their own Mappa Mundi were popular and widespread, more homogenous compared with the violently differing Cubes of their older selves that a less communicative population had enjoyed. Or was it endured?

For him it had been endurance. It was the perpetual Cube War he wanted to end, not free thinking. He had witnessed at first hand, and in all walks of life, the petty, banal, heartfelt, and bloody clashes of people with different Maps, different Cubes. What the defining memeplex happened to be was an incidental factor—a religion, a national identity, a public right-of-way, a jointly owned fence line, a water hole . . . the list was endless, but the result when the clashing Cubes came together was always the same.

There was even a form of mathematics that he, Isidore, and Alicia had developed between them, the Memetic Calculus, that described and predicted the outcomes of any amount of complicated ideas encountering each other for the first time. They resulted in one of four outcomes: acceptance (changing your own Map according to the new idea), tolerance (not changing it but tacking on the new information to your old Cube as a kind of handy reference), rejection (defining the new Map as utterly misguided and having no more to do with it), and attempted destruction (annihilate the threat of the new Map by killing all its hosts).

The last two were the ones Guskov hated. Both were triggered by emotions, generated in their own Cubes. Emotion was the master switch that Mappaware must come to play on most heavily. Alter the emotional portrait of a meme and you alter identity without the need for fancy fiddling with the hugely tangled and difficult definitions of neural pattern and synaptic timing.

His own identity had been a matter of expediency. Most people would have ferociously resisted the changes he had looked for and embraced. Many thousands every year died to protect their sense of identity rather than change and continue a physical existence. The very concept of your own identity was interlinked with the ideas of eternity, unchangeability, sanctity, and rightness. From anorexics to terrorists, the legions ready to throw themselves into annihilation to prevent the extermination of their own Maps was a phenomenon that enraged him with its pointless waste. And as long as the sacred self was enshrined as a concept that must not be tampered with or improved, the futile litany of torture and misery that accompanied it would, of necessity, go on.

Guskov looked along the lab at his staff, his companions, his conspirators. He didn't think any of them exactly shared his ideas, despite every communicative effort. Some Maps could not agree, no matter how you tried to fit them together. But they had agreed, in theory, that a mutable identity that embraced rational doubt and was prepared to reject any part of itself if proven wrong or unsuitable was preferable to a fixed dogma with no room for change. And he himself knew by experience that there was almost no limit at all to how a person could alter the entire structure of their selves, from values to language, and still remain aware that they were Themselves.

As the scheduled technical scans of Bobby X came to an end and the data began to be processed, it was time for the more traditional method of evaluation—a conversation.

Guskov walked along the back of the room and tapped Natalie on the shoulder.

"Since you're his chaperone," he said and held the door open for her.

She gave him a nod and went into the test room to clear away the scan gear and bring the other chairs forward so they could all sit in conference together.

Mikhail followed her and did his share. Bobby—Ian—sat and watched them with a constant and unwavering attention. His expression was unreadable, blank but fully engaged. Mikhail wondered what he saw.

Jude stood on the lowest bar of the gate at Theo Jones's Two-Fox Ranch and from the shade beneath his hat brim looked out over the corral at the circling horses. Theo was just behind him, sucking on a stem of old grass, letting Jude take his time. The paddock was dry and the grass all but ground up to nothing under the many hooves. Jude kept coming back to a graceful, powerful horse, its mane the same golden chestnut as Mary Delaney's hair. It had a white blaze on its face. There were no pale animals in the herd except a grey, but it was too dark for his purpose.

"That one?" Jones tipped his own hat back and nodded, extracting the grass stem for a moment. "Best one in the whole damn' herd." He was aggrieved, but there was nothing he could do. Jude handed over the best part of ten thousand and left an hour later on the nameless animal's back, riding the last ten miles across Jones's well-maintained pastures and woodland, up to the reservation fence line.

It was a long time since Jude had been in the saddle, but he hadn't forgotten how to ride. The horse, a mare, followed his leads easily and ran light on her feet, eager to be moving and full of the vigour of the bright day. His leathers creaked. He wore his father's necklace and bone-beaded jacket. He wore White Horse's old hat, which had been left at Jenny Black Eagle's house and so had escaped the fire. Good thing she had a head as big as his, he thought, and almost smiled. With the reins in one hand and the other resting easy, the mare's paces rocking and calm, he could have stayed like that forever, crossing the land, always going forward. But within what seemed like minutes they had found the trail that ran along the wire fence and were soon at the gateway and the dusty ride up into Deer Ridge.

He made her walk the last half mile. They stopped finally, panting in the noon heat, where the charred earth of the old house sat opposite Paul Bearchum's porch. Jude dismounted and tied the pony up to the mailbox. As she began to crop the grass close to it he walked inside, the brief lift of spirit he'd felt in the woods vanished into thin air.

He sat in the cool kitchen for the next half hour with Paul himself, drinking iced tea and listening to the sound of his mother in the other room, talking to other cousins. He and Paul said nothing, rested their glasses on the blue-and-white-check tablecloth, watched the world outside the open door. The day was sunny and bright with high, white cloud scudding in the distance. Gentle breezes ruffled the long, straggling grass heads that crowded next to the porch steps. Down the road a child played on a bright green tricycle. A chicken hawk sailed over the long, black ground where White Horse's home had stood, hanging on the mild updraught there, moving on.

"This case," Paul said at one point. "Will it ever make court?"

"I don't think so," Jude replied. They were talking about the case White Horse had tried to put together and which he had asked Paul to testify on. "I've got enough to start with and get a hearing; the program they used and a set of NervePath." He found himself unconsciously touching his head. "I can demonstrate the effect. But I need witnesses who saw the people that came, who saw them holding the scanner or saw it in their car outside Martha Johnson's store. I need links."

"Okay," Paul said, getting up for more ice. He was sixty-nine now and moved stiffly under his weight, taking his time. His hair still had dark amid the white, but his face showed all the years. "If you ask the others today they might change their minds."

"Maybe." And Jude needed to ID those people in the car. He had descriptions, not very good ones. He kept his mind on these things. They were having the ceremony in an hour.

Paul hadn't seen the car, but he had met one of the men involved when he was in town getting his weekly groceries. He could make an identification. As for the peanut butter, it was distributed via the store on a sign-out basis with the showing of a welfare card. Jude had collected samples of the contaminated batch, having toured that morning using a list of names on the dole register. He hadn't said why exactly, and nobody had pressed him for an explanation. Their dislike of his association with the Feds had mingled with their sorrow about White Horse and the mixture had made them stonily sympathetic. The fresh tins sitting in the back room of the shop on South Main had all tested clear. So he had that. Unfortunately Martha and her husband, who may have been able to confirm that the tins were contaminated while in the shop and not beforehand, were already in the burial ground on the southern face of the valley.

"You not on your own with this?" Paul asked.

"Don't worry about that." Jude still had the bastards who had thought White Horse would do the dirty work for them at the back of his mind. They could do their bit now. He planned to hand it across to one of their lawyers and he or she could stand up and get shot at for a change. But meanwhile he had to get more information.

In the other room the uneasy relationship between his wealthy white middle-class mother—a summer night's fling—and Magpie's remaining Cheyenne family seemed to have come to a quiet halt. Jude got up and took himself in there.

Squirrel, his youngest cousin and one of White Horse's closest friends, was sitting nearest the door. She made room for him on the sofa and he creaked down into it, trying to keep to the edge.

"We heard she drowned," Squirrel whispered.

Jude nodded.

"Drunk and drowned?" Jenny Black Eagle wanted to know, her voice hard and unforgiving.

"Yes."

The atmosphere in the small room bristled with resentment, tension, and anger.

"Murder?" Squirrel asked, looking up at him, her fashionable long-in-front haircut dropping across her eyes.

Jude closed his eyes and nodded.

Someone snorted derisively.

"Because of the case," Rob, Red Hat's son, said in his soft-spoken way, always calm. "She must have tried too hard."

"I'll follow it up," Jude said, staring down at his hands and then up into their dark, fierce glances. "I am doing." He looked at his mother, leaning back in the wicker recliner, her black suit a stoic plain shadow, her face very pale in this room of bright colour and darker tones. Her chestnut-dyed hair was tied up in a bun and on her lap her hat was similarly austere. She smiled at him with her eyes only.

"Then you'll go, too." Squirrel took hold of one of his hands unexpectedly and wrapped her own narrow one around it. "It isn't because of the coal oil?"

"No," he said quickly. "It's nothing to do with that."

"What, then?" Jenny said.

Jude wasn't sure what to say for the best. He didn't want them to know it was a military arms test for fear of what their reaction might be; mostly a reaction that would cause trouble and get people killed. Not that they would see it that way to begin with. And they'd have right on their side. "I think it's a secret research development. I don't know. I'll find out."

Jenny looked at him, her face neither trusting nor mistrusting. Her watch alarm beeped. "Time to go," she said and glanced at him as she stood up. "Paul told me you want witnesses."

He nodded.

"I'll find you some." She led the way out through the kitchen and into the street where the flatbed pickup bearing the body had arrived. Jude led the horse behind it, with the rest following them along the minor road that ran down towards the burial ground. He had a lot of people to thank, he thought as they reached the spot, just a stone's throw from the graves of the Johnsons. Friends and relatives had laboured to dig a pit seven feet wide and fourteen long.

The pickup stopped on the road and Jude handed the horse to Squirrel to hold as he took the front of the bier and led the way down to the sheltered spot overlooking the river valley. They set the wooden cradle on a stand and the blanket-wrapped body looked like nothing so much as a bundle of old clothes to Jude. He took off the necklace and his father's jacket and put them over it. He took off the hat and laid that across her chest.

Squirrel came forward and placed on the bier a silver belt she'd made. Jenny Black Eagle gave a book of poems, handwritten. Others came forward with small things: cloth, a cake.

Jude went down into the earth with it and saw that everything was set properly. He hauled himself out of it and stood on the side. Jenny put the pony's saddle in. Squirrel handed him the pony's rein. Everyone stood silently, even the priest, Father Younger, who'd come up from Missoula in case they had a last-second change of heart. Jude caught sight of his mother's face. She was shocked. Of them all, she was the only one who hadn't anticipated what was coming next.

He led the horse to the edge of the hole. It didn't want to go, but its pleasure in the day and its docility made it step close to when he offered it a mint from his pocket. From the back of his waistband he pulled out his gun. The click made the mare cock her ear in curiosity. She lipped his hand, looking for another sweet.

Jude hesitated. White Horse would never have shot an animal. She'd rather have died. Perhaps he'd have been smarter buying her a Subaru instead, but the warrior burial said horses for the next life and she'd been committed to that path. He brought the gun up where the horse couldn't see, and patted its neck with the same hand, starting to release the straps of the bridle from its ears.

But he didn't believe in any part of him that this was going to help. Of everyone standing there this horse was the best animal among them. He'd seen it run, felt its simple joy in life. It deserved to live, and he didn't believe there was any other world in which he and White Horse would get to ride it again.

Across the horse's sweat-marked back he saw the cousins, Paul, and the Tribal Chief watching him, their faces impassive, merely waiting. His mother had steeled herself and was rigid. Behind him Squirrel had taken a brace breath and was holding it. Jenny Black Eagle, who had once spat at him on the day he'd left to join the FBI, was at his other shoulder.

Jude looked down into the grave and up at the wild, blue sky.

He pulled the trigger.

At close quarters the shot was almost deafening. The crack made them all jolt, none more than the fire-coloured horse which took off in a gigantic leap over the grave, scattering Jude's cousins like ninepins.

Jude threw the limp leather straps of the bridle into the pit where the saddle rested and instead reached into his pocket, took out the keys to his Porsche, and tossed them in instead. Across the cemetery and the long sweep of field that ran down towards the lowlands everyone watched as the horse danced and leapt its way like a Chinese cracker, bounded over the low rail that marked Hawk and Joseph Benson's new vineyard boundary, and disappeared among the tall rows of trained grapes that traced across the ridgeline, following the sun.

Somebody, he thought it was Squirrel, giggled nervously and Jude himself started to laugh. He turned to see the cousins struggling to their feet, dusting themselves off. His mother had her hand clamped across her mouth, although he thought it was to hide a smile.

He jerked his head in the direction of the horse. "She never did wait to hear what I had to say."

Everyone except the Catholic priest was smiling or hiding a laugh behind their hands.

Jude stuck the gun back into the waistband of his jeans, bent down, and threw the first handful of earth. "Vohpe'hame'e," he said, his sister's name, the last time he would say it. They waited in case he had more to say, but it was Paul and the Chief himself who spoke the ceremony to free her spirit in the end. Jude got up and turned when it was done and the other hands had begun their work of scattering earth. His knees were painful and he was saddle-sore, ready to face whatever angry crap Jenny and the others were ready to throw about him ruining things. But as he staggered it was Jenny's hand that caught his arm to steady him.

"Come on," she said, a smile on her face that had lingered from the spectacle of the cousins gathering their dignity. "Let's go home."

"There's no difference," Ian was saying as the full team crowded around him in the testing area of the Sealed Environment. "Fundamentally all mass is energy and the quantum is the basic unit of information. When you see that, you realize the simple structure of the universe. Complexity is built of simple fundamentals, acting within information arrays whose range is determined by macrostructure."

"Whoa." Desanto, the cyberneticist and systems expert, held up her hand. Like the rest she couldn't help but bend closer to him, to see, to hear, to believe. "You're saying that particles at the quantum level are somehow restrained in their interactions by events on the Classical scale?"

"Gravity would be the case in point," Ian said, leaning back in his seat and wishing, at this moment, that he had a fat cigar to wag between his fingers. Never in his life had he had such an attentive, respectful audience. He wished his wife could have seen this, instead of the beery pub reminiscences that used to be the best talks he ever gave. But all she would have cared about gravity was that it kept her feet on the floor. Washing machines were more important. Actually, even now, the fragment of him that had stuck around in spite of his expansion wasn't sure that they weren't.

Isidore stumbled over his words. "G-gravity? You understand that?"

"Densely packed quanta develop a strong transdimensional harmony between them that propagates waves of attraction," Ian said, keeping the words simple, although they were inadequate.

The room was quiet. They were all looking at one another, but none of them were experts in the field. They couldn't naysay him and they didn't know if they dared agree. Nobody had so far come up with a theory of gravity that fitted both the theories of quantum mechanics and Einsteinian relativity. If they had, then the Theory of Everything would be in their reach and macro and micro universes fused into a model that predicted on both scales. It was worth . . . well, Ian thought it was worth at least a Nobel and a place in history. When he'd first realized what he was doing, sifting through matter and himself, he'd thought that maybe he'd quite like to have that. Now it was irrelevant on such a scale . . . He laughed.

"Have you got the figures on this?" Isidore was writing hastily.

"Not exactly," Ian admitted. "I don't do maths. I just . . . experience it."

"And is it right that the effect of an observer really changes the particles as though they're conscious?" Kropotkin asked tentatively.

"Consciousness is a macrophenomenon," Ian said, "which is why it's so difficult to take it apart and fix it up again. Macrostructures: once you've undone them, their complexity is thermodynamically susceptible, so you never do them up again exactly the same. You always lose bits. Particularly the longer you're—"

"Submerged?" Natalie suggested.

Ian nodded and his face became very heavy. "Yeah. The places where you have to put your information are themselves interacting all the time with the rest of the universe. Leave it too long and you drown, I guess that's the way to think of it. The little guys forget what they were doing." He grinned weakly at her. He wasn't feeling so great. It actually took concentration to maintain himself, like the effort of looking hard at one spot all the time. When he started to lose parts then he started to feel ill, and frightened. He longed to sink back under and drift in the endlessly changing, moving swirl, where it was safe and he would be allowed to forget.

"Mister Detteridge," Guskov said. "Would you demonstrate for us?"

Ian looked at him. *Detteridge.* Yes, he'd forgotten that. He nodded, glum, resigned. This wasn't the kind of thing he'd been thinking of, this performing-seal thing. He'd wanted a big showdown where he got his say and the white-livered scientists involved got to cower and be sorry . . . it was a dumb kid's fantasy, really. He felt ashamed of it. But he wasn't sorry about Dan Connor's body. That bitch had it coming.

Now he looked up into Mikhail Guskov's face and saw a person very alien to the one he himself had been when he was really Ian. This one had always been at arm's length from reality and other people. He was almost like Isidore there in that respect, but the quality of his distance was more intellectual than simply the result of a differently wired brain. He'd learned that people were predictable, that they had emotional buttons you could press to get what you wanted in a constantly reliable pattern. He'd understood that about himself and set about becoming invulnerable to such interference by holding no dream too close, no value too strongly. At the same time his manipulation of others had become an art. The best thing you could say of him was that he hadn't come to despise those who buckled under his pressures, and the worst was that he had realized the futility of attempting to escape the rules of his own unorthodox mind, but he wasn't going to give up trying.

"You don't know when you're beat, mate," Ian said to him, quietly, so that only the two of them and Natalie could hear it.

Guskov looked straight at her to see her reaction. She agreed.

"That's what I was trying to say before. You have to have some kind of map, at any given point in time. There's no such thing as the objective view from nowhere. And the map will always be an approximation. Even if you get it dead right, you'll never know that for sure—" She glanced at Ian and he nodded because the uncertainty of the universe went all the way down. She fixed her wonky smile on Guskov again, hopeful that he'd agree, knowing he wasn't going to because he couldn't.

"You can change all the ideas in the world and all the feelings, but you can't move beyond the limits of your vision. If you do, you end up like my meditation man—the lights are all on, but nothing's at home. You can't ever be free of meaning and every time you choose one it's a step in the dark."

"You're speaking from experience?" Guskov demanded.

"No, but I am," Ian said. "Get on with it, will you? I'm tired."

Mikhail and Natalie walked away together. Ian heard him say, "That doesn't mean that this project is futile. Far from it. Think about the possibilities beyond the simple use of control. Even control of the Selfplex. Think about what we could learn of ourselves."

"I was never arguing with that," Natalie replied as they passed the door into the control suite, watched by the others. "I'm arguing with the bit of you that can't give up on its dream of perfection. We aren't a perfectible race. We're better left trying to understand in our own ways than having it foisted on us by you."

"I think that a push in the right direction . . ."

The argument circled on. Ian could see both sides. He couldn't say he hadn't benefited from some of the systems. He couldn't say he'd have wanted it, either. But for the sake of stopping a war or saving a life, maybe it was worth changing a few minds, banging a few heads together. If they all had to change, maybe it wouldn't be for the worse.

He became aware of the two other women, Khan and Desanto, watching him as they got up to follow Guskov into the observation area, where whatever he was going to do wouldn't touch them. Their gaze was suspicious, fearful, and pitying.

Ian closed his eyes and waited for the word. The old him would have been sentimental. He would have missed this world. But now he looked forward to reunification with the free elements. The human desires meant nothing any more, only his debt to Natalie, and the rest he didn't want to remember. Burdened with this kind of slow, primate mind he was also stuck with never finding a way to comprehend the fullness of what it was he knew and saw. Even now, what had he said that began to explain? Nothing.

"Okay," said a voice from outside.

Ian opened his eyes. "What should I do?" Already he'd decided this would be the last time. No more trying. He was going to give up and go with the flow. They were already in a hell worse than anything he could achieve.

"Go," Natalie said.

He made eye contact with her through the partition and knew she understood his intention. Her eyes were full of tears. She was just below the threshold where he had started to reach into the deeper levels of the material world. Briefly, he wondered if people like them must always die this way, or if it was only him and his own reactions, built out of the man he'd used to be, Ian Detteridge, father of one, husband, ordinary man, not made for such a task.

"Go," she said.

He lifted his hand and waved to her.

"'Bye."

He let go.

Twenty-Three

Natalie read the message from Jude for the third time:

"Gov version of virus *not* the same as from Atlanta. Biological only. NP complete. Have got caught up this end in WH investigation. Stay cool."

At this distance, she had no extra insights into what was meant between the lines, if anything. She had to guess it, or make it up. She decided not to bother. She was in no position to help him, he was in no position to do more for her than this. And it was quite a bit.

It was eleven at night. She'd just woken up to the Pad's soft incoming-message chime after two hours' sleep. Since Ian's dissolution that morning the day had been a round of interrogations, analyses, and inquiries and she'd collapsed without eating when they'd finally reached a lull. Hungry, thirsty, and with a headache that seemed to occupy the entire space inside her skull, she washed her face and hands, then dragged herself along to the medical unit.

It was closed, but the room activated when she blinked into the retinal scanner on the access. To her right as she turned the vague, blue shapes of the gurney and lights in the operating theatre loomed, boxy and alien, from the shadows. She shuddered at the idea of someone collapsing in here. Their medical skills combined didn't add up to one good surgeon.

In the pharmacy several gunmetal-grey racks held the stores on auto-count and as she took down her aspirin the monitor in the corner recorded her transaction. It flashed, offering her some kind of US military emergency diagnostic programme. As she swallowed the tablets she peered down at the inventory next to it. She wasn't the first to visit for basic analgesics. By the looks of it Kropotkin had some kind of stomach ulcer, Khan was diabetic, and her father—she paused and blinked at the readout. Could that be right? That was more codeine than would kill a cat.

She was puzzled and still standing there when she heard a stealthy footstep outside. Just in time she turned and saw Lucy Desanto enter the room. Both of them were surprised but Lucy shrugged first and reached for the antacids. "Long day," she said.

Natalie held out her empty foils from the aspirin as evidence. "Too long."

"Want some coffee?"

"On top of those?"

"Just milk for me," Desanto said, but although she was making an effort to be friendly now that they were off duty Natalie was aware that Lucy's interest here wasn't really on the indigestion tablets or on her. She'd come to look for something else.

"Where's the bin?" Natalie made a show of looking for somewhere to put the packet.

"You'll have to take it with you." Lucy nodded at the door, expecting Natalie to go out first. She started chewing on the antacids.

Natalie passed her, close because of the restricted space betwen the racking, and saw her glance down with an involuntary eye-flick to a grey case on the bottom shelf. This, Natalie knew from her own use of other $BSL\text{-}_4$ facilities contained the Micromedica Universal Vaccine, an injectable nanyte suspension that was capable of killing any virus, bacteria, or parasite infection within hours. It was restricted to emergency use because of the extreme cost involved in its production—over a hundred thousand dollars a shot. Here it was a requirement because of the risk of NervePath infection, although its record against other nanytes was unproven. She'd automatically discounted it in her calculations concerning the dispersion of NervePath through the wider population because, although it might prevent infection or even clear a human system, there was never going to be enough of it in existence to make any difference on that scale.

But then, despite the pounding in her head, she realized that if Jude was right about Guskov, then his private version of Deliverance was capable of handling MUV. With just one dose of Deliverance you could vaccinate entire populations—meaning that on its own the system could save billions of lives and dollars. As she thought through the implications she carried on listening.

Behind her in the corridor Lucy was saying, "For what it's worth, I think you were right this morning, letting Bobby go."

"Ian," Natalie murmured, but turned around to smile at the older woman. "Pissed off Gusky and Kropotkin no end, not to mention my dad. Don't think they'll ever forgive me."

"It was the right thing to do," Lucy repeated. "We were using him. That was wrong. All the data we needed we'd got by doing the initial scan. He wasn't a freak-show act."

"Tell that to the others."

They arrived in the kitchen and its more cheerful lights came on as they walked in. Natalie found a kettle and began to heat some water before looking through the cupboards.

"I've never seen anything like that," Lucy said and then laughed at herself. "That's stupid. I've never even *imagined* anything like this."

Lucy was deeply uncomfortable with the explanations, Natalie thought, and trying to get some reference points, some comfort. "If it's any consolation, neither did I a couple of weeks ago." There were some crackers, which probably meant there was some cheese somewhere. She started eating a cracker. They didn't taste like the ones at home—too salty.

"Is he dead now?"

Natalie swallowed and tried to think. "Don't know," she said finally. "But he won't be back. Maybe there are bits of his information hanging around somewhere, but not enough to stick together and call a name."

"But what about, you know, the rest of it?" Lucy said. "Don't you believe in God? What about that? Did he ever say anything about it?"

"Not to me." Natalie began to see where this was going. In the refrigerator she found a lump of something that might be cheese and started to wrestle it out of its tough plastic packaging. She could feel the yawning hunger of Lucy's need for reassurance dragging her in, and knew that if she turned and was caught in it she was going to see that dead boy again. She began to hack at the plastic with a knife, trying to be patient despite her growling stomach, the headache, and the fact that she'd rather Jude was here than this awkward woman and the existential terror just under her surface.

"Please." Lucy was suddenly holding on to Natalie's sleeve. "You're like him. You must be. Halfway, at least. Don't you know?"

"Know what?"

"What's beyond this world. Spirit. It's never been proven or disproven, never even been linked with consciousness studies in most of the liberal universities. I mean, there must be more to it than just—"

"If there is—" Natalie stayed diplomatic "—I haven't seen it. I haven't felt it. There. That's all I know." She found herself clutching the plastic pack in one hand and the knife hilt in the other, resting both on the countertop. It was all she could do not to stab the other woman in the gut. "I know plenty of dead people. They've never come back. Not even a postcard." She hated the sound of her own flippant rebuff as she stabbed the pack, piercing it this time. Why couldn't Dan have been here? She'd have swapped him for the lot of them.

"Well." Lucy was reluctantly withdrawing now, seeing she wasn't going to get what she wanted. "If you do, you know, hear from him again . . ."

"He's gone. Why can't you accept that? It's perfectly simple," Natalie said, sticking bits of cheese onto biscuits, like a factory production line.

"Because I can't." Lucy's voice was tight and close to crying.

Natalie closed her eyes but it didn't prevent her view of the boy in the road, his left leg bent in the wrong way, his head on the tarmac, sightless, finished. She wanted Desanto off her back and out of her mind. She decided to lie.

"He's gone," she said, in her quiet, clinician's voice. "It was very quick. There was no pain."

She waited, holding on to the counter, for Lucy's own Catholic faith to take what she'd said and filter out of it a confirmation of her hopes.

"Thank you," Lucy whispered after a moment had passed. Again she held on to Natalie's arm, this time with a grateful clutch. "Thank you so much. I knew you could see. I knew it was going to be all right."

Natalie glanced back out of curiosity as Lucy was preparing to leave. She saw that Lucy understood her to have meant that her son had passed over and they would meet again, in some unidentifiable, bodiless way, in a beyond that was free of cares and lasted for eternity. Lucy believed that Natalie could say this for sure, as no other person in the history of Earth could have said it—except Jesus.

She felt bad suddenly and wondered which one of them was wrong. Could she prove Lucy's belief was wrong? What was so inspiring about thinking of Dan—good, happy, stupid, helpless, idiot Dan—as annihilated forever, without a single thing left behind except her thoughts of him? Lucy was comforted by her delusion. Natalie's bleaker view might be no more than a delusion, too.

As she hesitated, Lucy was walking backwards, smiling, thankful, then gone to be alone for a few moments, full up with tears and snot and sentimental visions of reunions and apologies and the ultimate forgiveness for her mistakes that Natalie was never, ever going to receive.

She felt the keen terror and rage at Charlotte's abandonment as if for the first time. And now Dad, what was he on? And this mad scheme she was caught in, captive of her own ideas . . . Dan gone, yes, gone, they were all bloody gone. Ian had simply faded away, blended atom by atom into the air. She would, too. They all would.

"I hate this!" Natalie bent forward and with one sweep of her arm sent the plate and crackers flying across the room. They crashed into the stainless-steel side of the cooker and the crackers scattered all over the floor. The plate didn't even break, because it was specially made not to. It spun around in a circle and then settled down with a few rings against the tiles before stopping.

Natalie picked up the block of cheese and bit the corner off it. It was rubbery, but okay. She looked down at the mess and sighed. Lucy's hopes were vain and that was all there was to it. She, Natalie, had lost nothing more than she'd already lost. And she was still standing, just about. She chewed reflectively as she located the dustpan and brush and cleaned up the spilled crackers. She was prodding a tea bag in its cup and drinking a glass of water at the same time when Guskov himself came walking in, wearing an ancient-looking tracksuit and thick socks. He reminded her of someone else's grandad.

"Mmn," he grunted, smiling and passing by her to take a can of vegetable-juice cocktail from the refrigerator. "What did she want?"

He was talking about Lucy, whom he'd met in the corridors.

"Comfort," Natalie said. "You know, that thing you think we'd all be better off without."

"Ah, na, na." Guskov popped the seal on his can after shaking it. "You're wrong. I want everyone to be able to have comforts that are real, not imaginary."

"You never did answer me when I asked you what 'real' was." Natalie took out the tea bag and flicked it into the wastebin. "What I really wonder is why you think you have an exclusive view on it."

He sat down heavily in one of the metal frame chairs. "But today you talked with Ian. You saw him dissolve into his component molecules. You heard him speak at length about the structure and nature of the physical world. He said nothing that leads me to believe that we as a species would not be better off recognizing the facts of our lives and rejecting the fantasies that make us behave with such degrading consequences."

"Yes. That's what I saw. But Lucy saw a miraculous event. Alicia saw a confirmation of her belief in a poetic final union with the rest of creation. Isidore saw a man disappear. My father saw a horrific vision of a person flying apart and disintegrating because of the weakness of his mind. We see it through the lens of ourselves. I still don't understand what it is you want to achieve with Mappa. Do you want us all to be the same? How could that ever happen, unless you impose closure, make minds run forever in the same tracks so they can't think of new ideas?"

"That is *not* the goal of the Free State!" he almost bellowed and smacked the end of his can on the table for emphasis.

"Then what *is* the program you're going to issue, after you achieve global NervePath infection by using your Deliverance technology?"

Natalie watched as his face showed shock for a moment before his expression changed gradually to a smile.

"That in itself would be a remarkable achievement. I don't anticipate complete coverage. Only about sixty percent, initially." His eyes sparkled with that essential fire that had always marked him out among others as brighter, tougher, and smarter. "As for the program . . ." He sighed and shook his head, pretending to read the can label. "I've thought of many things. First of all I was going to get rid of religions. When I was a boy they seemed like evil incarnate: arbitrary, judgemental, cruel, repressive. Then I found Communism, Socialism, Democracy and I saw that it wasn't the supernatural element at all that was causing this plague of memes that mark out divisions and give different values to human beings. It was in the way we saw ourselves as castes and tribes, the in-group and the out-group.

"I thought that the program should never allow the person to think of themselves as superior to others, that it should give the benefit of the doubt, generosity, kindness, make the social virtues stronger than our drives for selfish advancement."

He took another swig of the juice and scowled at the strong taste. "Celery." He pronounced the word carefully, his accent becoming more marked. "A disgusting taste when there is too much of it. Anyway, prison changed my mind about those starry-eyed visions of men and women.

"I began to understand that we are always living in pretend worlds, and their effect is to drag us away from the knowledge that we are animals with millions of years of evolutionary instincts that have made us successful. Whether or not we perceive those instincts as more harmful than good doesn't help us to remove them. We have had to develop intellectual defences to save us from their harm. Hence, we are dreamers and idealists. We have hope. We like the good guys to win so that we can feel all we have done is justified."

Natalie nodded. "Yes. And what use is a perfect understanding of the physical world to anyone but physicists? We're better off in dreams. People living their animal lives in families and social groups need dreams and ideals so they don't tear each other's faces off. But you didn't want to force them to live those dreams?"

"What, and be Pope of the world? No!" Guskov chuckled and smoothed his beard with one hand. "Our consciousness is a necessary evolutionary development that allowed individuals to experience themselves as separate entities, free agents, enabling them to change the world, instead of accepting it as part of them. Mappa Mundi is the final act of that long line of changes, and it must lead us into a future where we understand our power and limits, not where we carry on, blindly."

"So, you aren't going to remove self-awareness. What, then?" She was eager to know whether he did indeed have a master stroke that could prove beneficial, or whether he had managed to develop the tools for the job faster than he'd developed its goal.

Guskov put his can down and spread out his hands, looking at their tough, scarred backs and the half-tone skin that might or might not have been his original colour—he couldn't remember.

"Every purpose I have thought of I have rejected, because ultimately, in the Memetic Calculus, all changes made to the Cube create short-term shifts in outlook and perception that then, over time, always converge to the starting conditions. Within individuals great benefits can be seen, certainly, but in terms of large populations and multiple generations the calculus always returns the equilibrium of the origin as its eventual result. For any change of any kind that I have tested against it—nothing has any long-term impact. The Cube is robust. It heals itself. It regenerates lost memes."

"Doomed," Natalie said to herself in her cod-Scottish accent, as if Dan were there. "We're all doomed." She snickered and then heaved a long sigh. "And after all this."

At the table Guskov slid round in his seat and turned to her. "I hoped that you might be able to think of something."

"Why?" She was in the middle of biting the cheese again and almost choked.

"Because you're now out at the edge of the Cube. Your perception allows you access to information we've never had before. That means your own Memecube has already begun to shift. Bobby X reacted to it in his own way—he could find no future, because he saw no future for himself. He didn't have the ability to stretch his own Selfplex to accommodate what he saw. In his own words, he was already dead. But you aren't like him. You were always a believer-in-waiting, but with the strength to test your hopes to the limit."

Natalie explored the idea, moving her head from side to side as though shunting it back and forth. Her headache was in retreat. "Nice words," she said. "I sound like a hero. But if this is such a great idea, why don't you run the system on yourself? It's your project, and you're the master of mindshifting, not me."

"Myself, Kropotkin, and your father are already—" he paused and gestured vaguely at his head "—filled up, with older standard NervePath than is required." He smiled and finished his juice. "You didn't think you were the only one to use yourself as your central subject?"

So, Natalie thought, *this is what it comes to. All his planning, the years of calculation, the conviction of a lifetime.*

"You should never have come in here," she said, meaning the Sealed Environment.

"I saw that it might come to this." He was now crumpling the empty can, crushing the top down onto the bottom. "It wouldn't have been for a long time yet, but for that accident, the stupid Americans and their test."

"Deer Ridge." Natalie nodded. Of course, now she had the whole picture. Not wanting to let Guskov have all the power, the US had thoughtfully begun training others and pursuing a parallel program. Their mistake was in getting caught testing prototype systems on unsuspecting civilians. She wondered why they'd risked it, instead of sticking to simulation or else paying volunteers. But volunteers were a risky business. They had lawyers for that kind of thing when even the most basic field trial went astray, and the litigation fees for *this* scale of damage, plus the media exposure, would have finished the entire scheme.

Now the US government would expect Guskov to hand over a ready-made technology and to train personnel and oversee the production of specific programs for it. His work would be tested and verified before release. From that position there was no way he would be allowed to effect any variation. By staying here and keeping it to himself for as long as possible, his chances were better. There was logic to his plan. She had to admire his strategy. But she still didn't admire its aim.

"Supposing we used Deliverance as you suggest, but with a close-out program giving lifetime immunity," she said.

"But then all the potential benefits of therapeutic treatments like the one we gave to Ian will be lost," he replied.

That was not going to be it. She saw that. "Even so, your scheme seems like it can only cause a running battle between writers trying to impose their various maps on everyone else. There has to be some other way."

"I told myself that." He threw the remains of the can at the waste bin where it fell squarely on the rim and then slid down into the rubbish. "But I expected it to arise from the combined minds of everyone on the project—a long-term affair. A worldwide enterprise. Not this."

"And there's no way to get it out, even if we'd written one," she said, voicing his thought for him, although she already knew the way out. She wondered if he would dare to ask her, but although she knew it had crossed his mind he didn't say it. He had the Deliverance systems, the production capacity for a wide strike, enough stolen NervePath to kick-start it, and all he needed was a program, an idea, the Big Kahuna that would magically change the world.

She thought for a moment or two, watching Guskov. "But there's no way out."

"Of here?" But he'd known she hadn't meant that. The physical problem was trivial.

"Of ourselves. There is no way to become more than human. Selfware made Ian more of himself. It makes me—me, more of me. I'm not outside the Global Cube at all. I may be free within it, but I can't step outside it. Ian could step outside his own skin, but his problem always was that he couldn't step outside the Cube. When he saw things the Cube didn't address he couldn't fit those things into himself. That may not be true of all people. My yoga teacher said the universe came and sat inside you, the ocean poured into the drop, the drop didn't dissolve in the ocean. But I'm guessing that's easier to experience when it isn't a literal truth.

"It's as Ian said: human beings are macrocreatures with a limited range of perception. Expand it and your whole system can't process it into sense any more. When it becomes your actual world, instead of some knowledge on a page or in your memory, then you don't stick together." Natalie paused, looking down into her tea mug, sad with what she'd said but sure that it was true. "You jumped through so many hoops, but you can't jump out of your self. You never did. Isn't that so, Hilel?"

Guskov snorted and nodded, barely registering that she'd called him by his original name, leaning on the table, his energy still restless. "This old body and mind have been through a lot. If you count self as a continuity of experience, then no, I never made a leap into total unknowns. I was always remaking myself out of the old. Everything is like that. If there's a program that can help people become better navigators of our own Cubes, so that everyone can be free enough to let go of the old when its time has come and to let its boundaries spread, not get smaller, that would be the program I would send."

Natalie drank her tea and washed up the cup. On her way out she paused, bent down, and kissed his cheek above the rough line of beard.

"And that way we'd get to keep the best and not chuck the baby out with the bathwater." She straightened and stretched her back. "But you have to consider that there may be no universal solution."

"No bathwater?" He smiled and shook his head.

"The bathwater may be the best thing about us."

Mary Delaney could still smell the reek long after the cleanup squad had been through her apartment and scoured, scrubbed, bleached, and purified it down to the last toothpick. Clearly, the purpose of leaving Dan's body there was to destabilize her and let her know that someone who shouldn't have known anything about it was aware of her activities. Angrily, she had to admit to herself that it had been damn' effective. She couldn't stay there any more. She moved into a hotel and put the place up for rent.

The reports on Natalie Armstrong's exit from the bomb-squad truck had arrived. They were ridiculous, and explained nothing. "No detectable method of escape." What had she done, walked though the wall? But her speculating agents had combined this with the vanishing of Patient X and suggested that the accidents at the York Clinic might account . . . but Mary didn't have time to waste reading about their suppositions when they had no factual evidence. Corrupted officials were more likely to be guilty than superpowers, and if Guskov had decided to bring Armstrong in under his wing—which a tentative message out from the Environment suggested he had—there was enough money in mafia business to bribe anyone.

Several days had passed since Jude had been away for his sister's funeral. He'd returned to work and picked up his caseload slowly, but surely. The steady trade in illegally produced animals—mostly specially bred and patented strains of experimental mice—had taken up most of their time, and the rest had been spent tidying away the trails of the Guskov cases. He hadn't asked for the return of her file and she assumed he'd copied it, but she couldn't prove it when she searched his Pad databases. But Jude could easily have hidden it. They weren't on Special Sciences for nothing. And apart from the odd, joking, embarrassed reference to the other evening, he was almost on normal terms with her.

Meanwhile she waited for the forensic results on Dan's body and had the file itself scanned and dusted. It was when they arrived that she cancelled all meetings and shut herself away in her hotel room to think.

The file had Natalie Armstrong all over it. Including even some scribble on the back of the thing, a big pencilled mess around the very date on which it had vanished from Dix's Pentagon filing cabinet (locked, secured—no visible means, et cetera).

The body had traces of other DNA casually strewn about in it—not her own agents', and so far its owner was unidentified. Not from a United States database. Foreign. A white male Caucasian, aged about fifty years, blue eyes, average IQ, and cell nuclei that had incorporated NervePath structures as part of their mass. She didn't know who that was but she could guess.

She downloaded from Sequoia, Special Sciences' Net agent, all she could get from the Ministry about Patient X. But it left her no wiser. Guskov had Natalie now and Natalie might be more than just a brain with legs. Mary didn't know what to think about that. More important, she didn't know what to do about it. Mappa was her project and she didn't want him whisking it out from under her nose with some weird shit like this.

It was Thursday when Mary checked back with Dix at their regular weekly meeting. Her entire insides became solid stone-cold at the news that the government legal team were to appear in a preliminary hearing for a civil case lodged against them for personal damages for the total sum of ten billion dollars, brought by the Northern Cheyenne Nation and the townspeople of Deer Ridge, Montana.

"You're going to contest it, of course . . ." she began, looking at Rebecca Dix's grim expression.

"We're going to settle out," Dix said, almost toneless. "Ten B. No coverage in the press as condition. They'll take it. For Christ's sake, it's more than they'll see in any other lifetime."

"You offered them ten billion dollars?" Mary's mouth was hanging itself out to dry. "The case is hardly going. They haven't got enough evidence to go to trial. Otherwise, why isn't this a criminal proceeding? They're claiming that—"

"We're prepared to up it to twenty billion, if they hand over everything they've got. The goddamn oil deal on the land. We'll give them fucking Montana, but they have to settle out. Go tell that to your partner, and if there's still a case on Monday—" Dix made a chopping motion across her own neck and her stare at Mary became sharp "—you're out. I'm out. We're all out."

Mary left in a state of shock. She realized what the case's existence meant. There was only one possibility of a leak, one thing to go wrong. She ran down the corridor, startling the other people walking sedately there, and locked herself in the bathroom.

"Jude, you motherfucking bastard!" It was a gasp rather than a shout but she was so furious that she was almost unaware of slamming the wall with her right fist. The wall was tiled and behind the tiles, concrete. There was a crack as her middle finger broke.

She sat on the toilet seat, watching her hand swell and redden. When it finally began to hurt more than she could bear, she was calm enough to come out and get down to business.

Jude watched the hired driver taking his car away from the end of the street. The key to the U-Stor-It was still taped under the seat. He'd sent Jenny Black Eagle a message that would tell her what to do if the time came for that. He thought there was no way it would ever get public or go to court, but White Horse's case had at last got a hearing. The car, her new vehicle for the next world, was the last thing he had to take care of, and as it turned the corner and made its way into the northbound traffic he genuinely did feel a sense of lightness for the first time in weeks.

He didn't go back in straight away, but walked along the familiar streets, trying to figure out what to expect. The legal papers would be lodged by now, and if he was right about Mary, then he could anticipate some kind of visit very shortly. Not a friendly one. He'd feel bad about that if it happened. He hoped it wouldn't.

His hopes were dashed as a black and grey BMW pulled up to the curb a half hour later as he was on the return journey. Mary lowered the darkened electric window on the passenger side. She was wearing her sunglasses but her face didn't show any sign of feeling either angry or surprised.

"Get in," she said.

Jude looked the length of the street towards his apartment. No, there wasn't anything worth going back for. He opened the door and sat down in the soft leather. On the steering wheel he saw that she had two fingers taped up.

They both stared through the windshield. He sensed that she was searching for the right words and wasn't finding them. He had nothing to say either.

In the end she stepped on the gas and pulled away. He wasn't surprised when she crossed Arlington Memorial Bridge and then started to take roads out of town, moving south.

"I guess you've resigned, then," he said after a time.

She didn't turn her head. "I guess you have, too."

They didn't speak again. The roads led into Virginia towards the spine of the Appalachians. Finally, as evening drew on, they entered a National Park area, took a diversion off the Skyline Drive, passed two No Thru-road signs, and then the car stopped. Mary, who had driven without a pause, rested her forehead on the wheel as the engine muttered into silence. They were in a small settlement that Jude thought he'd seen signposted as Stone Spring. It meant nothing to him. The car was sitting on blacktop outside the Spring Laundromat. To his left the Bake'n'Bagel had already closed for the day. A stray dog, wiry and with an eye on the car, ran sniffing along the store fronts and then vanished through a clot of weeds on the corner. The place seemed uninhabited.

"Where are we?" he asked.

"End of the road." She took her gun out of its holster, checked the load, put it back, and nodded at him. "Get out."

He still had his gun, but not with him. It was back at the apartment, locked in the wall safe. He got out.

The sound of the car doors closing was a shock in the quiet. Apart from this single road he could see a few tracks branching away, perhaps to more secluded lots in the woods. Birdsong and the hum of insects gave the early evening a drowsy feel. The sun was just dropping through the trees on his left.

Mary led the way across the street and up the steps of a big grey clapboard house with white window frames and a turret at its road-facing corner. At her knock the door was opened by a man in a military uniform, although the entrance hall was so dark that Jude didn't see his insignia clearly.

She turned as soon as the door was closed.

"You'll stay here for now."

Jude glanced around. Apart from the guard on the door there was no sign of life.

"The guard will always be here. There are automated locks and security. If you try to leave you will be shot on sight." She gestured at his jailer and the man opened the front door again for her.

She held out her hand. "Give me your Pad."

He gave it to her and she put it in her jacket's inner front pocket.

Seeing that she meant to leave Jude asked, "What am I waiting for?"

Mary didn't pause in her exit, only glanced obliquely over her shoulder, not making eye contact as she replied, "Don't ask and you won't be disappointed."

She was halfway through the door when he added, bitterly, "You've got a fucking nerve, playing it like you're the one with a grievance."

She didn't stop.

The guard closed the door.

The house was very quiet.

Mary sat in the car with her head in her hands. She breathed through her fingers, trying for a long, slow breath, but she didn't get anything except gasping and drowning sensations until long after it was dark.

Twenty-Four

Natalie sat at her desk, staring into space. It was now three weeks since she had arrived. Ian's data had bridged the critical gaps in the program. She was left with the task Guskov had set her, but since that night when in some misguided moment of emotional breakdown she'd actually felt sorry for the wily old goat/idealistic old fool (delete depending on mood) she'd been doing a lot of thinking. She'd tried to figure out what kind of program she could write for the Mappaware that did everyone some good, nobody any harm, and prevented hostile interventions in the future. It was the equivalent of asking what it was that made people do bad things and trying to factor it out. Obviously, bad things had many definitions depending on which end of them you were at, and many causes—perhaps infinitely many.

She was staring into space because there was nothing to look at and she wasn't sure how long she'd been sitting there. Every so often she progressed and made notes. When she was stuck she sat and did nothing. Eventually solutions rose to the surface and became thoughts; she didn't care where they were coming from.

She thought that once Mappa Mundi was delivered the US and Europeans would go for a preemptive strike. It wasn't like nuclear war: nobody was going to die. In fact, from the joint security and governmental perspective things should improve no end. Human rights and the sanctity of individual personality didn't enter into it because governments had probably already convinced themselves that this was a kind of superdevice that would end all wars and turn the world into a kind of utopia.

Natalie knew that wouldn't happen, no matter what she wrote or what they wrote. But she hadn't given up entirely on finding methods that might cause a permanent shift in the Global Common Cube, which was a surprisingly small subset of the total Cube. And anyway, if things didn't work in time, she had it in mind that she could always stick MUV or NervePath carrying an immunization program into the Deliverance. That, at least, would help some people out until the technology was superseded.

The unique power that she had wasn't lost on her. If she wanted to she could write something so devastating that she'd make sure nobody ever figured a way out of what had happened in a million years. Potentially she had total power over anyone and everyone. She knew that even if this idea had no appeal for her, there were plenty right next door who might like it a lot, or they might like to trade it for a lifetime of security and luxurious peace. So she wasn't going to tell anybody anything from now on.

Recently, having junked days of effort hacking about with the Selfware, she'd turned on to Game Theory. Its analysis of human behaviour had evolved sufficient sophistication to mimic the complex and long-term minutiae of human social goals and planning, and using Khan's Memetic Calculus Natalie thought at last that she'd got something that was looking like it might be useful. It was a program that would create a strategic trend in the host mind, named after its function in all cases of dispute: Prefer Harmonious Compromise.

She knew that Kropotkin and Guskov and her father were all trying to write other systems—keeping back information as long as they could to try and forestall the others from gaining an upper hand. No doubt in distant bunkers other poor code-heads were attempting the same thing.

It couldn't be long before Desanto's anxiety tripped her into telling her masters that Mappa Mundi was about ready for use.

Prefer Harmonious Compromise had two elements, following Guskov's basic plan. It assessed an individual Selfplex, loosened it out to a state of open-minded, optimistic, rational doubt, and then installed an emotional gate system that preferred all conflicts to result in compromise and agreement. It made you capable of compromising and then it made you love it. It wasn't quite so rosy as to leave you devoid of all self-interest, however. Natalie hadn't weighted the feelings so hard that you'd trade your own mother for five magic beans, and it wouldn't leave you open to every salesman who came hyping his brushes—although there probably wouldn't be that sort of salesman in this future.

Then she felt bad about that.

Much as she would approve of using Mappaware to help people who were suffering, this idea of some kind of Universal Cure for What Ails Humanity made her angry. She wasn't sure it was a right way of thinking about the species. They were what they were, perfectly human.

Then again, here she was and here Mappa Mundi was, products of the same animals and their obsessions. Perhaps, as Guskov said, it was the natural evolutionary result of the function of their minds interacting with the Cube. Now the minds and the Cube were to become fair game for each other and a new stage in human history was about to commence in the traditional blood-and-violence fashion. He'd hoped it was going to be nice, but how realistic was that? And if identities were the casualties, would it matter? Would anybody even notice the difference?

Natalie hadn't noticed the Selfware changing her—except, of course, for the concentration span, the improved ability, the telepathy, the emotional temperance, and the apparent lack of any need for sleep. Apart from those things, she was the same. She missed Dan, she longed to see Jude, she was hacked off with her father, and she wanted to go home.

Actually, it was anger about Dan that kept her here, doing this. In his memory, something like that. Waiting to see if the people who'd killed him were going to show up so she could . . . well, it wasn't all worked out.

Natalie keyed off the system and sat in total silence. PHC, MUV, or immunize, or let the Americans have their way because they might not go for a global trial?

She wondered when it was that she would draw that date on Jude's file.

She wondered if Jude was okay.

She wondered when it was that she was going to switch her own Selfware back on and make Typhoid Mary's kamikaze run.

Jude had been in Stone Spring, shut in the house, for twenty days when Mary returned. Twenty days was longer than he'd ever believed he'd have to wait for her to come back and decide his fate. By this time the information pack he'd sent to the media would have been out, unless she'd found a way to stall it.

On his own he had little to do but watch TV and wonder exactly what it was he'd been doing during those five years with Mary. Who was she? What exactly was her position? Had she killed White Horse, or was she only a small player in the bigger pond? She must be an agent for the NSC, he reasoned, but his thinking was like the film on the surface of a septic tank. Underneath it emotions that had been deep and clear were now poisoned with the understanding of his own guilt and complicity, and with her betrayal of him.

He'd tried to get information from the guards and they were happy to show him how well hemmed-in he was, or to tell him gossip about the locals who walked past the windows. They thought the houses here that were owned by the army were training grounds for urban terrorist attack scenarios. Jude marvelled at their stupidity.

Mary's return was heralded by the sound of heavy engines. Jude was reading an airport novel at the time—his mind was incapable of paying attention to anything demanding—and got up at the sound to look down from the bedroom window. Along Main Street he recognized a marine troop carrier, several long, large trucks that probably contained equipment or possibly mobile laboratories, and finally a line of cars. The black and grey car stopped as it had before, at the Laundromat. Mary got out and looked up at the house.

Jude stepped back from the window. Despite his resignation to the situation his heart started to race as he heard the soldier downstairs open the door and start talking to his commander. They came up to get him and he was escorted on either side as they went out into the open air that smelled fresh following a day of rain. The clouds were just starting to break as Mary met them on the tarmac. She took off her sunglasses this time and met him face to face.

Glancing to either side, she looked at the armed guard. "Get lost."

When they were alone at the road's edge she said, "I want you to know this isn't personal. It's just business. It was you or the country. You didn't come first."

Jude nodded. "Well, that clears that up."

Her face contorted with hurt that she didn't seem able to confine. She lifted her chin and the sun caught her hair in that second, turning it the colour of liquid bronze. She was quite beautiful. Jude remembered why he'd liked her, even admired her. Mary was strong and she wouldn't let her own fear or feelings get in her way. He used to think that was cool.

"The project is finished," she said, screwing up her eyes against the sudden bright light that came glancing through the treeline. "We're here to close it down. Your friend, Doctor Armstrong, is in there."

Jude realized that she meant the Mappa Mundi project and, at her mention of Natalie, that she was jealous. He glimpsed a flash of humour in the situation but it didn't linger. He didn't understand what he was doing here.

Mary made a jerky movement of her arm. "Let's go."

He walked with her past the Dinette on the end of the row and along a country lane he didn't know. They were followed at a discreet distance by more soldiers. He had no doubt that any attempt at escape would be a pointless effort.

"So," he said. "You worked for the NSC."

A late breeze played with the leaves, just beginning to turn to the colours of fall—yellow, auburn, and red. It was peaceful here, he thought. Nice for a holiday.

"Not exactly." She kept her face rigidly toward the front.

"You know, Em, this play of yours doesn't suit you."

"No?"

"No. I used to like you."

"Did you?"

"Yes."

"And now you don't."

"You killed White Horse."

She said nothing.

"You cold, fucking bitch."

Then she stopped, pivoted on her heel, and smacked him across the face much harder than he'd ever have thought she'd be able to. The blow knocked his head sideways and he had to take a recovery step. The pain was a real wash of surprise, right across his jaw and through his teeth. His eyes stung.

Mary glared at him, "I loved you," she hissed, glancing self-consciously towards the patrol behind. "You would have been dead ten times over!"

"Thank you so much."

"Listen, smartass. Did it ever occur to you there was more at stake than your goddamn relatives' political bad feeling?"

Jude looked at her through eyes still streaming from the pain and shock of Mary's blow.

"This technology is going to change everything about the way we live on this planet. It has to end up in controlled, stable hands. Did you think about that when you spent all this time learning how to hate me?" Her pale face had become the stark white he'd only seen before on porcelain.

Jude straightened up, blinking. "I don't even know how to start hating you," he said, and it was the honest truth. He was shocked to the core, numb from the neck down.

She nodded and looked at the road. "I didn't want this to happen. It's the last thing I wanted. Why did you have to go and get all secret about the mind stuff? I would have helped you."

"I doubt that," he said.

They walked on. At last the gentle curve of the road became track-like and then, round a sudden bend, they were in the yard of a dull old house in the woods. The lab trucks were parked up, orderly, outside the garage. Mary led him up the steps and into the back of one.

As soon as he saw it in detail he started to get the idea. He turned to her then and grabbed her shoulder, spinning her around.

"Now wait a minute. This is a bit more like personal revenge, don't you think?"

She brushed his hand off her shoulder and stared at him with flat, zeroed-out eyes.

"This is business," she said, pushing him down so that he had to sit in the chair set up for him. "And that's all. You're a good negotiator. If you do your job, you and everyone else in there will be fine."

Jude watched the technicians behind her. The lab gear was all $BSL\text{-}_4$ Micromedica specific. He thought that he could see very well into the first of the control-unit boxes and that the man standing there was preparing something that looked very like a syringe.

"So." He tried to be calm and not respond to the galloping jolt of terror that was knocking the hell out of his insides. "They decided not to back your plans for global domination. Walt Disney must be spinning in his grave."

She snorted with derision. "It's not going to be like *It's a Small World*, Jude," she said, folding her arms across her chest. "We only want to use it on the people most likely to cause trouble. Unlike our Russian in there. He's got a real plan for a whole new modern lifestyle. You'll get the chance to ask him all about it."

Jude glanced through the door. The patrol were stationed outside, their guns at the ready. Mary spoke with the white-coated tech and then stood aside. She glanced at Jude as the man came forward.

"It won't hurt. Not for a long time. Thirty-six hours. Your choice. Get them to hand over everything and cooperate and everyone enjoys long life and happiness. Fail and every single one of you dies in there."

The tech was rolling up the sleeve of Jude's T-shirt. Jude stared at the hypo. The clear liquid could have been anything but he suddenly thought he knew what it was. If he hadn't been sitting his legs would have given out.

"Em, please."

The needle bit in. He felt the liquid build in his deltoid and then it was all over, as easy as that.

"You'll become contagious in an hour," she said, looking down her nose at him, fingers on her arms clenched so tight she must be cutting off all circulation. "Everyone will become infected by midnight. The payload will release in thirty-two hours from now for you, and thirty-two hours from first infection for everyone else. You then have another two hours, max, to come out while we can still save you. After that, nothing."

"What's the payload?" He was dizzy with nausea. Deliverance. She'd shot him full of that. He was her test subject, her guinea pig. He had no doubt it would work.

"Marburg," she said tonelessly. "Don't hang around." But the last phrase gave her away. Her controlled, smooth voice cracked on the last word and she had to bite it back.

Jude made himself stand up and be taller than she was. He moved closer, closer, as she fought to resist stepping back, until their faces were an inch apart.

He looked into her clear blue eyes and said, breath on her face, "How different this could all have been." It was all a play, no more than that. He'd lost. But he had the satisfaction of seeing her flinch as he almost kissed her and then turned away.

"Where's the door?"

Natalie thought she'd go and check if her father had taken any more huge doses of codeine. It was late, a day after she'd finished up everything that could be done on Prefer and she'd spent it going through the last rebuild of the whole Mappa system, checking for bugs and fixing them. Her mind felt on the fried side, but her body refused to feel sleepy. All it wanted these days was food, water, and one half-hour of meditative inaction in every four. The schedule was hard to take. She longed for a night of deep, dreamless oblivion in a part of her animal self that must have missed out when Selfware was doing its refit of her capabilities.

She had to admit she'd tried her best to use work as an excuse, but now it was all through and there was nothing left to face except the failure of herself and her father to form any kind of relationship of use. That and the unrewarding, strained relations with Alicia, Nikolai, and the others, all of them sick of the sight of each other, hating their work, hating their lives and themselves. The place stank of despair.

Inside the dispensary the tally on the machine showed that more of the same tablets had been checked out by Calum Armstrong. She was on her way out and trying to figure out how to start talking to him again when her attention was drawn down to the case of MUV. It had been moved.

A closer look revealed that not only had it been moved, the seals were broken. Natalie picked it up and brought it out onto the floor where she could rest it. She opened the flip locks. Two doses were missing from their positions in the high-density foam packing. The other canisters were still in place but the flashing red lights on their individual valves showed that every last one of them had been opened up and dispersed. They were all empty.

Natalie felt a rush of cold conviction that there was only one scenario in which this action made sense. She closed the case up and stepped immediately back to the dispensary workstation, using her codes to get as high up in the command levels as she could. It wasn't that high but at least it would give her full status readings on the environment's external and internal filtration systems.

"C'mon, c'mon," she muttered, smacking the side of the monitor with the flat of her hand.

After a longer delay than there should have been the Building Systems Screen came up. It showed readings that were all well within normal limits for gases and microbes. If someone had been in and shut down the alarm system or the filter checks then they'd done it so well that she couldn't tell if this screen was faked. But whether an infection showed up or not she knew it was going to be there.

She sent out a call for a general meeting.

One by one they assembled in the dining area, weary forms in clothes that looked rumpled and old, her father in his full lab suit minus its heavy headgear, Isidore the only one retaining an air of orderly neatness about his person in every detail.

Natalie sat at the head of one of the tables, the case concealed between her feet. When Guskov finally made up the quorum and the vague greeting and catching-up had subsided she lifted the case up and placed it in front of her, facing the others.

They looked at it for the most part with blank expressions. To Natalie's surprise it was not Lucy but Khan who recognized what was about to go down. Her smooth assurance ruptured with the tiniest of hairline cracks in expression running along the left side of her eye and cheek. Unable to help herself, she reviewed the events of her sabotage in her mind's eye. When she glanced up from the flight case at Natalie she'd got her composure sorted out. It took Nikolai to nudge the rest of them into noticing the powerful gaze between the two of them.

"What is going on?" Guskov demanded.

Natalie waited, but Alicia refused to speak.

"Doctor Khan has sold us out. Money talks," Natalie said. She flipped the catches and opened the case so that they could all see.

"But there are no biochemical hazards in here," Isidore pointed out after a second, his measured voice a calm flow of certainty. "Only the NervePath."

Kropotkin and Guskov paid no attention to his naivety. Her father stared at the lights. Lucy was the first to turn. She whipped around in her seat.

"Why have you done this?"

"What, sorry you were beaten to it?" Alicia snapped, sitting down, her shoulders high and her chin lifted defiantly, although Natalie knew she was scared now. So she should be.

Lucy was stunned. She glanced around, checking to see if everyone else thought the same of her. "All right now." She held up her hands. "I never believed in your plan, Mikhail, and yes, I sent some information out to keep the government up to date. What you're intending to do is absolutely wrong. But—" she turned back to Khan, more hurt than angry, and gestured at the case "—what's this?"

"I have two boys," Khan replied with the assured righteousness that she adopted during a demonstration of her work. "I have a husband. My parents are still alive." Her dark irises flashed at each of them—they had all been under the same threat.

"Don't forget the fifty million dollars," Natalie said with a false smile of cheer. "And the real estate."

Alicia's upper lip curled into a snarl. "You freak!" she spat, but nothing else.

Guskov was furious and because his anger was such a physical force he seemed to become the focus for the rest. He reached across the slim expanse of steel towards Khan and she shrank away from his touch. Standing up at his full bearlike height he stared her down until she became physically smaller but her defiance was smug.

"Desanto is right," she whispered. "Your idea is wrong. The Bobby X technology has to be kept secret. And it isn't for individuals to decide everybody's fate."

"And who is it right for then? You?" he said softly. He looked back at the case. "Two missing. I assume you already took one. Where is the other?"

Alicia had clammed up now. She wasn't going to say anything. As they waited they again looked to Natalie, to see if she could divine the answer, hoping that she could. Every single one of them was in shock. The sense of their disorientation and the creeping horror as they began to accept this twist was excruciating to her. On top of it the wild, futile hopes about the chance of salvation made her dizzy—she shut them out and shook her head. And then, in the silence, they heard the sound of the elevator doors operating from the highside entrance where each of them in turn had come in.

Natalie knew who it was. Before anyone had time to speak she was up and running. She negotiated the twists and turns of the corridors, slipping on the tough carpet and catching herself with a hand on the wall or the floor. Around the last corner she saw him walking towards her and her heart lifted in a leap of hope and the sheer pleasure of seeing him again. She flung her arms around him and hugged him close.

Jude was much slower to respond and for an instant he held his face away from her as though he wished they hadn't touched. But then he seemed to become resigned and embraced her in return, sighing.

Natalie looked up into his face and he shook his head fractionally.

She thought for a second that they'd found out about the NP and strove to see if it was true. Then she realized that wasn't it, and the understanding clicked home.

Twenty-Five

Jude laid out the government's offer in its stark terms. He was already feeling the beginnings of Deliverance's own symptoms: a heavy head, an aching back, his temperature starting to waver between chills and fever, but he ignored them as best he could.

"All of the NervePath hardware and all of the Mappa Mundi programs are to be left here within this network, intact and in working order. Each one of you will collect their personal items and exit, one by one, beginning with Mikhail Guskov. Any attempts to destroy work, or otherwise compromise the integrity of it, and they will not offer you your MUV shot." He flicked the card that he'd been handed, with its notes, onto the floor and looked up at their exhausted, incredulous faces.

"But they did want me to tell you that if you cooperate their rewards will be generous. Your families will remain unharmed, and you will have a successful career working with them in the future, including getting a place on some goddamned ethical committee they're setting up to ensure that the rest of the world doesn't think they're just following another Pollyanna foreign-interference scheme. Maybe you'd even get a place in the Mental Health Hall of Fame when this goes global."

"Mary Delaney sent you," Guskov stated, the most determined of all those here.

"Yeah." Jude nodded. He thought it was interesting they'd met again in these circumstances, him knowing all about this man and Guskov knowing and caring almost nothing about Jude's past efforts to pin him down. He wasn't as Jude remembered. He was younger, and stronger, more of a fighter.

For the first time, Jude sneezed.

Everyone jerked back in their seats or where they leaned on the wall. A nervous laugh ran between them as they saw their own reactions. Jude tried not to feel the shock of fear. He glanced at Natalie. Her small, heart-shaped face was set in a determined way, the steely colour of her eyes pronounced against her shocking red hair.

"Yes," she said. She looked at Guskov. "If you've got that other version of Deliverance, the one that can replicate Micromedica, then we have the lab equipment to extract some of the vaccine from Alicia's blood. Can you use it as a payload in a counterinfection? Will that work?"

He nodded. "Maybe. We'd have to start immediately."

"Alicia? Did you take both of the shots?"

Jude slowly pieced together what must have happened as they all started to organize themselves for action. Despite their antagonisms the sudden imposition of an external threat showed how seamlessly they'd learned to work together, first one and then another taking the initiative as their abilities decided. He and Mary had once been like that, he thought and sneezed again. It was harder this time and now his eyes and sinuses were starting to feel hot. Explosive aerosolization. Jesus Christ.

Natalie was leaning down next to him. She took his hand. "Come on."

Natalie led him into the control centre. She worked busily, setting up machines, tapping instructions.

Jude watched her, sniffing occasionally, his eyes starting to run. "What are you doing?"

"Fixing things," she said. "Although how well it turns out is anybody's guess. Still, that's always been the case." She picked up a handheld scanner, just like the one she'd shown him in her catalogue, pointed it at her own head, and pressed the trigger.

"What was that?"

"I've restarted the Selfware. If I go the same way as Ian then I can get out of here, and take something with me."

"You're going to go along with his plan?" Jude cleared his throat and then started coughing. There was a dry tickling in his ears and, seemingly, everywhere in his head. Even his lungs itched. "What's he going to do? Make everyone as mad as he is?"

"No. I think any changes will be short-lived but possibly beneficial." She was doing something else now that he didn't understand, her hands flashing over two keyboards at once. He sneezed again, six times in a row.

"I thought if I could make it straight into the lab I might be able to confine myself before I infected anyone," he said, swallowing on a throat that hurt.

"And what makes you think they're not pumping it in from outside?" She flashed him a quick, lopsided grin and then her face faltered and she became very still, poised as a cat, watching him as if he were doing a magic trick.

"What?"

"That woman," she said. "Is that Mary? The woman with the curly red hair?"

He nodded, a cold spark in his chest, and Natalie straightened up, her arms hanging loose at her sides and her mind suddenly very distant. He could almost see it rushing away himself, and he wasn't like her. "Why?"

From being a fast-moving streak of fire she was a small, still creature, hardly big enough or strong enough to do anything. He saw her take hold of the desk for support. Her face was like the wide-open sky.

"She killed Dan." Slowly the fast mind came back on and reanimated her. Her look became tougher, harder. Jude absorbed the news slowly. He nodded. It didn't even surprise him. His own feelings and thoughts about Mary had had plenty of time to fester in the house above this place.

"Listen, Jude." Natalie leaned forward and grasped his hands. "This is all a risk, but when we get out of here don't do anything you'll regret."

He thought she was trying not to do the mind-reading thing and instead was doing her best to be an ordinary human being. Unlike her he had no confidence about the last part—getting out—but he didn't say so. He thought that what she was proposing to do was equivalent to suicide, although he wasn't sure.

"And what about you?"

"I'm going to the dispensary and get you something for this." She smiled and for an instant he couldn't help but smile back.

But the medicine they had didn't do much against the Deliverance and within another hour Jude felt sicker than he'd ever felt in his life. He coughed and sneezed hard enough to rupture blood vessels in his throat and nose and in the lulls lay flat on the floor as around him the arguments and recriminations and the fear boiled together and became part of his fever.

He heard Guskov shouting about there only being enough for one dose to work in time. Calum shouting hoarsely when he found that Natalie had switched the system back on inside herself and her soft explanation that reasoned it was all for the best—hadn't he wanted her to be better? Nikolai and the others railing about the system of the Free State and how it hadn't been planned effectively. Natalie talking about some program she'd written that was going to manage fear, so that reactions of hate and violence would be curtailed.

It all sounded like a lot of very late after-the-fact theorizing. Inside Jude there was a kind of calm, when he wasn't retching or spitting into tissues or watching dark red appear in bigger and brighter stains in the wads of cloth he put to his face in an effort to stop the infection spreading so fast. His bones ached with the chills. He hoped he was going to have enough strength left when the time came to walk outside.

He wondered if the world could be made different by Mappa Mundi. Weeks ago he'd have said that was something that should be left to fate. But it shouldn't be in the hands of people like Mary, that was for sure. And when he thought about it, he didn't know who wasn't like Mary, in their heart of hearts: self-interested, hopeful, driven by fear.

Natalie cornered her father in the dispensary itself. He was in the act of swallowing two capsules when she walked in.

"What are you doing?"

"It's nothing, a headache."

He was old, she saw that now, because a piece of him had recently given up. He'd failed her.

"You've taken so many."

"I've had it for years." He put the rest of the pack in his pocket and sneezed. "Looks like your friend's done his job, too."

"We're all going out," Natalie said firmly. She took his arm. "You included."

"I don't know," he said. He was rooted to the spot. "If you're going to leave this way. I don't want to go. What's out there? Only more of the same."

"Dad, there's years of life left for you." But she was seeing the headache now, the pain of the trapped man inside a mind that had been set in a peculiar fixity for the last twenty years, the old NervePath system inside it a set of inert wrecks, like ships driven ashore to rot. Their malfunction had created a stasis of thought and produced phantom pain that came with it. Neurological damage, and not the fatal disease she'd dreaded, was to blame. He must have been trying out things when she was still in hospital. Trying to find a cure.

He shook his head. "Nothing changes," he said. "Work, living. It's all the same texture, the same clay."

"Come on, we can find a way." But she was talking to herself.

"We?" He shook his head. "Anyway, I think I've done enough. Don't you?"

"Dad, please." But, with a sinking heart, she knew that he was beyond persuasion. He'd decided and, as with all his decisions, he wasn't going to change.

Stunned, she tried to hold on to him, but he loosened her grip carefully. "Don't worry about me," he said.

"What about me?" she asked. "What am I supposed to do, knowing I left you here?"

"And what am I supposed to do when you've gone?" he said.

"There's no telling exactly what's going to happen." She was starting to be angry with him. "I may survive it and you may live to help more people like Ian. Of course, if you'd rather sit around feeling sorry for yourself then you can do that, too."

He caught her elbow as she was leaving. "Wait on there." His heavy face was weighted with the seriousness she knew very well. "Didn't you come here to get something for that agent out there?" He reached down a pack of Micromedica restructurant and handed it to her. "This is meant for wounds and the like but it's been known to aid cell growth and healing in other cases, too. It won't hurt to try it."

"Thanks." She took it.

"Friend of yours, is he?"

"Tried to be," she said.

"Go on, then."

It was so hard to leave him. She didn't know what to say. After a moment or two of nothing she turned on her heel and went. A curious dizziness almost stopped her halfway back to the dining room, but it passed. Then she started to sneeze.

Everyone had packed their things and was waiting to leave. The departure schedule listed that Guskov should exit first, then Natalie. But when they noticed she was missing they might change their minds. It was only fair to put this to the vote.

"What's the final program? Are you going to try for the Free State or have we met our match?" Nikolai Kropotkin asked as Guskov and Calum joined them last of all. Natalie sat next to Jude, who leaned into the back of his chair with his eyes shut, breathing heavily and shivering. He was wearing a borrowed sweater, but it made no difference. Everyone except Alicia was also in the middle of the primary stages. Shunned, Khan sat on the far end of the farthest table.

"Has everyone looked at the options?" Isidore was calm, wiping his nose on a tissue as if his illness was only to be a summer cold. "We should vote."

"We can use all the programs," Natalie interrupted as they began to talk around the variations of Guskov's ideas. "They can be the first options available. If your global network isn't so corrupt they've already decided to turn the entire system into a racket for making fast cash." She glanced at Mikhail. "Total immunization would be one. Selfware could be another, in a limited version."

"And send the NervePath out as an open system?" Kropotkin shook his head. "Then all that someone has to do is zap them."

"But that's all they have to do anyway," she retorted. "And their technology and programming is way behind. You can offer these straight away. We can soften the ground up, too, if we look for the short-term gains of using Prefer Compromise and No Fear across a wide spectrum of the population. And I thought, instead of sending it out empty, we can add information that can be downloaded complete to the user; a full knowledge of what it is and how it works. That way everyone is instantly informed about the Free State principles, so nobody can prevent them finding out they're infected. It can include localized knowledge about where and how to find new programs and how to prevent counterinfection."

She knew, as she'd said this, that it was news to most of them. They hadn't planned this far ahead—getting Mappaware to work had been the goal for so long that future developments had been something to muse about in idle hours, of which there'd been none. But she'd had the sleepless nights in which to think, and she'd put her mind to work. She knew that this could take a hold before the US and European agencies could prevent it. They, too, would be co-opted by its insidious spread, and then there would be, as Guskov had so rightly predicted, no worthwhile opposition to his ideas. In the years that followed what would come was unpredictable, but that was also true for the reverse situation, where the US got to wave its wand. All the options were bad, but she believed this one was the least rotten at its heart.

"And you've tinkered with this so that it won't cause a mass panic?" Kropotkin asked, acidic, but not entirely unimpressed.

"It comes with comfortable acceptance as standard," she said dryly, knowing how much she sounded like a cheap ad for cars. "Nobody is going to start a revolution. Nobody is going to go bananas and start cutting people's heads off."

She was interrupted by Jude starting another violent outburst of coughing that could have been laughing. The spasms were so violent that they would have thrown him out of a less stable seat. He held the wad of tissue that he'd been using for a while to his mouth and they all saw a sudden bright scarlet tint appear on it. He groaned as the coughing bout finally came to an end.

"What about the people who aren't infected, but know it's out there? How will you stop them?" he managed to whisper.

Natalie watched him with growing concern. The disease wasn't as bad as it looked—that would come when it opened its millions of tiny flowerets and released the Marburg virus. His question was a good one and she didn't know the answer.

"Jude," she said. "I'm going to leave soon. When I do, you should go out first and stall for time. Any lead I can get will be important. Then Guskov can go, and then the people left here can make excuses for me until it's obviously too late."

"We should all go out together," Jude said, with an effort. "Guskov in the front, but together. Otherwise they'll probably kill whoever is left in here. They won't wait if they think you've destroyed the information. They'll just come in shooting and ask later."

Alicia Khan spoke holding her arm where they'd taken a sample of blood as though it hurt. "I can't believe you're going to try this. What if it all goes wrong? The risk calculations are astronomically high. There are too many unknowable factors."

"In which case risk calculations are impossible," Natalie agreed. "Give us another choice that isn't like that and we'll take it."

"In the nineteen eighties everyone was convinced there was going to be nuclear war," Khan replied. "But it never happened. The strategic defence initiatives and the Cold War situation worked out. Nobody fired. Didn't you consider that this might be a technology situation like that one? Everyone has it, but nobody uses it? You sending this out there, untested, unverified—it's like Hiroshima. You don't know what it's going to do."

"They're already using it," Jude said from the floor. "Just like Hiroshima. It's already out there. I've seen it."

"I think we hardly need point out which nation was the only one to use a nuclear warhead aggressively," Guskov added, staring with the tight lips of contempt at Alicia and her second-rate head. "You have a history of shooting first against enemies with lesser power."

She rolled her eyes at this, thinking it a cheap shot worthy only of the standard response. "It ended the war."

"Yes," he said. "And that's not all it ended. It started this age, in which the deepest pocket and the smartest minds get to hold the guns against which there's no resistance."

"If Hiroshima and Nagasaki had been left alone, do you think that someone else wouldn't have used a nuclear device in a later conflict?" she retorted. "It would be the same, whoever used it."

"But if the USA had used it as a threat, instead of a reality, what then?"

"Ah, God, does the argument never get any further than this?" Kropotkin demanded, eyes watering as much with frustration as with the symptoms of the Deliverance.

"It's time," Natalie said quietly. She hated the idea as much as any of them but the bickering was starting to eat away at her determination with its constant circuits of hopeless emotional resistance. She felt the revulsion as much as any of them—hell, more so—she was well in its grip now and the sensations weren't the distant wallowings they'd been in the early days. Now she saw. Now she saw it all like Bobby had promised and it was terrible.

"Jude." She nudged him with her foot. "Get up. Let's go." She looked down at his wretched face, eyes bloodshot and surprised at her callousness, but he got up. Maybe he was able to see what she intended to do. Maybe not. She didn't care any more. The weight of so much responsibility made her unwilling to start sharing her troubles out for discussion. She knew there was only one way she had a hope of saving Jude. Mary Delaney wasn't about to deal him in on any late plea bargains—so she was going to take it.

Moving made him cough and behind her, even as she started sneezing in a string of belters that felt they were about to blow her face off, she heard the room's fragile peace explode with wet misery. She started to turn towards him as they cleared the door . . .

. . . And as she turned she looked inside and saw the fat, clear shapes of the Deliverance capsules dancing amid her own cells—easy to see, because they were the only ones that didn't talk to her, just sat there sending her T-cell response into a frenzy, raking up her hormones, guzzling her blood nutrients as if it was some goddamned all-you-can-eat happy hour. She saw how they held together and how she was held together and that there was a sameness there. She separated her information from theirs and she tore them apart . . .

. . . And as she finished turning, admiring the beautiful rainbow of colour particles inside the paintwork that managed to be such a dull beige to the ordinary eye, she said, "Listen to me. From now on you have about fifty minutes before this stuff can save you, if it can work a conversion like it did to me. I know what you're thinking." She put her hands out to his arms to stop his protest and locked eyes with him until he accepted what she saw brewing up in the dark storm inside his head. "And I want you to stall her better than that. Live for fifty minutes. Got that?"

His streaming eyes looked into hers with difficulty and narrowed as he tried to figure out what she was about. But like the rest of the world, there was no choice in the matter for Natalie. She knew how Bobby had done his undoing trick, the Indian rope job that let information pass freely between molecular organizations, in the single-electron fields. She didn't hesitate—she walked right through Jude and on her way she prayed that it worked, praying to any god, just in case, thinking, "This is what they used to call the Dance of Shiva, creation in its evolving form. It *is* like a dance. But not so much fun."

In transit she realized why it was that Ian Detteridge had followed her to help out; information is a state of energy and on the pass-through there were split moments where that energy belonging to Jude became hers and she was Jude Westhorpe. It was clearer from this side.

She turned around. Jude's back was to her. He was frozen to the spot in shock. She knew the feeling. She knew. There was no secret heart at the bottom of the world waiting to leap out and bite. There was nothing except minds and silence. But what could she possibly say to him to stop his headlong rush to that silence? What could make any difference at all?

Slowly he turned to face her. "Did it take?"

"Yes." She didn't need scanners now. She could see the decay in his right molar, the blood in his heart, the cringing lining of his guts that were suffering the anxiety and the fear. She could see, whether she wanted to or not. In a couple of years that stomach would turn ulcerous, and given a bit more stress the virus sitting in the nerve junctions of his face would leap out into cold sores that wouldn't subside without a truckload of acyclovir. She could see parts of him dying right there, breaking down and collapsing, bursting and exploding and dispersing into taints in the plasma. On his skin legions of flora and fauna were blissfully ignorant of the host state. On her skin no intruders existed. She'd lost them when she'd dispersed herself, and the same went for all her internal microbes that hadn't been opted-in by NervePath. *Remember that when you sell this system*, she mentally noted, *there has to be a way of reinstalling them . . .*

Jude was talking.

"Will you be back?"

She smiled. "I don't know. I'll try." She touched his arm, carefully, as though there was no intimacy between them, and saw him flinch. "I'm sorry."

He hesitated and she knew why—he thought that he'd remembered something. But for him the memory was impossible and his mind discounted it. "Sorry for what?"

"Never mind." She stood up on tiptoe and kissed him. "Goodbye, Jude."

He didn't say anything, but made a small nod of his head, fighting the urge to cough.

"You look better," he said, a kind of parting shot, trying to be up.

"Fifty minutes," she said, pointing her finger at him.

He nodded again, although she knew that he was thinking, *No chance of that. I'm sorry, too, but not this time.*

And she couldn't blame him, not for a second.

"Natalie?" It was her father, standing in the open doorway. She knew he suspected, although he hadn't seen what she'd done.

"Dad." She stepped across the huge, tiny space between them and held him tight. "I'm going."

"Be careful," he said, knowing it was pathetic, an offering of sound, nothing you could take with you.

"Always." And she closed her hand into a fist up in front of his face, taking hold of those words and then pressing her hand against her heart, to take them with her.

She turned away from them both and walked the length of the narrow corridor. At its end it was almost impossible not to spin around but she didn't do it. She turned right, towards the exit, but long before she got to it she was unpicking the information, letting the spaces open, travelling faster than she ever had before to her distant destination and as she travelled she lost information steadily, like tears falling into the gaps that lay, vast and empty, between one form of energy and another.

Twenty-Six

Jude watched Natalie go through a hazy world of pain as he had to start the endless bloody rounds of coughing one more time, but his thoughts that followed her were full of admiration for the strong way she set her back, head high on that small body. It was a suicide mission and she went straight to it, no last glances backwards as he was doing, mentally, all the time, into his memories of his own life.

He was vaguely aware of her father, upright but with the off-balance stance of a clockwork machine, stalled with a sudden failure of power.

When his coughing at last fell quieter, he panted out, "We should act now. While I can still talk."

Calum Armstrong looked at him as though only noticing his presence for the first time. "Yes," he said tonelessly, his face flat, expressionless. He went back inside the room. Jude stayed where he was. He didn't hear the elevator doors. He wondered briefly if Natalie might be there, around the corner, waiting, thinking, frightened, but his heart told him no, she'd gone; there was a flatness and a smallness in him that was like a kind of shutdown. Those areas of himself that had been optimistic and future-oriented were closed, their doors locked and the keys swallowed up in an ocean of grey tides whose waves were each as blank and identical as the last.

Jude thought of his life, and he wanted most of all to have it make sense to him, like a well-told story. Up to this point it seemed to lack plot and now, in its final hours, that distressed him, as Natalie had said it would, like there were too many things left undone and unthought-of. White Horse was beyond redemption. His father, too, was a footnote, a mystery, a clue pushed to one side for an eternal late-date with history that was never to come. His mother—she at least he had no unfinished deals with. How would she find out what had happened to him? Would the government send someone, or would he be a casualty in the papers? What story would Mary concoct? Maybe she would be the one to take her grey sedan up to Seattle, knock on the house door, and in her black suit say, "Ms. Westhorpe, we're so sorry . . ." But no. That at least he intended to conclude in a manner that he could die with. The misery of the symptoms in his head and body were nothing against this resolve. He would have it out with her. She was the pivot of the one strand he was still able to control.

It occurred to him that he was being stupid and melodramatic, but then, he hadn't expected a dramatic end and if that was what he was going to get, he wasn't going to waste it. For a second Natalie's promise of fifty minutes roamed around in his mind, looking for a home, but even if it held true he didn't think he'd last much longer, Marburg or no Marburg. It was a valiant effort, a two-fingered gesture in the face of fate, but it was only a gesture and its effects would be as permanent as a flick of fingers and the fall of a hand.

Guskov surrendered first.

Jude waited for him to clear the highside exit, counted the minutes as prescribed in the letter of Mary's demands, listened to the coughing, the sneezing, and the new and despairing silence of the science team as they waited their turn. Instead of Natalie emerging alone, they all went together. Jude stood at the front to lead them out and through watering eyes saw the lines of soldiers in full biogear, guns ready, who flanked each side of the elevator doors. He had no time to waste on them however, because Mary herself was standing in the sunlight of the driveway; he recognized her slimmer figure with the suit's green waistband cinched in tight, and through the polished faceplate of clear glass he could see the stark whiteness of her skin, touched into shadows about the eyes and mouth so that it seemed like her skull alone was looking for him.

The soldiers didn't move a muscle at the change of plans, but after a moment of indecision she stalked forward to meet him. There was no sign of Guskov, although there looked to be movement in the laboratory trucks parked up alongside the house, their paintwork now stuck with a few yellow leaves, the first of fall.

Jude made himself stand straight, his chest and throat feeling as though red-hot pokers had been reaming them out. He looked through the reflections of the trees and sky on her glass and into her blue eyes, still pretty, despite what lay beneath. The moment seemed to last a long time to him. He could smell the damp earth and feel the warmth of the falling sun, in each the promise of a night of rain, the growth of fungi, the fall of leaves, the beginning of rot and suppuration. In her face he saw her twisted emotions, lying far below the surface, like looking through a pool of deep water into the muddy bottom and seeing an ancient fish stir its fins. She looked on him with love, but one so long suppressed it had mutated into a form of possession.

He tried to erase the thought—he didn't want to pity her—but it was long in going.

"Where is she?" Mary asked, glancing past him with revulsion to the rest, who had been left to stand weakly sneezing and snivelling in a group on their own, like the cattle at Dugway, no help moving in for them until she said so.

"You mean Natalie Armstrong?" He was going to have to do better than that. He made himself duck his head and hesitate. "They thought she might go the same way as that other patient, X . . ." He made an expression that said it was something so awful to witness that he was finding it impossible to tell her.

"Is she still in the Environment?" Mary's voice through the filters was muffled into a soft sound he knew she wasn't feeling. Her body was knotted with tensions, rigid in its flat face-forward stance. He glanced again at her, daring her not to feel sorry for his wretched state.

"It's hard to say. We lost contact with her."

How long had it been? Thirty minutes? He wasn't sure, but his mind felt it was about twenty. Twenty to go. He hadn't got that long. Abruptly he realized his symptoms had got no worse. The histamine peak must be close.

"Jude. Where is Armstrong?"

"I don't know. I think she's dead." Which was the truth. Through the glass he saw Mary's face change. It said, *Why are you making this hard for both of us?*

He said, "It's hard because you made it that way when you decided to play me for an idiot. You got me. For a long time, you got me. Man, I must be the slowest guy you've ever come across. I'll bet you could hardly keep your pants dry you were laughing so hard—Guskov your pet study and me there rolling right along thinking *Hot damn! We're such unlucky people when it comes to getting the evidence*. So don't look at me like you deserve anything but the hard way."

Her mouth dropped open slightly and for once the comeback was slow to arrive. "Jude," she said. "What's wrong with you?"

He started laughing. He couldn't help it. He knew what she meant, but he couldn't stop it anyway and it made him start coughing and sneezing all over again and the spasms were so bad he ended up on his knees, doubled over and bright red all over his trousers and little dark clots of blood like jellies landing on the wind-stirred dust of the ground.

He saw one of the anonymous men in warfare gear come up to Mary with a scanner and take some readings from him. He saw her consult with him over headmikes and he saw, as the man came around for a second pass, the gun on his shoulder that was hanging close there.

He saw inside the man's mind a flurry of worries about the readings he was seeing and an anxiety about Jude that was fully justified.

Give me the gun, Jude insisted. *Hand it over like there was nothing wrong in it. Easy does it.*

Mary was turning to talk to a corporal who had arrived and was asking questions about how to deal with the infected cases, what to do about the infected Environment. Was she sure that the payload wasn't out yet. Was she ready to sign off the MUV shots . . .

Jude gratefully took hold of the heavy weapon as he was handed it, able to take off the safety, brace it, and set on the trigger with a dexterity he'd never had before. As he came up to standing straight the scan-man leapt away from him, only then realizing what he'd done. At the same moment the corporal reached for his own weapon and ten of the thirty armed soldiers who'd been watching the emerging scientists in horrified fascination turned around and focused their anxiety on him.

Mary turned.

"Jude!" She was surprised, really. She started to smile. "Don't be silly. Look around you. This isn't gonna work."

"Yeah, I see that." He straightened up to his full height and the gun felt good in his arms.

"For God's sake! Put it down. Don't make this worse. Don't you get it? It was never about you and me. It was security. It wasn't personal."

He'd heard her say that before. "You're wrong. It's always personal to the one on the receiving end."

There was such a fight going on inside her, between impulses that could none of them be satisfied. She wanted power, but to be liked. She wanted control, but not to take the blame. She wanted him to give in and a part of her wanted him to go ahead and finish it there because going on was harder, longer, and, ultimately, led nowhere she wasn't already at.

Jude made her decision for her. It was easy really. He only had to think of the fire smell of his sister's burned hair, the shiny, red skin, and the last note she wrote, trusting Mary as his well-known friend.

With the sensation of a sharp object being tugged out of his breastbone he took in a long breath and knew that he was free.

Selfware, it made you more yourself than you ever were. That was for sure. For the first time in his life he was certain that he was doing the right thing, the only thing, the justified thing. As he squeezed the trigger closed the peace inside him was indescribable in its relief.

Mary was flung ten feet by the shot as it punctured the suit and exploded inside her.

Jude watched her falling. The return of fire hit him ten times harder. The blows moved in him like a frenzy and he knew he was dead before his face hit the ground. It didn't matter, though. He was done here. He'd found the closing line, and he'd said it, and it was time to go before things fell apart in any one of a hundred anticlimactic ways. There wasn't even going to be time to say goodbye to anything of his world, but he watched it unfurling gently, like a long banner, streaming away from him into the forever lost spaces of the darkening, blue twilight as he fell. It didn't hurt and he was glad about that. It was like starting to dream and then sliding to a deeper place.

Natalie worked fast, not even pausing to talk with the people she'd met once they'd shown her their workstations. She installed the systems with a slam of disk into loader, a few keystrokes and then she left for the next destination. Five passed. Five, and four at least were full of people wanting to figure out how they could take a few percent off the top of the price and how to fiddle the system and how to use the stuff to make themselves more capable of shafting the next guy up the line, but that was okay, because she didn't want the responsibility of screwing everyone up all by herself and a few more Ray Innises would help the medicine of bitter knowledge go down better. She had hopes about No Fear and Prefer Compromise, but she hadn't got any hopes that the basic nature of the animal was going to change. When money grew on trees and everyone was in harmony, then she'd believe happiness was something you could design and sell. For now this would have to do, and whether it was the start of a new era or the death fits of the old one, she'd maybe never know.

Each time she travelled she bled information.

On destination seven the disks themselves she was carrying had become corrupt and the journey was at its end. Natalie looked at the wrecked object in her hand, perfect except for the fatal exceptions deep in its structure that had destroyed the program it had carried so far. She was like that, too, she knew it but, as Ian must have done, although she knew she'd lost she didn't know *what* she'd lost and so it wasn't that bad, not like being normal and realizing the magnitude of something gone.

She sat on a stone wall outside a terrace plantation on the subcontinent, tea bushes growing calmly around her in the velvety darkness. Behind her the packing factory and its secret heart of NP production machinery ground quietly into action for a long night's work. The scent of jasmine was heady and the sun gone ten minutes. The blue light reminded her of a long ago day, running through a wood and then, just as she felt an important thing was about to be revealed, the memory died.

She got up and walked a short way between the bushes, the stars overhead so bright, so distant. She watched one blueshifting away, another redshifting in. She still had one task to go. Was it true that time could be backtraced without unstitching her? She doubted that. How could you go back in time but retain your conscious states of memory? They relied on entropy and change in a linear timeline to exist. But the file remained a mystery—otherwise how had Jude got it? And there was that second in the laboratory where Ian had hinted to her that there might be a way back for him, a glimpse into the past when he was still a man with a family—he'd thought maybe he could relearn who he'd been, put himself together again. It was that theory she'd used when she'd tried to retain a copy of Jude in the crossover.

But if she was shot full of holes now then he would be, too, his data as useless as the disks themselves.

Natalie took them out of her pockets, those that remained, and flung them away into the plantation darkness. Across the Earth Jude was already dead. In America it was just starting to be evening and the sun set without him to see it. Dan was gone. She had nothing she wanted to come back for. So, why not try?

She stared up at the sky. A full moon hung overhead, silent and still, so quiet. Bats flitted across it in a delicate dance and she heard their sonar, felt it track and pulse against her skin. The insects they were hunting hung in ignorance between them, motes of life that flickered as though lit to her, and winked out as they joined the bats' collection, as simply as that.

She reached out to switch them back on.

To move through time in a backwards fashion means just one thing for a creature that can form intentions and actions in the forward direction only. You have to be isolated from the reversing process. You have to keep on moving into your future, as everything around you unpicks itself to the level of the past. Otherwise you will unpick yourself as well as the world, and because your understanding is an ongoing process, that will get undone, too. There is no backwards like a film played in reverse, because even that has to be seen in forward time. You might be subjected to a billion rewinds yourself, but you'll never know it, because such a concept of time's movement isn't possible to your one-tracked existence. You wouldn't even notice. How could you?

Natalie knew this and she had no idea how to isolate herself in a forward pocket, even with the quantum insights that Ian had promised. That there was a fatal contradiction in anything moving forwards and backwards at the same instance. She herself, as she was now, could not travel into any past. Ian had correctly said that time was misunderstood generally. It was an element of space, not a separate entity at all, but it was an element in which the three dimensions of her physical world shifted all together and she wasn't going to escape them taking her with them as long as she remained three dimensional.

Further, as she toyed with the problem, watching the insects, the mosquitoes and midges, the beetles and moths on the wing, heavy and blundering in their flight, she began to look beyond them to the stars. Redshifters were moving away. Their light was a longer wavelength because they were streaking off, stretching it out. Blueshifters were moving in, approaching, squeezing the waves closer as they came. To look at the night sky anywhere, even the moon, was to look at the past. The moon was milliseconds ahead of its apparent position. The stars were long gone. The light in her eyes that yielded the constellations and their pattern was a combination of billions of years, seeming to land here, in her mind, at a single, unified moment. Which is when she realized how to plot a course in time.

Complex entities were never going to make it. But information might make it back, and information, when combined into a sequence of directions, a program, activated at the right moment, could rebuild a simulacrum of Natalie Armstrong and execute a few important tasks before it decayed. The puzzle of what she'd written in her big scribble on the back of the Guskov File suddenly became obvious. It was a diagram of motes, travelling against the flow through three-dimensional space. Just as they could be linked across vast spaces and react to each other's states instantaneously, fundamental particles could be linked across time. She didn't need to bring those linked pairs together at any particular moment to create their bond. It could stretch into the past as easily as endure through the future.

No sooner had she imagined this than what seemed like a memory, not existing until now, but still her own, flooded into her mind.

It was weeks ago. She was in Washington, in the locked room where Mary Delaney's boss, Rebecca Dix, kept her private files. She was reaching into a drawer and extracting Mikhail's entry. She checked it quickly and then moved through the wall into the outer office, quiet at this hour of the evening. Using a pencil that had been left on the secretary's desk she wrote the date on the back and then sketched, roughly, just enough to jog her mind later on. All this took place in a kind of distant mode, where she was not fully present, but vaguely dreaming.

She encoded the file as information and restructured it at the guest house in York. Jude lay asleep on the flowery bedcover, as insensible as a lead block. She didn't want to wake him, because what could she have said? She laid the file, only a little damaged by its journey, behind him but then, in a moment of weakness, the look-back she'd not allowed herself in Virginia, she reached out to see if she could touch him one more time.

Jude, in his unsullied state, before he knew any of what was to come, started to wake up.

"I'm sorry," she said, to herself in the future as well as to him. "I'm so sorry."

It was goodbye, before it was even hello.

In the breathing, vivid darkness of the Kerala tea plantation the physical remains of Natalie Katherine Armstrong flew apart. They were caught for an instant, moth dust in moonlight, and then they were gone.

Mary Delaney, still sore from the operations, and with her right arm plastered and tucked up against her side—ironically protective of and protecting the same rib that had shattered and driven shards through every muscle in her upper body—felt a sense of triumph that was grimmer than the expression on any of the world's great old men troublemakers, who had all taken a black contentment in sending youngsters to their deaths in the name of freedom.

Superficially she was looking great. The Micromedica technology was a miracle worker. If anything the restructurants and the nanosurgery had improved what fast living and stress had done to her. She felt strong and competent as never before, but it was ruined by the one thing the bullet from Jude had shot out of her, and that was any capacity to feel pleasure.

She sat in her seat beside Dix in the White House Oval Office, watching the president and his advisers settle themselves for the agenda at hand, and she looked at General Bragg, who met her eye with an unflinching dislike that would have made an earlier version of Mary inwardly quail. But this Mary didn't bother. She stared him down, because she knew very well, in the wake of the upset, who had conspired to take the project and the country back to the Dark Ages and she had proof for whenever it was needed.

"Ms. Delaney?" the vice president said. "Would you care to begin?"

And she did, explaining in clear and easy terms the NSC plans for Mappa Mundi. The project was in. She had succeeded. Guskov had lost. They had won.

After the agreements to proceed were validated and approved she decided to take a walk along the Mall to clear her head. The fall weather had taken a sudden cooler turn and the air was for once fresh and almost invigorating. She was looking towards the Lincoln Memorial and the reflecting pool, thinking about nothing in particular, when a man sneezed near her. It was a violent sneeze and it shocked her into a jump that jarred her arm and rib cage together in a painful burst of sensation. She heard him say to a companion in an English accent, "Just got in from Europe. "Flu all over there. Bloody nightmare. Ugh. Mind you don't get it . . ."

"Sounds like an epidemic," the companion said breezily. "They have it in Asia, too."

"It always comes from there," agreed the sneezer and went on to another three violent convulsions.

Mary didn't know what had happened to Natalie Armstrong but the downloads from the Environment systems conclusively proved the disintegration of Patient X and she'd guessed that the US strike was going to be a counteraction and not the initiative. She quickly took a handkerchief out of her pocketbook and held it over her nose and mouth. Her MUV was still active, but she didn't like the idea of inhaling Deliverance, no matter what form it took.

On the Avenue she paused to get a taxi to take her back to the Pentagon. A Joint Chiefs meeting was taking place in an hour, as they prepared their strategy to deploy Mappaware. She was standing on the curb and a cab was coming, she was waiting and watching it, when she caught sight of something white and black suddenly approaching her out of the corner of her eye.

It made her heart jump and she turned rapidly, half expecting, in that horrifying way that happened ever since she'd lost her apartment, that it would be Jude.

She knew Jude was dead. Twenty-plus shots had made a real mess of him and she hadn't needed to look to verify the result. She had looked, though. She'd made herself glance down, sideways, as she was strapped onto a stretcher under the gentle autumn sky. He lay face down in the dry earth of the driveway. A lake of blood stained his clothes and the ground in vast, near-black marks.

The entire area had been sprayed, the earth removed, in an attempt to contain the blood and its fatal loads but even now she wasn't a hundred percent sure that they'd managed to get every Deliverance spore out of there. The house and its grounds were sealed off, soaked in bleach and microtech solutions, but so what? All it took was one animal . . . but she didn't want to think about that. She didn't want to think about Jude being flung into an incinerator, burning like a torch, his face and body shrinking and blistering in the incredible heat needed to destroy the NervePath and the Micromedica. But she did think of it. Every time she saw something in the corner of her eye.

But although she staggered this time, left hand raised to ward, there was nobody. The cab drew up to her and she reached for the door. She heard a voice, another English one, say "*Hola, Mary*," in a sarcastic way, but it seemed to be so close and whispered so quietly she wasn't sure.

Mary suddenly felt an extreme dizziness take hold of her. She grabbed the seat and the door handle. She couldn't feel her body. The views of the car swam and circled. She felt icy and then burning hot. Her emotions leapt out in a vast glut of inexpressible anger, lust, elation, and misery.

"Where to?" the Ethiopian cab driver was looking at her in the mirror with some frustration. She heard him, but the words took a strange route through her mind.

The next second everything was back the way it had been.

Natalie straightened her skirt, which was both familiar and unfamiliar, and looked down at herself, neatly attired, her case at her side, her gun in place. "Pentagon," she said, testing her voice, which worked as it always had.

Natalie/Mary watched the city pass by through the windows with fresh interest, despite the vile, lingering memories of Jude's death. He was gone, but she was still here, and in a position to do something good for a change, just like he, Ian, and Dan would have wanted. The complex question of who she actually was didn't seem very important.

Matter is only energy with information and identity was only information after all. Replacing some parts with others was child's play. Mappaware had proved it and she had taken her chance.

As she reached her office she greeted the secretaries and ordered an English tea—no changes there then. Sitting down she looked around her and reflected how very dull a room this was. Something should be done to brighten it. In the meantime she had work to do, determining that the US attempt to ruin the Free State would not come to any great shakes until the citizens had had the chance to see it for themselves.

The first thing she did however was to send a message to Mikhail Guskov at the military hospital where he was still undergoing observation to conclude his treatment and the removal of Deliverance from his system.

She wrote:

I doubt you can even imagine the full consequences of the system that you and I constructed. I cannot, and I have seen it. The coverage rate for PHC and NF has the greatest takeup of all the systems. Today I saw an article in the *Washington Post* that mentioned, "This strange uprise in net comms discussion groups about something called Mappaware . . ." No doubt you will have the new systems ready to release by the time I see you next week. The limitation numbers for the Selfware encoding are included in the attached file (MW1884), along with details of the stages in development each one should confer, including and up to sublimation. Please inform Calum Armstrong of my whereabouts as soon as you see him.

No longer, Mary Delaney.

Update

You're walking down the street, enjoying the sunshine and the freshness after a spring rain. You've had a good day at work and now you're returning home along the peaceful, broad sidewalks. It's more than a mile but you like to walk, it's good for you, and you get to pass the shops on the way, the post office and the bank. You can stop at the deli and get fresh fish, and ice cream for dessert. Right now you're passing the park. How beautiful the trees are here!

You see the group of children playing on the brightly coloured swings. The colours sing. Your son is there, on the blue swing, going higher than all the rest. You stop to look, wondering if you've time to go across and play a little kickball, when a mosquito whines around your head.

You bat it away, but for a second there you thought it was telling you a story. Something about a girl running out of the woods with her friend. Half-baked stuff they put in them these days—they're supposed to bring urgent news if they sting you for dinner. But at least this one, hopelessly data-corrupted as it is, has left you alone today. Some people will fill them up with any old rubbish.

Your son asked you for the third time today to get SlideKing. It's a new update, but first he'd need a higher grade of physical development and then the expensive base set of Physical Coordinator 4.2. But you could get it as a package. Maybe for Christmas.

The state shop is on the way to the deli. You just go in for a quick look in the catalogue. As always on the front cover is their big promotion—Selfware 10.3. It's supposed to be utterly painless, the greatest high, and best of all it's totally free. Nobody wants to die, but when you gotta go who'd want to just flake out instead of transcending the physical?

It gives you the shivers just to think about it but it's kind of comforting to know that all you have to do is load it and you're on your way. Nobody ever comes back to say whether or not it works, but interviews you've seen with those in the middle of transcending sure make it look good. You've been happy in your life and you know it when you see it.

Further on the sports gear checks out at a cool five hundred for everything your son hopes for. He'll have to be patient. Earlier on you saw the Adult page and there was a little something on there which even now you're ordering just for you and your lover. It's only ten and it promises a lifetime's orgasmic upgrading. You've had the earlier version and can't resist. Hey, what's life without a little indulgence now and again, eh?

As you pass the Quiet Space you see your neighbour's family gathered there with their singing bowls and their gongs, playing softly. In the middle of the garden a figure of light is gently rising, and fading as it rises. You think—of course—today is their great-grandfather's Blue Day. You wave at the form, hoping you're not too late, and it seems to wave to you. Your neighbour turns at the sight and sees you, comes to invite you to the party, bring the whole family along. There are tears in his eyes but of joy, not sorrow—he can hear what his father is thinking, can see what he sees. Creepy, but, man, better than the old style.

The sun is going down, red and large, the heat softening, and the midges crowding as you reach the door of your house. Another mosquito whines past—one of the dissident forms from some hacker breeding pen. It whispers in your mind with stinging doubt—are there wars out there, with killers converting mothers to slayers and children to spies? Somewhere the mosquitoes are telling stories of worse than bears in the wood. Somewhere there are people living lives of starvation and slavery at the hands of cruel masters who enjoy the depravity their technology is able to bring. Yes, somewhere. Believe it.

Whack! Slam those suckers! Pesky things.

Such a thought could ruin even the best of days, couldn't it? Used to, before you got a news pilot to filter what you heard and thought. Sometimes there are get-togethers here where you can take off all the programming and experience life raw, firsthand, no censorship, the old style. Sometimes you do this, now and again, but less as time goes on. You used to think it was necessary, shriving even; that it kept you really human and in touch with what mattered. (It embarrasses you to remember.) Aren't we all such assholes when we're so serious and young?

And these things aren't happening today, to you, right now.

Comfort yourself.

Live your life.

Today is a beautiful$_{\text{YOU*}}$ day$_{\text{ALLDAY*}}$.

---

*The parameters YOU and ALLDAY are used subject to patent law and licensing agreements with the International Free State of Mind Trade Administration.

About the Author

Justina Robson is an author from Leeds in Yorkshire, England. Her first novel, *Silver Screen*, published in August 1999 in the UK and in 2005 by Pyr®, was shortlisted for the Arthur C. Clarke Award and the BSFA Award, and the Pyr edition was nominated for the 2005 Philip K. Dick award. Her second novel, *Mappa Mundi*, together with *Silver Screen*, won the Amazon.co.uk Writer's Bursary 2000 and was also shortlisted for the 2001 Arthur C. Clarke Award. A third novel, *Natural History*, a far future novel, placed second in the 2004 John W. Campbell award and was shortlisted for the Best Novel of 2003 in the British Science Fiction Association Awards and nominated for the 2005 Philip K. Dick award. Vist her online at www.justinarobson.com.